THE
SILENT
DEAD

BOOKS BY MARNIE RICHES

THE
SILENT
DEAD

MARNIE RICHES

Bookouture

Published by Bookouture in 2022

An imprint of Storyfire Ltd.
Carmelite House
50 Victoria Embankment
London EC4Y 0DZ
Uniter Kingdom

www.bookouture.com

ISBN: 978-1-80314-148-0
eBook ISBN: 978-1-80314-147-3

PROLOGUE

With sorrow tightening its grip on her heart, she kissed the freshly washed curls on her small son's head.

'Have a lovely day, Lukie-baby,' she said. 'Nanny'll pick you up just after lunch, because she's taking you to the dentist while Mummy goes to work. You can do colouring-in at Nanny's after, and she said she'll let you help her bake.'

Tears stood in Luke's eyes. He reached out to her. His chin dimpled and his lower lip drooped. 'Please don't go, Mummy. I think I've got a tummy ache.' He placed his hand on his belly.

'Come on. You're a big boy now, and there's nothing wrong with you. Time to go to school,' she said, looking to the teacher for support.

Kindly Miss Dale kneeled down and smiled. She caught Luke's attention. 'Hey, Luke! I've got an important job I need you to help me with. Why don't you say goodbye to your mum and come and help me give out some crayons to the rest of the class?'

'Miss Dale needs you, Lukie,' she said, taking the teacher's surreptitious wink as the cue to back away. 'Go on. Show her what a clever, sensible lad you are.'

She swallowed down the pain of separation. Term was already three weeks in, and parting had become no easier. In truth, her youngest child didn't look old enough to be going to school. His brand-new grey-and-blue uniform was way too big for his tiny frame, and those pristine shorts with their patch pockets and sharp creases hung below his bony knees. Part of her wanted to push her tiny boy on the swings and take him to playgroups in church halls and coddle him indefinitely. But that energy bill wouldn't pay itself, and the house insurance was due to renew. School meant she could finally take on longer shifts at work.

'Say goodbye to Mummy, Luke.' Miss Dale started to wave. 'And let's go and find those crayons.'

Luke nodded, clearly reluctant. 'Bye-bye.' A tear tracked its way over his pink cheek. He waved half-heartedly.

She locked eyes with Miss Dale. Could almost hear the woman telling her to just turn and leave quickly. 'Have fun. Love you.'

Finally, she tore herself from the classroom door and headed to the school gate. Didn't look back, because she knew the mayhem it would cause, and they'd have to start the goodbye rigmarole all over again.

As she got into her untidy old Volkswagen, she breathed a sigh of relief. Checked the time. She had just under three hours until her shift at the biscuit factory began. Fine. It would give her time to put a wash in and search for new house insurance quotes online. Do her neighbour's hair, as promised.

She checked her phone. No word yet from her daughter. It had been days. She made a mental note to call her on WhatsApp when she was on her break. *Don't panic about Kylie*, she counselled herself. *She'll be fine. She's a grown woman, and she's having the time of her life. Let her have the freedoms you never had.*

Nodding at her own wisdom, she started the engine and drove home. There was even a parking space right outside her house today. Maybe things were looking up.

As she put the key in the lock, she peered through the bevelled glass pane in the front door. Was that a shadow passing across the hallway or were her tired eyes playing tricks on her?

Frowning, she opened the door as stealthily as she could and held her breath. The blood rushed in her ears. Her heart beat so wildly that her body swayed slightly, in time with its insistent rhythm. Should she call out or try to ambush any intruder?

Opting for the latter, she closed the door softly behind her and tiptoed down the hallway. Set her bag and keys silently on the half-moon hall table. Taking the fake chrysanthemums out of the large Chinese-style vase that sat on the table, she lifted the vase above her head. She was ready to defend herself.

Walking from the hall to the kitchen to the living room, she scanned every surface, every curtain, every cushion to see if anything was out of place. But it was as she'd left it. The only sound was her breath – now ragged – and that gushing, rushing in her ears.

A floorboard creaked. She looked up at the network of fine cracks in the living-room ceiling. Was someone in her bedroom, overhead? Her arms were screaming in complaint as she held the vase up, ready to bring it crashing down on some intruder's head. She lowered it, still poised to defend herself though.

Climbing the stairs, avoiding the ones that creaked, she checked the two bedrooms. Empty. Then the bathroom. Also empty. Sometimes the house just made noises. Sometimes, especially when she was exhausted and overwrought, she imagined things. The shadow was nothing, she told herself.

Padding back downstairs with the vase weighing heavy in her hands, her breathing returned to normal and her heart rate slowed. She set the vase back on the half-moon table and stuffed the fake flowers back inside. Checked her reflection in the hall mirror. She was dark under her eyes. Luke's struggle with separation anxiety at school was definitely getting to her. Kylie's radio silence didn't help. She felt alone in the world, shouldering her mothering responsibilities without any support beyond the odd school run reluctantly done by her parents.

Sighing, she kicked off her sneakers, stuffed her feet into her fluffy slippers, made her way through to the kitchen and put on the kettle. Dropped a teaspoon of instant coffee into a cup and put a slice of bread into the toaster. Added another slice. She felt like eating today to stuff down all her feelings of losing control. Maybe she'd have some of that damson jam her mother had made.

Reaching into the larder cupboard, she retrieved the sticky jar and set it down on the small kitchen table. Took out a highball glass for juice and set it on a coaster next to a place mat. Put out a knife for her toast. Poured boiling water into her coffee cup, ignoring the sensation of the hairs standing to attention on the back of her neck.

She carried the coffee to the table, along with two slices of toast on a plate, and sat down heavily onto the rickety old chair. Suddenly, she felt a stinging sensation in her thigh.

'Ow!'

Was there a wasp beneath the table? She slapped at her leg and pushed her chair backwards abruptly, stumbling. Feeling woozy as she leaned over, she tried to catch a glimpse of the thing that had stung her. It was then that she saw the man, sitting cross-legged beneath the table, clutching a spent syringe.

'Surprise!' he said, staring out at her. He was smiling.

She opened her mouth to scream, but medicated sleep was rolling in like dense fog, silencing her tongue, paralysing her limbs, smothering her thoughts. It wrapped itself around her and pulled her to the floor.

She saw her attacker crawl out from his hiding place. He was coming for her, and there was nothing she could do to stop him.

ONE

'I know her,' Jackie said, catching her breath at the startled expression on the dead woman's face. She crouched to get a better look, wincing as her own battered body reminded her that it was not long since she'd given birth under difficult circumstances. 'I know exactly who she is.' She studied the fine lines etched into the woman's once plump, youthful skin.

'Eh?' Dave asked absently.

Jackie glanced up at her partner. With one latex-gloved hand, he was holding the handwritten note the neighbour had found on the kitchen table. In the other hand was the empty bottle of sleeping pills. She looked at him expectantly until he gave her his full attention.

'I said, I *know* her. Claire Watkins.'

'That's not the name the neighbour gave the uniform.' Dave set down the evidence of a life taken early and took out his notepad. '*Rachel Hardman* I've got written down here.'

Shaking her head, Jackie looked back at the dead woman, noting the cheap miniskirt and the washed-out T-shirt she was wearing. Supermarket fashion, by the looks. Her mottled legs were bare. On her feet were fluffy slippers. There was no visible bruising on her body, no smashed-up furniture or broken glass. No obvious signs of a struggle or there having even been anyone else in the house at the time of death, Jackie reasoned, judging by the mealtime place setting for one – untouched toast, undrunk coffee and a solitary empty highball glass. 'I don't know about the surname – maybe it's her married name.' She peered at the dead woman's left hand. 'No ring, mind.'

'Divorced?' Dave offered. 'Or maybe it's just a different woman, given *she's called Rachel Hardman.*'

'Shove your sarcasm, David. This is Claire Watkins, I'm telling you. My old school pal.'

Jackie swallowed hard at the sight of the dead woman, lying as if asleep on the well-scrubbed kitchen floor. In seeing her friend, it felt like Death himself was holding up a two-way mirror for Jackie – one side revealing a youthful past; the other reflecting back at her a grim here-and-now and Jackie's own mortality. *Dead at thirty-nine*, she thought, remembering all that had happened in her last case. *That could be me.*

'Rachel was her middle name,' she said softly. 'And I know that because she was overweight at school. Not really big, but just a bit... well, chunky. But it was enough for the other kids to call her *Eclair*. She got given the nickname in the first year, during lunch. We had eclairs for pudding. Claire ate three... So it just stuck. Poor love tried to get them to call her Rachel after that, but nobody would. It was always Eclair Watkins. And now she's dead in a council house in Gorton.'

As she got to her feet again, her knees cracked. Carrying all that weight for almost nine months at nearly forty had not done her joints any favours. 'The Claire I knew was nowhere near depressed enough to end it all.'

Dave raised an eyebrow. 'When was the last time you saw her... *if* this is who you say it is?'

Puffing the air out of her cheeks, Jackie thought back to a time when she'd been a schoolgirl – always one of the last to be picked for netball; always preferring Fatboy Slim and Jamiro-quai to the beiger musical offerings of Ace of Base and Boyzone; always with her head in a book rather than her nose in everyone else's business. The daughter of a failed artist, shrouded in the mystery of a terrible family tragedy, Jackson Cooke had sought to mark herself as different from the other kids because she *had* been different. And she and Claire Watkins – the shy, smiling, robustly built girl who was ostracised by the alpha girls – had formed an alliance of sorts. Sitting together at lunch. Sharing a table in the library during free periods. Failing as a pair at PE.

'Jeez. I haven't seen her since the last day of sixth form. I tried to keep in touch, but she never returned my calls. Eventually, life got in the way, and I forgot all about her. And now here she is.'

Picking up the letter from the small kitchen table, Jackie read the solitary word that had been printed in a shaky hand, in ballpoint pen. Her heart felt suddenly leaden in her chest.

SORRY.

'Just "sorry". That's it.' She kneeled down again and looked carefully at the expression on Claire Watkins' haggard face. 'Who was she apologising to? Do we know?'

'There's no sign of a phone, so we don't know if she's got a partner... kids. We should question the neighbour. Find out who's next of kin,' Dave said. He pointed to the hallway and the front of the house with his pen. 'Neighbour's still in the lounge with the uniform.'

Together, they made their way through to the cramped living room, where an ashen-faced, dishevelled old woman was perched on the edge of a sagging IKEA armchair. She dragged hard from a cigarette wedged between two shaking, gnarled fingers. Tears stood in her cataract-green eyes as she looked up at them.

'Detective Sergeants David Tang and Jackson Cooke,' Dave said, showing his ID. 'We need to ask you some questions, if that's okay, love?'

The old woman looked through Dave to Jackie. 'And then can I go home? Only I've got the council coming to fix my boiler.'

Jackie took a seat on a sofa that was covered in cat hair. Alice seemed to sneeze every time she was near cats or dogs. Jackie made a mental note to run a lint roller over her coat before she returned home. Just the thought of her four-month-old baby daughter, sneezing repeatedly and struggling to feed because her little sinuses were on fire, made Jackie's leaky breasts ache.

She folded her arms across her chest. 'I can imagine this is very traumatic for you, Mrs...?'

'Dolan. Theresa Dolan.'

'Mrs Dolan.' She glanced at Dave, who was taking notes. 'So, do you want to tell me how you came to find your neighbour?'

The old woman stubbed out her cigarette in a saucer. 'Me and Rach have keys to each other's houses, you see. Because we're both on our own, like. And she was going to do me hair this morning.' She scratched at yellowed hair that looked as though it hadn't seen shampoo or hot water in at least a week. 'She works at a biscuit factory, but she's a marvel with hair. Said she did a stint as a mobile hairdresser, when her daughter was little.'

Jackie remembered her friend being top of the class in chemistry and biology. Destined for medicine. Perhaps it wasn't Claire Watkins after all. 'So, what happened? Did you let yourself in?'

'Well, I knocked at half ten. She said, "Come round at half ten, Theresa, cos my shift doesn't start 'til late." But nobody answered. So I give it 'til quarter past eleven, and I thinks, something's up here. It's not like Rach to mess me about. And when I comes back round, I sees the cat. Freddy. He was ravenous, I could tell. And I thinks, Freddy's not had his breakfast, which doesn't seem right, because he's a greedy little sod, that cat. I save my scraps for him, like. So that's when I lets myself in and sees Rach on the floor like that.' She sobbed just once and seemed to swallow her anguish down in one gulp.

Jackie looked at a shelving unit in the corner of the small room. On it were photos: mainly sun-faded school photos of a girl, growing bigger over time until in one large, framed portrait, she was posing like one of the influencers on Instagram – all pouty lips and right leg bent demurely to slim her already slim silhouette, clutching bobbing metallic pink balloons that said she was eighteen. On a separate shelf were brighter, more current photos of a small boy. Curly-haired, gap-toothed and freckled. No man. 'Does Rachel have family? Children? An ex?'

Mrs Dolan nodded. 'Her daughter, Kylie. She's working away in Spain at some nightclub. Gives out tickets or something, Rach said. And the little boy – Luke – he's in school, far as I know.' She lit another cigarette, looking at the flame from her lighter through watery eyes. 'Poor little beggar.'

'What about a boyfriend?'

The old woman shook her head. 'Nobody. Rach got divorced from the little boy's dad about two year ago. Kylie's dad's... I don't know. They never married. I don't think the girl has any contact with him, but you'd have to ask her yourself. It's not my business, and I never seen anyone coming round regular like. Not when she was married to Greg. Not since they split, neither.'

'Any idea where we can find Greg?'

'He's in the wind. Shacked up with some new woman in Liverpool, I heard.'

Jackie nodded ruefully, thinking of her own soon-to-be-ex-husband, Gus, who was 'shacked up' with the pneumatic school-run yummy mummy, Catherine Harris. *Forget about Gus. Focus on work. Gus isn't going to pay your bills. He never has.*

As Jackie considered what to ask next, her gaze fell onto a bookcase in the hallway. On the bottom shelf were fat, leatherette-bound tomes. Photo albums. Perhaps old photos would reveal more about the enigmatic Rachel Hardman.

She turned back to the neighbour. 'Would you say Rachel was depressed?'

The old woman frowned. 'Worried about money definitely. Lonely maybe. But depressed?' She inhaled so hard that the cigarette halved in size. 'Never. I seen that note and I couldn't believe me eyes. First I knew of it, and me and Rach have been close for years. I'm like a nan to her.'

At Jackie's side, Dave rubbed his black eyebrow with the end of his pen. 'Does Rachel have any other living relatives apart from her children? Mother? Father? Siblings?'

'Yes, I know what "relatives" means, son.' The old woman still failed to meet Dave's gaze. There was a barb to her voice. 'I've been speaking English longer than *your* lot.'

Jackie sensed Dave's discomfort by the way he stiffened slightly in his seat, but outwardly, he remained cool and unruffled. She wondered how he managed to bite his tongue whenever they encountered a class act like Theresa Dolan.

'Her mam and dad live northside, I think. They do the odd school pickup, now little Luke's started school, but she's not that close to them. I met them once. They're snobs.'

As Jackie ushered Mrs Dolan out of the door, she calculated how old Claire Watkins must have been during her pregnancy to have a daughter who was already twenty-one years old.

'Twenty-one,' she said aloud. 'She must have been pregnant in... sixth form.'

'What's that?' Dave shouted through. He'd returned to the kitchen to take photos.

'Nothing.'

Jackie picked out a couple of the photo albums from the bookcase – the ones that looked the most dog-eared and covered in dust. Sitting on the bottom step of the narrow staircase, a flick through the first revealed photos mainly of a little girl who couldn't have been more than three years old. The girl's mother was in only a handful, carrying even more weight than the Claire Watkins that Jackie remembered, and far less than the size twelve or fourteen that she now appeared to be, lying life-less on the kitchen floor in those figure-hugging supermarket clothes.

Opening the other dusty album, Jackie gasped. 'Jackpot!' The photos within had become unstuck from the adhesive pages, but it was clear they were mainly school snaps. Halfway through, Jackie called to Dave. 'Have you got a minute?'

He joined her in the hall, leaning over the banister. 'What have you found?'

Jackie turned the album around so that Dave could clearly see. He took out his reading glasses and perched them on the end of his nose, squinting at the staged image of a sixth form: row after row of teenagers, ascending in height, smiling uncer-tainly at the camera. The name of the school and the year on the mount was written in gold lettering.

Jackie pointed triumphantly at a girl with a round face. 'Claire Watkins.' Then she pointed at a girl with dark hair and a surly expression, standing next to her. 'Me. Me and Claire. Our school-leavers' photo. See? I never forget a face. Claire *Rachel* Watkins. She must have been pregnant when this was taken. *That's* why I never saw her again. *That's* why she wouldn't return my calls.'

Dave shook his head. 'I hate it when you're this smug.'

'You hate it when I'm right.'

'And you had terrible hair.'

'It was the noughties. I'd put a tenner on it that you had terrible hair too.'

Her partner patted the short black spikes of his hair. 'My hair's never been less than awesome.'

He padded back into the kitchen. Jackie followed, silently registering an almost overwhelming pang of grief at the untimely death of her school pal. Remembered them both laughing like drains on the upper deck of the bus into town, at the end of the school day. With swim bags at their feet, stuffed full of damp towels and swimming costumes from an earlier lesson, they had put their swim-caps and goggles on, ignoring the strange looks from the other passengers. Full of schoolgirl-silliness and light-hearted mischief. It felt like only yesterday, yet decades had passed since. How had Claire come to take her own life?

With cracking knees, she knelt beside the body again. 'So, we're assuming an overdose, right? Suicide.'

'Judging by the empty bottle of sleeping pills and the note. Seems fairly cut and dried. There's no forced entry. Nothing to say she was murdered. Maybe she dropped the boy at school, came home and had a final barbiturate breakfast.'

'But there's no phone. That's weird, right? And she'd still bothered with breakfast.'

Peering into her friend's open mouth, Jackie noticed that there was something stuck low down in her gullet. She felt her skin prickle with anticipation. 'Hey, come here. Look at this, will you? Tell me what you think.'

Dave crouched beside her and illuminated his torch so they could both see inside Claire's mouth more easily. 'There is something in there. Maybe some of the pills got stuck and she choked. Maybe that's why she's got that look on her face.'

'Not your usual though, is it?' Jackie said. 'Not after a bottleful of sleeping pills.'

She gingerly lifted Claire's miniskirt for signs of bruising or anything that would indicate that this had not been a straight-forward episode of a desperate woman taking her own life after all. At a glance, there was not a single blemish on her skin. But as Dave switched his torch off and Jackie turned away, she caught sight in her peripheral vision of a tiny red dot on the outside of Claire's thigh. 'Would you say that's a pinprick?'

Frowning, Dave pushed his glasses up his nose and exam-ined the mark closer. 'Could be anything. Blocked follicle? Birthmark? A spot she'd picked. No idea.' He backed away and got to his feet. 'Looks fairly straightforward to me. My money's on suicide.'

'But only Nick Swinton can say for certain,' Jackie said.

She took out her phone and dialled the forensic pathologist. When she got through, she could hear disconcerting sawing and banging in the background. 'Am I disturbing you in the middle of a post-mortem?'

Nick laughed. 'Not at all. It's my morning off. I'm at the rifle and pistol club. Came to oversee some renovations. Jack of all trades...'

'Shall I call Cohen instead?'

'No. No. Fire away. What's eating you?'

Jackie looked at the anguished expression on her old school friend's lifeless face. 'We've come to give a suicide the once-over. Turns out I know the deceased. But here's the thing, Nick. I've got a nasty feeling it's not suicide at all. I think my friend was murdered.'

TWO

'First thing's first,' Jackie said, picking up a sheaf of bills and written correspondence from the cluttered kitchen worktop, all addressed to Rachel Hardman. 'We need to find contact details for Claire's next of kin and deliver the bad news. Daughter, parents or ex?'

'If the daughter's in Spain,' Dave said, 'maybe we should start with her folks. We've not got addresses for them or the ex. Let's have another scout round, see what we can find and take it from there. You look for any filing knocking about. Maybe there's an address book.'

He moved into the hallway, opening the door to a cupboard beneath the stairs. Clearly found nothing of interest and closed the door. 'You really think this isn't a straight suicide?' Dave asked.

'I do,' Jackie said, quickly ascertaining from the pile of post that her friend had racked up a credit-card bill of over six thousand pounds and owed United Utilities upwards of five hundred in unpaid water bills. Her financial situation looked precarious, but surely it hadn't been bad enough to warrant suicide. 'I mean, I admit it's decades since I last saw Claire, but she was never the depressive type. And what mother would abandon her four-year-old?'

'Depression's not picky.' Dave started to climb the creaking stairs to the bedrooms above. 'And it can pounce without warning. Listen, I'm going to see what I can find up here.'

'Well, I don't like any of this,' Jackie said beneath her breath, glancing over her shoulder at her school friend's legs, splayed beneath the kitchen table. *Claire, Claire, you had everything as a teen and just couldn't see it. How did you end up like this?*

Opening the kitchen drawers, one by one, she came across some official correspondence regarding child maintenance.

'I've got an address for the ex – Greg Hardman,' she shouted up to Dave. 'Looks like he *is* in Liverpool. An address in Bootle. Near the docks, I think.'

She wondered what sort of husband Greg Hardman had been to walk away from his wife and infant son. A philanderer? A weak man who couldn't cope with commitment? Or maybe Claire had thrown him out for being a drunk; a gambler maybe; a controlling bully. Could it be that he was implicated in her death? Even if this did turn out to be a straightforward suicide that required no further investigation, Jackie resolved to personally find out how her old school friend had come to end her short days, alone on the kitchen floor. A trip to Liverpool surely beckoned, on or off the books.

'Still haven't found a phone,' Dave shouted down. 'But she's got quite a collection of toys in her bedside cabinet, and I don't mean she's been to Hamleys. She could open her own branch of Ann Summers.'

'Dave, you're being crass,' Jackie said. 'Just remember that's my friend you're talking about, and she's dead. Show some respect.'

Another memory resurfaced – this time of Claire weaving Jackie's hair into an accomplished French plait in a quiet nook of the library, during a free period. She could still feel the tickling sensation of Claire's busy fingers, twisting her hair this way and that; could feel the warmth of the sun on her as it shone through the tall library windows. Claire had always had skin like a peach, and the golden light had given her a pre-Raphaelite radiance.

Jackie moved to the living room and looked around for a landline phone. Nothing. She pulled up the loose seat pads on the armchair and sofa to see if there was a mobile phone or some other item of interest underneath. There were only crumbs and the odd hair.

'Where the hell's her handbag and phone? What woman doesn't keep those to hand at all times?' she asked the photos of the adult daughter. It was only then that it struck her that the daughter looked familiar – not like Claire but reminiscent of someone else Jackie had known from those school days. One of the boys from the nearby boys' school perhaps? She made a mental note to go through the photo albums again, when the opportunity arose.

Peering through the murky living-room window at the litter-strewn street, she sighed with relief at the sight of Nick Swinton's forensics van approaching. Opposite, the neighbours were already twitching their net curtains. The sight of Nick, as he got out of the van and started to pull his white protective all-in-one over his normal clothes, was enough to bring those neighbours out of their houses and up to their front garden gates, where they exchanged knowing looks. Loving the gossip.

Jackie opened the front door.

'DS Cooke!' Nick beamed at her as he ambled up the path, carrying his kit. 'We'll have to stop meeting like this. Fourth death in a week and it's only Wednesday? People will start to talk.'

Jackie rolled her eyes but couldn't muster a grin today. 'This is Manchester, Nicolas. Let them do their worst.'

'Show me what you've got?'

Jackie led Nick inside and stood sentry by the sink while he crouched next to the body.

'I couldn't believe it, after all these years,' she said. 'Sixth form leavers' day was the last time I saw Claire Watkins alive. Bright as a spark, she was. Top of the class in Physics and Maths. I thought she'd achieve great things. Get a fabulous job; make a good marriage. Turns out she was living under a different name in a damp council house in Gorton. Not a leading scientist after all. Just another single mother in George at Asda clothes. Now she's dead, leaving two kids behind – one an adult; one a toddler. What a waste.'

Nick was carefully studying Claire's face. 'You can speculate about people's private lives all you like, but you rarely guess the truth. They always surprise you.' He took out a torch and illuminated it. 'So, you said you thought you saw something in her throat?'

'This is why I called.'

Shining the light down Claire's gullet, the pathologist frowned. 'Oh, ho ho. What have we here?' Taking a pair of tweezers, he reached inside and, with some effort, presently pulled out something cylindrical and covered in mucus.

'What the hell is that?' Jackie asked. She kneeled beside him as he held the object up to the light.

'Your friend's swallowed a bitter pill, all right.' He dropped it into a see-through sample bag, and it became clear what it was.

Jackie gasped. 'A roll of money, tied with an elastic band?' She stared at the Queen's distorted, tightly rolled face.

'Doesn't look like any suicide I've seen before,' Nick said, swabbing Claire's throat.

'It's been staged, hasn't it?' Jackie waved her hand over the empty bottle of sleeping pills and the single-worded note on the table.

Nick raised a bushy eyebrow. 'Someone's certainly gone to some lengths to disguise foul play. And yet they've left a roll of five-pound notes behind as some weird calling card.'

Jackie felt the hairs on her arms stand to attention. Inside the latex gloves, her palms grew damp with anticipation. 'I *knew* it wasn't suicide.'

At that moment, she visualised having to work overtime; coming home late to her children, who were already spending too much of their time with her mother, Beryl, or else with their father, Gus, at Catherine Harris's place – Percy and Lewis, fighting with Harris's beast of a son, Taylor, and being plied with dayglo drinks that were little more than syrup. Jackie's boys needed more stability in their lives, not less. And Alice...? Her four-month-old baby daughter deserved a mother who could give more than freezer bags full of pumped-off breast milk. A grandmother and an estranged father who was too involved with his silicone-breasted new squeeze were no replacement. Yet a murder case would demand almost all of her.

The sound of Dave clomping back down the stairs pulled her from her reverie.

'Nothing obvious of interest upstairs,' Dave said. 'What have I missed?'

Nick held up the sample bag containing the roll of money. 'This. Either your suicide OD'd on fivers, or you're looking at murder.'

Jackie wagged her finger at her partner. 'See? What did I say? I told you things felt off. I knew it!'

'Another case where you've got personal involvement,' Dave said. 'Venables is going to hit the roof.'

Casting her mind back to the huge case they had recently solved at enormous personal cost, Jackie closed her eyes. Lucian encroached on the here and now: memories of her Down syndrome kid brother before he was taken; bittersweet imaginings of him as an adult, his hand on her shoulder and a smile on his innocent face. Her heart still felt like it had been torn in two. 'Tina Venables can go to hell. Whatever corners she tries to get us to cut this time... I owe my school friend better.'

She opened her eyes. Lifted the hem of her friend's miniskirt and showed Nick the tiny red spot. 'Tell me what you think of this. First impressions. Needle puncture mark?'

Nick pursed his lips and frowned. 'Maybe. Let's get her back to the ranch, and I'll know more once she's had the full belt and braces. I've got two more ahead of her in the queue, but I'll get to your pal as quick as I can. In the meantime, I'll call my team and get them to go over this place with a fine-tooth comb.'

'Okay,' Jackie said, slapping her knees resolutely and getting to her feet with a grunt. 'I'll ask the uniform to get some tape round the place. Until you say otherwise, Nick, we'll treat this as a murder scene.'

Dave sighed. 'I'm not looking forward to telling a four-year-old that his mother's never coming home. That bit of the job never gets easier.'

It wasn't hard to track down Claire Watkins' parents. They lived in the same 1930s semi-detached house in Prestwich that Jackie had occasionally visited as a schoolgirl.

'God, it hasn't changed,' she said as they pulled up outside. 'Even the net curtains are straight out of the eighties.'

Dave took a swig from his Manchester City water bottle and belched. 'You've been here before?'

Jackie nodded. 'Fish fingers and chips and a couple of hours spent listening to music, while we bitched about school and pretended to do our Maths homework. I got invited back for tea a few times. Ironic really. Back then, I was the rough kid from Queen's Road. The mother thought I didn't see her checking my bag before I went home.' Jackie blushed hot with indignation as the memory of Mrs Watkins foisted itself on her – all pleated skirt, sharp elbows and whispered suspicions of petty theft. 'I think she thought I'd run off with her porcelain figurine collection. Now I live a few streets away in a house twice the size, and her daughter's ended up dead on the floor of a dump that looks pretty much like the shoebox I grew up in. Why the hell did she let her only child fall into such destitution?'

'Sounds like a right charmer.'

Opening the car door with a resigned sigh, Jackie nodded. 'She doesn't deserve the news we're about to deliver though.'

The weed-free, block-paved driveway was empty. The lawn beside it would put a bowling-green groundsman to shame. Its borders were filled with jaunty lilac asters that nodded in the unseasonably warm autumn breeze. The Watkins family liked order in their small lives, Jackie remembered. All of that was about to change.

Just as she was poised to press the bell, the toot of a car horn made her start. She looked around to see a small silver hatchback pulling onto the driveway. In the driver's seat, she recognised Debbie Watkins, wearing a look of undisguised suspicion on her fully made-up, ageing face.

The car came to a standstill and the engine fell silent.

Debbie Watkins got out, frowning. 'Can I help you? We don't want to buy anything,' she said.

'Don't worry. We're not selling,' Jackie said, flashing her ID. 'Police. Detective Sergeants Jackson Cooke and David Tang.'

Debbie's eyes widened. 'Police?' She turned back to the car and opened the rear door. Leaned inside and started to fumble with something.

Jackie could hear the excited chit-chat of a small child. Sure enough, Debbie helped a small boy out of a car seat and set him on the ground. He carried a brightly trimmed school bag that was almost as big as he was. It had to be Claire's son. Luke. He had her eyes. Jackie swallowed hard at the thought of breaking the news.

Clutching the little boy's hand, Debbie Watkins gave Dave a cursory once-over and then studied Jackie with a laser-like intensity. 'Jackson Cooke. That name rings a bell.' Her eyes narrowed then, though a quizzical smile played on her peach-gloss lips.

'Can we come in please, Mrs Watkins? We need to have a word. It's about your daughter, Claire.'

The smile faltered. 'Nobody but us has called her Claire for years. She's gone by her middle name, Rachel, since she was seventeen. You were at school with her, weren't you?' Even with the make-up, it was clear her colour had drained. All the lady-of-the-house bluster had dissipated.

'That's right. Me and Claire were pals. I came here a few times.'

'You'd better come in.'

Mrs Watkins ushered them into an overheated conservatory and then settled her grandson at the table in the adjacent dining room. Once she'd furnished him with some colouring materials, a glass of juice and a side plate containing what looked like lumps of cheese, she stepped into the conservatory and pulled the door to behind her.

'Has she been shoplifting again?' Without waiting for the answer, she opened the conservatory door and stepped outside. Shouted up to an open window on the first floor that sported obscured glazing. 'Leonard! Leonard, you'd better come down.' Stepped back inside and turned to Jackie. 'My Leonard's been retiling the littlest room. Now he's semi-retired... He gets a good reduction at B&Q for being a pensioner.'

Jackie noted the smell of potpourri coming from a bowl of coloured wood-shavings on the windowsill of the conservatory, conjuring the memory of Claire as a teen, sneezing uncontrollably and miming sickness at the cloying smell of her mother's kitsch choice of dust-gathering air freshener. She swallowed down a lump of sadness, wondering what her friend's story would turn out to be.

'Tea? Coffee?'

Jackie folded her hands in her lap. 'Like I said, Mrs Watkins—'

'Call me Debbie.'

'This isn't a social call I'm afraid, Debbie.' She tried on the familiarity for size but it pinched like ill-fitting shoes.

They sat in awkward silence until Leonard appeared. Jackie remembered him as a tall, overweight, perpetually harried second-hand car salesman – earning too much for Claire to qualify for a free place at the private school she'd attended with scholarship-winning, poor-kid-on-the-block Jackie; not earning enough to cope comfortably with the extra financial burden. Now, as he entered the conservatory dressed in spattered overalls, he seemed shrunken by age or his wife or both.

'These are detectives,' Debbie explained. 'They're here about Claire.'

'What's she done now?' he asked, plopping down onto a wicker armchair. His tone was indulgent.

Taking a deep breath, Jackie delivered the bad news. 'Claire was found dead this morning. I'm so sorry for your loss.'

Claire Watkins' parents reached out for each other's shaking hands. Leonard uttered a guttural groan and grasped at his stomach, doubled over, as though the news had been a physical sucker punch. Debbie remained sitting bolt upright, blinking hard.

'Dead? How?' she asked in a small voice.

'On the face of it, it looked like suicide.' Jackie took out the baggie that contained the scrawled, one-word suicide note. 'Does this look like your daughter's handwriting?'

Debbie glanced down at the *Sorry* that had been inked on

the scrap of paper. She shook her head. 'Claire didn't write this. My girl wasn't suicidal.' She thrust it back into Jackie's hands.

Jackie felt her cheeks flush hot. She was a veteran detective who had only relinquished the responsibility of a detective inspector because she had fallen pregnant unexpectedly and knew she'd never be able to juggle twin boys and a newborn. Yet here she was, blushing and struggling to find the words.

'The circumstances around her death are suspicious, I'm afraid.' Dave spoke with professional detachment. 'We're going to have to conduct an investigation.'

'Wait, suspicious? Suspicious how?'

'We'll have to conduct a post-mortem examination. I'm sorry. And we'll need to ask you a few questions.'

Debbie Watkins clasped her hands to her perfectly made-up face and started to shriek. 'No! No, no, no. This can't be happening. Not to my Claire.'

Her anguish cut through Jackie, manifesting itself as a jabbing pain just behind her right eye. She found she was grinding her molars together painfully. Then she realised why. Here was yet another mother having to mourn the untimely loss of her child. Was Debbie Watkins really any different from Beryl?

The door to the conservatory opened and Luke walked in, looking startled. 'What's wrong, Nanny? Why are you crying? Are you hurt?'

Debbie held her arms out, and the boy scrambled onto her lap, hugging his grandmother like a frightened koala.

'Please don't cry, Nan.' Tears rolled onto Luke's cheek, even as he tried to wipe at Debbie's streaked mascara.

Debbie took his small hand and kissed his knuckles. 'Oh, my baby,' she said. She stroked his hair. 'These police officers are here to tell us that your mummy's...' Her voice cracked. She closed her eyes momentarily. When she opened them, tears fell afresh. 'Mummy's had to go and live with the angels, in heaven. She's going to be watching over you from up there, my love.'

Jackie balked at the brutality of watching a boy who was little more than a toddler process the news of his mother's death. At first, he nodded, frowning, as if he'd been told an important secret. Then it started to register with him.

'So, Mummy's not going to pick me up?'

'No, Lukie. Mummy's never coming home.' Debbie started to keen, clutching the boy tightly to her. 'I'll never see my girl again. Oh, sweet Jesus, give me strength. Oh, I can't—'

'Never? Wait. Did Mummy die, like Peter the goldfish?' Luke started to shake and sob.

Across from them, Leonard quaked with grief, clutching at his knees in an eerie silence that was punctuated only by a singular loud sob as he exhaled.

Jackie reached out, wanting instinctively to place a comforting hand on Debbie's shoulder – to take the boy from her and cuddle him, as she cuddled her own boys – but she knew there was nothing she could do to sweeten this most bitter of pills. 'Please. Debbie, Leonard. Let us do our best for Claire. I'm going to be working on the case, and I promise you, I'll get to the bottom of her death.'

Debbie let her hands drop from her face. She nodded. 'I want to see her.'

'You will. I'll arrange for you to come and formally ID her. And her daughter, Kylie, needs to be told. She has to come home from Spain straight away, and we have to speak to her ASAP, so if you have her contact details, please let us have them. Now, tell me. When was the last time you saw Claire?'

Shaking her head, as if trying to shake a memory loose, Debbie looked to Leonard. 'Last Thursday? Yes. Last Thursday. Her and Luke had dinner here. But I spoke to our Claire at half seven this morning to wish her luck with Luke. He's been having a bit of separation anxiety since he started in reception, and it's been upsetting her.'

'So, she seemed alright then?' Jackie wrote in her notebook.

'Yes. Dreading the tears at the classroom door, but fine otherwise.' She gulped visibly.

'Okay. Right. Now, who could have wanted to hurt Claire? Her ex-husband? Greg Hardman?'

'Him?' Debbie said. The sudden sneer on her anguished face spoke to an acrimonious split. 'He drained our Claire of everything. Money, energy, hope. Sucked her dry like a vampire, he did. And then he did a disappearing act. On to his next victim. That parasite never cared enough to hurt her.' She examined her nails, seemingly oblivious to the tears that plopped onto her skirt.

Jackie watched her, wondering how these bereft parents could have allowed their only child to misstep so dramatically without intervening.

As if Debbie had read her thoughts, she leaned forwards and locked tearful eyes with Jackie. 'Listen, before you judge us... I love my daughter with all of my heart – loved. But Claire's always been – *was* – contrary as hell. If we said black, she'd say white. She... I don't know.' She shook her head and tutted. 'From the minute puberty kicked in, she turned into this quiet rebel. I told her, "Lay with dogs, Claire Watkins, and you'll get fleas," but would she listen? We offered help. We tried.' She turned to her husband. 'Didn't we, Leonard?'

Leonard nodded.

Satisfied with his response, Debbie turned back to Jackie. 'But Claire wanted her independence, and she took advice from strangers before she'd listen to us – that's why she moved all the way to Gorton on the say-so of some fly-by-night pal, who disappeared off the scene soon enough.'

'Well, it wasn't entirely down to her pal. We did throw her out on her ear,' Leonard said softly.

Debbie shot him a withering glance. 'No we did not! She refused our offer to get her and Kylie fixed up with a nice place over this side of town.' She turned back to Jackie. 'We tried and tried, and the arguments... It was a pressure cooker, and my Leonard's got heart problems, so... Claire left by mutual consent.' She held her hands up, fingers splayed. 'She didn't want us interfering anymore.'

'She called you overbearing,' Leonard said, wiping a tear with his sleeve.

'Claire wanted to learn from her own mistakes, she said.' Debbie seemed not to hear her husband. 'And the only good things that came from her terrible judgement were my grand-kids.' She sat up emphatically. 'So you can speak to that waste of space Greg Hardman, but don't expect the response of a husband or father.'

'Anyone else?' Dave asked. 'Who else might have wanted to harm your daughter?'

Debbie and Leonard exchanged a glance that appeared to be loaded with the intrigue of some shared secret.

In unison, they replied, 'Kylie's dad.'

'Can you give me his name?' Jackie asked, poised to note it down in her pad.

'What? You mean you don't remember him?' Debbie asked.

'Should I?'

'Didn't you know?'

'Didn't I know what?' Jackie looked from Leonard to Debbie, wondering who could have fathered Claire's daughter, given there had been no boys on their radar at an all-girls school.

Then she realised why Kylie's face was so familiar and she shivered as the blood in her veins seemed to slow and rapidly turn to ice.

THREE

'Why the hell wasn't he prosecuted? That's what I want to know,' Jackie said as she took the slip road onto the M60 and headed south, towards the peaks. Angered by the Watkinses' revelation, she floored the Ford, as if breaking the speed limit would somehow demonstrate her solidarity with the world's exploited women. 'You're talking about a teacher of thirty, abusing his position and getting into a clandestine relationship with a seventeen-year-old girl.'

'Pervert,' Dave said, scrolling absently through his phone. 'But it went on a lot, back in the day, didn't it? Let's face it. There was a PE teacher at our school who—'

'She was vulnerable, at that!' Jackie didn't want to listen to Dave's dismissive anecdotes. Her head swam with the enormity of the revelation. 'A bullied girl, looking for acceptance off anyone who'd give it. You met her mother, didn't you? Don't be taken in by the tears. Back in the day, she was the type where nothing's ever good enough – chip, chip, chipping away at her daughter's self-esteem. Small wonder Claire was willing prey for Mr Travis, the handsy Maths teacher.'

Dave fell momentarily silent at her side. He shook his head. 'If a teacher tried anything on with my daughter...'

Overtaking a sluggish heavy-goods vehicle, with a spurt of speed that the ageing Ford could barely spare, Jackie started to piece together a more accurate picture of her old school pal's life. 'So Claire gets knocked up in upper sixth, and her prissy parents are outraged. Maybe old Leonard tried to stand up for his baby girl, but Disapproving Debbie eventually turfed her out on her ear when Claire wouldn't play nicely.'

'And, if the parents are to believed, when they came after this Mr Wandering Hands for child maintenance, it all got nasty.' Dave took a ball-shaped object wrapped in tinfoil out of the glovebox and started to unwrap it.

'Jesus, Dave! No Scotch eggs in the car. What did we say?'

He bit into the rancid-smelling snack and shrugged. Spoke with his mouth full. 'My blood sugar's low. Maybe you should have a bite.' He waved the egg towards her.

'Pack it in, will you?' She batted his hand aside, silently admitting that she *was* ravenously hungry. Breastfeeding had always given her an insatiable appetite.

She thought of baby Alice then, enjoying nap time and oblivious to the fact that her mother was miles away in a car that stank of Scotch egg, trying to solve the probable murder of an old friend.

'Let's just think this through. Claire's found with money stuffed down her gullet, and the father of her eldest has apparently got previous for wrangling over maintenance payments. But the daughter Kylie's grown up now, isn't she? Still, this death feels like it's about money.'

'Or sex,' Dave said. 'Could your pal have been a working girl?'

As she pulled off the motorway and onto the A57 that snaked its way through the Peak District to Buxton, Jackie realised how little she actually knew about her friend. Claire Watkins had transformed into Rachel Hardman. What kind of woman had the painfully shy, academically able girl really become? 'I just don't know. You think you know someone at eighteen...'

'At eighteen, I was an idiot kid from Hong Kong, with spots and a Man City obsession. I thought I was going to somehow make it big in Hollywood and marry Lucy Liu. Truth was, I was terrible at acting, and I didn't know anything outside of school and serving in Dad's pharmacy on the weekend. Now look at me.'

Jackie navigated a hairpin bend as they climbed up and up through the peaks. The bracken was already turning golden on the steep hillsides on their left. She squinted as the September sun turned the reservoir below to liquid silver.

'I didn't think that at almost forty, I'd be raising a newborn and twin boys of nearly ten on my own. Going through a divorce, with my mother living in the basement. I certainly didn't think I'd be a cop, trying to gun a substandard car up and over the peaks, partnered by a man who stinks of petrol-station snacks.'

They rounded a corner and Buxton appeared, nestled in a valley below.

'Get Clever Bob on the phone again, will you? We need anything he can get on this Travis creep before we knock on his door.'

Dave dialled Greater Manchester Police's database expert, who was anything but, and whose nickname was a cruel gift of HQ's gallows humour. 'Did you get anything on this Phil Travis then? We're a couple of minutes from his home address.'

'Put Bob on speakerphone,' Jackie said, following the satnav onto Travis's anonymous-looking street and pulling up several doors away. From her vantage point, she could see his unre-markable York-stone terrace. It didn't look like it housed a sexual predator.

'He's clean,' came Bob's nasal voice through the speaker. 'No criminal record.'

'Nothing on the sex offenders register?'

There was silence on the line.

'Bob?'

Bob cleared his throat. 'My login's not working for some reason.'

Dave slapped the dashboard. 'Oh, come on! Seriously?'

'As soon as I find out, I'll call. I swear.' The line went dead.

Dave looked at Jackie, wearing an expression of disbelief. 'Can you believe that? He put the phone down on me. On *me*.'

Jackie sighed and held her hands up. 'That's cutbacks for you.'

'Yeah. Bob cutting back on brain cells.'

'Listen. Let's make this snappy,' she said. 'We've got a long day ahead of us and we've still got to get over to Liverpool to see the ex.'

Just as Jackie wondered if travelling to Buxton in the hope that Phil Travis would actually be in had been a fool's errand, she heard footsteps on the other side of the front door. There was the sound of several locks being undone. The door was cracked.

'Yes?'

'Phil Travis?' Jackie thrust her ID towards the miserly gap. She couldn't even make out her old Maths teacher's face. 'Detective Sergeants Jackson Cooke and David Tang. Can we have a word please?'

The door closed.

'Seriously?' Dave knocked hard on the door again. 'Police. Open up please.'

This time, the door opened fully, and Jackie saw immediately that her old teacher had aged significantly. He was still thin, but the fifty-two-year-old version of Mr Travis sported an almost perfectly round, buoyant beer gut that looked strangely welded onto his wiry frame. His thick dirty-blond hair had all but gone. He was dressed in jogging pants – baggy at the knees – that looked as though they hadn't seen the inside of a washing machine in a while and a white shirt that was stretched too tightly over his gut.

'Jackson Cooke,' he said, showing yellowed teeth in a smile that didn't reach his eyes. 'I never forget a student. My word, it's been years. Twenty years? To what do I owe this honour?'

'Can we come in please?'

They were escorted into a spartanly furnished, clean house that was devoid of all clutter or trappings of a personal life. It was wholly at odds with Travis's scruffy appearance, Jackie mused.

'Take a seat.' Travis ushered them onto a small sofa at the back of the house. By the window was a desk with a computer. On the monitor was a screen from an ended Zoom session.

'Not working?' Dave asked, taking out his notepad.

Travis smiled. 'I work from home. I'm a Maths tutor these days. My students are from all over the world. Been up since 4 a.m. today, would you believe it?' He yawned, as if to illustrate his point. 'A student in Korea. His father's a diplomat.'

'Why did you close the door on us, Mr Travis?' Dave asked.

Jackie sat in silence, observing the way Travis's eyes narrowed and his pupils contracted.

He gripped his knees. 'I realised I needed to end my teaching session.'

'We didn't hear you walk away.'

That yellow-toothed grin was back. 'I'm light on my feet.'

He turned to Jackie. 'My word, where did little Cookie go? You're quite the sophisticated woman now, Jackson. Detective sergeant, did you say? Are you married? Children?'

'Mr Travis – Phil – we're here to talk about Claire Watkins, or Rachel Hardman, as she now calls herself.'

Travis blinked hard. His lips moved, as though he were rehearsing what to say. 'I remember Claire.' His tone was one of wistful reminiscence, but that calculation was still behind his eyes.

Jackie held her hand up. 'Let's just cut through any pretence, Phil. We've just come from Mr and Mrs Watkins' house. We know you're the father of Kylie – Claire's eldest child.'

'Ah.' Travis looked down at his slipper-shod feet. His pallor gave way to flushed cheeks. 'It—It's... Sometimes things are more complicated than they appear.'

'I don't see anything complicated about a thirty-year-old teacher taking advantage of a sixth former. But we're not here to dwell on the abusive nature of your affair with Claire in 2001. I want to talk about the here and now.'

'Ask away. I have nothing to hide.'

'Ask what?' Dave said. He pointed at Travis with his pen. 'You know we're here to talk about the mother of your child, but you haven't shown a shred of interest in why.'

'You're baiting me, Detective.'

Jackie suppressed the urge to reach over and slap Travis. 'Claire's been found dead. Under suspicious circumstances. We're expecting a murder verdict, but first, I'd like to hear about the last time you saw Claire, and the current nature of your relationship with her.'

Travis's Adam's apple rose and fell in his throat. A sheen of sweat appeared on his balding pate. 'Murder?' He blinked repeatedly. 'What do you mean?'

'When was the last time you saw her, Phil?'

'I've not seen her in years. Honestly. Our relationship – the attraction was mutual. It was an intense, whirlwind romance that ended badly. I couldn't offer Claire the stability she wanted. I wasn't ready to be a father or to commit to someone... like her.'

'You mean, you used her sexually, and then abandoned her and your child – refusing to pay maintenance, we've been told.'

'I *did* try to be there for Kylie. I *did*. I didn't abandon her. Whatever the Watkinses have told you, it was nothing like that. It's just that I had to move school.'

'You were found out, weren't you?' Jackie narrowed her eyes at Travis in an accusatory manner. 'Summers rumbled you.'

Phil Travis nodded, looking wistfully out of the window that faced onto the nondescript garden that contained little beyond a shed and some wheelie bins. 'It was suggested I move. Old Summers wasn't far off retirement and had a lucrative consultancy lined up on some educational think-tank or other. I don't think he wanted a stain on his reputation, so he suggested I move to a boys' school in Surrey. But Debbie Watkins still made sure she made as much trouble for me as possible, even when I was three hundred miles away. I just had to throw in the towel and start doing agency work at an adult education college. After that, I could barely afford to feed myself, let alone give Claire money. I sent cash, whenever I was flush; on Kylie's birthday and Christmas, but...' He shook his head.

'When did you move back up north?' Dave asked.

'Five years ago? Kylie was pretty much grown-up by then. She didn't want anything to do with me, and neither did Claire. I honestly haven't seen either of them for about five years. I went round to her place in Gorton. She'd just married some bloke called Gary or Gav or something.'

'Greg Hardman,' Jackie said.

Travis nodded. 'Yeah. Him. There was a bit of a scene. We locked horns a bit, but I soon realised I was wasting my time. If Kylie doesn't want to see me, there's no point pushing it. I understand. I've not been there for her because her grandparents did nothing but drip poison in Claire's ear.'

'But you didn't want to be a part of her life, did you?' Jackie wrote in her notepad, *5 years since last saw C – check with daughter? Self-pity.* 'You wriggled out of paying formal child maintenance. The Watkinses told me you dumped Claire when she was pregnant and cut her dead – financially and romantically. So I'm hearing two different stories here.'

Standing suddenly, Travis folded his arms. 'Claire was browbeaten and eventually hung out to dry by her parents. You want to find a scapegoat for her death? Maybe look at them before you point the finger at me.' The loathing dripped from his every consonant. He walked to the living-room door and held it open expectantly. 'Thanks for coming.'

'But the Watkinses said—'

'I don't care what they said. I've told you, I haven't had any contact with Claire for five years. Ask Kylie. I've not even set foot in Manchester since before the first lockdown. Talk to that mouth-breathing husband of hers. Maybe he killed her. Maybe he'd had enough of his interfering in-laws.'

Dave got to his feet. 'What exactly *have* you been doing over the last forty-eight hours?'

'Tutoring. Eating. Sleeping. Rinse and repeat. Up at four. Bed by midnight. I haven't left the house for so much as a pint of milk. Check my fridge. It's empty.'

'So you've got nobody can corroborate that?' Jackie asked, slipping her notepad into her bag and scanning the room one last time before she was ushered out. There were no photos on the shelves or the walls. No evidence of a significant other or of family or even friends. Travis was apparently a loner, living an austere, monk-like existence. Jackie didn't buy it.

'Oh, yes. Of course I have.' Travis nodded. 'If you want, I can give you the contact details of all of my students and their parents.'

He took a battered wallet out of his jogging-bottoms pocket and removed a business card. Thrust it towards Dave. 'Here are all my business details. *First Class Formula* – Philip Travis, qualified tutor in Maths and Further Maths, for A level, IB and all international equivalents. My phone number's on there, and like I say, if you want my client list for the last forty-eight hours, you only have to ask. They'll vouch that I was teaching online. And when I wasn't, I was ordering in food, which the local Indian takeout will confirm.'

He left the living room and disappeared off into the back of the house. Returned bearing a takeout menu and pressed it into Dave's hands. 'There you go. Ask for Ahmed.'

'Oh, I will.' Dave gave his own card to the disgraced Maths teacher. 'And I want you to send your clients' contact details through to me by end of play today please.'

Without the conclusions of Nick Swinton's careful post-mortem examination, Jackie had no real idea what kind of murderer they were looking for. For now, at least, they were done with the man that had started Claire Watkins on the path to ruination.

'We'll be in touch,' she said, nudging Dave towards the front door.

'Nice seeing you,' Travis said.

Jackie didn't deign to answer.

Returning to the car, she plugged Greg Hardman's address into the satnav. 'Okay. Liverpool, here we come. Let's see if Claire's taste in men got any better with the passing years.'

Dave glanced back at Travis's house before pulling away from the kerb. 'Somehow, I doubt it.'

FOUR

'Mr Hardman?' Jackie stood on the step to Greg Hardman's terraced house in Bootle. An insistent, icy wind whipped in from the neighbouring Irish Sea, as though the weather gods were trying to cleanse this impoverished area of Liverpool of its long-held vices.

Greg Hardman was a wall of a man, built from nominative determinism and sheer malice, by the looks. Dressed in a plasterer's utility trousers and plaster-splattered T-shirt. 'Who wants him?' His dry, thin lips cracked as he spoke. He clasped a rough hand to his jaw and winced.

Jackie and Dave held up their IDs.

'Greater Manchester Police,' Dave said, placing himself between Jackie and Greg the hard man, though there was a good six or more inches between them in height. 'Can we come in please?'

'Well, I've just got in from work and I've got to get changed and get to the dentist. I'm due a root canal and I'm in bloody agony. So, not being funny, but what do you want? You've not come about my little lad, have you?'

'No. We're not here to speak to you about Luke, Mr Hardman,' Jackie said. 'It's your ex-wife that we'd like a word with you about.'

Hardman looked over his shoulder, into the living room beyond, where a TV flickered in the corner. He turned back to them and lowered his voice. 'It's a bit awkward, like. My girl doesn't like me so much as mentioning Rachel. She's the jealous type, you know. And me and Rachel have been water under the bridge for three years.' He frowned and then winced, rubbing his jaw again. 'She's not been done for shoplifting again, has she? Because they dropped the charges last time, but only after I paid for the bloody lot and begged that boutique to go easy on her, on account of her depression.'

So she was depressed, Jackie thought. *Or is Hardman our murderer, trying to frame Claire's death as suicide?* She started to drum her fingers on her thigh, feeling the patience leach from her like the sands of an egg timer running out. 'Let's go inside please. This is not a conversation to be had on the doorstep, Mr Hardman.'

The living room of the cramped terrace was filled with kids' toys and a hot-pink crushed velvet corner sofa that was too large for the space.

'Who's that, love?' the girlfriend asked, blithely painting claw-like nail extensions sugar pink as she watched some daytime American drama. Her lips were swollen and pitted with red marks, as though she'd had a bad reaction to injected filler. She looked up at them and her over-made-up face fell. 'Hey! I don't want no truck with the bizzies. Why'd you let them in, Greg?'

'It's all right, love,' Hardman said. 'They've just got a couple of questions. Nothing to do with us.'

Beside the girlfriend, a large baby sat in a playpen in front of the TV, gumming a chocolate bar, unperturbed by the brown drool that spooled copiously onto its playsuit.

'Nice snack for a baby,' Jackie said as she followed

Hardman through to a grubby kitchen at the back of the house. 'You know that their teeth come through rotten if you give them chocolate as babies?'

'You what?' The girlfriend looked at her blankly, batting her thick, black false eyelashes.

'Hope you've got the child registered with a good NHS dentist.'

The girl issued an expletive under her breath and continued painting her nails.

Hardman shut the door to the kitchen and took a seat at a small table. 'Well?' He checked the time on his phone. 'Can we make this quick, like?'

Jackie sat opposite him; Dave leaned against the sink.

'Claire – or Rachel, as you probably know her – has been found dead,' she said, watching Hardman's every reaction to the news. 'We're sorry for your loss.'

The colour drained from his florid face. 'Dead? How?'

'Murder,' Dave said, clearly pulling no punches now that they had a potential killer in their midst. 'We found her on the kitchen floor of her home in Gorton.'

'But what about my Luke? Where is he?' He glanced nervously towards the door. 'I can't have him here.'

'Your son's with your ex-wife's parents,' Jackie said, wanting to shake Hardman. 'By the looks of the parenting going on in your front room, I'd say it's just as well.'

Thoughts of feeding Alice started to encroach on the grim here-and-now, and she folded her arms over her chest. Even mere musings on her beautiful daughter needed to be protected from the likes of Hardman and his slovenly girlfriend. 'Now, you're clearly not moved by the news that your ex-wife is dead, but we'd like to know where you were this morning, between 8.30 a.m. and 10.30 a.m.'

Hardman rubbed his face with those shovel-like hands.

'Easy. I was at work. I start at eight. You can ask my site supervisor.'

'Where are you working?' Dave asked.

'A new block of flats.'

'*Where?*' Dave stepped towards him and bore down on him. The difference in stature meant nothing now.

'Manchester. By the old Boddingtons Brewery site. I know how it looks, but like I say, you can check with the boss-man. He'll tell you. I was in bang on time, and I never left.' He locked eyes with Jackie. 'You might not believe me, but I'm telling you: I'd never lay a finger on Rach. I loved her. I would never have left if she hadn't thrown me out because of...' He jerked his thumb in the direction of the living room.

'That's not the story I've heard from her parents.' Jackie wrote in her notebook: *Another sob story.*

'Those two? They're conniving, meddling old bastards. You shouldn't trust a word that comes out of that Debbie's mouth. She gave her daughter more heartache than I ever did. And Len's just a spineless waste of space.'

'So it's not true that you slept around on Claire... I mean, Rachel... and left her in the lurch with a baby? An infant son you decided you wouldn't have anything more to do with.'

'I'm not denying any of the sleeping-around bit. I'm a red-blooded male, aren't I? But I did try to be in my little boy's life. It was Rach who pushed me away.'

Hardman looked down at the white plaster caught beneath his fingernails. He opened his mouth to speak, but no words came out for a moment. Then he found his voice again. 'Look, I didn't kill her. Just because I was a bad husband and a rubbish dad doesn't mean I'm a murderer. You speak to my boss. I'll give you his number. You'll see I've got a cast-iron alibi.'

He started to write a telephone number on the back of a spent envelope with a worn-down IKEA pencil that had been wedged behind his ear.

'If we need to speak to you again, make sure you give us the number we can get you on most easily please.' Jackie held her hand out expectantly, while he added his own number to the scrawled details of his site manager.

As the door shut behind them, the girlfriend snorted loudly with derision.

'Drives me mad the way nobody respects the police anymore,' Jackie said, clutching her coat tightly to her to fend off the freezing Irish Sea wind.

'We're the pigs, the feds, the bizzies,' Dave said. 'We're not part of their gang – we're on the outside, looking in. That's why it's *our* job to solve the crimes *they* commit.'

Jackie nodded as they climbed back in the Ford. 'A cop's perspective is like putting a special lens over gen-pop's version of reality, isn't it? We get to see the unvarnished truth beneath the shiny façade.'

Dave brought the screen of his phone to life and started to input Greg Hardman's details. 'Ha. Like Facebook. Living their best lives, my arse.' He looked thoughtfully through the windscreen out at the run-down outskirts of Liverpool. 'They all think they can hide their disappointments and failures and dirty little secrets from us. Question is, what were Rachel Hardman's dirty little secrets?'

'We need to find out if there's been any murders or suspicious deaths with the same MO,' she said. 'I'll call Nick and ask him to check through his post-mortem records.'

She dialled the forensic pathologist, who picked up quickly.

He answered with a smile in his voice. 'Jackie. How far away are you guys?'

'Why?'

The forensic pathologist's voice was tinny, as though he was calling from the tiled, subterranean examination room of the morgue. 'I'm starting on your girl in the next hour. If you want to observe, you'd better come now.'

FIVE

'This feels so intrusive,' Jackie said, standing at the foot of Nick's slab, looking at the naked body of a woman she had once called her friend.

Nick Swinton nodded, making the first incision. 'I understand if you don't want to stay.' He began the process of revealing the layers beneath her yellowed skin, where bacteria were already starting to unmake the muscle and coagulated blood that had made her a living, breathing mother of two. 'In fact, have you told Venables what you're dealing with yet?'

Jackie chewed the inside of her cheek and looked away, preferring not to see the stopped heart that had once beat strong for Ronan Keating, trigonometry and pink Nike sneakers. 'She's demanded an update on the "suicide". Dave's in the car park, breaking the news to her that we've just been landed with another murder.'

'Oh dear. Better you than me.'

With the heart removed and placed reverentially on the scales, Nick turned to revealing the contents of Claire's bloated stomach. 'And how's little Alice doing?'

Jackie took a step back as the gas was released. 'Can we not talk about my baby right now please? Maybe save it for when you come over for lunch. In fact, let's not talk about food either.' She wished she'd put more VapoRub beneath her nose.

'So you don't want to know the contents of your friend's stomach?' With practised hands, Nick sifted through the digestive remnants of Claire's last day.

'Pills?'

Nick shook his head. 'Nope. There's hardly anything at all, except maybe some undigested meat left from a meal from the previous day – chicken, maybe – and certainly not pills. If she'd taken barbiturates in a quantity large enough to kill her, there would definitely still be partially digested remnants in this stomach.'

'So the suicide thing was definitely staged.'

'Seems that way, eh?'

Watching the forensic pathologist take her friend apart as though he were dismantling a car's engine, stripping her down to her component parts, Jackie thought again about the tiny pin prick she'd spotted. 'Has the toxicology report come back yet?'

'Nothing so far, but I'll check before you leave. I need to establish a cause of death, and so far, nothing's leaping out at me. But I'd put time of death between 8.30 a.m., after she'd dropped her son at school and, say, 10 a.m. A slightly smaller window than my initial guess.'

Just as Nick was poised to study her friend's lungs, Jackie heard someone clearing their throat in the room beyond, where the bodies were kept in refrigeration. 'Jackie. You got a minute?'

It was Dave, anxiously peering in at the macabre post-mortem scene. 'Venables wants to speak to you ASAP.'

Nick waved merrily at him. 'Not coming in to say hello, David?'

Dave blanched and took a step back towards the door. 'You're all right, mate. I'm laying off body parts for a while.' He patted his stomach. 'After the last case... I just don't think they agree with me.'

Jackie left her school pal in Nick's experienced hands and headed back with Dave up to the land of the living, where the air was fresh and warm.

'What did she say?' she asked as they walked over to the car.

'Call and ask her yourself.' Dave unlocked the Ford and rummaged in the glovebox, retrieving a second Scotch egg. 'The smell of the chemicals in there makes me want to eat meat every damn time.'

'You're a pig. I feel for Hannah, being married to such a heathen.' Jackie rummaged in her bag for her work phone but pulled out her personal device first. Bringing the screen to life, she saw there was a text from her soon-to-be-ex-husband. Her hands shook as her pulse started to race.

Got a gig in Stoke. Can't do school run. Also, tell your solicitor to up her life insurance. Mine's coming for her. Gus.

A bead of sweat tracked its way from between her shoulder blades to the waistband of her well-worn suit trousers.

'You okay, Jack?' Dave asked, slamming the passenger door and leaning against the car. 'You look like you've seen a ghost.'

'Yeah. The Ghost of Christmas Future,' she said. 'Where Gus fleeces me for every penny, and me and the kids end up in the poorhouse, while he lives in our family home and decorates it with wall-to-wall collectible guitars and Catherine Harris's stripper-shoe collection.'

Dave grimaced. 'That bad?'

But Jackie was in no mood to go into further detail about her split with the feckless father of her children, who had opted to be a stay-at-home dad but who had subsequently decided he'd rather be staying at the home of one of the school-run mums.

She dialled her mother, who picked up just before the phone went to voicemail.

'What is it? I'm at the hairdresser's.' The irritation in her mother's voice was audible above the whine of hairdryers, the salon chatter and the sound of someone singing a Motown classic out of tune. 'I thought it was time I got my roots done. I can't just give up after what happened, can I?'

'Where's Alice?'

'With me of course. She's in her car seat. The backwash girl fancies herself as an *X Factor* contestant. She's singing to Alice, and our baby's loving every minute of it.'

'Good. Listen, Gus has left me in the lurch with the boys, at the last minute. Can you pick them up? Please?' Jackie dug her fingernails into the palm of her hand, knowing that her mother wouldn't appreciate the change to her routine.

'Why can't you do it?'

'Me and Dave have just copped a murder enquiry. I'm at the morgue. I just can't get to the school in time, and I've got to get back to HQ. There's no way round it. Sorry.'

On the other end of the phone, her mother tutted loudly. 'Oh, Jackson! I wish you'd stop treating me like a glorified babysitter. I had to apologise to that teacher yesterday for Percy digging a fork into Taylor Harris's arm at lunch. I mean, I told her I wasn't surprised, seeing as that Taylor looks like a pig.'

'Mum!'

'Well, he does. He's like an oversized bacon joint in a V-neck jumper, that kid.'

Jackie found herself giggling. 'You can't say things like that.'

'Clearly. The teacher certainly wasn't impressed. She had a face on her like a bulldog sucking on a wasp. But that's the problem, Jackson. I should be free to be an obnoxious old boomer if I want, because I'm *not* Percy's mother. You are.'

Squeezing her brows between her finger and thumb, Jackie nodded. The old lady was right. Percy was having to deal with major upheaval at home, as well as the assessment process for ADHD by the school's special needs co-ordinator. He needed his mother's support.

'I'm sorry, Mum. I know you're shouldering way more responsibility than you should, and I really appreciate everything you do. But you, of all people, should know what it's like to parent on your own. Gus is unreliable at best.' She waited for the 'told you so' response but breathed out with relief when it didn't come.

'You married a carbon copy of your dad.' It sounded like a statement free from judgement, for a change. 'Okay. Leave the boys to me. I'll leave your dinner on a low light in the oven.'

'There's bags of breast milk in the freezer for Alice. I'll be home as quick as I can.'

Jackie hung up, wondering how long she could feasibly juggle a job that demanded too much with a baby and two nine-year-olds who realistically needed all of her. Then she remembered her school friend – a young life, cut short by someone who'd stuffed money down her throat, leaving her wide-eyed and stone cold on the kitchen floor.

Come on, Jack, the imagined voice of grown-up Lucian said. *You can juggle. You've got this. Claire's children matter too. Who's going to get justice for them, if not you?*

Realising imagined Lucian was right, Jackie crouched against the car and called Venables.

'Ah, finally.' There was no softness to her superior's voice.

'Dave said you wanted to speak to me.' Jackie squeezed her eyes shut, knowing instinctively what would come next.

'Tang tells me a straightforward suicide is now a murder. How do you explain that?'

'I didn't stuff a roll of fivers down the deceased's throat,' Jackie said, rolling her eyes.

'I've got them dropping like flies in Longsight and Moss Side because of some new gang turf war, and you go looking for *another* case to solve? A suicide with a note and everything!'

'Tina, I—'

'And as if that's not bad enough, I hear you have a personal connection to this dead woman.'

Jackie got to her feet and glared at Dave, who was perched on the bonnet of the car, texting, by the looks. 'It's not what you think. I only know the deceased from school days. So don't make me pass this case on to someone else. I'm perfectly capable of—'

'Give it to Tang. He can partner up with Malik. You can join Connor on the gangland thing.'

'The line's breaking up.' Jackie held the phone close to her jacket and rustled the fabric. 'Sorry, Tina. I can't hear you.'

But she could still hear her superior's irate voice on the other end. 'Are you disobeying a direct order, Cooke?'

Flushed through with adrenalin from the confrontation, Jackie ended the call. If she didn't engage with Venables, she couldn't be taken off the case. She slid the phone back into her bag. 'Thanks a bundle, Dave.'

Dave held his hands up. 'You can't keep something like that from Venables. And anyway, the last time you got involved in a case that had a personal connection, I almost lost you.' He screwed up the packaging from his Scotch egg and walked away from her, towards a bin.

Jackie followed him. She reached out to grab him by the shoulder and thought better of it. 'I'm not a child. I'm a professional.'

Stopping in his tracks, Dave turned to her. 'It's not just you who suffers when you're put in danger, you know. It's the people around you too.'

'Come on, Dave. It's the job. It's risk that we knowingly sign up to—'

'You don't know what it was like for me and Malik, combing

the city and coming up with nothing. Thinking you were dead. How do you think your kids would feel if Venables has to make that call because you've got in too deep again, except law of averages says this time, you're never coming home?'

Jackie was just about to castigate her partner for making a morality judgement that she neither wanted nor needed when Nick Swinton emerged from the hospital exit, wearing a fresh set of scrubs.

He strode over to them with purpose, waving a sheaf of paper. 'Hey. I've finished your girl and I've got the toxicology report back.' His eyes shone with intrigue.

'And?' Jackie laid her hand on his forearm to get a look at the paperwork. Noticed Dave's enquiring look and let go of the pathologist. 'What's the verdict?'

'She had been jabbed in the thigh. There was Rohypnol in her bloodstream.'

'Cause of death?' Dave asked.

'That roll of money. She choked to death. My guess is, someone doped her, inserted the cash in her throat while she was out cold, and she came round just as she was choking.'

'Any sign of sexual activity?' Jackie batted away the image of her school friend fighting for her last breath, perhaps as her murderer stood idly by and watched.

'Yes. No signs of a struggle though. So either she'd had consensual sex some hours before death or else her attacker had raped her while she was out cold. But that's not all. I've just had a word with Cohen. We checked back through the records of suspected suicides we've both worked on, where there's been an open verdict or a verdict of death by misadventure recorded.'

'Go on.' Jackie held her breath. The blood rushed in her ears.

'There was a death by misadventure just over a year ago. A woman in Didsbury – Faye Southgate – found dressed up in fetish gear, with a roll of tens down her throat and a plastic bag over her head. Cohen did the post-mortem and concluded that it was an auto-erotic thing gone tragically wrong.'

'Any Rohypnol in her system?'

'I don't remember the details offhand. But I'm pretty sure your lot just put her down as a rich divorcée, enjoying a big weekend in on her own.'

The furrows in Jackie's brow deepened. 'The roll of money down the throat... that sounds like a serial killer's calling card to me, not some kinky game. How wasn't that flagged as suspicious? Which detectives worked the case?'

Nick rubbed at a wayward eyebrow and shrugged. 'Who do you think?'

Jackie locked eyes with Dave and groaned. They both spoke in unison.

'Hegarty and Connor.'

SIX

'Close the door.' Back at HQ, Tina Venables was sitting behind the desk that had once been Jackie's, surreptitiously trying to jack up her seat so that she would preside over the meeting like a giant.

Jackie stole a glance at her watch. Gone seven. She should be at home now, supervising the boys' homework and bathing Alice before bedtime, but conducting door-to-door enquiries in Claire's street had gobbled up the rest of the afternoon, and then Venables had demanded an in-person update from them both.

'Look, can we make this snappy? Only, I really need to go, Tina. By rights, I should be on maternity leave.' She sank into the too-low visitor's chair and put her hands over her sore breasts. 'If I don't get home and feed Alice, at this rate, I'm going to end up with mastitis.'

Venables wrinkled her nose and held her beautifully mani-cured hands in the air. 'Eeuw. I really don't need details thanks.' She looked in vain to Dave for corroboration. 'And you opted to come back early.'

'You were short-staffed. Everyone was down with Covid.'

Jackie looked down at her own work-worn hands and visualised the forest of dirty feeding bottles that would require scrubbing and sterilising when she got home. She winced when she accidentally touched a florid scald, inflicted at 2 a.m. when she'd lifted the lid of the still-steaming steriliser, looking for a fresh bottle.

'You needed the money. Let's not dress it up. Anyway, enough of that. Tell me about your involvement with this murder.'

Jackie sighed. 'Claire Watkins. Goes by... went by the name of Rachel Hardman – her middle name and her married surname. I went to school with her. That's all. Haven't seen the woman since sixth form. First thing I know since leavers' assembly is that she's dead on her kitchen floor. It looked like suicide...'

'Empty bottle of pills and a note just saying "Sorry",' Dave said.

'But she'd choked to death on a roll of money that was inserted in her gullet.'

The corners of Venables' mouth turned down. 'Kinky sex gone wrong?'

Jackie dug her nails into the palms of her hands beneath the desk, thinking of little Luke, sobbing into his grandmother's bosom. 'I don't think my friend was like that.'

Venables pursed her lips. 'But you said you hadn't seen her since sixth form. That's a good couple of decades ago at least. So you couldn't have actually known what your friend was like, could you? She could have been a prostitute. Maybe a trick went badly wrong.'

'She died between 8.30 a.m. and 10 a.m.'

'So? A breakfast trick.'

Looking at her superior askance, Jackie could barely stifle the urge to roll her eyes. 'A *breakfast* trick? Entertaining clients in her own home? Are you kidding me, Tina? Is that the kind of detective work that got you my old inspector's job?'

Venables leaned forwards and pointed accusatorily. 'Hey! Greater Manchester Police is in special measures because we're sinking in a high tide of crime. Understaffed. Underfunded. I'm just trying to encourage my detectives to solve a few of the murders that come our way.'

'GMP is in special measures because too many cops in this place are incompetent and cut corners, Tina.' Jackie folded her arms resolutely, unwilling to give in to the woman – a woman she'd trained alongside – who had stepped up to fill her shoes as soon as she had stepped down.

'I'm a woman in a man's world, Jackson. This job is no picnic. I'm just trying my best.' Venables looked almost hurt. Almost.

Jackie was aware of Dave at her side, bouncing his foot as he often did when she and Venables clashed.

'What's clear is that this is no suicide. It's murder, but it's something above and beyond your usual domestic,' he said. 'Watkins or Hardman – whichever you wanna call her – had Rohypnol injected into her thigh. Nick Swinton reckons there's an apparent auto-erotic death in Didsbury with the same money-down-the-throat MO.'

Venables fixed him with a hawk-eyed stare. 'So we're into serial-killer territory? Again?'

'This is Manchester,' Jackie said. 'You're talking nearly three million people in Greater Manchester alone. We're living in the most violent city in the UK, and our murder rate's not far behind London's, which is three times the size. You said we're drowning in a high tide of crime. You said it. So, odds are, more than one serial killer a generation is going to come along. Simple stats.'

Venables rose from her chair and placed her hands territorially on the desk, leaning into them. She spoke in a low, deadly voice. 'Well, you're screwing up my simple stats. If we weren't short-staffed, I'd—'

'Yeah, yeah,' Jackie said, getting up from her low visitor's chair and slinging her bag over her shoulder. 'Spare me. Me and Dave solved a career case not four months ago. Even if you wanted to get rid of me, you couldn't now. So just let us get on with the job.'

'Find me a murderer.'

'We will.'

'Start with the red-light district. Sounds to me like these two women were on the game, if money and drugs were involved.'

Jackie blinked hard at her superior. 'I've told you. Claire Watkins was no prostitute.'

Venables smoothed a lock of her perfectly bleached bob behind her ear. 'You want to do good detective work? Maybe *you* should stop making assumptions. I want you down Back Piccadilly and Strangeways, asking questions. Take Malik. Those girls will know if there's a rogue punter with an axe to grind.'

'Tomorrow night,' Jackie said, slapping her hands onto her knees. 'The dead can wait. I'm exhausted. Right now, I'm going home to see my family.'

'Are they asleep?' Jackie whispered.

Beryl grimaced and muted the television. 'Keep your voice down, will you? They played merry hell with me at bedtime. I've only just got Alice off.'

'Sorry. I tried to make it back in time.' Acknowledging the sinking feeling that she'd missed yet another opportunity to kiss her children goodnight, Jackie padded into the kitchen. She slipped her suit jacket off and hung it on the back of a kitchen chair with a sigh. Washed her hands with almost scalding water at the kitchen sink.

The house smelled of her mother's cooking. Lentils and cumin, with a top note of baby's wet wipes and nappy sacks, coming from the trash. Jackie swallowed a lump of sorrow at the thought of being a guest in her own home.

Opening the oven door, she donned an oven glove and took out the searingly hot plate covered in foil. At least it smelled good. She removed the foil. 'Dried-out korma. Nice,' she said beneath her breath.

'Well?' Beryl said, appearing in the doorway to the kitchen. She folded her arms expectantly.

'It's lovely, Mum,' Jackie said, shovelling a forkful into her mouth. Her stomach growled, and she realised she hadn't eaten since breakfast. 'Thanks. I really appreciate it. Did the boys eat?'

Beryl took a seat beside her at the kitchen table. 'They eat for ten men. I think they're going through puberty early, those two. So, what kept you so late?'

The truth tantalised the tip of her tongue along with the curry. 'Like I said. Me and Dave copped a murder.' She knew Beryl would remember Claire Watkins; knew the old lady would love the gossip about snobby Debbie Watkins' daughter; was itching to tell her what had become of her enigmatic friend. But she'd learned her lesson about sharing details of her cases with her family. There were rules for a reason. 'You know what it's like. All hands on deck until someone's arrested or else the trail goes cold and the boss loses interest. I've got a late tomorrow.'

Her mother slapped the table. 'Oh, come on, Jackson! For God's sake. I'm going to the Albert Hall tomorrow night with Punk Sue. There's a seventies nostalgia night. It's been booked for months.'

Jackie sensed the waves of fury emanating from her mother and suddenly felt like her body was fading and losing its substance like a dying star. A dry sob forced its way up and out.

'I'm sorry. I'm so sorry, Mum. It's just...' She pushed the plate away and covered her face with hands that shook with the sudden wave of sorrow and stress that engulfed her.

Beryl's arms encircled her tightly from behind. The old lady spoke softly into her ear. 'Hey! What's all this? What's eating my girl? Has that feckless, philandering jerk Gus been having another go at you?'

Shaking her head and then nodding, Jackie willed the sadness and strife back into Pandora's box. 'Oh, he can go to hell for all I care. I'm not scared of him.' Had her mother seen past her bravado to her raw heart and the unfettered dread beneath?

'He's a coward and a bully, that one,' Beryl said, releasing her from the bear hug. 'He'll back off, don't you worry.' She took a seat at the table and patted Jackie's hand. 'And if he doesn't, I'm going to get Big Mavis from the gym to break his legs. And that slut he's shacked up with. Big Mavis will do anything for fifty quid and a giant bar of Cadbury's.'

Jackie chuckled. 'Big Mavis is seventy, Mum.'

'Doesn't matter. She's half Danish and the size of a house. In body pump she squats with twenty kilos on her shoulders. You should see her thighs. They're very robust, the Scandinavians.'

'Oh, Mum!'

'I'm telling you. She could crack that weedy ex of yours in the nick of her arse.' She screwed the spent foil emphatically into a tiny ball and let it drop to the table. 'Like a walnut.'

'That's fighting talk.' Jackie allowed a smile to ease its way across her anguished face. She imagined the scene of Gus being manhandled into compliance by Big Mavis, and the horror of the day seemed to fade, just for a moment.

Her mother nudged her conspiratorially and winked. 'Now eat up. You need your strength to get the milk supply for tomorrow restocked. If I'm missing my seventies nostalgia night, the least you can do is leave Alice with a couple of pints of Mama's best.'

The old lady got to her feet and filled a pint glass full of orange squash. Placed it by Jackie's plate. 'But first, you'd better rehydrate. You've got to look after yourself, Jackson. I know you're keeping the roof over all our heads, love, but you can't afford to neglect basics like food and drink. Not when you're still breastfeeding.'

'Huh. That's a joke.' Jackie felt the sorrow welling up, ready for a second onslaught. She looked over to the fridge-freezer and saw the family photos pinned to it – Lewis, Percy and her; the boys cradling Alice; Beryl burping the baby after a bottle; Alice asleep in her Moses basket; Jackie and Lucian as toddlers. Beneath the photos were samples of the boys' clumsy artwork, stuck to the fridge beneath a 'Go to Goa' fridge magnet that her father had brought back from a trip with his on-off girlfriend, Valeria.

'I'm missing out on family life. I'm nothing but a robot. When I'm not working these ridiculous hours and spending all my time either with the dead or with the scum of the earth, I'm a dairy cow, hooked up to a pump. Being a cop is in my blood now. I need to get justice for people like Claire. Like Lucian. But I'm never getting any proper time with the kids.' She dabbed at her eyes but realised they were still dry. 'I'm so torn. I feel like a satellite, lost in space.'

'This too shall pass,' Beryl said. 'Remember. You've got through far worse.'

Pulling her plate back towards her, Jackie made a second attempt on her dinner and downed the squash. Realised then that her mother was right. 'Thanks.' She finished her last forkful and kissed her old lady on the head on her way to the sink. 'You're a star. And I'll make the nostalgia night up to you, I promise.'

· · ·

With Beryl back in her basement flat, Jackie crept upstairs, careful to avoid the steps that creaked. The boys' bedroom door stood ajar. She stepped into their sleepy realm, savouring the lingering smell of bath time and slightly damp boys. Lewis was cocooned in his duvet, snoring gently, his hair sticking up in tufts, as Gus's had before his hair had begun to thin on top. Percy's arms and legs were splayed above and below the tangled bedding, bearing testament to a sleep full of adventurous dreams. Here were her glorious twins – relegated to second best by their father and short-changed by their overworked mother.

She sighed and moved on to the baby's box room, which still smelled of the fresh paint Nick had carefully applied while she and Alice had been in the hospital. Tiptoeing over to the cot, she peered down at her baby, still swaddled inside the Moses basket, which had been placed on top of the hand-me-down mattress from Dave and Hannah's youngest.

'I love you, my babelicious babba,' she whispered to her sleeping daughter, whose cherubic face was just discernible in the thin shafts of light that sneaked around the edges of the blackout blind.

Jackie allowed herself a smile. She exhaled deeply, relieved that the house felt full, even without Gus.

She padded through to the master bedroom and turned on the lamps. Only in here did it feel like something fundamental was missing. Jimi Hendrix's biography still sat on Gus's night-stand, as did his blister pack of antihistamine, in case of those hay-fever attacks he sometimes suffered from in the middle of the night. It was as if her soon-to-be-ex-husband had merely stepped out for the proverbial pint of milk, never to return.

'Good night, arsehole,' Jackie said beneath her breath.

She showered the day from her new mother's body, and once she'd set by as much milk as she could for Alice for the following day, she sat on the bed that had once been the beating heart of the marital home but which now felt too big for one.

From her bag, she took the file she'd pulled on Faye Southgate, the Didsbury divorcée who had met a sticky end in a leather studded harness, with a ball-gag strapped to her head and a roll of ten-pound notes wedged down her gullet.

'Now, Faye. Let's see what sort of secrets are kept behind Didsbury's stained-glass front doors.'

Pushing all thoughts of Gus and Catherine Harris aside, she began to read the post-mortem report. It told a tale of a thin woman in her early forties whose heart had been too big for her body, thanks to decades of heavy drinking and hard drug abuse, almost certainly masquerading as acceptably middle-class hedonism. A drinky with lunch. A couple of lines after dinner. Conservative estimates by Jackie who had never taken drugs in her life, apart from Migraleve and the odd ibuprofen.

'Two kids. One C-section,' Jackie said, reading the history that her dead body had narrated. 'Evidence of intercourse shortly before death. Like Claire. But physical signs of playing rough. Bruises on the inside of your thighs, eh? Were those invited in some BDSM game or were you attacked?'

She read on, noting how the hairs on her arms stood to attention as the strange aspects of her death and the toxicology results were related in clinical detail.

'Rohypnol in your bloodstream. There we go. This is the same set-up.'

Slapping the report down on the bed, she took out her phone and thumbed a text to Dave.

Definitely got a double murder on our hands.

SEVEN

'Why wasn't this investigated as a murder?' Jackie asked Venables.

Jackie had passed a fitful night, thinking about the case. Now she was faced with having to challenge her boss, who looked like she might melt the furniture at any moment with her indignant glare.

'You crossed a line yesterday, criticising my inspector's instincts. Now you're suggesting I've ignored a murder case?' Venables got to her feet and folded her arms over her red power-suit jacket. She was all burgundy shellac nails and shoulder pads this morning – the armour she wore to brief the new commissioner.

'Well, I'm not going to mention the wrongful conviction in the Scott Lonsdale case.' Jackie looked down at the now-shiny knees of her own drab grey trouser suit; an ill-fitting relic from before the twins had been born. She'd already moved the button on the waistband twice.

'You were on that team too.' Venables sat back down, as though Jackie had punctured her with the implied criticism, letting all the hot air out. 'I didn't see you speaking up at the time. You were just as happy to—'

'Look. I'm not here to point score, okay?' Jackie held her workworn hands up. 'It's just that the case of Faye Southgate was never picked up as a murder.'

Venables rolled her eyes. 'Is that the rich divorcée who died in an asphyxi-wan—?'

'She had a roll of money down her throat and Rohypnol in her bloodstream.' Jackie slapped Cohen's report onto the desk. 'You could explain the blockage in the throat as some kind of asphyxiation thing gone wrong, but nobody knocks themselves out with a date-rape drug in the middle of a...' She searched for the right word. 'An erotic adventure. In any case, Faye Southgate had had sex – rough sex, at that. Just because she was found trussed up in fetish gear doesn't mean she wasn't murdered.'

'Oh, come off it, Mrs High and Mighty. You'd have come to the same conclusion as me.'

'No. I wouldn't. Because I'm a detective sergeant in Major Crimes, and it's my job to ask difficult questions.' At that moment, Jackie wished Dave hadn't drawn the straw that meant he was sounding out their counterparts in Vice to see if they'd heard tell of some syringe-wielding pervert who had been giving the city's working girls a hard time.

Getting to her feet again, Venables waved her hands dismissively and marched to the filing cabinet. 'Whatever. Hindsight is a wonderful thing, right?' She opened a drawer and started rifling through, as though Jackie was disrupting some important admin. 'Just get down to the red-light district and make sure you and Tang come back with some answers. Okay?'

'I'm going to look into Faye Southgate's life. And I want Bob to comb the database for similar cases that might have gone... under the radar.'

Venables pulled out a file with something bordering on

unbridled hostility and slammed the drawer shut with a bang that made her flinch. 'Just do your job, Cooke. And don't go all vigilante-with-a-personal-axe-to-grind   on   me.   This   is Manchester, not a superhero film set, and I can't afford to have a detective with your level of experience off sick or blocking up the morgue. Besides, your children need you.' She flushed red and studiously looked at the file. 'Now get out.'

'Bob.' Jackie stood over her colleague, Clever Bob, who was sitting at his desk, surrounded by the usual forest of monitors. They displayed differing grainy footage of the law-breaking scum of Manchester's sodden earth, caught on CCTV in some act of theft, bodily harm or other drug-related skulduggery.

'Jackson Cooke, as I live and breathe.' Clever Bob swivelled round to greet her, his left cheek bulging. A telltale banana skin in his right hand.

'Bob, don't talk with your mouth full. It's like watching washing going round in a tumble dryer.'

'Breakfast.' Bob swallowed, looking contrite. 'I was gaming late into the night and overslept. You know how it is. Now, what can I do you for, O slayer of slayers?'

'Can we not mention that? Please?' Grim scenes revisited Jackie's memory in terrifyingly sharp resolution and full colour.

Bob dropped his voice to a whisper. 'You going to make nice with the new commissioner and get rid of Venables? Everyone I speak to would sooner see you sitting back at that desk.'

Jackie perched on a clear corner of his desk. 'My circumstances haven't changed, Bob. You just can't parent a new baby and two unruly boys – solo, at that – and be Queen of the Heap at work. My kids are getting two-star service as it is. I sent the boys to school in last week's shirts this morning.'

'Sprayed the armpits with Lynx?' Bob asked, grinning.

'How did you know?'

Bob sniffed his own tank top. 'Works like a charm, even at my age.'

He must have noted Jackie's look of exasperation because the grin slid from his waxy-looking face. 'Come on then, Detective. What am I looking for?' He held out his hand for the list Jackie was clutching.

'I need you to search the database for cold cases,' she said. 'These are the commonalities me and Dave are interested in. Single mothers, actively dating women, maybe working girls. We're looking for cases where it was a suspected suicide, but an open verdict or misadventure was recorded. If there's detail of something being stuck in the women's gullets, so much the better.'

'Another serial killer on the loose? We've only just caught the last one!'

'T.I.M., Bob. T.I.M.'

He looked at her blankly. 'What you talking in a funny accent for?'

'"This is Manchester". Like in the film *Blood Diamond*, except that was Africa and I'm not Leonardo di Caprio?'

'Ah, I get it,' Bob said, smiling weakly and clearly not getting it.

He brought up the Greater Manchester Police's database and plugged his login details into the system. A message flashed up, denying him entry. Jackie knew better than to wait for Clever Bob to figure it out.

She made her way down to the car park, where she rendezvoused with Dave by the Ford. 'Any joy with Vice?'

Dave rubbed his forehead. 'There's never any shortage of pervs and crazies in the red-light district. Rolls of money shoved down women's gullets didn't ring any bells, even though that would fit with the transactional vibe. *But* the Vice guys did give me some food for thought about Rohypnol.'

'Go on.' Jackie got into the passenger side of the car and buckled up.

Slamming the driver's side door shut, Dave took his notepad out of his breast pocket and read through what was written there. 'Date rape. Right? We knew Rohypnol was the drug of choice for spiking girls' drinks in nightclubs. But there's a new thing where little shitbirds jab girls in the thigh while they're on the dance floor.'

'So they can rape them once they're woozy?' Jackie asked, vaguely recalling an article in the newspaper that she'd read over Beryl's shoulder about the danger of young men covertly administering Rohypnol to unwitting girls on university campuses.

'No. It's not even about rape. It's just about incapacitating women for twisted sort of kicks, I guess. Schadenfreude, like. Apparently, there are groups of women-hating blokes on the Dark Web called incels or something.'

'Involuntary celibates,' Jackie offered.

'Yeah. That's it. They all sit there in chatrooms, hiding behind some avatar, hatching plans to do bad stuff to women because they're hacked off that nobody will willingly sleep with them.'

Jackie tried to picture the sorts of men that would fantasise about hurting women because of their own sexual inadequacy. 'I'm guessing these are real bottom-feeders. The kind that look okay but have the personality of angry molluscs or look like they've been cobbled together from spare body parts and still can't hack a straightforward conversation with the opposite sex.'

Dave chuckled. 'You guessed it. Clever Bob types, but not remotely as nice. Screwed up, embittered, misogynist... violent.'

'Poor Clever Bob. Don't lump him in with those losers. He's a bit dim and nerdy, but he's got a lovely girlfriend. You're talking about a different league here – toxic masculinity at its worst.' Jackie thought about Gus then. Did her soon-to-be-ex embody toxic masculinity? No. For all Gus was a philandering, money-grubbing jerk, he was a world away from men like that. Jackie had always been able to sniff a woman-hater from a mile away. She had kissed enough frogs as a young woman after all.

'Yeah. Scumbags, like I say. But it's worth looking at the incel angle, *if* Venables will let us do our jobs properly.' Dave plugged Faye Southgate's Didsbury address into the satnav. 'But for now, let's start with a victim we *know* is somehow linked to your Claire Watkins' death.'

Didsbury felt more like a well-heeled part of South West London's zone three or four, as opposed to a Manchester suburb. South of the city, they turned off towards the 'village' before they hit the M60 outer ring road. Immediately, they were plunged into a rarefied world of Victorian villas and chi-chi wine bars.

'The women are thinner and blonder out here,' Jackie noted, thinking about her own drab undyed hair and the baby belly that would take a good year to shift, since she had no time to consider her diet or exercise, beyond running after criminals and her sons. 'Look at them, with their pert bottoms in their £200 leggings. Sweaty Betty, indeed! I bet they've never broken a sweat in their lives.'

'My Hannah wants to live round here,' Dave said. 'She wants a cleaner and a gardener and a regular manicure.'

Jackie started to laugh. 'What did you tell her?'

'I reminded her that Chinese families don't do Didsbury. Especially not when the main breadwinner is on a measly cop's salary.'

'You might win the lottery.'

'And pigs might fly. I don't even play the lottery. Not after Hannah found out I lost a grand on the gee-gees.' He wiped his top lip and blinked fast. 'Still got Premium Bonds though.'

'Okay. So are you telling me that if you won the jackpot – a cool mil – you'd stay in Levenshulme?'

Dave's laugh was mirthless as he turned into the narrow street full of large Edwardian family houses where Faye Southgate had lived, and where her children were apparently still living, but now with their formerly estranged father. 'I'd get as far away from Levvy as possible, me. I'd go to Wilmslow or Bowdon or Hale. I'd get a house with a garden so big and walls so high, I wouldn't be able to see the thin blond people from my poolside sun-lounger. On a Sunday, I'd roll up in my Bentley – personalised number plate of course – I'd rock up to Glamorous Restaurant and order more dim sum than I could eat, just so everyone would know Dave Tang, millionaire badass, was in town.' He dusted off his collar, grinning at his fantasy.

Looking up at the house, however, Jackie felt as though a long shadow of grief had blotted out the weak autumn sun.

'Let's hope we get some answers, Captain Badass.'

As they walked up the garden path, Jackie saw a man looking down at them from the window of the attic room. The unexpected sight sent a shiver down her spine.

Dave pressed the doorbell. 'They know we're coming, right?'

Jackie nodded. 'I called ahead.'

After a couple of minutes, a figure loomed behind the stained glass of the front door. It was opened by a man in his forties who looked nothing like the strange character Jackie had spotted in the attic window.

'Police, right?' the man asked. He was well dressed in slacks and an expensive-looking shirt with a cashmere sweater draped over his shoulders in a considered manner. He held out his hand. 'I'm Miles Southgate.'

Jackie showed her ID. 'Detective Sergeants Cooke and Tang. Can we come in? We have some questions for you, as I explained on the phone.'

Miles Southgate ushered them into a living room that smelled of wood polish and was furnished with minimalist designer pieces. The floor was oversized parquet. The walls were a rich grey. It looked nothing like the hotchpotch that was the Cooke household.

Taking a seat on the uncomfortable sofa, Jackie wondered that this was a place where children were being raised. 'No stains,' she said.

Miles looked at her askance. 'Sorry?'

'Nothing. Now. We'd like to talk to you about Faye's death.'

Their host flushed. 'I've already been through all this months ago. It's very hard for me... I don't really want to dig up all that unpleasantness. Faye changed.'

'In what way?' Dave asked.

'Before the split, she was homely and loving and warm. Then I came out to her.'

'Came out...?'

'I realised I was gay. It was difficult. We'd been married for thirteen years. That's not the sort of thing you can easily drop into the conversation over dinner, you know?'

Jackie looked at the shelving in an alcove beside the chimney breast. On it were photos of three attractive children – two girls and a boy. Trophy photos in chunky, contemporary frames – not just of the children but also of Miles and his partner, perhaps – the man from the upstairs window – dressed in pastel-coloured clothing; by the sea, grinning with perfect teeth. If there had ever been photos of Faye, these had been removed.

'Was the split acrimonious?' She wanted to ask if he'd been sleeping around with men behind Faye's back but bit her tongue. It wouldn't do to let her own cynicism about men's fidelity poison her professionalism.

Miles laced his fingers together. 'You could say that. Yes. She felt it was a betrayal of trust. I had lied for a long time. I think that's why she went off the rails.'

'Explain to me what you mean about going off the rails,' Jackie said.

'The dating. The partying. The drugs. Have you seen her Facebook page? It's quite some time since she died, but I've not taken it down yet. So people can leave messages. Condolences. That sort of thing.'

Jackie made a note to check Faye Southgate's social media. 'Go on.'

'Well, it was embarrassing. I mean, every other day, she was posting selfies of her fawning all over some bloke or other, or her drinking espresso martinis with her bimbo friends. Posing and pouting and trying to convince everyone she was living her best life.' Miles Southgate's judgemental words dripped with disdain. 'And that was nothing compared to what she was really getting up to behind closed doors, spending all my hard-earned money on...' His eyes narrowed as he fell silent.

Dave cleared his throat and shifted his position in his seat. 'What *do* you do for a living, Mr Southgate?'

Miles sat up straighter then. 'I'm an entrepreneur.'

'Meaning...?'

'I create business startups and then sell them. Tech mainly.' He folded his arms tightly across his chest.

'Business good?'

He nodded. 'Oh yeah.' But looked away from Dave, towards the door.

'You got a nice pad of your own, I'll bet. A man like you. Clutter free.'

Miles unfolded his arms and looked down at his outspread fingers. 'Well, I've moved back in here since Faye... For the kids. You know? Stability. It's hit them hard.'

As Jackie watched the behaviour and listened to the words of this bereaved ex-husband, it occurred to her that he was revealing only a carefully cropped picture of his life and relationship with Faye. 'Who was the man upstairs, when we walked up the path?'

Shaking his head, Miles stumbled over his words. 'Well... I—'

'In the attic. I saw him. Looked in his thirties. Receding. He was wearing a pink and navy polo shirt.' She leaned closer. 'I'm sure you know exactly who I'm talking about, because he's in your house, he looked a bit too middle class for a burglar and to be honest, I don't believe in ghosts.'

'It's Clive. Clive Douglas. He's my... a friend.'

'Not a partner?'

Miles checked his watch and got to his feet abruptly. 'If you don't mind, I've got an important conference call to join.'

Jackie packed up her bag and stood to leave, but Dave stayed put on the sofa, drumming his pen against his notebook, tongue in cheek.

He cocked his head to the side. 'So you don't know anyone who might have tried to hurt Faye?'

Holding the door to the hallway open expectantly, Miles frowned. 'Should I? Faye's death was misadventure, wasn't it? A silly, hedonistic experiment gone horribly wrong.'

'And did she know a Claire Watkins, aka Rachel Hardman?' Jackie asked, following their host into the hall.

By the time Dave hoisted himself off the sofa, Miles was already unlocking the front door. 'I really haven't got a clue who Faye was rubbing shoulders with after we split. Apart from the kids, our lives took off in completely different directions. But I'll let you know if anything comes to me.'

He slammed the door on them without fanfare or farewells, like a man who had better things to do.

Jackie looked up at the attic window – no longer anyone looking down at her. 'Does this feel off to you?' she asked Dave.

Dave unlocked the Ford and looked back at the house. 'He's definitely hiding something. The question is what?'

EIGHT

'Right. Husbands,' Dave said, switching on his monitor.

Jackie sank onto her chair and flung her bag beneath the desk. 'Yep. Both women had pretty lousy ones, and Miles Southgate was definitely hiding something. So how about you check out Greg Hardman's alibi—?'

'They're bound to have some digitised clocking-in records on a building site that big.'

'Exactly.' Jackie nodded, starting to make a mental checklist of websites that would potentially yield useful investigative information on a risk-taking entrepreneur who had hidden his true identity for decades. 'And I'll start taking a closer look at Faye Southgate's ex and his pal Clive.'

As Dave dialled the number that Greg Hardman had given them, Jackie first checked that Miles Southgate didn't have a criminal record – he didn't. Then she looked at the records of his business activity on the Companies House website.

'Oh. You've been a busy boy,' she said, raising an eyebrow at the numerous entries for companies where Miles Southgate was listed as the CEO or a director. The records went back fifteen years, showing where companies had been set up and then later, in some cases, dissolved. More often than not, Jackie could see that Miles had resigned.

Frowning, she turned to Dave, who had just got off the phone.

'Hardman's in the clear,' he said. 'His alibi checks out 100 per cent. He turned up on-site at 7 a.m. The site security guy has it on CCTV. He turns up and doesn't leave 'til after lunch.'

'7 a.m. is too early to have killed Claire,' Jackie said. She shrugged. 'Onwards and upwards, right?'

Dave grinned. 'More like sideways and backwards, where me and you are concerned.'

He took up his notebook and thumbed through the pages he'd written at the Southgates' house. 'If you're doing Miles, I'll move on to this Clive.'

Nodding, Jackie focussed once more on the Companies House entries for Miles Southgate on her screen. She turned back to Dave. 'What does it mean when someone keeps setting up and dissolving companies?'

Dave peered at her screen. 'I'm pretty sure it usually means they're either just bad at business and keep having to fold or else the directors argue to the point that they can't carry on.' He poked at the gelled spikes in his hair. 'My cousin fancies himself as Mr Entrepreneur. He's forever setting companies up, making a pig's ear of the finances and having to shut up shop because he's broke.'

'So, like bankruptcy?'

'Not sure bankrupts can then start new businesses in their own name.' He pressed his lips together and looked thoughtfully at the photo of his family that sat on his desk. 'Actually, thinking about it, my second cousin *did* go bust in 2012. According to my mum, he's since set up a couple of companies in his wife's name, his mother's name... you can basically rope in anyone who's willing to be listed as owner.' He chuckled. 'I'm glad I didn't inherit the entrepreneurial gene. I may not be earning megabucks, but at least I haven't got the headache of wondering where my next meal's coming from or if the bank's going to repossess my house.'

Nodding, Jackie turned back to her computer. 'Miles Southgate's living in the family home. Do we think that's genuinely to give the kids some stability or is there another motive?' Her fingers flew over the keyboard, and she brought up the government's bankruptcy and insolvency register. 'Okay, Miles. Let's see if you've been a sensible boy with your pennies.'

Jackie plugged Miles' name into the search engine.

'Bingo!' she said, clapping her hands together.

'Bankrupt?' Dave asked.

'You bet. Declared bankrupt two years ago.' She searched for his previous address online and found Miles had been living in a luxurious, newly constructed apartment block in Cheshire's footballer-belt, where each three-bedroomed unit – including that belonging to Miles – had sold for over £1.5 million, according to Rightmove. 'The bank will have foreclosed on his flat, if he'd gone bump. Faye's death must have been a cause for celebration, if he'd been forced to downgrade to cheap rented accommodation. Now I'm beginning to wonder if poor Faye had any life insurance.'

'Check her will too,' Dave said. 'See who the beneficiary was. I'll look at Clive. See if he's financially tied to Miles.'

Jackie called Miles Southgate.

When he picked up, he sounded cagey. 'Detective. I thought I'd answered all your questions.'

'It's my job to ask questions,' Jackie said. 'And I need the name of Faye's solicitor – I assume she left a will.'

'She did. Yes. It's the same firm she used for our divorce. Black, Black and Fein. Her divorce solicitor was the senior partner, Sam Black. Can't remember the name of the one who dealt with probate.'

'Did you benefit from the will, Mr Southgate?'

There was a pause on the other end of the phone before he spoke again. 'She left everything to the children. Obviously, I'm now their sole parent, so I'll act as a trustee for their inheritance until they reach eighteen.'

'No other trustees?' Jackie frowned, wondering if she was trying to shoehorn a theory that Miles had killed his wife for money into a hole where it simply didn't fit. Could a lone, unpoliced trustee, who was also the surviving parent, blow their children's inheritance?

'Are you trying to insinuate I'm spending my own kids' money on coke and toy boys?'

'I just need to— It's just that I can see you've run into financial difficulties, so I need to rule out—'

On the other end of the phone, Miles sounded indignant. Was it bravado or had she really insulted him? 'I know what you're doing. You're trying to frame me, as some kind of immoral, spendthrift ex-husband who murdered his wife for the life insurance.'

'*Did* Faye have a life-insurance policy?'

Now Miles sounded aggressive. 'Hey! Now that's enough. You're the detective. You want to know all of this stuff? Do some detecting work, and speak to Black, Black and Fein. I'm not going to help you besmirch my good character. And anything else you want to ask me? You can go through my own solicitor.'

The line went dead.

Jackie put the phone down and looked over to Dave, who was reading through the Facebook page of Clive Douglas. 'Miles Southgate's got a wasp up his backside, and no mistake. Refuses to tell me the terms of Faye's will, can you believe it?'

'Clive Douglas checks out fine though,' Dave said, pointing to his monitor. 'Him and Miles only met about six weeks ago, judging by their social-media accounts, so it's unlikely there's been any lovers' plot between the two of them to get their hands on Faye's estate. Clive has no criminal record or financial bad track. He's a music teacher at a further education college. Seems legit.'

Gazing at a photo of Miles Southgate on Clive Douglas's Facebook feed, where Clive's arm was draped around Miles' shoulder and the two were posing on some smart-looking roof terrace, Jackie considered their next step. 'I think I need to speak to Faye Southgate's probate solicitor at Black, Black and Fein.' She checked the time on her watch. 'The office is in Spinningfields. I think we've got time to swing by there before we hit the red-light district. Don't you?'

The waiting area of Black, Black and Fein was slickly furnished with smart black leather sofas and the obligatory glass-and-chrome coffee table.

'Smells nice,' Dave said, picking up a glossy car magazine and flicking through idly. 'Smells of furniture polish instead of Connor's feet.'

'This is what hundreds of pounds an hour buys you,' Jackie said.

She looked past reception to the open-plan space beyond. A maze of workstations was surrounded by offices that all sported internal windows, affording the occupants a view of the brisk efficiency of their junior colleagues and admin staff.

A woman walked towards them with her hand stretched out. 'Detectives? I'm Kerry Dent, the associate that deals with probate. Follow me please?'

Jackie and Dave were taken to a small meeting room and offered coffee.

'There's really no need,' Jackie said. 'We just need some information from you about the will of Faye Southgate. Like I said on the phone.'

Kerry Dent opened the file she'd brought into the meeting

room and turned the legal document on the top to face Jackie and Dave. 'It's all here. Mrs Southgate left everything to her children – evenly split.'

'With Miles Southgate as the trustee?'

'We also act as trustee and have arrangements in place to check in with Mr Southgate regularly and to monitor cash flow from the estate.'

'So Miles Southgate can't spend his kids' fortune on fast cars and designer clothes?' Dave asked.

Kerry Dent shook her head. 'We'd ask questions.'

'Any life insurance payout?' Jackie asked.

'Half a million. All to the children. Evenly split.'

'But Miles Southgate's been declared bankrupt.'

Hooking her sleek black bob behind her ear, Kerry Dent smiled. 'He's still the children's father. He's their legal guardian. And if there were any impropriety with the legatees' finances, we'd know about it.'

'Tell us about the Southgates' split,' Dave said, folding his hands behind his head.

The solicitor treated him to a show of pearly teeth. 'Oh, Sam Black was the lawyer acting in that. I did do some work on the case – that was before I moved to probate – but Sam was the lead. He's one of the bosses.'

At that moment, a man knocked at the door to the meeting room. He looked to be in his mid-forties and was dressed casually in cord trousers and a cardigan, Jackie noted. He looked nothing like a solicitor.

'Come in.' Kerry beckoned him in.

The man opened the door and stood at the threshold smiling. 'Kerry. Sorry to interrupt, only I've got to go now.'

'Oh, Andy, hi.' Kerry turned to Jackie and Dave. 'Sorry. This is Andy Dewhurst. He's a social worker from the Children and Family Court Advisory and Support Service. He investigates children's living arrangements in the case of acrimonious splits to help the court decide who gets custody.'

'But you deal with wills now,' Jackie said.

'Our paths still occasionally cross when a divorced client dies in an untimely fashion and there's a bit of a wrangle over where the children are to go.'

Jackie clicked her ballpoint pen on and off and then pointed to the social worker. 'Did you work on the Faye Southgate divorce, Andy?'

The social worker frowned momentarily and then shook his head. 'No, I don't believe so. Doesn't ring a bell. I only get involved when the parents can't agree on custody arrangements or there's some suspicion of abuse.'

Kerry shook her head. 'The Southgates might have argued between themselves... I mean, divorcing couples rarely break up entirely amicably because there's money and usually children involved. But Faye and her ex-husband were pretty straightforward compared to many of our family-law clients. Miles Southgate let Faye have everything. I think he felt guilty, because he came out. That's a big secret to keep, right? But the family home was in Faye's name anyway. It was all in her name. She was the financial powerhouse in the relationship because she came from a wealthy family and inherited well herself. They argued bitterly over custody of the children at first. But eventually, they came to an agreement. Miles backed down and just took the kids every other weekend and one night during the week, every fortnight, if memory serves.' She narrowed her eyes. 'Something like that. He wasn't especially happy, but it's pretty standard, as access arrangements go. Faye was holding all the cards, after all.'

Jackie locked eyes with the social worker again. 'Andy, isn't it? Andy, did you or a CAFCASS colleague ever get involved professionally in a split between a woman called Rachel Hardman and her husband, Greg?'

Dewhurst muttered the two names beneath his breath and

looked up into the CCTV camera installed in the upper corner of the room. 'Rachel Hardman...'

'Sometimes known by her maiden name of Claire Watkins.'

He shook his head. 'Sorry. No. Like I say, we only get involved in the most complicated cases.'

'It was just a thought. Thanks.' Jackie smiled, registering a sinking feeling in her heart.

When they emerged from the steel-and-glass building, Jackie allowed herself a hearty sigh.

'You okay?' Dave asked.

She shook her head. 'Just a bit disappointed, I suppose. I thought we might be onto something. But there's absolutely no evidence that Miles Southgate was anything more than a terrible businessman who copped lucky financially when some other chump murdered his wife.'

'It's never that easy. Take heart, Jack,' Dave said, popping a stick of chewing gum into his mouth and offering her one. 'We'll find this son of a bitch, or we're not Tang and Cooke, Greater Manchester Police's finest.'

NINE

Sitting in their Ford in a squalid backstreet behind Piccadilly, waiting to rendezvous with Shazia Malik, Jackie took out her laptop and dongle.

'We've got a good hour and a half to kill.'

'There was no point going back to HQ,' Dave said, opening a bag of Marmite-flavoured crisps. 'Not when the working girls come out to play soon. And I'd rather sit here, eating crisps, than get cornered by Venables, banging on about some new idiot theory she's dreamed up.'

Jackie grimaced at the smell emanating from the crisp packet. 'I don't know about you with your evil snacks, but I'm gonna use my time to do some proper police work. We need to look at Claire's and Faye's social media to see if there's a murderer lurking among their followers and friends. Maybe they had friends in common or lovers... stalkers. Who knows? ' She logged into her own Facebook account and searched for Claire Watkins' profile. It was easy to find. She started to scroll through her old pal's scant posts.

Claire had joined as Rachel Watkins in 2009. At first, the feed had shown the odd family photo – Claire with her young daughter by the pool in Spain; Claire blowing out the candles on a cake, flanked by her parents; an updated profile photo, where Claire's few 'friends' charitably declared how hot she was, even though she looked decidedly worn out and somewhat haggard from weight loss. There were a few inspirational memes about the pursuit of happiness – the mawkish kind that made Jackie bilious – and a few about diet fads. Eventually, Greg Hardman started to show up in the posts, his arm wrapped territorially around Claire's shoulder. There was the obligatory 'Rachel Watkins is in a relationship with Greg Hardman' post, followed by a snap of them in their Sunday best, on the steps of the local registry office. The transformation to Rachel Hardman was complete.

Swiftly, Luke appeared, and Greg disappeared. The number of inspirational memes for the broken-hearted increased rapidly, followed by defiant, rallying cries to all other single laydeez out there. But there were no more photos of other men. No new boyfriend. No male friend or colleague from the biscuit factory where she'd worked, who looked like he might be something more. The only non-family member who did appear regularly in photos was a woman Jackie recognised immediately. '*Katie Pritchard?*'

'Who?' Dave asked, peering down at the photo of Claire, in a tight embrace with a woman who was wearing a headband with fluffy pink stars, suspended at the top of springs that sprouted from the headband like insect antennae.

'Another girl I went to school with. Katie was good at art and mixed with a slightly different crowd. I knew she spoke to Claire a bit, but I had no idea they were close. Certainly not this close. Claire's tagged her as her "bestie" and "BFF" on Facebook. Who'd have thought it?'

Suddenly compelled to google Katie, Jackie learned that she was working in marketing at a large insurance company nearby. 'I don't believe this. She's at the Co-op. I'm gonna call her.'

Jackie dialled Katie Pritchard, who answered with a chirpy voice.

'Hello, Co-operative Insurance marketing. Katie speaking.'

Jackie was momentarily flummoxed. Katie had had a high-pitched, almost squeaky voice at school, but this woman had the deep, gravelly voice of a long-term smoker. 'Katie. Yes. This is Detective Sergeant Jackson Cooke calling.'

'Who? Wait a minute. *Jackson Cooke?* Are you *the* Jackson Cooke that went to Manchester High?'

Jackie chuckled and blushed. 'I sure am. Katie... you sound so different. So grown-up.'

'I *am* grown-up. Bit too grown-up. Ha. But why are you calling?'

'Listen, can I meet you in the foyer of your workplace? In about ten minutes? I won't take up much of your time. I know this is out of the blue, but it's important.'

With the impromptu meet scheduled, Jackie took her leave from Dave and hastened through the Northern Quarter to the bottom of Oldham Road. She made her way down to the giant Co-op building that dominated the city's northern skyline – a big glass-and-concrete orb that kept a watchful eye on the goings-on in the city. Katie Pritchard was sitting in reception on an uncomfortable-looking, brightly coloured sofa. She was dressed in a skirt suit, with her hair in a chignon. A world away from the hippy chick who had excelled at portraiture in sixth form.

She rose to meet Jackie. 'Jackson Cooke. Who'd believe it, after all these years?' Held out her gym-toned arms. 'How the hell are you?'

Jackie returned the awkward embrace. 'Old. With a million kids, a failing pelvic floor and an impending divorce.'

Katie laughed. 'You haven't changed, Jackie. Funny. Join the club – the divorce club. Ha ha. My pelvic floor's still as tight as a drum at least, but God knows how long that will hold out, eh?'

Jackie then showed Katie her ID. 'Look, it's lovely to make contact again after all these years, but I'm afraid this isn't a social call.' She took a seat on the sofa in the otherwise empty waiting area.

Sitting down next to her, Katie's brow furrowed. 'How do you mean?'

'It's Claire.'

'Who?'

'I mean Rachel. Rachel Hardman. Claire Watkins. Whatever you want to call her. I'm afraid she's been murdered, and I'm one of the investigating detectives.'

Tears welled in Katie's eyes. 'No.'

Jackie nodded. 'I'm afraid so.' She could almost touch the woman's sorrow. It seemed to thicken and chill the air around them.

'Did she suffer? Did my bestie suffer?'

'She was doped, so it's possible she wasn't entirely sure what was going on. But no matter what, I'll find her killer.'

'When did she...?'

'Yesterday. I've spoken to her parents, her ex and Kylie's dad.'

Katie's cheeks flushed pink. 'Oh, *him*.'

'I take it you knew about Handsy Travis.'

'That pervert should rot in hell.' Katie's soft features hardened.

Jackie cleared her throat. 'Look, Handsy Travis's alibi checks out. So does Greg Hardman's. But I need to know, Katie, was there anyone else in Claire's life who might have wanted to hurt her?'

Katie stared through the giant plate-glass window at the neat, landscaped approach to the building. She turned back to Jackie. 'I dunno. I mean, she was doing online dating.'

'Which dating sites?'

'Not sure. Tinder, definitely. Connection, possibly? Match, at one time... We used to swap notes on the guys we talked to. But she's sensible. *Was* sensible. At least I thought so.'

Having gleaned all the information she could from Katie, Jackie exchanged work numbers with her friend and took her leave, promising to keep her abreast of any developments in the case.

As she exited the building, she thumbed her phone into life and saw that there was a missed call and a new voicemail. Clicking on the voicemail, she listened to a woman's voice on a bad line. The woman sounded young and nasal – sniffing as if she'd been crying.

'Hiya. Er, this is a message for Detective Sergeant Jackson Cooke. It's Kylie Watkins. I'm the daughter of Rachel Hardman.' Jackie held her breath as she listened. 'You left me a message to call urgently. Well, my nan already told me the news about Mum. So...' The girl's voice warped and wavered as she started to cry. Then she started to speak in a halting manner once again. 'Sorry. I, er... Sorry.'

There was the sound of her blowing her nose. 'I've tried booking a flight home, but there's nothing for a few days. Erm. Yeah. I'll get back as quickly as I can. Anyway, I'm going to try ringing you again later, because I want to know what's gone on, and I need to know our Luke's okay.'

The girl took a juddering breath in and breathed out hard. 'Er. Listen, I'm going to email you Mum's social-media logins, because Nan said you needed them urgently. Luckily, she wrote them all down and gave them to me to keep safe. She was always forgetting, see? So I'll email those now, and I'll call again later. Bye.'

Jackie exhaled slowly, now listening to the blood pulsating in her ears. She opened her emails and refreshed her browser.

Watched as an email from Kylie.Watkins123@gmail.com popped into her inbox.

'Here we go,' she said beneath her breath.

She read through the short email. There were the logins for Facebook, Twitter, Instagram and Claire's Outlook account. 'Brilliant.'

Jackie jogged all the way back to the car to find Dave licking the inside of a second crisp packet.

'How'd it go?' he asked, shards of crisps clinging to his chin.

'Most useful hour we've had in a while. Kylie Watkins has just sent all the logins through for her mother's social media.'

'Result!' Dave said, wiping his mouth with the back of his hand. 'You do Facebook. I'll do Twitter. Deal?'

Jackie passed the details on to Dave. As she logged into Facebook as Claire, her heart drummed out a lively tattoo. She skimmed through the same feed yet again, wondering if there had been more private and revealing content that she'd not been privy to as an outsider. But there was nothing.

'Come on, Claire. I don't believe you were living like a nun,' Jackie said.

She clicked on the message facility and came across a thread that made the hairs on her arms stand on end. This was surely it.

TEN

Claire had been chatting to someone called **Guy** Schön, whose photo was so perfect, he could have been a model.

'Okay, Claire. How likely is it that a single mother from Gorton was being chatted up by a male model?' Jackie performed a search on the photo and was unsurprised when there was a match with a Gucci model, who looked not unlike the actor Jamie Dornan. 'Oh, Claire, Claire, Claire. You daft girl. Let's see what Guy Schön had to say for himself.'

Over the course of a thread that started in February and ended only days before Claire had been found on her kitchen floor, Jackie read how her friend had been wooed – or more likely catfished – by this fraud of a suitor.

> *Hey, Rach. Can I call u Rach? It was so good to meet u in the chatroom last night. Been thinking about u n that hot profile pic of urs. Guy.*

> *Hi Guy. Lovely to hear from you. You're a very handsome man yourself. What brings a man like you to my inbox on a wet Friday night? Rachel x*

There was a proliferation of flirtatious emojis that did away with any irony or need for guesswork. Jackie could see this relationship had begun on a strictly sexual footing. Down-thread, it occasionally meandered into standard relationship territory, where Claire would moan about her day and Guy would make comforting noises, never revealing anything concrete about his own life. But mainly, it was essentially sexting. The question was, *where* had it started? What chatroom had Guy been referring to?

'Laptop,' she said beneath her breath, picturing the tab that would handily reveal Claire's browser history.

She reached for her notes to see what she'd written down at the crime scene.

'No laptop. No computer. No phone. Sounds off.' She looked at the profile photo of Guy Schön. 'Are you our murderer, stalking your prey through the long grass of the internet, Mr Catfish?'

Jackie made a note to get access to her old pal's bank account to double check which dating sites she'd been paying subs to. Perhaps gaining access to her various dating profiles would open up a world of online filth and danger dressed provocatively.

Her thoughts then turned to Faye Southgate. She brought up the Didsbury divorcée's social-media accounts. Miles Southgate had not had the passwords, and access had not yet been granted to the police by Facebook, Instagram or TikTok. But what could the public see?

'Come on, Guy Schön. Where are you?'

Facebook revealed nothing of Faye's life beyond cocktails with the girls; the odd fun-run for a major children's charity, where Faye looked amazing in Lycra; a raft of photos of her posing coquettishly – all pouting lips and the obligatory one leg bent, like a demented flamingo; and many, many snaps of Faye with her long hair balayaged in ash blonde and tonged to perfection at some expensive salon or other. She'd been 'living her best life' according to the commentary that accompanied the photos.

'No photos of the kids or your actual private life visible to the public. Not totally stupid then,' Jackie muttered, realising that if Faye Southgate had taken part in charity fun-runs, she had almost certainly been a more sympathetic character than the image-obsessed Barbie she'd chosen to construct online.

'But "living my best life, 24/7" wasn't your true story, was it, Faye?'

Jackie was suddenly overwhelmed by an aching sense of loneliness, coming from those staged photographs. She recognised it in herself, though her life was otherwise full-to-bursting with family and work. It was a symptom of the newly divorced, akin to those amputees she'd read about, who could still feel their arms or legs and were dismayed to remember that those intrinsically important parts of themselves had gone for good.

Instagram was her next stop. Jackie found Faye's account – @NotThatSouthgate. There, at least, Faye had let her guard drop somewhat. Photo after photo revealed her sitting on plush velvet chairs, pouting for the all-seeing, all-judging lens. She'd been taking those selfies in some fancy eatery, where the walls had been covered in smoky mirrors, reflecting her dining companions. Over the course of several months, in the same hangout, she'd unwittingly snapped the reflections of six different men. They were beefy, bald and well groomed.

'You had a type, didn't you, Faye? The opposite of your ex.' Jackie wondered how Faye could have put enhancing filters on the photos, and yet she'd apparently missed that her dates had been caught on camera. 'Or maybe you want your followers to see what's you're really up to.'

She looked through the list of Faye's 500-plus followers and noticed that Miles had been among them.

'Were you trying to make your gay ex-husband jealous? Oh,

Faye. That was never going to work.' Jackie thought about the slightly ghoulish-looking Clive Douglas. 'That ship had already sailed.'

Jackie looked at Faye's other Instagram followers, looking for Guy Schön. He was not among the bewildering array of monikers. But she did notice a Guy Sympa. Somewhere in the mists of her half-forgotten schoolgirl memories, a light switched on.

'Come on, Jackie. There's got to be a connection.' She stared at the names, written in her pad and underlined twice. 'Two *Guys*? Both with foreign-sounding names, beginning with S...?'

Plugging the names into her search engine, Guy Schön threw up a cameraman in Luxembourg and some unprepossessing middle-aged German on Instagram, who looked nothing like a Gucci model. Guy Sympa was a similar dead end.

A knock on the passenger window of the car snapped Jackie abruptly out of her reverie. She looked up to see Shazia Malik, grinning and waving through the glass.

Jackie rolled down the window. 'Shaz. Punctual as ever. Ready for an evening of trawling the red-light district?'

Shazia chuckled and toyed with the fringes on her navy hijab. 'Beats working the case I've been allocated. It's a snore-fest.'

Jackie was about to put her laptop away and get out of the car when something occurred to her. 'Shazia, I want you to tell me what springs to mind when I tell you two names. Okay? Only, there's a connection between them, and it's on the tip of my tongue, but...'

Shazia leaned on the sill of the window, idly waving at Dave. 'Sure. Fire away.'

'Guy Schön and Guy Sympa.'

Chewing her lip, Shazia frowned. Then the frown dissipated, giving way to a delighted smile. 'Guy Nice. Schön is nice in German. Sympa is nice in French.'

'Nice Guy,' Jackie said. 'How didn't I see that? Shaz, you're a genius!' She treated her junior colleague to a hearty thumbs up.

'I did French and German at GCSE. Easy when you know how.'

'You'd better get in the back and make yourself comfortable, because I want to finish up here before we go on a tour of Manchester's working girls.'

With Shazia installed in the Ford, Jackie went back through the names of Faye's and Claire's friends and followers on social media but could find no additional mention of the enigmatic Nice Guy. Rattling her fingers across the keyboard in frustration, she thumped the Ford's dusty dash.

'Bank details and computer access,' Jackie said, staring at the women's Facebook profile photos, displayed in separate windows, side by side on her laptop screen. 'That's what I need. This isn't about trawling the streets for a weirdo. This all started online.'

'What did?' Dave paused his Twitter trawl and glanced over at her.

Jackie looked at her partner thoughtfully. 'You mentioned incels, didn't you? The creeps who hate women.'

'Involuntary celibates.' Dave nodded. 'Why? What have you found out?'

Bringing him up to speed on her catfishing Nice Guy theory, she and Dave contemplated the photo of the muscular male model that had been used for Guy Schön's Facebook profile.

'My guess is we're looking for a stalker type,' Dave said, putting his phone into his jacket pocket and lacing his hands together behind his head. 'Mid-twenties dork, poor hygiene, maybe on the spectrum.'

Jackie turned to Dave, askance. 'David Tang, I would have expected more from you than a harmful stereotype.

Autism doesn't sentence you to life as a stalking, no-pals loser.'

'Oh, come on, Jack. You know exactly what I mean. These lads just can't cut a conversation with a woman.' He waved dismissively.

'That's down to dysfunction and toxic masculinity, not being on the spectrum,' Shazia said.

Jackie glanced back at her junior colleague and nodded. 'Exactly right, Shaz.' She turned back to Dave. 'My point is, we shouldn't make assumptions about Claire and Faye's murderer. But I do think the incel and chatroom thing is where we're headed, and we're gonna need Clever Bob to do stuff *off* the books.'

'Why? Because Venables has got it in her head that we're looking for the new Yorkshire Ripper?'

'Exactly.'

Dave pressed his lips together until the colour drained from them. 'Well, let's not rule anything out. Vice gave me the names of two working girls who were prepared to speak to us. Daisy and Shereen.'

Jackie nodded. 'Let's keep our eyes and minds open. Bring on the night.'

ELEVEN

Over the next few hours, they worked their way from side alley to backstreet, approaching the reluctant prostitutes, who more often than not turned their backs on them and hastily tottered off in their stilettos to find a kerb or a corner where they could ply their trade without appearing to collude with the police. Where they did get willing interviewees, they were met with: 'Nope. Nothing out the ordinary. Sorry, mate.'

'Don't know what you're talking about. I'm not on the game. I'm waiting for a friend.'

'Weird punter? Ha. They're all weird, love. If they wasn't, they wouldn't have to pay for it, would they?'

Feeling the cold night air of autumn start to bite through her coat, Jackie stamped her feet and watched the passing cars slow as their drivers assessed the wares on show. Some would stop and roll down the passenger-side window, asking what the girls did and how much they charged. Jackie felt her heart sink every time a girl got into a car and drove off.

Presently, Dave returned from talking to a couple of male prostitutes. He rubbed his upper arms. His breath steamed on the air. 'Any joy?'

'Not yet,' Jackie said, glad that her children were all sleeping soundly at this hour, unaware of Manchester's nocturnal dirty secrets. 'What did Vice say your two girls look like again?'

'Daisy's white, young, mousy hair. Wears head-to-toe pleather. Shereen's mixed race and normally wears a floor-length white Nike puffer.'

Jackie glanced down a section of the street they hadn't yet covered. She spotted a car, slowing by the kerb. It came to a standstill and a woman – little more than a girl – got out. Jackie nodded towards her, noting her pleather miniskirt, tight pleather jacket and cheap heeled boots as she strutted back to a doorway. 'That our girl?'

'Maybe.' Dave approached the prostitute. 'Daisy?'

Daisy emerged from her sentry post, all clacking chewing gum and neck full of love bites, visible in the nicotine-yellow light of the street lamp. She was no more than twenty. 'Who wants to know?'

Dave held his ID up. 'Detective Sergeants Dave Tang and Jackson Cooke. Major Crime Unit. Joanne Young from Vice said you were willing to speak to us about problem punters. A man who might have been pushing his luck with girls. Weird stuff. Violent. Strangulation maybe.'

Jackie noticed how Daisy looked again up and down the street, as though she were expecting someone to be watching her. 'Would you like to sit in our car with us? Are you worried about a pimp?'

'Are you kidding?' Daisy said, full of bravado and a crooked-toothed sneer. She folded her thin arms across her low-cut top. 'I'm my own boss, me.' She flicked her high ponytail indignantly. 'I'm just worried one of the other girls might see me and think I'm grassing.'

'Joanne said your pal Shereen would be willing to talk to us too,' Dave said.

Daisy nodded. 'I'll text her. We want paying though. Lost income and all that.'

Within a minute, a tall, mixed-race girl swaggered towards them. She wore a long Nike puffer coat. Bare legs and heels looked incongruous beneath it. Jackie could see in the sulphurous light that the girl had beautiful bone structure and large, long-lashed eyes, but working the streets had stripped her of a youthful exuberance, leaving her eyes dead, with dark circles beneath.

'Shereen?' Dave asked, showing his ID.

'Might be.' Shereen looked Dave and Jackie up and down. 'If the price is right.'

'Thirty each,' Daisy said, holding her hand out. 'Or we're not talking.'

'Thirty for both of you,' Dave said.

'Price just went up to forty each.' Shereen stuck a balled fist onto her hip.

The price was agreed.

'So come on. Tell us about the punter,' Jackie said.

Daisy took out a vaping pen and dragged hard on it. A plume of strawberry-scented smoke billowed from her nostrils. 'Creepy little arsehole. I gets in his car after we shook on a price, and he drives me to a building site. I mean, that's nothing new, because they mostly want to go somewhere quiet like, where they can't be seen. But then he wants me to play dead and tries to ram some pill in my mouth.'

Jackie mulled over the girl's revelation in silence. How similar was this attack to the intravenous administration of Rohypnol inside the victims' homes – victims who weren't working girls?

'What did you do?' Dave asked.

'I bit him, didn't I? Nearly took his finger off. I had to get tested and everything, because I drew blood. But I bit him and ran. Lucky he was too busy fussing over his hand to come after me.'

Clearing her throat, Jackie mentally compiled a list of questions to ask the girl. 'Did he show you cash, before you agreed to provide... services rendered?'

Daisy nodded. 'Yeah. I normally ask for payment upfront, but this one waved a wad of cash in a money clip. He agreed to pay more, but only if he paid after.' She looked down at her scuffed boots. 'He scammed me. If you're lucky, you live and learn, Shereen says.'

Jackie turned to Shereen. 'And what about you?'

'Yeah. I've had a run-in with this guy,' Shereen said.

'Can you describe him?' Dave asked.

'He's about six foot... no, less... well, actually, I don't know how tall he was, because he was sitting in his driver's seat. But he drove a Toyota.'

'What kind of Toyota?'

Shereen shrugged. 'A family car. Silver maybe. It was dark.'

'Go on.'

'Anyway, so he was a white man. Mid-thirties, I'd say. Short hair. Receding a bit. Old-fashioned metal-framed glasses. Dressed like a geek.'

'A geek?' Jackie asked.

'Yeah. V-neck sweater with a shirt underneath. Dressed like someone's granddad, know what I mean? But he had these, like, beady intense eyes. And he wanted me to pretend I was dead. Like Daisy said. Same routine.'

'Did he try to drug you?' Dave asked. 'Knock you out?'

The girl nodded and clutched her puffer closer. 'Yeah. Except when I went with this guy, he had a drink bottle. Like a thermos thing, yeah? He said it was gin and tonic, but I smelled it, and it wasn't right.'

Jackie wondered briefly if Rohypnol smelled of anything at all. She made a note to ask Nick Swinton. 'Did you drink it?' she asked.

Shereen shook her head. 'No way.' She glared at Jackie. 'What do you take me for? I wasn't born yesterday. I knew he was trying to spike me, and Daisy already told me she'd had this weirdo, so I was on my guard, like. I tried to push the thermos away, but then he gets nasty and tries to pour it down my throat. He ruined my new dress, man. And this wasn't no Primark rag. I got it from the designer section in TK. First time on.'

'I presume you got away from him unhurt,' Dave said.

'Damn right.' Shereen took the vaping pen from Daisy and dragged on it. 'I know you two are the pigs and that, but I don't mind telling you I carry means of defending myself, and I ain't afraid of doing some damage when punters get cheeky.'

'Did you mark this man in any way?' Jackie asked. 'Any way we'd recognise? A cut that might scar? A black eye?'

She shook her head. 'Me and Daisy compared notes, and we reckon it's the same guy. We asked some of the other girls if they'd come across this creep, but they all said no. So maybe he's just... starting out.'

Jackie could feel frustration mounting. They had a rough description of a man who could be a thousand men – a man with an interest in role-playing sex with women who were out cold. But what about the roll of money? Owning a money clip was not the same as trying to ram a roll of notes down a woman's throat.

'Did he do anything else out of the ordinary? Did he try to tie you up?'

Both girls shook their heads.

'He didn't have a chance,' Daisy said. 'We both got away, didn't we, Shereen?'

More nodding.

Dave exhaled heavily, frowned and pressed his lips together. 'Did you get a name maybe?'

'I don't ask for names,' Daisy said. 'I just take their money.'

But Shereen spoke over the top of her friend. 'Col,' she said. 'He said he was Col.'

TWELVE

'Hush little baby, don't say a word, Mama's going to buy you a mockingbird...' Jackie started to sing the lullaby to Alice as her infant daughter grew sleepy on her breast. She stroked her downy hair and marvelled at those tiny eyelashes, fingers, rosebud lips. How could something so tiny and perfect be the outcome of such a traumatic pregnancy?

Jackie uttered a prayer of thanks to a god who seemed only to listen selectively. It had been a good day. She and Dave had a potential lead in this Col, who could feasibly be Mr Nice Guy. Now Jackie was back home, revelling in the peace of the place and the knowledge that her children were all safe, under the roof that she provided.

Alice's intermittent sucking came to a standstill. With cracking knees, Jackie got up from the armchair in the corner of the nursery, stealthily carried her to her Moses-basket-in-a-cot set-up and lowered her onto the mattress. The baby girl jerked from the feel of the cold surface against her back, fists balled tightly and eyes squeezed shut. Jackie held her breath, not daring to move, lest her daughter wake and want to start the feeding rigmarole all over again. Her heart beat wildly at the thought but not wildly enough to wake little Alice. The baby slept on.

Creeping back to her own room, Jackie breathed a sigh of relief. She looked at the bedside clock – 5.13 a.m.

'Oh, what's the point?' she whispered, fully awake now.

Under a steaming hot shower, she thought of all she had to do on three or four hours' snatched sleep. She had to see if Bob had unearthed any banking information on the victims that might be of use, and she made a mental note to follow up any dating-website leads for Claire and Faye; she had to get Bob to look into the records of any kerb-crawling men matching the description of Col – perhaps Vice would know more; she had to duck out of work several times during the day – once to visit her divorce lawyer in the city centre, a second time to take Alice to see the health visitor at the local health centre, and a third time to pick up the boys from school and have a chat with Percy's teacher about his escalating behaviour in class.

Jackie felt the weight of responsibility pulling her down, down, down yet again. She turned the shower off and raised a finger to draw a flower or a heart in the steam on the door, as she usually did, but couldn't find the optimism to do more than smear her hand across the glass.

She dried and dressed herself and padded down to the kitchen to put a pot of coffee on. Switching on her laptop, Jackie decided to log into her bank account to see if she would be able to pay the water bill without going into overdraft. She plugged in her username and password.

'Come on, Santander. I know my balance is going to be a car crash. Hit me up.'

Her account page loaded and for the first time that morning, Jackie smiled. With her finances now uncoupled from Gus and his profligate spending, she was finally in the black.

'I don't believe it,' she said, staring at the balance of £1,074.23. 'A couple of months on my own and I can pay the water bill without worrying about the bailiffs? It's a minor miracle.'

Jackie got to her feet and poured her coffee. She drew a heart in what little froth there was and started to sing the old Destiny's Child classic that celebrated being an independent woman. She had, in fact, bought the house she was living in. She had, in fact, bought the shoes she'd shortly be wearing, as well as the car.

'Thank you, Beyoncé,' Jackie said, throwing a move that demanded much from a new mother. She took a brioche out of the bread bin and kissed the photo of her kid brother that was attached to the fridge door by a magnet. 'Love you, Lucian.'

Perhaps things were looking up for Jackson Cooke.

By the time Gus rang the bell at 8 a.m. in advance of the school run, however, the rosy glow of financial solvency and independence had worn off.

'Have you sent all your wage slips to my solicitor?' Gus asked, standing on the doorstep in the drizzle.

'You smell of wet dog,' Jackie said, cradling Alice in the crook of her elbow. 'Doesn't Catherine Harris own a washing machine, or is that just her natural odour rubbing off on you?'

'You're very hostile, Jackie,' Gus said. He remained on the step, despite the fact that the shoulders of his red jacket were growing dark with moisture. 'You wanted a divorce. You're getting one. I'm just asking for what's rightfully mine.'

'I wanted a divorce because you ran off with Taylor Harris's surgically enhanced mother. And every time you ask for a cut of my salary or ownership of the house that *I* bought for this family, you're taking food out of the kids' mouths. *Your* kids' mouths. Way to go, Gus.'

'I've always done the overwhelming bulk of the parenting.' Gus's lips thinned to a mean line. He stuck out his pigeon chest.

'Even once the boys went to nursery, you wouldn't get off your backside and get a part-time job. You had a good seven years of sitting in your pants, watching daytime TV. And playing gigs in pubs for the price of a round of drinks doesn't buy school uniforms for two growing boys.'

'I was the glue that held this family together. This house is my home.' He poked himself emphatically in the chest.

'Well, you should have thought of that before you started scouting the school-run mums for an upgrade and making yourself at home in Harris's bed.'

Behind her, the boys were fighting on the stairs.

'Those are my shoes!' Percy yelled at Lewis. 'Get off them, butt plug!'

Jackie swung around. 'Percy Rutter! Don't let me hear you using language like that ever again or I'll wash your mouth out with soap!'

Percy responded with gales of forced laughter and swiped his brother over the head with his lunch pack.

'Mum! Percy's got my shoes on,' Lewis yelled. 'Just because he got his all scuffed up, playing footie on the tarmac. *And* he's nicked my homework and put his name on it.'

Turning back to Gus, Jackie eyed her soon-to-be-ex-husband, wondering how their marriage had disintegrated into this scene of domestic discord. No, actually she knew how it had come about. It wasn't just Gus's selfish, lazy streak. It was also her job, with its long, long hours and emotional demands. To be a cop's spouse, you had to be nothing short of a saint.

'Look, I can't stand here, arguing in the rain,' she said. 'Come in, sort out your sons and then get them to school. I've got to see to Alice. Mum's banging on about some emergency appointment at the chiropodist, because she's got a funky toenail, but I need her to take the baby. It's mayhem.' She felt the red mist start to descend. 'You've landed me with all this bloody responsibility, Augustus Rutter, four months after giving birth to your daughter. And all you can do is stand on my doorstep with your hand out.'

She could see Gus opening his mouth, ready to come back at her with some biting retort. Here she was, a single mother being exploited by a man who expected simply to take what he wanted from her. How different was she from Claire Watkins and Faye Southgate, she wondered? 'Actually, no. Don't come in. Get the hell out of here, in fact. I'll sort the kids myself, like I sort everything else. And my solicitor will be in touch about your latest claim for cash. And don't expect me to just roll over and give in to your demands.'

'But I—'

'I don't want to hear your pathetic excuses. I've had three hours' sleep, and I'm carrying the can for three generations. So, turns out I don't need you putting a dampener on my already demanding day.'

She took a step over the threshold and pushed Gus off the step. 'Go back to Catherine Harris and her wet-dog smell. Go on! Bye-bye.' Jackie slammed the door in his face.

'Get your own shoes on, Percy. Now!' she shouted.

Her wayward son, always so keen to push the boundaries, looked up at her in wide-eyed silence. He merely nodded and pulled off Lewis's shoes.

'I don't want to hear a word out of either of you. Now get your shoes on, get your bags and coats, and get in the damn car. Right?'

'Hey! What's all this commotion?' came her mother's voice from the top of the stairs that led down to the basement flat – Beryl's domain. 'Jackson? What's with all the shouting?'

Jackie found there were tears rolling onto her cheeks. She felt suddenly like a dripping pressure cooker that was ready to blow. 'Take the baby, Mum. I've got to go.'

'But the chiropodist!' The perfectly groomed Beryl looked at her askance. 'I need my pedicure. I've got a fungal—'

'I'll be back in time for the health visitor appointment.'

Handing Alice to her mother, Jackie kissed Beryl on the

cheek, kissed the baby and stroked her peach-like cheek with a wistful longing in her heart. Ushered her chastened boys out of the door. 'Alice's milk's in the fridge, and I've washed the pram blanket.'

She closed the door behind her, willing her tears to stop.

'Mum?' Percy began.

'Car. Now.'

As she drove the boys to school through a bottleneck of similarly harassed school-run parents and commuters, Jackie thought about the stereotypes of cops that she'd read in crime thrillers from time to time. Damaged sorts, who struggled with addiction and mental-health issues. They never seemed to have to juggle kids and work and ironing. They were almost always loners or else alluring bad boys. How glamorous their self-indulgent lives seemed compared to hers.

'Being normal is hard enough,' she whispered beneath her breath.

Jackie delivered her sons to the already empty school playground – late enough, at least, not to have to face Catherine Harris, flanked by the other alpha mums.

By the time she got to HQ and found a decent parking space, Venables had everybody in a team meeting in the big meeting room. Jackie swore beneath her breath as Venables turned towards her and beckoned her inside.

THIRTEEN

'Jackson,' Venables said, pointedly glancing down at her watch. 'So nice of you to finally join us.'

'Sorry, Tina. The kids...'

Jackie looked around the meeting-room table. She took her place next to Venables, flanked on the other side by Dave. Shazia was diagonally opposite, with Bob facing her.

Venables cleared her throat and turned away from the whiteboard, on which she'd written 'Prostitute-killer update' in red marker. 'Right, Cooke, Tang and Malik. You're first up. What have you lot got for me after trawling the red-light district?'

Rereading the title on the whiteboard, Jackie frowned as Dave gave an account of meeting Daisy and Shereen.

'So these girls mentioned a Col – short for Colin, I'm guessing,' he said. 'He tried to dope the girls. The encounters took place between the time of Faye Southgate's and Claire Watkins' murder, so that fits, and it sounds vaguely similar to the MO of our murderer, but...'

'It's a bit of a stretch,' Jackie said. She pointed to the board. 'And I don't think it's helpful to decide this is about a prostitute killer, Tina. There's no evidence that Claire Watkins or Faye Southgate were selling sex. None. So let's not make assumptions, eh?'

Venables leaned against the tabletop, ignoring Jackie and fixing her gaze on Shazia. 'Malik! What else?'

Shazia blushed. 'Col drives a silver or silver-blue Toyota. Maybe an Avensis saloon. That's it.'

'Good,' Venables said. She wrote 'Col' and 'Silver Toyota Avensis?' on the whiteboard. Then she turned to Jackie. 'Let's not assume this isn't our guy, eh? The mayor has got wind of this case. The press won't be far behind. So the pressure's on this department – on me – to solve the case. How can Manchester attract funding from business and central government when people can't walk the streets at night?'

Jackie was tempted to come out with a smart retort about Manchester long being the nation's most violent city and about Venables looking for a lazy win, yet again, but steeled herself not to rise to the bait. 'This Col is interesting, but I want to look into the online dating that both victims took part in. They were both in touch with a man calling himself Nice Guy in two different languages – Guy Schön or Guy Sympa. Uses a stock photo of some Gucci male model to chat up women. Bob's been looking into the victims' bank details, for evidence of online dating sites, haven't you?' She nodded at Bob.

'Roberto?' Venables asked. 'Care to enlighten us?'

Bob was drinking from a bottle of a dayglo orange liquid that was masquerading as fruit juice. 'Ah yes.' He slammed the bottle down. 'Bank deets for the victims.' He turned his attention to his laptop, clicked on the mouse pad and brought up on the whiteboard PDFs of bank statements. Turned to Jackie. 'I can put them on a stick for you.'

'Do me a favour,' Jackie said. 'Just give me old-fashioned printouts. I got three hours' sleep. The less time I spend staring at a screen, the better.'

'And you asked me about previous cases that might have similarities.' Bob rubbed the stubble on his weak chin.

'Oh, here we go,' Venables said.

'Just doing due diligence, Tina. We need to do more of that, not less.'

Venables fell silent then, agitatedly flicking her nail extensions.

Glancing at the bank statements of Claire and Faye on the whiteboard, Jackie could already see a couple of entries that made the hairs on her arms stand up. But Bob was looking at her expectantly, still waiting to tell her about previous cases. 'Well?'

He cleared his throat and glanced nervously at Venables. 'Well, there's just one from 2015. A woman in Worsley. Marie Grant. Forty-nine, mother of three grown-up children. Abusive ex-husband.'

'Have you got the post-mortem report?'

On the whiteboard, Bob replaced the bank statements with the report in question.

'Zoom in on the findings please,' Jackie said.

She read aloud from the whiteboard. 'She had benzodiazepine in her system but no remnants of sleeping pills in her stomach. Who's the forensic pathologist that did her?'

'Old Maclean,' Bob said.

'Didn't he retire ages ago?' Dave said.

'He found a pound coin in her gullet,' Bob said absently. 'Mad, eh?'

Jackie thumbed her chin thoughtfully. 'What was Maclean's verdict? Murder?'

Bob shook his head. 'Nope. Misadventure.'

Jackie jotted the details in her notebook, hardly able to believe that such a bizarre death could have been interpreted as anything other than murder. 'So Maclean concluded she was spaced on sleeping pills and accidentally swallowed a coin and choked?'

'How the heck can you *accidentally* swallow a coin?' Shazia asked.

'It was Christmas time,' Bob said. 'Could have been baked into a Christmas pudding, couldn't it?'

'I'm sure Maclean knew what he was doing,' Venables said. 'Let's not put two and two together to make five, shall we?'

'Tina, I think it's a link worth looking into,' Dave said. 'Just because there's years between the deaths doesn't mean a killer wasn't cutting his teeth on this Marie Grant.'

'Fine,' Venables said, getting to her feet. She wrote Marie Grant's name on the whiteboard and put a question mark next to it. 'So, Cooke and Tang, keep looking into our first two victims, and also this new woman. Bob, I want you to try to find a Col on the database that might match the description the working girls gave.'

'What about me, boss?' Shazia asked. 'Do I help Connor with his Burnage stabbing or Jackie and Dave? I'm happy to help Jackie and Dave. I mean, it sounds like they've got their hands more than full.' The eagerness in her voice was unmistakeable.

Venables checked her notebook and shook her head. 'No, Malik. Today, I need you to follow up on the death of an ultra-Orthodox woman from North Manchester who apparently had a seizure and fell downstairs. She died last Sunday. The parents wanted her buried on the Monday before sundown, but the cause of death wasn't cut and dried, so she was sent for an MRI and bloods, and then whacked in the fridge. The results are due back today, so given you're an ethnic and she's an ethnic, it makes sense for you to pick that up.'

The enthusiastic glow to Shazia's face dimmed. Jackie could see her mouthing the word 'ethnic'. The girl shifted in her seat and pulled the sleeves of her jumper over her hands.

'Don't look at me like that, Malik. It's good experience for you. Jews aren't allowed post-mortems without a genuine suspicion of foul play, demonstrated by a dodgy blood test or MRI. See? You've just learned something new, thanks to me.' Venables beamed at them all. 'You're welcome.'

Jackie sighed with relief as the meeting was concluded.

Wondering if old Maclean had done a half job of the post-mortem examination, given he'd been long overdue retirement, Jackie asked Bob to print out the entire file. She followed GMP's inept computer expert back to his forest of monitors and gave him the profile of Col – the problem punter. As Bob checked the database, she sat in the visitor's chair, stationed at the end of his desk, and pored over the hard copy of the file.

'Marie Grant lived alone with her kids,' she said. 'The kids had been at their paternal grandparents' for a sleepover. If she did choke on a Christmas pudding – which sounds more than a bit of a stretch to me – there was nobody to ask. But these notes show no remnants of your mythical Christmas pudding in the house, no sign of a break-in and no evidence of a struggle.'

Bob shrugged. 'Stranger things happen at sea. Know what I mean?'

Jackie stacked the paperwork into a neat sheaf and slid it into her bag. 'Looks like this case never made it past the uniforms who attended the scene. It's like what almost happened with Claire Watkins, aka Rachel Hardman. They spotted some sleeping tablets and assumed it was suicide or accidental overdose. And because of that, murder might well have gone under the radar for seven years. Seven!'

Swivelling round to face her, Bob narrowed his eyes. 'You really think this is connected to your other two?'

'Maybe. Yeah. I mean, it's a very similar scenario. She's been knocked out and there's money rammed down her throat.'

'But it's literally just a couple of months since you caught the last weirdo.'

Jackie held her hands up. 'What can I say? Femicide is massively under-investigated, especially in older women who aren't likely to grab headlines. It's bad enough now. Seven years ago, it was even worse.'

'Zoe calls it bias,' Bob said. His girlfriend Zoe's insight made him seem positively enlightened.

'Exactly. And sometimes, it's just hard to know what you're looking at with death. People don't go in convenient, obvious ways, and we've got a police force and forensics service that sometimes aren't as joined up as we'd like – especially when murderers move between counties. It can take years before patterns are spotted and a detective in one force joins up the dots with another.'

'So you've got a clever killer here?' Bob swigged from a new bottle of dayglo orange drink.

Jackie considered Bob's words, privately wondering if there was some kind of stimulant in his drink that was making him particularly astute today. 'Yeah. Yep. He knows how to sow the seeds of doubt over the cause of death – enough to cover his tracks. If Marie Grant *is* connected, our killer has definitely been capitalising on human error in a complicated justice system.'

Jackie stood to leave. She paused to look at Clever Bob, surrounded by his hi-tech gadgetry. Bob was a man who often couldn't even generate a PDF, yet his insight had triggered something in her detective's brain. *A clever killer.* She couldn't articulate why that was important, but she mentally pinned it, feeling certain her colleague had touched on something significant. It would keep.

'Listen, I'm going to be looking for dating websites and singles' chatrooms that the victims visited,' she said. 'Will you hit me up with an avatar or whatever they call it for a spoof dating account?'

Bob grinned and winked. 'Spoof? Yeah. Sure. Okay then.'

'Just because I'm newly single, doesn't mean I'm looking,

Robert. Especially not with a tiny baby to look after, and especially not with a killer out there.'

She arrived back at her and Dave's booth, where her partner was sitting with his back to her, intently searching for something on the internet. In silence, she took her seat and fanned out the three years' worth of bank statements she'd collected from Bob. Scanned through the list of expenditure and income on her old friend's main current account.

Dave turned around. 'How's it going?'

'Well, at a glance, I can see that Claire Watkins had a subscription to Connection.com, and she's paid for Tinder Gold.' Jackie sighed. 'What's the bet that this got her killed?'

'I thank God every day that I met Hannah before the internet really got going. All it took in the old days was a nightclub and four pints.'

'You told me Hannah was your mum's best friend's daughter, and that the old ladies totally engineered it, Mr Boombastic Luva-Luva.'

Dave blushed and turned back to his keyboard. 'Well, I'm just glad I don't have to do online dating. Put it that way. A short-ass Chinese man with a job that takes twelve hours out of his wakeful day doesn't really bring all the aubergine emojis to the yard, or whatever it is the kids do now.'

Jackie put Tinder in the Google search engine. 'What does DTF mean, do you think?' She mulled over the possibilities and rolled her eyes when she realised. 'Ugh. When did everything become so transactional? And how is this any different to Back Piccadilly?'

'The men don't pay for it on Tinder,' Dave said, clicking his mouse.

How must it feel to have every man judge you on your looks alone and immediately swipe you away? Jackie thought, imagining her own profile up there, visible to every man in the country who was looking for a quick and easy conquest. Would she fare any better than her school friend? She shivered with distaste, feeling like she was looking at a picture of her own bleak future.

Taking Faye Southgate's bank statements, she noted a plethora of direct debits. A lease agreement with Mercedes, TV channel subscriptions, family gym membership, milk deliveries from a local dairy, a weekly farm-shop veg-box subscription, private school fees, piano lessons, football coaching subs, two different tutors, astronomical life and critical illness insurance... In among the regular payments were trips to the hairdresser, meals out, shopping for clothes, the nail bar, car valeting services, massages, osteopathy treatments, intimate waxing, unspecified 'aesthetic' treatments, which Jackie took to be Botox and fillers. The list of outgoings was dizzying. But in among the necessities that made a Didsbury divorcée turn heads were three dating memberships: eHarmony, Connection.com and Tinder Gold.

'I've got a link,' Jackie said, showing Dave the paperwork that, hours later, was covered in highlighter pen. 'Connection and Tinder.'

'Is that where we'll find our Nice Guy?' he asked.

'Time will tell,' Jackie said. 'We need to apply for Claire's and Faye's login details and get hold of their archived chats. In the meantime, Bob's going to knock together a fake profile for me.'

'For you? Wait! What do you mean?'

'I'm going online dating, and I'm going to catch us a killer...'

FOURTEEN

'What do I think of the MRI?' The consultant radiologist on the end of the phone sounded impatient. 'What do you mean, *what do I think*? Don't you pick up your voicemails?'

Shazia swallowed hard as she brought the screen of her phone to life. She saw the missed call and voicemail icons in the top left-hand corner. Could Connor see her blushing?

She turned away from her temporary partner and lowered her voice. 'I think there must have been a bad signal or something, Dr Mumtaz. I've not had anything through.' She winced at her own lie. How had she not noticed a missed call and voicemail? Sheer fatigue perhaps, as she tried to juggle obligations at home with these long, long hours. 'Anyway, the main thing is that we're talking now, so why don't you just give me an overview? Did anything weird show up in the scan?'

'If by weird you mean untoward, then yes. There's a blockage in Esther Glickman's throat that requires further scrutiny.'

Shazia thought briefly of Jackie and Dave's case. 'You don't have any ideas on—?'

'I can't tell what it is, so the body will have to be retained for post-mortem examination.'

Shazia squeezed her eyes shut and pinched the bridge of her nose between her index finger and thumb. 'The family aren't going to like it. Her burial's booked for this afternoon.'

'Well, I'm not getting involved in the religious politics of a suspicious death,' the consultant said, firing his words out at speed, as though he were late for something more important. 'You're the detective, Detective. I'll forward my report to the necessary parties, shall I?'

Thanking him, silently hating him for the way he'd talked down to her, Shazia hung up. She looked at the blood test results that had been emailed over, wishing she'd paid more attention in biology class. She then put in a call to Nick Swinton, whose only advice was that she tread carefully with the family.

She covered her face with the fringed end of her hijab and groaned.

'What's eating you?' Connor asked.

'You don't fancy a lovely trip to Broughton Park, do you?' Shazia restored her hijab to its former perfection and tried her utmost to give Connor her Bambi eyes. 'There's this old Orthodox Jewish couple whose daughter has just—'

'Nice try.' Connor laughed and turned his back to her. 'I'm quite happy writing up some lovely paperwork about three delightful little Burnage boys who stabbed their pal to death on the way home from school.' He waved. 'Jews and Muslims are more or less the same thing, aren't they? All family, and the women covering themselves up. You'll be in your element. Have fun!'

Glaring at Connor for his insensitivity and ignorance, Shazia picked up her bag and marched out.

Half wondering if anyone either in the police HQ building (or at home, come to think of it) actually ever saw her as anything more than *that* girl – the Muslim recruit who ticked the diversity boxes; the skinny Asian goody-two-shoes who never drank or swore; the dutiful daughter who made everyone proud but who was still expected to pitch in with the care of her grandmother, her siblings and her younger cousins – Shazia drove out to North Manchester's Orthodox Jewish community.

The house of Esther Glickman's parents was nestled between the colourful, rubbish-strewn streets of Cheetham Hill and the outermost reaches of leafy Broughton Park. The further Shazia drove from the melting pot of Cheetham, the fewer Asian faces she saw, until the hijabi women and the men in shalwar kameez gave way to Jewish men who wore large black hats, with sidelocks flowing over their shoulders, and dowdy-looking women, wearing long-sleeved black clothing and almost identical wigs. Most were pushing trollies, with toddler siblings reluctantly tagging along.

Pulling up outside an overextended 1930s semi-detached house with an old silver Toyota Previa people-carrier on the drive, Shazia got out and took a deep breath. When she rang the doorbell, it was answered by an ashen-faced woman in her late fifties who wore a crocheted snood over her dull hair.

'Mrs Eskowitz?' Shazia produced her ID. 'I'm Detective Shazia Malik. I attended the scene of your daughter's death?'

'Yes, yes. Of course. Come in.'

Stepping over the threshold, though she could hear small, shrill children playing somewhere in the house, Shazia smelled more than just stale cooking smells on the air. She caught the unmistakeable whiff of grief. A sheet hung over a large framed object in the hallway – a mirror perhaps? It was the same in the austere living room that contained only four large sofas – so like her own family's home, where practicality in accommodating an extended family was king. There was a blanket covering what she presumed was another mirror over the fireplace. In the back room, many men were gathered, holding prayer books and swaying almost as one in fast-mumbled prayer.

'Come through to the office,' Esther Glickman's mother said.

She led Shazia through a doorway to an extension. It was a long, thin room where the walls were clad ceiling to floor with shelving, stacked with leather-bound books – gold, embossed Hebrew lettering covered their spines. The only artwork she'd seen in the house was religious, and in here, it was the same, with a framed photo of some Rabbi or other and an old-looking portrait of an Orthodox Jewish man, carrying the sacred scrolls of the Torah, the only decorative objects on the wall – again, not dissimilar from her own home, where extracts from the Quran were displayed, written in beautiful scrolling calligraphy.

'Mrs Eskowitz. I'm so sorry to come back and intrude on your grief,' Shazia said.

Mrs Eskowitz's hand shook as she patted her snood. 'It's a busy time. We've got the burial later. Esther's ex-husband is flying in from Israel.' She pulled a handkerchief out of her skirt pocket and started to wring it in her workworn hands.

Before Shazia broke the news that she knew would reduce the Eskowitzes' world to ash and rubble, she saw an opportunity to do a little more digging into Esther Glickman's life. 'I never realised ultra-Orthodox Jews could get divorced,' she said. 'I thought you were in it for life.'

Some colour blossomed in Mrs Eskowitz's wan cheeks. 'It's called a "get". The rabbi has to approve it. It's a whole shebang.' She waved her hand dismissively. 'Even the most devout are only human.'

Toying with her few bangles, Shazia cocked her head to the side. 'Can I ask why Esther divorced her husband – Shimon, isn't it?'

'That's a private matter,' Mrs Eskowitz said, smoothing her fingers along the collar of her white polo neck.

'Please. It's really important.'

'Important for what?' The mother's eyes swam with sorrow. 'Your questions won't bring her back, will they? They won't give her five children their mother back. And anyway, my Esther had a seizure, didn't she? That's what the doctor who pronounced her dead said. She always had a weak heart, the GP said.' She looked wistfully into the distance and then turned her focus back on Shazia. 'Why do you need to know?'

There was no way round it. Shazia tugged at the cuff of her sleeve. 'I'm afraid the MRI scan showed a blockage in Esther's throat. I've not had her blood-test results back yet, but the blockage on its own points to her death being suspicious.'

'Suspicious? She had a seizure, fell down the stairs and broke her neck. Her eldest had taken the younger children to the park. They came home and found her at the bottom of the stairs.'

Shazia dug her short nails into the palms of her hands. She tried to imagine her own mother's reaction, if she'd died in the same circumstances. Torn between the expectations of a judgemental and tight-knit community and the desperation to seek the truth. 'Look, I – of all people – know why you want to get Esther buried today. My lot's the same. We bury our dead before sundown, wherever possible. But... sometimes there are extenuating circumstances, and we all have to observe the law.'

Mrs Eskowitz's eyes widened. 'You think she was murdered?'

Shazia bit her lip. 'We don't know. But the authorities need to examine her body.'

At that point, Mr Eskowitz burst into the office. 'No way. My daughter's body is not being tampered with. The rabbi will never allow it.'

Getting to her feet, Shazia tried to assert her authority. 'I'm fairly certain even the most Orthodox of rabbis have got a mandate to follow the letter of the law. There's a blockage in

Esther's throat and we need to see what it is. We're currently investigating a number of murders and—'

'Oy, gevalt!' Eskowitz clutched at his heart and said something in Yiddish, Shazia presumed, that she didn't understand. He then lifted his hands in the air, his voice questioning and high-pitched. 'Are you saying my daughter was *murdered* now?'

'Well—'

'A seizure, the doctor said,' he cried. 'I don't want some goy cutting her up on a mortuary slab.' He looked down at his wife.

Mrs Eskowitz simply held her hands over her face and started to weep.

Shazia had to redeem the situation. 'Did... was Shimon Glickman ever violent towards Esther?'

'I don't think this is appropriate,' Mr Eskowitz said. His prayer tassels, which hung beneath the waistband of his trousers, shook with indignation. 'Shimon Glickman is many things, but—'

'Did he ever raise his hands to your daughter or the children? We'll need to rule him out of our enquiries, if it turns out that Esther was... murdered.'

'Shimon was difficult.' Mr Eskowitz scratched at his beard. 'He wanted custody of the children, at first. Some social workers started to get involved. But we persuaded Shimon to give up the ridiculous fight and leave Esther alone to raise their family. It was the right thing to do.'

'A mother should look after the children,' Mrs Eskowitz said in a small voice. 'Anyway, Shimon moved to Israel soon after the divorce. How could he have hurt our girl?'

Mr Eskowitz, the bereaved father, was as vocal in his grief as his wife was restrained. He waved his arms emphatically as he shouted, 'This feels like a witch hunt. You're looking for scandal where there is none. It's always the same. Pointing fingers and wild accusations from you *Guardian*-reading types. Jewish women are beaten and kept down. Jewish men are pariahs and bullies. Everybody's wondering what the Jews are up to, behind closed doors, as though we mix gentile children's blood into our flour to make dough.'

Shazia's head swam with stress. She could see these people were grief-stricken beyond reason. 'We don't want to carve her up,' she said. 'We want to examine her properly. Esther's definitely got something lodged in her throat. That's medical fact. And if she was my daughter or mother, I'd want to know if she lost her life by accident or if it was snatched away from her in a cold-blooded act of violence.'

The Eskowitzes fell suddenly silent. Shazia was aware of a crowd of men who were gathered just beyond the doorway to the office, peering in. The father locked eyes with one of the elders, whose white hair and long, long beard perhaps marked him out as a rabbi. The elder nodded.

Mr Eskowitz squeezed his wife's shoulder. His voice was now so quiet he was almost inaudible. 'Okay. You can retrieve the blockage.'

FIFTEEN

'Right, Mr Nice Guy, let's see what you've been up to,' Jackie muttered as she entered the online dating worlds of Claire and Faye.

Swiftly issued warrants and the mere mention of murder had had the admin and legal departments of the relevant dating sites bending over backwards to grant them full access to the victims' accounts and archived chat.

'He might not even be on there,' Dave said, leaning back in his chair with his hands behind his head. 'Guy Schön mentioned a chatroom, not a dating website.'

Jackie looked wistfully at Claire's heavily filtered profile photo. 'Well, even if there is another platform where they'd been talking, I'd put my money on it that this is our killer's main hunting ground. Both victims paid subs to Connection and Tinder Gold.' She felt a pang of nostalgia, remembering the bright girl with terrible self-esteem whom she'd befriended at school.

Exhaling hard, Jackie accessed the chat archive for Claire's Connection.com account. She gasped when she saw thirty or

forty separate threads – all with different men. They had all
begun similarly, with the men approaching Claire.

*Hey, beautiful. I saw ur pic n wondered if ur into fun times
with a solvent guy.*

Hi, gorgeous lady. I'm looking for love. Are you?

*Hi babe. I normally date tall, model-like girls, but something
tells me ur up for sexy times.*

Jackie made vomit noises.

'That bad?' Dave asked, wheeling his chair up to hers to
look over her shoulder.

'Worse. Look at all those aubergine emojis.' She read on. 'And
Claire tried her hardest to have sensible conversations with them. I
mean, three of these sleazeballs say they're doctors. Four are
accountants. Four!' She'd opened the correspondents' profile pages
in new tabs. Now she clicked from one to another, revealing middle-
aged men wearing summer shirts, sat on balconies with palm trees
or a sunset in the background. Almost all were wearing sunglasses.

'Any man wearing shades is married and looking for an
affair,' Dave said.

'You think?'

He nodded energetically. 'Oh, I don't think. I know. A
friend of a friend, who goes to all the City matches, boasts about
it. He goes online just to sext with women, and occasionally, if
they're gullible enough, he hooks up with them. His poor wife
hasn't got a clue, and any of those photos of men in shades could
be his profile pic.'

Jackie thought about Gus with Catherine Harris. She shook
her head. 'Disgusting, amoral behaviour. What the hell is wrong
with these men?'

'It's not just the men,' Dave said.

She glared at her partner. 'Really?' Didn't try to hide the sarcasm in her voice.

'Well, mainly men. But people basically do stuff like that when their relationship is dead, but they're too cowardly to leave.'

'Or when they're murderers, scouting for easy victims.'

Jackie kept scanning through the suggestive correspondence held between Claire and the men who had initiated conversations. In each instance, she noticed the men cut Claire dead after brief exchanges. 'What's the word again, when these losers leave women hanging?'

'Ghosting.'

'Yep. That's the one. Well, Claire was ghosted pretty quickly by almost everyone she spoke to. Everyone except this guy.' She pointed to an account held by someone calling himself NiceGuy452. 'Photo's the same as the one on Facebook. Here's our Guy Schön.'

'Can't believe she didn't cotton on that the account was fake,' Dave said. 'Now I come to think of it, I did German at school before GCSEs, and *schön*... well, you don't have to be linguist of the year to know it means nice, as in, beautiful or attractive.'

'Claire didn't do languages.'

'She could have looked it up online.'

Flicking to the screen that displayed Faye Southgate's Connection.com history, Jackie thought about how she'd believed Gus was 'just at rehearsals' night after night, when in fact, he'd been philandering. 'Women believe what they want to hear.'

She looked at the avatars of the men that Faye had been speaking to and spotted NiceGuy452 immediately. He was the one groomed and sculpted male-model-type in a sea of out-of-shape, ageing lotharios, who wore ill-fitting shirts and Ray-Bans.

'Here we go. Here's our man, signing off some pretty steamy exchanges as Guy.'

'Doesn't he use a Facebook account with Faye called "Guy Sympa"? Dave asked, raising an eyebrow at some of the fruitier chat.

'That's right. If he's our killer, it seems pretty clumsy to use variations of Nice Guy as his moniker for all his communications. I mean, all we had to do was join the dots, and then find out who's paying for this account.'

Dave folded his arms and looked at the string of emojis at the end of the last missive between NiceGuy452 and Faye's moniker of RedHotMama_40. 'Maybe he's just not that clever. But let's not jump the gun, because we've got to get control of his account and get hold of his bank details first. I don't know much about catfishing, but I think the good ones cover their tracks pretty well.'

'It looks like their chat quickly migrated to WhatsApp, judging by what's written here, and we don't have Faye's phone.'

Dave was right. Jackie could feel the dead end looming ahead. 'Their chat and any clues that might have given us died with Faye.'

'Same with Claire,' Dave said. 'No phones. No laptops. The murderer's clearly taken them, trying to cover his tracks – assuming the murderer *is* this catfishing Nice Guy. There's a limit to what we can track through phone billing. We can't get transcriptions of texts or WhatsApp messages without having the physical devices, because the messages aren't stored on servers, and the killer must have known that. Not so stupid after all.' He picked up a biro and drummed it thoughtfully on his front teeth. Pointed the pen towards Jackie. 'What's the bet that the chatroom Guy mentioned in his Facebook messenger conversation with Claire is private, by invitation only, unsearchable, end-to-end encrypted... the works?'

Jackie groaned. 'Technology's supposed to help us be better detectives, but half the time, it makes everything more complicated. Maybe my mother's got a point. Maybe "modern life is rubbish", as she's so *very* fond of reminding me.'

Together, they checked Tinder Gold and found the same Guy on there, though he hadn't had an exchange with either Claire or Faye on the app, despite both having swiped right to initiate chat.

'Okay, it's time to fish for a catfisher,' Jackie said. 'I've just got to get knee-deep in this and see what bites.'

Keeping one eye on the clock as her appointment with the health visitor neared, Jackie created her fake account on Connection.com.

She uploaded the photo Bob had emailed over, impressed with the Photoshop job he'd done, miraculously merging about five different stock photos of women's faces into one believable yet utterly fictitious avatar. Or had it been his computer-whizz girlfriend, Zoe, doing it as a favour? On balance, she suspected the latter. Bob simply wasn't skilled enough to have made something so convincing.

Now Jackie was LucyLoveU247, a thirty-year-old slightly blousy blonde, with large blue eyes, a round, pleasing face and sugar-pink lipstick that enhanced a quizzical smile. Her profile said she was divorced and devoted to her six-year-old son. This was an attractive but not-show-stopping woman who was looking for love, ultimately, but who didn't mind having a good time in the pursuit of romantic bliss that would mend her recently broken heart.

'What do you think of this?' she asked Dave. She sat back and admired the short profile description. 'I've tried to made LucyLove a mixture of Claire and Faye. A mother, but game for an adventure.'

Dave looked down at his hands and cocked his head to the

side. 'I don't think you should do this,' he said. 'Venables will hit the roof for a start if you put yourself in harm's way.'

'I'm trying to lure a serial killer,' Jackie said, placing a hand over her chest where her partner's disapproval stung. 'I'm safe because none of this is real. It's only online.'

'But that's where it started for Faye and Claire,' Dave said.

Jackie could almost feel his accusatory stare boring into the side of her face. She didn't meet his eye. 'I'm not stupid. But I do want to get the son of a bitch who cut my friend's life short, and I want to see him locked up so he can't steal the futures of any more women.'

Dave held his hands up. 'Just be careful then. Keep me posted on any developments. And for God's sake, don't agree to meet anyone in person, unless we go together – preferably with backup.'

With her paid accounts ready to use, Jackie immediately searched both Connection and Tinder Gold for NiceGuy452. Yet that username was nowhere to be found.

'Eh? What? Hang on...' Jackie stared at the screen, dumbfounded. She had only just been looking at Nice Guy's profiles. How could it be that the accounts were no longer available? Unless... 'He's taken down his account!'

'Who has?' Dave asked.

'Nice Guy. One minute he's there. The next...' Jackie found herself in the grip of paranoia. A cold sweat started to break out on her back. 'Do you think he could see his account was being viewed?'

Dave steepled his fingers and nodded slowly. 'I think those dating sites tell you if somebody's looking at your profile.' He snapped his fingers. 'Yep. In fact, thinking about it, you should have switched on the incognito mode when you looked at his profile.'

The enormity of what she'd done suddenly dawned on Jackie.

She pressed her hands to her hot cheeks. 'I am *such* an idiot. I accessed NiceGuy452's account as Claire and Faye, didn't I? Well, if he's our murderer, he knows full well that both women are dead.'

'So he's put two and two together...'

'He knows the police are onto him.' Jackie nodded, feeling her lips prickle and that cold sweat track its way down her back. 'My avatar's a total waste of time. He's definitely taken his account down now. Slippery piece of crap.'

Though the clock was ticking and her health visitor's appointment beckoned imminently, Jackie called the customer services line of Connection.com. She eventually got through to a man who announced he was called Tom. He spoke with all the social-media soundbites and bluster of a teenager.

'I'm waiting on a warrant coming through to access Nice-Guy452's details,' Jackie explained. 'But he's a suspect in a murder investigation and I need access expediting, before somebody else loses their life.'

'My hands are tied,' Tom said. 'Until we get that paperwork through, we've got an obligation to protect the data of our subscribers.'

Drumming her fingers on the desktop, Jackie could see that there were fifteen minutes before she would have to leave. 'Put me through to your manager please.'

There was an audible tut, followed by a sigh. 'Can you hold for a minute please?'

Jackie listened to annoying, seemingly endless hold music, frustrated that even the police got short shrift when it came to customer service from online companies. 'Come on, for heaven's sake, you incompetent—'

'Detective Sergeant Cooke?' A woman's voice cut the hold music dead.

How much of the insult had this manager heard? Jackie wondered, feeling the blush spread across her cheeks. 'Yes. I'm investigating a double murder and need to get the—' There'd been a click on the line, and now this was followed by the flat-line beep that signalled the call being disconnected.

'Damn it!' Jackie slammed the phone down, feeling like her killer had just wriggled out of her grasp, aided by bureaucracy. She slammed the phone receiver down again and then thumped her desk.

'Woah! What's got into you?' Dave asked.

'Idiots. Computer-says-no idiots, slowing our investigation down. That's what's got into me.'

Dave spun around, wearing a look of triumph on his face. 'Well, here's something that might cheer you up. I've been looking into the archived paper-based case file of Marie Grant. And I've found something you're gonna wanna hear.'

SIXTEEN

'Speed dating,' Dave said. With a click of a mouse, he brought up a website for a company called Instant Attraction that looked like it had been put together at least a decade earlier, judging by the clothes that the people in the photos wore. 'Marie Grant went speed dating.'

Jackie looked over his shoulder. 'Eh? How do you know that?'

Dave pointed to a robustly built red-headed woman in one of the photos on-screen. She was sitting at a table, grinning at a man, whose back was to the camera. 'That's Marie Grant, right there. Spoke to one of the daughters, Lisa, while you were on with the Connection people. I've arranged for us to interview her later, by the way. But I mentioned the online dating thing, and she said her mum never did *online* dating – Marie Grant didn't care for computers – but she *did* go speed dating.'

Jackie looked at him blankly. 'Remind me again what...?'

'The women each sit at a table with a number, and every time a bell rings, a new man comes to her table to talk. Three minutes each.'

'How do you know all this, David?' Jackie searched her

partner's face for signs of extra-marital subterfuge but found none.

Dave gave her a disparaging look. 'How do you *not* know this?'

'Listen, I've spent the last ten years living with a musician and twins – one of whom is a Percy. Oh, and there's my mother in the basement, entertaining her various bus-pass-bearing boyfriends, not to mention the occasional drama of my drippy hippy of a dad, dropping back into our lives whenever it suits him to come back "on-grid". Chaos doesn't quite cover it. Unsurprisingly, I've never had the time to learn about things that don't affect me.'

'Yeah, yeah. Jackson Cooke. Special by name, special by nature. I get it. Anyway, get this...' He tapped the screen. 'Marie Grant was such a regular at Instant Attraction that she agreed to be in the photos for the company's website update, back in 2014.'

Studying the delighted-looking woman, who had looked good for her age, Jackie stroked her chin. 'Are you thinking our Nice Guy was out looking for victims back in 2015?'

Dave nodded. 'Stands to reason. Marie Grant choked on a pound coin and had been doped. The MO's pretty much the same.'

'And she was a single mother. Same for all three women.' Jackie mulled over the similarities, nodding. 'That's the profile of his ideal victim: single mothers from Manchester, out looking for new love. Rich or poor, it's the common denominator. But any dating website or organised dating activity is full of women like that. So why such a gap between murders, and why these three in particular?'

'Maybe this Nice Guy was someone who'd pursued the women in real life.' Dave leaned back and laced his fingers together, cradling his head. He stared intently at Marie Grant's image. 'I'm thinking, he started with Marie and maybe intended it to be a one-off. Maybe he was scared of getting caught. Maybe he killed more in-between, and we just haven't made the connections yet. I'm guessing he'd known them, made a move on them, got rejected and then started catfishing them until they agreed to meet their mystery Nice Guy admirer. They thought they were hooking up with a hot date. Turns out, they were being ambushed in their own homes.'

'He couldn't have catfished Marie.' Jackie looked at the photo of her on the website, noticing how physically similar she'd been to Claire Watkins. Busty. Of a type. 'Her interactions were all face to face.'

'So he stalked her, old-school. He stalked the others online.'

'Then he killed them,' Jackie said. 'But there's still the issue of the cash down the throat. It feels symbolic. And is there a link between the three women? You've got Claire, a packer in a biscuit factory; Marie Grant, a dinner lady in a canteen; and Faye Southgate, a one-time legal secretary turned lady of leisure. Did they know each other? If so, how? Did they owe their killer money? Or were they all just in the wrong place at the wrong time?' She shook her head. 'I've got to get those dating-website bank details for our Nice Guy, and we should definitely go and see the organiser of this Instant Attraction.'

Dave turned away from his screen and locked eyes with Jackie. 'After your appointment at the health visitor's, we'll swing by Marie's daughter, Lisa, in Worsley. I'll try to get hold of the guy who runs the speed dating. He's not going to remember every customer who's ever walked through his doors, but he'll have paperwork from people who have paid to book online. Bank details. That sort of thing. If any of it tallies with Nice Guy on the dating websites, we know we've got our prime suspect.'

. . .

For the first time since the case began, Jackie felt excited. She drove home, barely noticing the traffic queues en route, caused by roadworks. All she needed were Nice Guy's bank details, and she felt certain they would have their man.

Yet, hadn't Bob said the one thing that was niggling away at the back of her mind? *You've got a clever killer here.* The excitement and deep satisfaction of knowing her investigation was on the right track started to wane. It all felt too easy. Jackie had always had to work harder and for longer to solve cases. She could hear echoes from the past: Beryl lecturing her that *a dollar doesn't come for free, Jackson*; berating her for being a lazy, corner-cutting child.

It didn't take long for Jackie's thoughts to wander to self-recrimination. She was a bad mother. She entrusted the care of her infant daughter to the desperately damaged and self-obsessed Beryl. She short-changed her boys – especially Percy, who demanded so much because he needed so much. She swallowed a lump of cold, hard, guilty grief as she acknowledged that she'd short-changed Gus, too, treating him like an unpaid lackey; downgrading the importance of his musical aspirations, because her own job was Important, with a capital I.

She thumped the steering wheel in frustration. Accidentally hit the horn and was forced to apologise to a bewildered old dear in a Miss Marple hat, driving a Fiat 500, who clearly thought she'd committed some terrible traffic misdemeanour.

By the time Jackie met Dave outside a fine-looking detached house in Worsley, she'd wept openly in front of the health visitor and had actually given voice to her suspicion that she had a touch of the old post-natal depression.

'How did it go?' Dave asked, popping a piece of chewing gum into his mouth as he looked up at Lisa Grant's house. 'The visit, I mean.'

'Fine,' Jackie said, feeling her bosom throb painfully at the thought of having had to hand Alice back to Beryl. 'I've got two hours before I'm meant to be having a heart-to-heart with Percy's teacher over his... behaviour.' She exhaled hard. 'So let's make this count.'

Lisa Grant answered the door with her mobile phone pressed to her ear. She looked around thirty and was wearing jeans and a cashmere sweater. Her hair was cut into a no-nonsense bob, her face devoid of make-up. As she barked instructions into the phone at someone who sounded like an assistant, she barely glanced at Jackie and Dave's ID; merely ushered them impatiently into the Edwardian house, past a grand-looking living room – all storm-grey panelled walls, mustard-gold chesterfield sofas and an expensive-looking enter-tainment system – and into a large office. By the tall bay window, the office contained an oversized antique-looking desk with a chair large enough to accommodate a Bond villain. To the side was a mid-century modern black leather sofa, and on the opposite wall, a long, retro rosewood meeting table that looked as though it had cost the GDP of a small country.

Lisa Grant's come a long way from a dinner lady's terraced house, Jackie thought. She looked at a framed picture that hung on the hall wall, opposite the office doorway. It was a blown-up copy of a magazine cover for *Construction Weekly*. The cover star was Lisa, wearing a hard hat and hi-vis waistcoat and standing with her arms around another, similarly attired woman who looked a good decade older. They had been photographed by the grand entrance of a brand-new glass-fronted high-rise in Manchester's city centre – caught from below so that the tower loomed above them. 'The unstoppable rise of Grant-Hardcastle Developments,' read the headline.

A power couple. No kids, no mess, no chaos. Jackie crossed her arms over her slightly leaking bosom. *Everybody too busy being successful to look out for lonely old Marie.*

With the assuredness of someone much older, Lisa Grant waved her hand dismissively, gesturing that they should sit at the meeting table. She positioned herself at the opposite end, like a benevolent dictator, and ended the call.

'You wanted to talk about my mum?' Lisa finally looked at them both.

'It's come to our attention that your mum's death was...' Jackie tried to think of the right word. 'Troublingly similar to the more recent deaths of two other women – both single mothers.'

'We need to ask you some questions about Marie's life,' Dave said.

Lisa nodded. Looked down at her phone when it pinged. Clearly distracted. 'My mother led a simple life,' she said. 'She choked on a Christmas pudding, the pathologist said.'

'Well, that's not entirely true,' Jackie said, shuffling uncomfortably on the hard seat. She wanted to slap her hand on the tabletop to get this woman's attention but realised that, for all she was young to enjoy such success, Lisa Grant was not one of her nine-year-old sons. 'She choked on a pound coin. The death was recorded as misadventure, but she had sleeping meds in her system. Certainly enough cause for suspicion.'

'It was a good while ago,' Lisa said. Her phone rang shrilly then. 'Sorry, I've got to take this.' She turned away from Jackie and Dave, facing instead onto the front garden. 'Well? Did they pass it?' There was a pause. 'Damn! For God's sake, Neil, I pay you to get these things past planning. Do your job. If the neighbours didn't like it, tweak it. And make sure you throw them a bone to keep them quiet.' She ended the call and turned back to Jackie, red in the face. 'Sorry. Go on.'

Jackie could feel the vibration from Dave's foot, tap-tapping impatiently against a table leg. She laid a placatory hand on his arm. 'Did your mother have a boyfriend or a love interest that she might have mentioned? Someone from her speed dating maybe.'

Frowning and puffing air out of her cheeks, Lisa pressed her lips together, as if looking back into the past was hard work. 'Steve. She once mentioned some guy called Steve. Think he was a mechanic. Or was it a postman? I can't remember.'

'Any photos?' Jackie asked. 'Maybe you still have your mother's phone?'

Lisa shook her head. Finally, her hard features softened. 'I loved my mother, but my childhood was... it wasn't a picnic. Some stuff went on. Long story. Made our relationship complicated. I was a handful, growing up. I know I was. Anyway, she got on better with my brother, Kev, and my younger sister, Sacha. But Kev's in Australia. Has been since Mum died. Sacha's moved to Scotland with her boyfriend.'

'And your father?' Dave asked.

'What about him?' The light seemed to dim in Lisa's eyes.

'How was his relationship with your mum?'

Glancing down at her phone, Lisa licked her front teeth and closed her eyes ruefully. 'My dad hasn't been on the scene since we were kids.' She opened her eyes again and fixed Jackie with a penetrating stare. 'I was seventeen when she eventually kicked him out. He drove Mum mad. Gaslighting. Controlling.'

'Violent?'

'He never needed to hit her because he beat her into the ground with his words. And he had me.'

The implications of what Lisa had said made the air feel heavy.

Jackie looked at the woman quizzically. 'You mean, he...?'

'Abused me.' Lisa took a deep breath and exhaled hard. 'My dad had been sexually abusing me for years. Mum found out and kicked him out. It was the bravest thing she'd ever done, and I'll always be thankful that she believed me and not him. He was brilliant at covering his tracks.'

'I'm so sorry. That must have dreadful. And how was it, once they split? Did your mum tell the police about the abuse?'

Lisa shook her head. 'No. She was scared of retribution. He turned really nasty as it was, and the divorce proceedings... I remember they were a nightmare. At first, he fought for custody of us kids. He did it just to be difficult, because he wasn't interested in raising us, nurturing us – he was only ever motivated by control and exploitation. Once he realised she'd never give us up, he dropped us like a tonne of bricks.' She crossed her arms emphatically.

'Do you ever have contact with him now?' Jackie wondered about an abusive father and husband who had been good at covering his tracks. Could this be their murderer?'

'He's been dead five years. Heart attack. Shame he didn't suffer for longer.' There was a hint of satisfaction in Lisa's half-smile.

'Oh. Okay. I'm sorry.'

'Don't be. I'm certainly not. I hope he's rotting in hell. He ruined our family. I mean, Mum leaned on me and Kev too heavily, after the split. For years, we were expected to fill a Dad-shaped hole – for her, for Sacha – and it was too tall an order. We had our own lives to live, right? I'd decided I wanted to sink all my energy into seeking my fortune instead of chewing over the past. So I encouraged Mum to get out and meet people.' The colour drained from her face. 'I never realised – if what you're saying is true – that my advice could have cost her her life.' Those hawklike eyes were suddenly glassy with tears.

'Going back to Steve, could you describe him to us?'

Lisa shook her head. 'If she told me about him, I wasn't really listening. Mum was one of life's great natterers. She'd just go on and on, so me, Kev and Sacha, we all zoned out. I'd just started out as a property developer, and to be honest, I was too busy thinking about my business.' She exhaled hard and glanced at a WhatsApp message.

Jackie was sorrowful at the thought of how these dead women had lost their lives, simply because everyone had rendered them so invisible that they'd jumped at the first show of interest. Too bad the interest had come from a killer.

'Steve,' Jackie said, later that evening, as she and Dave headed into the city centre to meet with Doug Barnes, the owner of Instant Attraction Speed Dating. 'We've got a speed dater called Steve, a catfisher called Guy and a kerb-crawler called Col. They could well be one and the same person. In fact, I'd put money on it that Steve and Nice Guy are the same man. But we're no closer to catching our killer. How long before he takes another life?'

SEVENTEEN

'2015 is a long time ago for a busy entrepreneur like me,' Doug Barnes said, dragging a table across the upstairs function room of a downtown bar that was normally the stomping ground of stag parties and scantily clad girls, calling for shots, shots, shots. 'I help Manchester find love every Friday evening from 8 p.m. without fail – complimentary glass of Prosecco included. But I don't think I'm going to be able to help you with customer details from seven years ago. Sorry. No can do.'

Jackie wrinkled her nose at the smell of stale alcohol. Empty bars were strange places. They reminded her of the newly dead – an eerie, soulless facsimile of what they should be. 'Well, how do people book with you?'

Doug straightened his back with a crack and ran a hand through heavily sculpted hair that was beginning to thin on top. He looked like an average, middle-aged dad, dressed in young men's clothing. 'They book and pay online. It was the same back in 2015. I always had a special on – book three nights for the price of two. Bring a friend and they get in half price. That sort of thing.'

He walked over to another table and dragged that into a

different position, forming the end of an S shape that ran the length of the bar. 'I always keep the last seven years' records for tax purposes.' He handed some numbers to Dave. 'Here. Make yourself useful. Number the tables, will you? One to fifteen.'

'Do you remember Marie Grant?' Dave asked, placing the numbers on the tables.

Now busy putting tealight holders on each table, Doug's eyes moved from side to side, as though he were scanning his memories for signs of Marie.

'The redhead on your website banner,' Jackie said.

'Yep. Yep. That's right. You mentioned her on the phone,' he answered Dave, ignoring Jackie entirely. 'Yeah. I remember Marie. Course. She was a regular. Larger than life.'

Jackie grabbed two tealights from him and set them down on a table. 'Mr Barnes, it's important you give this your full attention. Marie's a potential victim in a murder investigation.'

Doug looked at her askance, finally realising the enormity of their visit. 'Murdered? Poor cow. I noticed she'd stopped coming, but I thought she'd just met Mr Right.' His brow furrowed. The half-smile on his face was fading fast, leaving only confusion and perhaps grief tugging the corners of his mouth downwards.

'Well, I'm afraid it's not quite the happy ending you thought. Now did she ever pair up with a man called Steve?'

Doug sighed. 'I told you. I don't know –. 2015's like a lifetime ago. I get hundreds of single men coming through my doors every year. Probably a stack of them are called Steve. It's a popular name.'

Dave approached Doug from behind and slapped a territorial hand on his shoulder. 'Do us a favour, pal. Check your records. If you don't have them, ask your accountant. If he doesn't have them, what do you say we have a nice chat with the boys and girls at HMRC and they can check your records for you? Maybe a nice little audit will jog your memory.'

Even under the artificial lights of the bar, it was clear that the colour in Doug Barnes' face had leeched clean away, leaving him ashen and waxy-looking. He nodded. Glanced over at the laptop that lay on the table by the door. 'I'll just check, shall I? I think I might have archived that year.' He took a seat behind the table and opened the laptop.

As he searched his files, Jackie looked around the bar, wondering what speed dating was like. She pondered whether or not you could get the measure of a man inside three minutes. Beryl always said that first impressions counted for a lot, because that was your gut telling you what your head or heart might later gloss over. If she faced the killer in a speed-dating scenario, would she – a time-served detective – be able to sniff him out inside three paltry minutes?

At his table, Doug chuckled. 'Would you believe it? I found them straight away. Fancy that!' All that entrepreneurial bluster had gone now. His voice was shaky.

Dave stood sentry behind him and peered over his shoulder. 'Come and look at this, Jack. Doug here has got scanned copies of the paperwork from everyone who matched on the night.'

'I keep good records for safety reasons, as well as the taxman.' Doug's Adam's apple bounced around in his thin neck.

'Financial records?' Jackie asked.

'Most payments are made online. I get a few that are cash on the night but...' His mouth seemed to slacken as he skirted around a lie.

It was clear that Doug Barnes – Manchester's answer to Cupid, in trousers that were a little on the tight side for a man in his forties – had undeclared income to hide. Perhaps he was even laundering money for someone. But Jackie wasn't inter-ested in any tax-dodging scam. She wanted to find the mystery Steve. 'Steve. Steve and Marie. That's who you're looking for. Focus please.'

With a few more clicks of the mouse, Doug nodded and

smiled, as though he'd been given a last-minute reprieve from the executioner's blade. 'Here we go. Marie and Steve. Daters write notes about each other to jog their memories, if there's a match. I take the bottom copy. Marie wrote that Steve was funny and reminded her of an actor. Steve...' He squinted at his screen. 'He just wrote "nice".'

'Print that off for us, will you, pal?' Dave said, clapping him on the back rather too hard. 'And find us Steve's bank details, showing his full name and address.'

With the paperwork thrust at her by an eager-to-please Doug, Jackie looked down at the online payment form from Marie's date. Finally, she had something to go on.

'Steve James. Steve James from Timperley.' She rolled the paperwork tightly into a baton and slapped her left hand triumphantly. 'Got him!'

On the way out, she took a leaflet for Instant Attraction, hoping Dave didn't see.

On the way back to HQ, Dave drove while Jackie sat in the passenger seat, checking her emails.

'Shouldn't we just go to this guy's address right now?' Dave said. His knuckles stood proud as he gripped the steering wheel. The tendon in his cheek flinched.

'It's not enough,' Jackie said. 'Not yet. Give it while. I want to see the name of the guy behind the Connection.com and Tinder Gold accounts.' Her gut was clenched tight, as if it knew something that she didn't yet. 'Let's see if that's Steve James too. Then we pounce – with backup. Venables will go mad if we screw up an arrest.'

She could see that she had 4G connectivity, yet the phone was slow to load her emails. Suddenly, several plopped into her inbox at once. 'Yes!' she cried. 'The warrant's in. We can pull the financials off the dating websites.'

Checking her watch, she realised that yet again, despite having spent a chunk of the day trying to persuade the school's special needs co-ordinator to bring forward Percy's assessments for dyslexia and ADHD, and despite a trip to her divorce lawyer to endure another round in the infernal battle to secure the best financial and domestic circumstances for the children, she wouldn't get to enjoy the simple pleasure of tucking them in. Her stomach growled in complaint. 'Swing by the kebab shop, will you? I've got to eat if we're going to pull a long shift.'

En route, Dave pulled up outside a 'Tasty Fried Chicken, Kebab, Pizza, Curry' that promised the culinary world in a poly-styrene container. As they ate by the roadside, Jackie dialled home.

Beryl picked up just before the voicemail kicked in. 'Is that you, Jackson?' She was just about audible above the sound of boys arguing and Alice screaming.

Jackie's chest ached at the sound of her disgruntled baby girl. 'Is Alice okay? What's going on, Mum? Is she ill?'

'Is she buggery,' her mother said. 'I'm trying to feed her but she's windy as hell.'

Visualising the contents of the medicine cupboard, Jackie spotted the necessary remedy in her mind's eye. 'There's a bottle of Infacol in the—'

'Oh, for heaven's sake. She's just hocked up an entire bottle on a pocket of wind. Jesus! It's all over my lilac palazzo pants.'

Jackie could visualise the mayhem. 'Mum, she's just got colic. That's all. It'll pass.'

'I'm going to start weaning her in the morning.'

Alice started screaming again. She could hear Beryl patting the baby on her back to bring the wind up. Hey presto, Alice belched and the screaming stopped.

'You're *not* going to start weaning. Do you hear me?' Jackie could feel her pulse racing. 'She's too young. It's bad for them.'

Her mother wouldn't be told, however. 'I weaned you and

Lucian at three months and you were both fine. Alice is a full month older. I'll just put a bit of rusk in her milk.'

Jackie shouted, almost spitting out her mouthful of char-grilled chicken. 'You bloody well will not! You're supposed to wait 'til they're six months old.'

'Why? Give me one good reason why?' Beryl had started to sound like she was enjoying winding Jackie up. The boys were still arguing in the background.

Throwing a thick wedge of lemon out of the car with such ferocity that it hit a passing drunk, Jackie rolled up her window fast and yelled: 'Allergies, Mother! Because of bloody allergies. And don't give me that bull that nobody had allergies in the eighties, because I had asthma and Lucian had eczema. Alice is my baby and I say no f—'

The line was dead. Beryl had hung up.

'I've got to get some time off to spend with my kids,' Jackie said. She wiped her sleeve angrily across her tearful eyes.

Dave was watching her in silence, intermittently chewing lettuce that was hanging more out than in his mouth. 'Jack... I don't know what to say. You came back to work too early, man. Hannah took a year off with each of ours.'

Turning to her partner, Jackie glared, feeling frustration building within her to become something rather more combustible. 'Hannah is married. To you. I am getting divorced. From Gus. Big sodding difference, David.'

Looking down at his kebab, Dave folded the wrappings around the half-eaten meal. 'I'm sorry.' His voice was little more than a whisper.

Jackie grabbed his wrappings as well as her own, got out of the car and dumped them in a waste bin. She got back into the passenger seat. 'Just drive.'

.   .   .

When they got back to the station, their floor was still buzzing with various teams working late. Shazia was writing up a report. Connor was on the phone. Venables was still in her office, staring at her computer.

'The city that never sleeps,' Jackie said under her breath, wondering if she might meet a rich man if she went speed dating. Rich enough to give her the maternity leave she needed.

She sat on the edge of her desk and dialled the customer-service department of Connection. After being put through to several juniors, some of whom sounded like they were in a far-flung call centre, Jackie eventually reached the manager she'd spoken to earlier.

'I'm sorry, Detective, but I'm about to leave for the evening.'

'Well, I'm not that fortunate, and neither are the dead women whose murderer I'm charged with finding.'

'Accounts is shut. They're back in tomorrow.'

'I don't believe you, and I have a warrant. Now *please* get me my information.'

It took twenty minutes or more for the manager to get back on the line and end Jackie's stay in hold-music hell.

'Detective Sergeant Cooke? Yes. It's Mandy. I pulled a few strings. Have you got a pen and paper? The man you're looking for is a Steven James.'

Jackie punched the air. Steven James was definitely the man who had speed dated Marie Grant, as well as the man behind Guy Schön and Guy Sympa, who had catfished both Claire Watkins and Faye Southgate. Jackie had her murderer. 'Okay. And his address?'

'Well, hang on. Here's the problem. There seems to have been an issue with his direct debit. The payments are still coming out to us, but there's discrepancy, and our accounts people have been looking into it.'

'What kind of discrepancy?'

'Well, the bank-account name doesn't tally with his name,

which is fine, because maybe someone else has bought him a membership as a treat. But...'

'Yes?' Jackie's gut felt leaden. *It* knew there was something off. She sensed it too.

'There's a flag on his account because it's in a woman's name – Beatrice Grey – and when my colleague looked into it, they discovered Beatrice Grey has been dead since 2018. It's a stolen identity.'

Jackie put the phone down, feeling like the air had been knocked out of her. She turned to Dave. 'We need to get out to Timperley fast.'

'What's wrong?'

'I think we're being led a merry dance here. Steve James is a master of identity theft, if his bank account is anything to go by. We've got to check out that address.'

At that time of night, there was little traffic on the road, but it still took them an agonising forty minutes to get out to the Cheshire borders, thanks to roadworks.

'We're looking for Bingham Grove. Number forty-one. Should be next left,' she said.

Dave took a left in silence and slowed down. 'Number two, four... odd numbers are on the other side of the road.'

Eyeing the 1940s semi-detached houses, Jackie could hear the blood rushing in her ears. Steve James might have fake bank details, but if this was his address, they could get their man tonight, come hell or high water.

You can keep your gut instincts, Mum, she thought. *This is all down to careful detective work. Logic. Deduction. Calm rational thought.*

'Hang on,' Dave said as they reached the end of the road. He angled the car so that the headlights shone on the number by the last house's front door.

'Number thirty-nine?' Jackie said.

She realised then that it *had* all been too good to be true; too easy.

'There's no forty-one here,' Dave said.

Jackie thumped the dash in anger. 'We've been played for fools. Our Steve James is fiction.'

EIGHTEEN

'Listen, Gus. You'd better come over. We need to talk about Percy.' Jackie left the voicemail for her soon-to-be-ex-husband and set her phone down on the kitchen worktop.

'Mum! Percy's just drawn boobs on the table with a Sharpie!' Lewis yelled.

Jackie turned around to find Percy grinning at his artwork, then idly spooning cornflakes into his mouth as if he hadn't just vandalised the kitchen table. Next to him, Lewis's brow was more deeply furrowed than a nine-year-old's should be.

Dampening a cloth and plucking the cream cleanser from the under-sink cupboard, Jackie sighed. 'Percy, for the love of God, stop doodling on the furniture.' She yawned and started to scrub at the offending ink. Kissed both boys on the tops of their heads. 'Especially not boobs. Nobody needs a side order of boobs at mealtimes.'

'What can we do today, Mum?' Percy asked. 'Can we go swimming?'

Jackie thought about the last time they'd gone swimming as a family. Hadn't Percy tried to drown his pal Will in the name of practising his 'life-saving moves'? 'No. No swimming today – I'm out of swim-nappies for Alice.'

She looked over at her baby daughter, who was lying on her quilted playmat, batting at the soft toys that dangled from brightly coloured padded bars, criss-crossed overhead. A rush of love swept away Jackie's fatigue. She padded to the baby, kneeled down and blew a raspberry on her belly. 'Ooh, Mummy loves you, little girl.' Turned to her sons. 'And you two rascals. I love you too. It's so good to be with my babies.'

After hitting the dead end in the hunt for Steve James, Venables had insisted Jackie go home and spend a weekend with her children, leaving Shazia and Clever Bob to continue looking for the mystery kerb-crawler, Col. Exhausted and desperate to be with her children, Jackie had been relieved to be given permission to down tools.

She'd slept fitfully until the small hours, after the long and fruitless shift. Steve James loomed large in her exhausted mind, taunting her from the shadows, telling her that she was a bad cop; that she was wasting the first precious months of her daughter's life, trying to catch a killer who was smarter than she'd ever be. The sun had begun to rise when she'd finally fallen into a deep sleep. Only two hours later, Alice had woken her, crying for a feed. But the exhaustion was a small price to pay for being with her family.

'How about Laser Quest?' she asked the boys.

'Mum, you're the best!' Lewis shouted, punching the air.

Percy leaped out of his seat and jumped on Jackie's back, smothering her in kisses. 'Yesssss! Best mum!'

'Mind your sister, Percy.' Jackie got to her feet with creaking knees, with Percy still clinging to her back like an oversized koala. 'And get down.' She chuckled at the mayhem. Vital. Full of love. Almost overwhelming. It felt like life in its most concentrated form.

When Gus appeared on her doorstep about an hour later,

the colour in the house seemed to drain away. In the kitchen, he sat sullenly at the island, gazing intently at the fruit bowl full of unpaid bills – noticeably emptier these days. Jackie moved the bowl out of his line of sight then continued to rub Alice's back.

'So, we need to talk about Percy,' she said, trying to pat the baby's wind loose. 'I spoke to his teacher yesterday. It was embarrassing.'

'Our son's not an embarrassment to me,' Gus said. His foot bounced up and down on the bar stool.

'This isn't a competition, Augustus. It's parenting. You should have been at the meeting and you weren't. Percy's at risk of being excluded from school.'

'But he's got ADHD, right?'

'Well, we won't know that until he's been assessed. I had to fight the good fight on my own, back there. The wait to see a psychiatrist is almost a year. Anyway, biting Taylor Harris is *not* ADHD.' Jackie wanted to shake Gus for all he'd undone by sleeping around. 'He doesn't bite other kids, does he?'

'He's always acted up though.' Gus was smiling now. 'It's not the first time he's got into fights or answered the teachers back. He's the kid who likes climbing on and jumping off things. He'll probably end up a famous mountaineer or free-diver. He's spirited is all.'

'Rubbish. I knew there would be something underlying the biting and I've finally got to the bottom of it.' Jackie visualised the teacher's concerned, contrite face as she'd confessed to a litany of subtle bullying episodes that had been brushed under the carpet until Percy's biting incident. 'Percy's been picked on by Taylor for months – ever since you took up with his mother.'

Gus got to his feet and held his hands out to take Alice from Jackie. 'Now who's talking rubbish? Look, just give me the baby. If you like, I'll take the boys to the park.'

Jackie shunted her chair back, away from him. 'Don't side-step the issue, Gus. Our son is traumatised by our split and your girlfriend's child. Acknowledge it. We need to give more thought as to how we give our boys a soft landing during this divorce. And you need to sit down with Catherine and talk through what she's going to do about Taylor.'

Gus threw his hands up in the air. 'Taylor's chill. What can I say?'

'Taylor's *chill*? How old are you exactly? Twelve? You're not our boys' pal. You're not Taylor Harris's pal. You're a grown adult. Act like a damned parent, Gus. And be loyal to your own flesh and blood before you take the side of somebody else's brat. Taylor's sly. He undermines and winds Percy up. Does crappy things and then blames Percy for it. Makes fun of his dyslexia in front of the rest of the class. Miss Godber told me. Percy's been taking it and taking it, and then he'd had enough. That's when he got bitey.'

Rolling his eyes, Gus started to nod. He sat back down. 'Okay. I'll have a word. You're right. Percy's my boy, and God knows I love him. I didn't realise this was going on. He's kept it quiet. Lewis never said anything either.'

Alice started to gurgle and giggle. Jackie kissed the tiny girl on the top of her fluffy head and passed her to Gus. 'It's not up to Lewis to keep you posted, is it? Talk to your children, Gus. Spend less time trying to keep Catherine and Taylor Harris amused and more time parenting properly. Okay? You like to think of yourself as the main carer, but since we split, Beryl's doing your share of the hard graft. And my mother's too old to be lumbered with this kind of responsibility, right?'

Looking down at Alice, Gus appeared crestfallen. When he looked up, there were tears in his eyes. 'I'm sorry for everything, and I miss you, Jack. I miss what we had.'

Jackie moved to the fridge and took out a punnet of strawberries for her overdue breakfast. Should she dignify Gus's overtures with a response? She stared at some yoghurt, waiting for the moment to pass.

'Did you hear me? I said I miss you. I miss us.'

Continuing to look into the fridge, Jackie willed herself to keep her voice calm to avoid startling the baby. 'It's too late for that, Gus. And if you ever cared about me, you wouldn't be trying to squeeze me for every penny I earn. You'd have some self-respect, and you'd get a job.'

'Who would look after the kids?'

'Me, Gus. *I* would look after my kids. Except I couldn't afford to take longer than the eighteen weeks at full pay, because Alice came early, and *you*' – she turned back to him but couldn't keep the barb out of her words then – 'won't get off your backside and contribute financially to this family. All you're capable of is taking. Take, take, take.'

Gus opened his mouth to speak but was silenced by the appearance of Beryl in the doorway.

'Play nicely, children,' Beryl said. 'I've got a date tonight and I don't want any stress showing up in my recently Botoxed face.' She smiled in that tight way that Jackie found perplexing in women who spent too much time and money at the aesthetician's. The mischief was still showing in the old lady's eyes, however. 'Juan, the forty-five-year-old gym instructor, thinks I'm fifty, and I'm not going to disabuse him of that notion thanks to you two bickering fools stressing the filler clean out of my wrinkles.'

Perhaps realising that Beryl would make his life even more of a misery if he hung around, Gus made his excuses and left, leaving Jackie to enjoy her much needed time off with the children.

'Do me a favour, Mum,' she said as she rubbed noses with Alice. She spoke in a sing-song voice that all babies seemed to love. 'Be careful. There's a killer out there, targeting single mothers.'

Beryl patted her freshly coiffed hair. 'Oh, I'm much too old to worry about being mistaken for a single mother, Jackson. I'm a glam-ma.'

Jackie realised she should be keeping the details of the case to herself but acknowledged that her mother's safety came first. 'Just... just be sensible. Don't leave your drink unattended. Wear jeans, not a skirt or anything with bare legs, so you can't be jabbed with Rohypnol.'

'Ooh, it's funny you should mention that,' Beryl said, snapping her fingers. 'My pal Deidre from circuits... she said her granddaughter got jabbed on the dance floor at a university disco. Can you believe it? Jabbed in the thigh! On a dance floor, packed with other kids! Talk about brazen.'

'What happened to her? Did she pass out?'

'You bet your bottom dollar she did. Hit the deck, Deidre said, right in the middle of an Ed Sheeran number. Poor kid fell awkwardly and broke her collarbone and her little finger.'

Jackie grimaced. 'But she wasn't dragged off by some nut, right?'

Beryl stole a strawberry from the bowl Jackie had been preparing. She shook her head vehemently and popped the strawberry into her mouth. Spoke with her mouth full. 'No, nothing like that. Her friends called an ambulance straight away.'

'Where was this? It wasn't Manchester, was it?'

'Newcastle or Durham, or one of those places where they never wear a coat, even when it's freezing. Maybe it was York. I don't know. I can't remember. But Deidre said the local police arrested one of those scruffy little Herberts that sits on a computer all night long, talking to other virgin boys about how much they hate women. A *brain cell* I think they call them.'

'Incel, not brain cell,' Jackie said.

'That's right.' Beryl pointed at her triumphantly. 'The police found this young stalker and his bottom-feeding pals had been writing the most appalling things about Deidre's granddaughter and her friends in some chat forum or other. I mean, graphic, sexual things that would make your toes curl. Violent too – planning how they were going to attack Deidre's granddaughter because she was beautiful and would never look twice at the likes of them. It's jealousy, isn't it? Jealous of these girls' beauty and vigour. Nasty little arses. I hope their penises drop off. They don't deserve a woman.'

Jackie chewed on a strawberry and swallowed it down. Showed the next one to Alice and let her play with it until she tried to squish it between her tiny fingers. 'Funny you should mention this. Me and Dave were talking about incel groups in relation to the murders we're investigating. My boss, Venables, had us haring off down a blind alley, talking to prostitutes in the city centre. She was convinced that the dead women were on the game, or that it had something to do with the sex industry. That's come to very little... so far. But then me and Dave got onto this online dating trail – you know? Connection and Tinder and that sort of thing.'

Beryl, senior queen of Tinder, nodded knowingly. 'Tinder has a lot to answer for. That's all I'm saying.'

'Right. So it looked like we were actually going to find the killer,' Jackie went on. 'And I put the incel thing on a back-burner. But now we've hit a dead end with both of the other lines of investigation, and you've just given me my next place to look. Cheers, Beryl.' She kissed her mother on her perfumed helmet of hair. 'You wouldn't have made a half-bad detective.'

'If that was the case, Jackson Cooke, things wouldn't have turned out the way they did with our Lucian.' Beryl's Botoxed, blank expression soured.

Jackie set Alice on her playmat by the kitchen TV and hugged her mother in silence until Beryl pushed her away.

'Leave it, Jackson. You can't undo the past, and you're going to crush my hair.'

.   .   .

Once Beryl had gone to put on her make-up, Jackie thought about infiltrating the world of incels. This was surely their next port of call. She allowed the thrill of the chase to wash away her sleepiness, her post-natal ennui and her motherly guilt. She thumbed out a text to Dave and Bob.

Come round mine this p.m. to go Dark Web-hunting? Bring Zoe. Will provide beers. J

NINETEEN

'Hannah is not happy with you,' Dave said, brandishing a four-pack of Corona beer as he stepped over the threshold. 'She says you owe her one.'

Jackie stepped aside to let him through. 'Tell her she'll have to get to the back of the queue. Everyone wants something off me at all times. But thanks for coming.' She slapped her partner on the back affectionately. 'Maybe I'll babysit for you guys, if either of us ever gets the same night off, and I'm not breast-feeding and it's not *my night* with the kids. Actually, forget I ever said that.'

As Dave headed for the back of the house, Clever Bob drew up outside. Jackie waved to Zoe as she emerged from the passenger side. Bob's cyber-whizz girlfriend was dressed in something long and handknitted that looked like a fisherman's net. She had rainbow glitter Dr Marten boots on her feet. There was still enough light to tell that today her blunt-cut bob was dyed jade green.

Bob bounded up the path enthusiastically. He rubbed his hands together by way of greeting. 'Exciting times, Jackie. Exciting times.'

'Keep your voice down, Bob. The kids are in bed.'

Zoe stomped up to the front door, bearing a bottle of what appeared to be supermarket value cooking wine. She pushed it into Jackie's hands. 'I missed a D&D game for this.' Patted the laptop under her arm and grinned. 'But trawling the Dark Web for killers sounds like much more fun. Good to see you.' Unexpectedly, she pecked Jackie on the cheek. 'Hope you got some vegan snackage in.'

Presiding over the out-of-hours gathering at the kitchen table, Jackie looked longingly at the beers Dave had brought, but with Alice's milk supply to consider, she'd had to settle for a pint of squash instead.

'Right. Incels,' she said. 'Where do we start?'

Zoe had her laptop open already and was poised to plug the relevant information into the search engine. 'Reddit, 4chan, Facebook... There's so many, and there will be a load of incel-hosted chatrooms on the Dark Net. But what exactly are we looking for?'

'How about starting with NiceGuy452?' Dave suggested. 'Steve James is another possible – those are the pseudonyms our suspect has been using.'

'You should look for chat about Claire Watkins, Rachel Hardman, Faye Southgate and Marie Grant,' Jackie said. 'Those are the victims' names. You never know.'

Cracking her fingers, Zoe nodded. 'Okay. We're going in. Now I've trolled these pieces of crap before, just for fun on a wet Tuesday night. And I can warn you, this isn't going to be pretty.' She looked at them all, one by one. 'Ready? Brace yourselves.'

As the next couple of hours unfolded, Jackie found herself clutching her stomach, wondering what sort of future lay ahead for her boys in this world full of toxic masculinity. The comments she read had her reaching for a beer after all, reasoning that she had enough milk in the freezer to get Alice through the next twenty-four hours.

'What's all this business about Stacy and Chad?' she asked Zoe.

Dave and Bob had all moved to Jackie's side of the table, and the three of them were now crowded round Zoe's laptop, so that she was forced to elbow Bob out of the way to get a better look at the screen.

The chat was flowing between several incels:

This Stacy at college won't even look at me. She said I couldn't sit next to her in the canteen because she was saving the place for a friend. The friend never even came. She was lying. She made me look stupid in front of everyone just because I'm not a six-foot, muscle-bound Chad like her boyfriend. She's only with him cos he drives an A Class and has money. It's always about money. They're nothing but whores. This Stacy is a whore, batting her eyelashes and flicking her hair every five minutes at any Chad that passes.

She's a dumb bitch needs taking in hand, dude. You need to show her what it feels like to be bottom of the heap. Overpower her fat ass.

Zoe scrolled slowly down the page they were all reading. 'Stacy is what these losers call any attractive woman. Chad is basically a catch-all name for any sexually successful man – so, any man who isn't completely crazy and socially incompetent.'

The conversation about the 'Stacy' in the canteen became more sinister.

'Are they really egging this boy on to attack the girl? To rape her?' Jackie asked.

'That's not all,' Dave said. 'Read down to the bottom.'

The aggrieved incel started to talk about his feelings:

I feel so lousy that I'm thinking about ending it all. No woman will give me the time of day. None of them will ever sleep with me. Maybe I'd be better off dead.

Dude, if you're going to kill yourself, make sure you take down some bitches with you. Kill some kids while you're at it, like the gentleman, Elliot Rodger. Do it! Do it! Everyone will respect you for showing these bitches the consequences of their arrogance and entitlement. You'll go to incel heaven.

'They're encouraging each other,' Bob said. 'Can you imagine if an impressionable teenage lad joins a group like this because he's lonely and takes all the bragging from the other boys at school to be God's honest truth?'

'If we were to be believed, when we were at school,' Dave said, taking a thoughtful gulp of his beer, 'everyone lost their virginity at thirteen. We all lied. But this sucker's gullible as hell. And if he belongs to a group like this, small wonder he can't get a girl.'

Jackie shook her head. 'It makes me sick to my stomach. How is this any different from those chatrooms where they recruit suicide bombers for ISIS?'

Zoe turned to her. 'Good point. Very little difference at all really. These chat forums are the places where mentally ill men – young men, generally – come to find outlets for their frustrations. They can't make life work, so they go online and fantasise about a parallel universe where they're the alpha male. Except it always involves sexual violence.'

Hearing Alice making gurgling noises on the baby monitor, Jackie stood up and rubbed her numb legs. She walked over to the monitor and held it to her ear, trying to distinguish between Alice-about-to-wake-up-and-scream-the-house-down noises and the sort of soft grunting that babies did intermittently in their sleep. It was the latter. She realised she'd been holding her breath and exhaled with relief.

'This is all very well,' she said, 'but we haven't seen anything about injecting girls and women with Rohypnol yet, have we? We haven't seen any mention of Nice Guy or the victims. There's nothing about stuffing money down the women's throats, though it's obvious that these incels see women as transactional and money-obsessed.'

'I can take you deeper,' Zoe said. Her fingers rattled across her keyboard, and they entered the dark side of the internet where the Stacys and Chads almost certainly never went.

Jackie heated through some vegan pizza and dished it out for her guests.

'Hang on,' Zoe said, her mouth full of pizza. 'There's a chat group here, going on about jabbing girls with Rohypnol on the dance floor.'

Biting heartily into her crust, Jackie felt the hairs on the back of her neck stand to attention. 'Oh, this is exactly what my mother was talking to me about this morning. That happened to one of her gym buddies' granddaughters at university.'

They all stared at the screen with renewed hope of this site yielding their Nice Guy.

'No mention of your victims,' Bob said.

'This is all chat by college kids,' Zoe said. 'There's nobody talking about targeting grown women, and certainly nothing about single mothers.'

'It's no good,' Dave said. 'Let's move on.'

Another hour passed fruitlessly and Jackie started to yawn. All she wanted to do was lie in her bed and go to sleep. Yet by inviting her colleagues and Zoe round, she'd started the ball rolling on an investigative process that ideally they ought to see through.

'Do you think we'll ever get through every last chat on every last UK-based site?' she asked. The conversation between incels on the site that Zoe was currently visiting had taken a turn for the racist. Jackie wondered how much more hatred she could stomach.

'No way,' Zoe said, chuckling. 'This is the tip of the iceberg. There are thousands and thousands of these creeps out there. It's a contagion.'

With her enthusiasm flagging in earnest, Jackie was relieved when Alice's cry could be heard on the crackling monitor.

'Look, you guys. I'm going to cuddle my baby,' she said. 'I need a break from this. If you haven't found anything by the time I get back down...' She glanced at the kitchen clock – 2.15 a.m. 'We should call it a night and reconvene another time. I'm wiped out, and we're getting nowhere.'

Upstairs in the nursery, she found Alice crying – half-asleep, half-awake. Desperate for the baby to sleep through the night now that she was four months old, Jackie fought against the impulse to pluck her out of her Moses basket and start feeding her. Instead, she held the tiny girl's hand and stroked her brow.

'Shhhh, shush, shush, shush, little girl,' she whispered. *Please go back to sleep*, she said silently, almost as a prayer. *You'll wake Lewis and Percy and I just don't have the band-width for that. Not tonight. Not after an afternoon of tween fighting at Laser Quest.*

Sure enough, Alice's mewling started to abate, giving way to contented gurgling. The gurgling lessened, and before long, the baby was back to sleep.

'Oh, thank you, Lord,' Jackie whispered, imagining Lucian placing an encouraging hand on her shoulder. She reached up to put her hand on his, then remembered that he wasn't there.

Heading back downstairs, avoiding the floorboards that creaked, Jackie was about to call time on the incel hunt when

Dave turned around to face her. He was grinning and beckoned her close.

'We've found him. We've only bloody found him. At least, I think so,' he said.

Jackie took her seat, no longer tired. She read the conversation on the chat group. The main contributor was an avatar that was a cartoon character. 'Hiro Shishigami? Who the hell is that? Is this a Japanese incel group?'

Zoe shook her head. 'Nope. It's Manchester-based, judging by the content of the various threads. Hiro Shishigami is a super-violent anime character. A high school kid turned mass murderer. Our guy has just used that as his avatar.'

'Okay.'

'Anime's very popular,' Bob added. 'Especially among Millennials and Gen Z. They can't get enough of it. Zoe reads it, don't you, love?'

'Sure do. But you're gonna wanna see what this Hiro Shishigami says to the other members of the group.' She pointed to the screen.

Good news. The bitch at work finally got what was coming to her, and I was the one that gave it.

Well done, bro. Tell!

I set a trap that I knew she'd fall in. Got her talking online and then went to her house. Gave her some of that sweet, sweet sleeping juice, right in her thigh. Then I rammed the truth home to her.

Yes! You are our hero, Hiro! Go, Shishigami, incel warrior. What did you do? Did you show that bitch who's boss? Did she thank you for it?

*Better than that. I took all the hurt and rejection and stuck it
down her throat 'til she gagged. She didn't think I had it in me.
I wasn't good-looking enough. Wasn't rich enough. So I made
her eat her words.*

'I don't believe it,' Jackie said, clasping her hand to her chest
and backing away from the screen. She tried to imagine Claire's
terrified last moments, as she choked to death on her kitchen
floor, with her attacker standing over her. She blinked away a
tear. 'We've found our man. Please tell me we've found our
man.'

'It's going to be tricky to work out who Hiro Shishigami is,'
Zoe said. 'People don't go to these dark places unless they've got
something they really want to hide. I don't need to remind you
how your last case panned out, do I?'

Jackie pressed her lips together, balled her fists and pushed
them hard against her mouth. *I can't give up the search. Not
now. Not with us so close,* she thought. 'We need to move hell
on earth to get the name and address of this dirtbag,' she said.
She laid a hand on Zoe's shoulder, just as imaginary Lucian had
laid a hand on hers. 'If anyone can do it, Zoe, you can. The law
doesn't count under this roof. Not tonight. Not in this scenario.
Hack the damned chatroom and tell us who Hiro Shishigami is.'

By dawn, Jackie was shaken awake. She'd fallen asleep on the
little sofa in the corner of the kitchen where the boys sat to do
their gaming.

'Jackie! Jackie! I've got a name.'

She opened her sticky eyes to see Zoe's exuberant face.

'Really? Tell me!'

'Tyler Fleming.'

TWENTY

'Okay, Bob. Let's see if our Mr Fleming has graced the inside of a cell before,' Jackie said.

The weekend had felt all too brief, but Jackie had savoured every moment of spending quality time with her children.

Now, on a drizzly Monday morning, to put their investigation back on a legitimate footing, Bob plugged Tyler Fleming's name into the Greater Manchester Police's database. A result came up immediately.

'Here we go,' Bob said. 'Tyler Fleming. Thirty-two years old, single, lives in Denton. He's on the sex offenders register. Sounds about right.'

Jackie looked at the photo of a mousy-haired man who wore rectangular metal glasses frames with Coke-bottle-bottom lenses that made his eyes beady. She scanned the report that had been filed some five years ago by a colleague. 'He was caught kerb-crawling near a girls' school, offering girls a lift. Then he exposed himself to them when they wouldn't get in the car. What a charmer.' She remembered the working girls' story of Col, the punter who'd tried to force them to swallow a sedative so that they could play dead all the more effectively. She turned to Dave. 'Could this be our guy?'

'Only one way to find out,' Dave said, yawning. 'Let's find out his address and get round there.'

Denton was much like every East Manchester neighbourhood on a Monday mid-morning – full of red-brick housing, discount shops and ordinary people loping along aimlessly.

They found Tyler Fleming's house in a cramped terrace, not far from the main road. From the street, it looked well-tended but old-fashioned, with pristine net curtains adorning the windows in a horseshoe shape that pointlessly allowed any passer-by to peer in. Ceramic ornaments were visible on the windowsill of the living room. A hanging basket full of artificial pansies hung by the front door.

'It's like something out of a time warp,' Dave said, peering through the windscreen of the Ford at the unprepossessing house. 'Like the 1980s just kept going and going.'

'What's the bet that Tyler Fleming lives with his grandparents?' Jackie asked, trying to guess their suspect's circumstances on the basis of the curtain choice.

'Let's find out, shall we?' Dave switched off the engine.

As Jackie pressed the doorbell, Dave peered in through the living-room window and then glanced up at the front bedroom window.

'No sign of Fleming,' he said.

Jackie heard the shuffle of carpet slippers. 'Someone's coming.'

The door was cracked open – a hefty-looking chain preventing it from opening any wider. 'Can I help you?' an elderly lady asked.

Jackie smiled and showed her ID. 'Detective Sergeants Cooke and Tang. We'd like to talk to Tyler. Is he home?'

The woman scrutinised the ID, clearly not believing a word Jackie said. 'Closer please. I left my reading glasses in the lounge.'

Holding the ID to the gap, Jackie waited until the woman was satisfied that they weren't some kind of con artists, out to trick Manchester's gullible senior citizens into parting with their meagre pensions.

Finally the door was opened. Their interrogator was a tiny woman wearing an apron over a navy pleated skirt and a lilac bouclé jumper. A large gold cross and several gold belcher chains hung around her neck. On her feet, she wore old-fashioned burgundy slippers, trimmed with fake fur. She looked to be in her late seventies. The polar opposite of Beryl the glam-ma, Jackie mused.

Dave looked beyond the woman to a narrow staircase, carpeted in swirling-patterned Axminster. 'Can we come in, Mrs...?'

'Edna. Edna Collins. Tyler's my grandson. I hope he's not in trouble.' Edna craned her neck to look beyond Dave to the neighbouring houses, clearly fearing twitching curtains and the ensuing wagging tongues. She ushered them inside.

The house was as Jackie had expected – a snapshot of the mid-eighties that was kept in pristine condition, as though it was an homage to the best of times in Edna Collins' life. She wondered that so much hatred could flourish within these floral-wallpapered walls.

Edna led them into the front room, and Jackie's appraising gaze passed over a drystone fireplace paired with an unsightly black canopy that housed a gas fire. On the mantle were family photos, lovingly framed in silver and dominated by a boy wearing Coke-bottle-bottom glasses – Tyler. On the wall were horse brasses and a framed poem with a cross in the bottom-right corner. Ornaments had been carefully arranged on every available surface – figurines and Swarovski crystal nick-nacks.

At first, the room seemed empty, filled only with a strange hissing sound. Jackie jumped when she finally made sense of the sight of an old man, sitting like a statue in an easy chair in front of the TV. Dressed in a floral shirt that wasn't dissimilar to the Hawaiian shirts that Dave insisted on wearing, he was hooked up to an oxygen machine, with tubing protruding from his nostrils. Only his eyes rolling to the side, to see who these visitors were, gave away the fact that he was still alive.

'This is my Bert,' Edna said. 'Say hello, Bert.'

Bert raised a finger in acknowledgement.

'Now tell me why you want to see our Tyler. He's a good lad.' Edna sat primly on the edge of a matching easy chair, next to Bert. She patted the old man's hand.

Jackie chose her words carefully, not wanting to horrify this clearly doting grandmother. Did she even know Tyler had a criminal record? Or maybe she did, and she was one of those women who would forgive their errant descendants anything. 'We just need to eliminate him from our enquiries.'

Bert started to cough and slowly turned to them. 'What sort of enquiries? Has he been flashing again?' He wheezed the words with clear disdain.

'Don't talk about our Tyler like that, Bert. He's a lovely boy, and he's had a lot to deal with, growing up.' Edna caught Jackie's eye, as if they might form some sort of motherly bond. 'My daughter...' She blushed and sighed. 'Our Tyler was an assistant manager at the factory until...' Her words hung awkwardly on the artificially freshened air. 'He's labouring on a building site, now. Over Clayton way. It's good honest work.' She treated them to a dazzling denture smile.

Dave took out his notebook. 'You got an address for this building site?'

Edna was midway through giving Dave the address when something struck Jackie.

'You mentioned a factory. Which factory?' she asked. 'Which factory did Tyler work at?'

Looking up at her with a bemused smile playing around her lips, Edna laid her liver-spotted hands on her lap. 'Why? What's these enquiries you're making anyway? Because our Tyler just sits in his room all evening, talking to his friends on his computer. He has pals all over the world. He's very popular, is our Tyler.'

Jackie looked in her notebook at the pages she'd written on meeting the working girls, Daisy and Shereen. She read out the dates when the girls had complained about being attacked by Col, the rogue kerb-crawler. 'Do you remember if Tyler was at home on those evenings, Edna?'

Getting to her feet with audibly cracking knees, Edna flip-flapped out of the living room. 'Hang on,' she shouted. 'I'll check the calendar.'

She returned bearing a 'Celebrated Garden Roses' calendar and leafed through to the dates Jackie had given her. Nodded sagely. 'Those were both Thursdays,' she said. 'And Thursdays are shepherd's pie night. We watch *Gardener's World* on telly together. Sometimes, he takes me to bingo. I like routine, you see. I need it, cos of our Bert. He can't be left, but my next-door neighbour looks in on him if I'm at the bingo.'

Feeling that interrogating Edna was an investigative cul-de-sac, Jackie and Dave took their leave from Tyler Fleming's doting grandmother and clearly less committed grandfather. They headed out to Clayton, to the address of the building site that Edna had given them.

'He's basically under house arrest,' Dave said. 'No surprises that he's weird.'

'Makes you wonder what the story is with his mother. Edna clearly had an embarrassing family secret there. And she was so slippery when I tried to pin her down on where Fleming used to work and his whereabouts on those dates I gave her.'

They pulled up opposite the building site, which was a part-built side extension on a semi-detached house. Jackie noticed a silver Toyota Avensis, just like the one Shereen and Daisy had described. It was parked outside, next to a white Transit van.

'There he is!' she said, spying the mousy-haired, bespectacled Fleming.

Their suspect was shovelling sand into a cement mixer, out front, while a solitary bricklayer trowelled mortar onto a wall on the upper floor. The bricklayer didn't even look up when Jackie and Dave crossed the road, but Tyler Fleming clearly knew detectives when he saw them.

'Tyler—?' Jackie said, poised to show her ID.

Fleming dropped the shovel and ran before she could even say his surname.

'Oi!' Dave yelled, sprinting after him down the street.

Jackie caught sight of Fleming ducking into a tight alleyway between the houses that she guessed led from front to back. Instead of following Dave, she clambered beneath the scaffolding and through the newly built doorway at the back of the extension. She ducked to avoid scraping her scalp on a low-hanging scaffold nut and shot out into the back garden. There was a gate at the end, covered in ivy, with a padlock hanging open on an old rusty hasp. She yanked the padlock out of the hasp and flung it aside, opening the creaking gate. Poked her head out and caught sight of Fleming streaking along another alleyway that ran at the backs of the houses. It was a warren of a place.

'Stop! Police!'

Just as Jackie reached the place where the alleys crossed, she crashed into an already panting and puffing Dave.

'He went that way.' She pointed to where she'd last seen Fleming. 'Follow him. I'll try to head him off the other way.'

'Okay. Be careful.' Dave hared off down the alley that Fleming had taken.

Jackie spied another garden gate and tried the handle. It opened with relative ease – unlocked but half-blocked by wheelie bins. With her baton drawn, she negotiated the bins, some soggy turf and an assortment of motorbike parts strewn over a hardstanding at the side of the house. Nobody home at least. She emerged out front in a new street.

As she turned left and right to get her bearings, she heard Dave shout. There was the sound of a scuffle ricocheting off the brick walls of the tight-packed street. Jackie's heart thudded against her ribs. Was Dave hurt?

Holding her breath lest she give her position away, Jackie crept along a cut-through that seemed to lead in an entirely different direction. It felt claustrophobic and dark, with the walls of two-story houses closing in on both sides. Deeper into the cut-through she went, until the walls became mercifully lower as houses gave way to gardens. *Where the hell am I?* she thought. *And where is Dave?*

Jackie held her baton out in front of her, as though it was a wand that would magically deliver Tyler Fleming.

The cut-through opened up suddenly on both sides to another alley. She looked to her right. By the time she heard the crack of a branch under someone's foot to her left, it was too late.

Tyler Fleming pounced.

TWENTY-ONE

'Not a word,' he said, gripping her tightly from behind – one arm around her chest, the other around her neck. His breath smelled of stale coffee.

Jackie craned her neck in vain in an effort to see her attacker; to somehow reason with him. 'You're making it worse for yourself, Tyler. I'm a detective. Do you know what happens to people who attack cops?' Her legs felt like jelly, blood rushing to her brain as she tried to fathom a way out of this dangerous situation. Where was Dave? Had he been injured or worse?

'I'm not attacking you. It's self-defence,' Tyler Fleming said. 'Because I know you want to hurt me, and then turn the tables and make me look the bad guy. Women are wily like snakes. But I'm not stupid. So drop the baton, bitch. Drop it now, or I'll strangle the life out of you.' He tightened his grip on her, lifting her off her feet.

Letting the baton fall to the ground with a clatter, Jackie spoke as loudly as she could in the hope that someone would hear her and come to her aid. 'You're hurting me. Let me go. We only came to ask you some questions relating to one of our cases,

Tyler. Let me go, and we can talk like civilised adults at the police station.'

'Oh yeah? Really. You must think I'm stupid. Well, I've got an IQ over 100.'

She needed him to loosen his grip just enough to get her elbow beneath his ribs or her leg wrapped around his ankle enough to throw him off balance. But he was strong. Too strong for her. *Think, Jackie! Think!* Maybe she could say something to distract him. Yes, that was it.

'It's about your gran,' she said. 'She's in terrible trouble, and this isn't helping her.'

'What do you mean she's in trouble?'

What the hell could she say now to convince this psychopath to let her go? 'Grave danger, and you need to act fast to save her from harm. I can't tell you more until you let me go, can I?'

Her half-spun yarn was enough of a distraction to make Fleming loosen his grip. Jackie knew she had a split second to react, and she had to be quick and decisive in her defensive moves.

She stepped out to the side, kicked her left leg behind him, bent forwards and cradled his knees. Pulling upwards with all her might, she toppled him onto his back. He went down onto the alleyway cobbles with a sickening thud, his thick-lensed spectacles skittering across the cobbles. Jackie grabbed her baton, and before Fleming could get to his feet again, she'd straddled him, holding it tightly against his throat.

'Nice try, smart arse. You're under arrest. Now, I want you to put your hands where I can see them. I'm going to roll you onto your stomach and cuff you. Are you going to behave?'

She read him his rights. Looking down at him as she did so, Jackie could see that he matched the description the working girls had given her. She was sure she had her Col, and she'd put money on it that the silver Toyota was his too.

'What exactly am I under arrest for, you mad cow?' Fleming yelled. 'You attacked me.'

'Assaulting a police officer. Now roll over, you ugly little pimple, before I rearrange your features with my baton.'

'You knocked my glasses off! I can't see. I'm visually impaired. This is disablist.'

'Never mind that. You'll get your glasses in a minute. First thing's first. Where's my partner?'

Fleming did as he was instructed and looked down the alleyway as Jackie cuffed his hands together from behind. 'There,' he said. 'There's your stupid partner.'

Jackie looked up to see Dave jogging towards them. Except he was more weaving than jogging, and she could see from the slick of blood at the side of his head that he'd taken a beating.

'You okay?' she shouted.

Dave nodded. 'More or less. This creep knocked me out.' He stumbled towards them.

Jackie put her face close to Fleming's. 'Oh, we're going to have a lovely time with you in an interview room.'

Processing Fleming had been a trial, as he'd complained and resisted every step of the way. Now, however, they were finally ensconced in the stale-smelling interview room, with its cheap office carpet and furniture, bolted to the floor. The sound recorder was running. At Jackie's side, Dave clutched an ice pack to his head.

'I hope that hurts,' Fleming said. He jerked his head in Jackie's direction. 'It's pretty low that she wound me up about my gran and knocked my glasses off.'

'Answer the question, Mr Fleming,' Dave said. 'It's not difficult. Did you know Claire Watkins, Faye Southgate and Marie Grant?'

Fleming shook his head. 'Never heard of them. I don't consort with whores.'

Jackie resisted the urge to screw up a piece of paper from her pad and throw it at his head. She could see he was going to be as obstinate as possible. 'We know your avatar in your incel group is Hiro Shishigami. You talked about giving a woman' – she read from a printout of the chat that Zoe had given her and which Bob had later claimed credit for during a team catch-up with Venables – '"sweet, sweet sleeping juice" in her thigh. Tell me what you were referring to, Tyler.'

'I don't know what you're talking about, and I've never heard of Hiro what's-his-name. Sounds Japanese. You've got the wrong guy.' He smiled. 'And I'd like a solicitor.'

'This will be a lot easier if you just help us, Tyler. Think about how your gran is going to feel when she hears we're talking to you in connection with three murders. All female victims.' Dave placed the photos of Claire, Faye and Marie onto the table with some ceremony. They had been taken in the women's respective homes, when the police had first arrived on the scene. 'All drugged – two of them jabbed in the thigh with' – he looked at Jackie, as if for corroboration – 'that sweet, sweet sleeping juice?'

Jackie nodded. 'Rohypnol. Barbiturates. Yep. The medical terms for sleeping juice, I believe. And all three women had something rammed down their throats.'

She looked down at the printout again. 'Now, you said in your little incel chat group that you'd rammed all your hurt and rejection down this woman's throat. "Stuck it down her throat 'til she gagged," you wrote.' She jabbed at the printout with her index finger. 'I've got it here, in front of me. In black and white.'

Fleming crossed his arms and shook his head. 'Nothing to do with me. I don't know what incel group you're talking about, but—'

'Oh, don't worry,' Dave said. 'Proving you're Hiro Shishigami's gonna be easy once we've seized your computer equipment. We've got colleagues over at your gran's house now. They'll be tearing the place up, I expect.' He winced visibly. 'Poor Granddad. Bet he won't enjoy that. All that dust in the air from a thorough search, and him on oxygen and all.'

Fleming leaned forwards. 'I want a solicitor, or I'm not saying another word.'

Some hours later, Fleming had been assigned a legal-aid solicitor, whom Jackie assessed to be no more than five years out of college, if that.

The internal phone rang, and Jackie's pulse rate accelerated. She picked up, praying that their fast work would yield equally speedy results. A smile spread across her face as the receptionist gave her the happy news. She looked over at Sophie Higham, Solicitor – a woman so new to the merry-go-round of legal aid and criminal law that she'd written her name on her boss's business card. Jackie snapped her fingers and pointed. 'Time for our line-up.'

'I'm really not sure about this, Detective,' Sophie said, fingering the lapel of her grey polyester suit.

'Not sure in what way?' Jackie asked. 'If Tyler wasn't the man that my girls were accosted by in the red-light district, then he's got nothing to worry about, has he?'

As uniforms were summoned to the interview room to take Tyler Fleming to line up with the hastily assembled decoys, Jackie and Dave made their way to reception to meet Daisy and Shereen.

One of the detectives from Vice was standing with them, frowning as though she were guarding state witnesses in a regicide case.

'Joanne,' Jackie said, placing her hand on her colleague's

arm. 'You're a star. Thanks for picking up our lovely ladies so quickly.'

The Vice detective motioned to the working girls that they were to follow Jackie. 'Not a problem. Now *you* owe *me* one, and that's the way I like it.' She winked.

Shereen and Daisy were clutching their coats tightly shut and looking around them with undisguised suspicion and disdain in their eyes. Wearing micro-miniskirts and stilettos, during the day, with bruised, bare legs, they stood out as prostitutes. The gazes of the other waiting citizens were judgemental – the men's admiring in some cases.

Jackie thought Shereen and Daisy looked like vulnerable girls. 'Don't worry,' she said. 'Nobody will think you're informants, and this gets you a free pass, next time you get picked up for soliciting.'

'Damn well better had do,' Shereen said.

'Let's get this over with,' Daisy said.

One at a time, the two girls click-clacked in their heels into a darkened room where a large window faced onto an identity parade of men.

'They can't see you,' Jackie told Shereen. 'Just have a good look at them and tell me if you can spot the punter who wanted you to play dead and tried to drug you.'

'That's him.' Shereen pointed to Tyler Fleming. 'Definitely. Them glasses and that hair... Like a curly mullet.' She had her hand clasped to her mouth. She spoke through her fingers. 'Cruel, thin lips too. Number three, definitely.'

'You sure?' Jackie asked, feeling warmth spread throughout her empty stomach.

'Dead sure.'

Jackie repeated the rigmarole with Daisy. It took no more than a minute for her to point out Fleming.

Daisy nodded. 'The other fellers are all too big or too brawny. It's the hair and glasses that give him away. It's him.'

'Sure?

'Yep.'

Feeling triumphant, Jackie parted company with the girls and made her way back to the interview room. For a few minutes, she and Dave were alone.

'He's Col. I feel pretty certain about that,' she said.

'Question is,' Dave said, rubbing his head, 'would a jury believe the testimonies of a couple of prostitutes? And the evidence linking him to one of the murder victims is circumstantial as hell at the minute. We need more. We need to link him to the name Steve James and to the bank details of the old dead woman – the identity he used to float the online dating accounts.'

'We'll get it,' Jackie said, squeezing his arm. 'If it's there, we'll get it.'

Sophie, the legal aid solicitor, returned first. Tyler Fleming was brought back to them moments later, and he was in a foul mood, struggling against his uniformed escorts.

'This is a fix,' he shouted. 'It's bull!' He locked eyes with his legal aid representative. 'And you're useless too. What's a girl with chicken tits in a cheap suit going to do for a man like me? Nothing! I need a male lawyer. Someone with balls. Someone who knows how the damned world works.'

'Can I have a word with my client please?' the solicitor asked. Her mouth settled into a grim line. Perhaps Sophie wasn't so naïve after all.

Jackie and Dave stood by the snacks dispenser in silence, waiting to be readmitted.

'Do you think he *is* our man?' Jackie asked presently.

Dave turned to her, touching the scab on his forehead gingerly. 'I agree he's probably Col. But we at least need to establish a link between him and one of the victims.'

Nodding slowly, Jackie sniffed resolutely. 'Hiro Shishigami mentioned that he worked with the woman. But I can't see a woman working on a building site, can you?' She took out her phone. 'His gran mentioned a factory. We need Fleming's employment history fast, and I've got a contact at HMRC who can help. One of my dad's unlikely old squeezes. She's near to retirement, but...'

Half an hour later, Jackie and Dave were still grilling Tyler Fleming, who now looked a good deal more contrite after the conversation he'd had with his solicitor, but who was still refusing to co-operate. Jackie felt her phone vibrate inside her jacket pocket. She took it out. On the screen was a text from her father's old conquest, Scouse Frances.

> *Tyler Fleming's last place of employment was Vanguard Biscuit Factory in Trafford. He was given his P45 four months ago. Give my love to your dad. Frances.*

Jackie slid the phone to Dave and pointed to the information.

Dave nodded almost imperceptibly. Beneath the table, his foot started to bounce up and down.

'Tell me, Mr Fleming, where your last place of employment was, because Hiro Shishigami wrote that, "The bitch at work finally got what was coming to her, and I was the one that gave it."'

Fleming looked at his solicitor.

'It's a matter of public record,' she said. 'Tell them, Tyler.'

He cleared his throat. 'Vanguard Biscuits in Trafford.'

Jackie tidied her documentation together, trying to keep the excited smile inside. 'Funny that, because one of our victims – Claire Watkins, or Rachel Hardman, as she came to be known – worked at Vanguard Biscuits too.' She smacked her lips together and frowned. 'Now tell me. If I called their head of human resources now, what would they tell me was their reason for sacking you, Tyler?'

Tyler Fleming looked down and ran his finger over some graffiti etched into the table. He said something inaudible.

'What was that, Tyler?' Jackie asked.

'Sexual harassment.'

'Of whom?'

'Rachel.'

'Sorry? Can you say that clearly for the recording?'

He sighed. 'Rachel Hardman.'

TWENTY-TWO

'I'll ask you *again*,' Dave said, clearly wishing he could wipe the insolent expression from Tyler Fleming's face. 'Where were you on the fifteenth of September, between the hours of 8 a.m. and 10 a.m.?'

Tyler Fleming leaned back in his chair, stretched and yawned. Beside him, his legal aid solicitor looked at Dave without blinking.

Finally, Fleming spoke, rolling his eyes, the boredom audible in his voice. 'I've already told you. I was at home. Speak to my gran. I was online by nine. There's no law against that.'

Jackie listed the estimated times and dates of death for Faye Southgate and Marie Grant. 'Well? Where were you then?'

Fleming shrugged. 'How the hell should I know? It was ages ago. At work maybe, or at home. Am I supposed to know all this? My every movement during every waking moment, going back years? *Really?*' He looked to his solicitor.

The solicitor cleared her throat and fixed Jackie with a challenging stare. 'My client spends a lot of time online when he's not at work. You'll be able to get everything you need from his electronic devices or his grandmother. You're the detective, Detective. I suggest you do some detecting.'

Taking a deep breath, Jackie wished Venables was not watching them from behind the two-way mirror. Out of the corner of her eye, she could see Dave gripping the table edge.

'Let's start again,' he said. 'Do you know a Faye Southgate or Marie Grant?'

'Who?' Fleming's expression had set into a sneer.

'Faye Southgate.' Jackie placed on the table a photograph of the Didsbury divorcée when she'd been alive. In it, she was holding a glass of wine and pouting at the camera – her Facebook profile picture.

Fleming shook his head.

'Speak for the recording please.'

'Nope.'

'What about Marie Grant?' She placed a photo of Marie beside the snap of Faye. In it, Marie was dressed to impress. On the back, she'd written 'Megan and Tom's wedding, 2014'. Jackie tapped her index finger on the photo. 'Ring any bells?'

Fleming leaned right in towards the recording equipment. 'No.' His voice was loud enough to make his solicitor jump. He treated them all to a self-satisfied smile.

Feeling her pulse speed up and pound in her throat, Jackie opened her file again and took out a pink piece of paper covered in blue writing – new paperwork they'd only just found when sifting yet again through Doug Barnes's hard-copy records from 2015. 'Recognise this?'

'Nope.' Fleming answered before he'd looked at the sheet of paper. When he did look down at it – albeit cursorily – a rash of red blotches appeared at the base of his neck.

The solicitor held up her hand. 'Sorry. What's this?'

'That is the sheet that Tyler here filled in during speed dating, back in 2015,' Dave said. 'Instant Attraction. Runs out of the function room above the Imperial Bar on Princess Street.

Still very popular I'm told, now that Covid restrictions have lifted.'

'I've never been speed dating in my life,' Tyler said. He scoffed. 'That's for old people.' Then he picked up the sheet and read it with narrowed eyes. '*Col?* Who the hell is Col?' He flung the paper back down towards the table. It drifted off the edge, landing on the ground.

'Col's one of your pseudonyms, isn't it, Tyler... or should I say Hiro Shishigami, or maybe Steve James?' Jackie reached down and placed the sheet back under Fleming's nose. 'And we know you're Col because you perfectly match the description that a couple of working girls gave us about a punter who wanted to stuff sleeping tablets down their throats and get them to play dead. Col. That was the name they gave. There's also the small thing of them having ID'd you in a line-up too.'

'That will never stand up in court, and you know it, Detective,' the solicitor said.

'Looks like Col here had his three minutes in the love seat with Marie Grant.' Jackie tapped her finger on the scrawled notes.

Marie – Yes. Fat, chatty, nice.

'I'm wondering if, when Marie inevitably didn't match with you, you took matters into your own hands, broke into her home, doped her and choked the life out of her by stuffing a pound coin down her gullet.'

'That's not my handwriting!'

'We can get that checked by an expert.'

'Please yourself. You lot are fantasising,' Fleming said. 'I have no idea who this Col is, and like I say, I've never set foot inside the Imperial Bar, let alone gone speed dating.'

Jackie wondered when the legal aid solicitor would speak

up for her client, but she was looking intently at the side of Fleming's head instead.

'What's your middle name, Tyler?' Dave asked.

'I haven't got a middle name.' Fleming was smirking again. 'Check my birth certificate.'

'Oh, I did,' Dave said. From the file, he teased out a birth certificate. On it was registered the birth of Tyler Fleming.

Fleming pointed to the piece of paper. 'See? No middle name.'

'Ah, but that's not the full picture, is it?' Dave pulled another certificate out of the file. 'Because your mother added a middle name a few weeks after your birth. Want to know what your middle name is?'

Fleming got up and leaned forwards so that he was almost nose to nose with Dave. 'I haven't got a middle name.'

Dave turned the second document around and pushed it towards Fleming. 'Just because you destroyed your second certificate by doctoring your birthdate so you could get into a nightclub when you were seventeen doesn't mean the second certificate doesn't exist.'

Jackie looked over to the solicitor and saw realisation dawning on her face.

'Tyler Colin Fleming,' she said. 'We spoke to your mother – she didn't say "Hi" by the way. She *did* explain she'd wanted you to take her surname of Collins, but she and your dad came to an agreement weeks later that Colin as a middle name would have to suffice – the closest thing to your mum's maiden name.'

At her side, Dave grinned and laced his hands together behind his head. 'She's quite a piece of work, your junkie mum. No wonder you're still living with your grandparents in your thirties.' He winked.

Fleming flushed bright red. 'Y-You're making this up,' he said, looking from Dave to Jackie to his solicitor. 'I-I'm being fitted up. *This* is why the police needs defunding.' He jabbed at his alternative birth certificate with his index finger. 'Not because Black Lives Matter and all that rubbish. It's because men like me are getting singled out all the time. White, working-class men are the most vulnerable group in the country because everything's about women and the ethnics.'

'Lovely,' Jackie said. 'Keep it up. This is going to play nicely in court. We've got an established link between a hostile, *racist* habitual liar on the sex offenders register and two dead women who both rejected your advances.'

'There's the motive,' Dave said. 'Coupled with your incel forum shenanigans, where you publicly talk about ramming things down women's throats, I don't think we'll have much of a problem getting a murder conviction.'

'This is all conjecture,' the solicitor said. 'There's absolutely no established link with Faye Southgate, and the rest is... You're browbeating an innocent man. Now if you don't mind, I need time to talk to my client.'

After Jackie and Dave left Fleming and his floundering legal representative to bicker in peace, they walked back towards Clever Bob's workstation, accompanied by Venables.

'He's definitely our man,' Venables said. 'Good work in there, Tang, with the birth certificates.'

Jackie drew breath, instinctively wanting to challenge her superior for giving Dave the credit for work they'd done as a team. But she realised it was pointless. Venables saw her as competition. They clashed. They always had. And Venables never lost an opportunity to play one of her subordinates off against the other. *Don't rise to the bait, Jackie*, imaginary Lucian said.

'We're a long way off making this stand up in court,' Dave said.

'Dave's right,' Jackie said. 'The Facebook, Tinder Gold and

Connection accounts for Nice Guy go nowhere. They're registered to a Steve James, but Steve James doesn't check out at the
address given, and there's no way of linking Steve James or the
dead old lady's bank account he's been using to Tyler Fleming. I
have no doubt that Tyler Fleming is Col, the kinky punter our
working girls ID'd *and* Hiro Shishigami from the incel forum,
who described the MO of our killer pretty accurately. But
there's just no way of connecting him to Steve James, even
though Steve James *and* Col are both listed as speed daters who
met with Marie Grant. There are some really sophisticated
spoofing techniques at play here. Identity fraud on a grand
scale. *Is* Tyler Fleming, aka Col, this Steve James? Or is Steve
James another incel, and Tyler Fleming is just copycatting him?'

Dave nodded vigorously. 'We've got quite a few pieces of
the jigsaw, Tina, but they're all bits around the edges. We're
missing big chunks of the main picture in the middle.'

Venables slapped him on the shoulder, not even making eye
contact with Jackie. 'I have every faith in you, Tang. Keep at it.'

'Can this wait?' Bob asked, barely even looking round to
acknowledge Jackie's arrival. 'Only I've got to get through some
CCTV footage from a City match for, like, yesterday.'

Jackie pulled up a chair and peered over Bob's shoulder.
'Which match? The one with the stabbing?'

Bob nodded. He pointed to the blurry, slowly moving image
on the screen. 'See him?' His finger landed on a Black fan – a
young man, wearing a Tottenham scarf. 'He's the one that gets
stabbed. See them?' His finger hovered over a small group of
white youths in City strips, who were clearly shouting taunts at
the Tottenham fan. 'They're the accused. They've just been
sent to Strangeways on remand. Trial's not coming up for
months, but I've been asked to get this footage edited and
enhanced ASAP.'

'Black guy's not alone,' Jackie said. She pointed to some blurry figures standing nearby. Their body language was defensive – all balled fists and craned necks. They too were wearing Tottenham regalia. Jackie suddenly felt like a radiographer, able to make out the fine detail in an ultrasound image that looked like nothing more than static to the uninitiated.

Bob paused the footage and turned to Jackie. 'You're not going until I help you, are you?'

'Did the Black kid die?' Jackie asked.

Bob shook his head. 'He's still in intensive care.'

Jackie raised her eyebrows. 'Well, he's alive. That's something.' She turned her thoughts away from football. That was Dave's domain, and Dave was off talking to Marie Grant's neighbours, to see if they had any long-lost leads to offer the case. 'Now, you know this Tyler Fleming creep that we've got in custody? Well, we've got to prove a link between him and Faye Southgate – one of the victims. Our case is still mashed potato, if I'm honest.'

'No forensics?'

'No fingerprints, no DNA. Not a sausage. Problem is, we've got to get as far down the rabbit hole as we can before our guy kills again.'

Bob leaned in and spoke with a conspiratorial air. 'Leave it to me, Jackie. I'm you're man, or Robert's not your father's brother.' He winked. 'Now, what do we know about this Faye, and what do we know about your incel?'

Jackie presented Bob with all the login details she and Dave had finally been given by the accounts people at Gmail, Facebook, Twitter, Instagram and TikTok – legacy information that had been hard to come by. 'Faye Southgate was a dedicated exhibitionist, looking to be loved.'

'And your incel?'

'Tyler Fleming. Middle name's Colin. Goes as Col or Hiro Shishigami. We know Faye Southgate had contact with Nice

Guy, but we haven't checked for Tyler or Col or Fleming or the Japanese moniker.'

Bob logged in as Faye Southgate and retrieved a jar of pickled gherkins from his desk drawer. Wordlessly, he unscrewed the lid, took out a fat cucumber and bit into it with a crunch. The pickling juice dripped onto his lap.

Jackie watched the ritual in stunned silence. Why did her male colleagues all have such terrible eating habits? 'Well?'

Bob chewed noisily. 'I'm checking her TikTok account – wow. She had a *lot* of followers, considering all she goes on about is scented candles and the gym.'

'She was a big supporter of a local children's charity,' Jackie said.

Bob wasn't listening. He put the jar back into his drawer, but the entire area now reeked of vinegar. He wiped his hand on his trousers. 'No Colins or Cols.'

For the next twenty minutes, Bob looked through all of Faye's social-media accounts but couldn't find anyone among her followers or correspondents named Tyler or Col or who had the surname of Fleming. No Hiro Shishigami. 'Not looking too promising this.'

Jackie rubbed her face and exhaled heavily. 'There's got to be something. He's got a connection to the other two women. How about you search the followers she's blocked? Is that possible?'

'Leave it to Clever Bob.' Bob's fingers were a whirr of blurred movement. He logged into an app called Sendible and suddenly had an overview of all of Faye Southgate's social-media accounts. 'I should have done this first really, but I find it very confusing.'

'But you're the cyber guy.'

Bob looked at Jackie blankly and then turned back to the dashboard. 'Right, let's see...' Before long, he'd accessed a list of everyone who had followed, unfollowed or been blocked by

Faye. 'Here we go,' Bob said. '@Cool_col88. Ooh, eighty-eight is a Nazi thing. Means *Heil Hitler*. H is the eighth letter of the alphabet, see?'

'What happened to Cool Col then?'

'Blocked for sending filth.' Bob brought up a number of screens that showed archived chat. 'See?'

Col had indeed sent a string of sexually explicit messages via Instagram and Twitter, and Faye had subsequently blocked him.

'How do we know Tyler Fleming is @Cool_col88?'

Bob shrugged and scratched his head. 'I'd have to read my notes again. I've got it written down somewhere. Tell you what, I'll give you a shout later. I promise.'

Wishing fervently that Bob actually lived up to his nickname and that the police wasn't so overstretched and under-resourced, Jackie went back to her desk. She looked at the photo of her children, but she was thinking about Tyler Fleming – the suspicion that Claire would never have let a workplace sex pest into her home willingly still niggled.

Before she could jot her misgivings into her notepad, her internal phone rang. Bob was on the other end.

'Bob. What did you find out?'

Bob's voice was tremulous. 'Cool Col *is* Tyler Fleming. Faye Southgate was hassled by him and she blocked him.'

Jackie smiled uncertainly. 'Sure?'

'Hundred per cent.'

Perhaps they had their man after all.

TWENTY-THREE

'This your first time down here?' Nick Swinton asked.

When Shazia tried to speak, the words seemed reluctant to come. She swallowed hard. Her mouth was dry. 'Y-Yep.'

'You don't have to be down here, you know. You could just pick up the report afterwards. I know this aspect of the job isn't for everyone.' The forensic pathologist smiled at her, and when he did, the harsh overhead lights didn't seem quite as harsh.

Pinching her nose, though there was hardly any bad smell at all from a cadaver that had been first refrigerated, to allow an MRI, and then ceremonially washed, in anticipation of finally receiving a Jewish burial, Shazia steeled herself to look at the body on the slab.

Esther Glickman had been de-shrouded and was lying naked, awaiting this final indignity. Her rounded, stretch-marked body spoke to a life spent tending to children's needs – cooking and baking and washing and wiping – as opposed to her own, pounding the treadmill or spin bike at the gym. Her dull, thin hair bore testament to being covered for most of her adult life by the hair of another or else a headscarf, not dissimilar to Shazia's.

'It's all right,' Shazia said, smoothing the edge of her hijab where it skimmed her forehead. 'I want to be here for her. I feel...'

A memory of Shazia's cousin's untimely funeral presented itself to her, vivid and raw, as though Aisha had been hit by the car only yesterday, rather than five years earlier. Tended in death by womenfolk in the community. In the ground before sunset. The hit-and-run killer had never been found. Shazia shook her head, trying to dispel the image of Aisha, wrapped in a shroud – imagined, in any case, as she'd never been allowed near her cousin's body, and no female relatives had been allowed to attend the burial itself. 'I feel a sense of duty to her mother to act like a chaperone of sorts.'

'But she's got those already, standing outside. Jews don't leave their dead alone until they're in the ground.'

'Well, let's just say, I never realised how similar a Jewish burial was to a Muslim one.'

Nick sighed. 'You're getting personally involved, aren't you?' He held Esther's head between his strong-looking latex-gloved hands and prised her mouth open. Peered down her gullet and took up a long pair of tweezers. 'A word to the wise, Shazia: don't. In a job like this, you can't afford to, for your own sanity's sake. Learn to compartmentalise.'

Reaching in, Nick frowned. Then his features softened and his hand jerked, as though something buried deep had dislodged. 'Aha!' He withdrew something foul-smelling that was roughly the size and shape of a lip balm.

Wrinkling her nose, Shazia drew closer. 'What on earth is that?'

Nick dropped the object into a metal dish. 'Not a prune or a date stone. Not a chicken bone. Nothing that could legitimately have got stuck. This, Shazia, is exactly what I thought it might be when I got the MRI scan through. Look.' Using his tweezers, he removed an elastic band that had bound the object so tightly.

Unfurled the contents so that the Queen's face was visible. 'Voila.'

'Money,' Shazia said softly.

'And I hear the bloods came back, showing Rohypnol in her system too.' Nick rounded the slab and leaned in to get a closer look at Esther Glickman's thigh. He pointed to a tiny black spot that stood out among the purples and yellows, where her blood had drained from the top of her body, settling along the bottom. 'She's been jabbed. See? Like the others.'

'Others?' Shazia asked the question, but she already knew the answer.

'The murders that Jackie and Dave are investigating.'

Shazia nodded. She took a step backwards and appraised the body of the dead woman in the florid livery that heralded the start of decomposition. 'I don't believe it. How has an ultra-Orthodox Jewish woman been targeted by a killer who stalks his victims through online dating websites? I mean, *how*? The women in that community don't mix with men unless it's their immediate relatives. They don't dance together. They don't pray together.'

'How indeed.' Nick systematically photographed the body and the money that had come from Esther Glickman's throat. 'Wasn't the initial cause of death supposed to be a seizure?'

'Yep. This is a long way from a seizure.'

'I bet her family's going to be devastated all over again when they find out she's part of an ongoing murder investigation. Murders that seem to be sexually motivated at that.'

Shazia thought about Esther Glickman's ultra-religious parents and the austere house full of sombre, praying men, all dressed identically with their full beards and formal black suiting beneath tasselled prayer shawls. Serious men, obsessed with observing religious laws and decorum in all things. 'They'll be in denial. This is a total can of worms, open and all over the floor.'

The hairs on her forearms stood to attention as she suddenly realised that the roll of money and the jab to the thigh meant that Venables would surely give the nod to transferring her from Connor's uninspiring supervision to Jackie and Dave's case. She tried to stifle a smile as, in that moment, she imagined herself solving the murders single-handedly. She could already see her photo on the cover of the *Manchester Evening News*:

MANCHESTER'S FIRST FEMALE ASIAN DETECTIVE TO BRING DOWN SERIAL KILLER RECEIVES KEY TO THE CITY.

Deep down, she knew her fantasy was the stuff of super-hero movies. But it made the onerous task of standing there, in that sterile environment with the dead body of a murdered woman, a little more tolerable. It made the prospect of having a difficult conversation with Esther Glickman's family a little more bearable. It made Aisha's death fractionally less frustrating. Finally, Shazia Malik would be the one to get the answers for the difficult questions.

'You okay?' Nick asked. 'You seem a bit...'

She shook her head. 'Fine. I'm fine. Thanks, Nick. Thanks for making this... I thought it was going to be...' She squeezed her eyes shut momentarily. 'I did it. You helped me through my first one.'

Nick picked up a handheld saw and cocked his head to the side. 'Well, to be fair, you've not really seen the full monty. But there's no rush. This is Manchester. Murder's as perennial as the grass.'

There was an atmosphere of celebration when Shazia got back to HQ. She walked in to find Jackie high-fiving Dave. Even Venables was joining in the frivolity, grinning at everyone.

'Beers after work beckon,' Dave said.

'Hey. Hang on. Don't be getting carried away.' Venables' smile started to falter. 'You've got a prime suspect, but that's as far as it goes.'

Jackie was perched on the edge of her own desk, sipping a coffee, still looking happier than she had in a while – all the happier for witnessing her boss finally giving a hoot about dotting the i's and crossing the t's, instead of pushing to get a quick conviction. 'Tina's right, Dave. We've got a lot of holes in the case still. The judge would throw it out as a circumstantial flight of fancy at the moment. We've got to produce the computer records that corroborate the fact Tyler Fleming is Hiro Shishigami, for a start.' She counted out the tasks on their investigative to-do list on her fingers, one by one. 'Then we've got to prove he's also Steve James *and* Guy Schön or Sympa or whoever the hell is the catfishing avatar on not just the dating sites but on Facebook too. We've got to establish beyond a doubt a link with the dead old lady's bank account.'

Jackie set down her coffee and clasped her hands to her face. That cheery, twinkly-eyed look had all but disappeared now. 'And there was no sign of a break-in at Claire's house. Given Fleming harassed her at work, would she have let him in willingly? My God. There's a mountain to climb, and that's assuming he doesn't have alibis for all three murders.'

Shazia had quietly paced around to her desk, to where Connor was peering over the partition, clearly revelling in Jackie and Dave's triumph as if it was his own – especially when Dave had mentioned beer. She set her bag down, mulling over the implications of what she'd just discovered in the mortuary. It would keep – at least until Venables had returned to her office.

When the jubilation had settled down, Dave had gone on the hunt for takeaway menus and Venables had stalked out of sight in those idiotic stilettos she wore, Shazia slipped around the partition and loitered at Jackie's side. For the second time that day, she willed herself to speak, but the words wouldn't come readily.

Jackie looked up at her, inhaled sharply and pressed her hand to her chest. 'Shazia. You gave me a fright.'

'Sorry.'

'Is everything okay?'

Placing a hand on the desk to steady herself, Shazia took a deep breath and then spoke. 'Look, I'm really sorry, but I've got some news you're not going to want to hear.'

Jackie swivelled round in her computer chair to face her colleague. 'Like what?'

'I've just come from a post-mortem – a Jewish woman, who I thought had died of a seizure. I was looking into her death, remember?'

'Yes. I remember. And?' Jackie's colour started to drain, leaving a sickly pallor in its wake.

Shazia explained the findings of the blood test and the MRI. Then she described what Nick had found when he'd extracted the mystery blockage from Esther Glickman's gullet. 'She's one of yours,' Shazia said. 'Rohypnol in the bloodstream. A pinprick on the thigh points to her being injected like your women. A roll of notes in her throat.'

The moments of ensuing silence as Jackie studied Shazia's face felt like they stretched on for hours.

'But we've just charged a lad from an incel group,' Jackie said finally. 'A lying, stalking little turd who wooed lonely women in online dating sites and then killed them in their own homes. He's the perfect suspect.' She sank in her seat and sighed heavily. 'Except he was, until you introduced an Orthodox Jewish woman into the equation. How the hell...?'

'Sorry.' Shazia toyed with the cuff of her jacket.

Jackie rubbed her face. 'Why are you apologising? It's not your fault. But this does feel like it's come from nowhere.'

'I know. She lived in this really insular little world. A load of kids. Hassidic, ageing parents, living just across the street. Nobody farts without the rabbi's say-so. I mean, we should get hold of any computer equipment and her phone – I assume the ultra-Orthodox are allowed all that.'

'They're not Amish, Shazia,' Jackie said.

'Well, okay. Get her devices and see if maybe she was living a double life, but...' She shrugged.

'What else do you know about your victim?' Jackie took out her notebook and straightened up in her seat.

'She *was* divorced. Does that help?'

'This is going to be a horror show, right?' Shazia asked a short while later as Jackie drove them over to the Broughton Park home of Esther Glickman's parents.

Jackie nodded. 'The very religious don't like to acknowledge wrongdoing, if it can be avoided. They'll take it as an insult that we want to dig around into Esther's private life, because it casts shade on her. They might say we're harassing them. Who knows? I've not had to deal with this sort of case for a good long while.'

Shazia pressed the bell, her stomach churning as she heard footsteps padding to the front door. The door was opened by Gilda Eskowitz. She looked smaller than she had only days earlier. The sclera of her eyes were blood-shot and dull, as though she had died along with her daughter.

'Come in,' she said. 'Come through. We're having a rest while we can. The house has been packed with people from the community, coming to mourn with us.'

She shuffled ahead and led them into Joel Eskowitz's office. 'The police are back.'

Taking off his glasses, Mr Eskowitz rubbed his eyes. He barely seemed to take it in when Jackie introduced herself as the

DS heading up the murder investigation. She gave him an over-view of what had so far come to pass.

'So, I realise this might be hard for you, but we're going to need you to help us with our investigation, Mr Eskowitz,' Shazia said. 'We're going to need access to Esther's devices – laptop, PC, phone. Anything like that. We need to establish if and how she knew her murderer.'

Mrs Eskowitz slumped onto a chair and started to weep quietly. 'How could someone have done this to my Esther?' she said. 'I don't understand. She was nothing like... She couldn't have got involved with a stalker. An *incel*, you say? Someone on the internet who hates women and then tricks them into meeting with him? My Esther would *never* meet a non-Jewish man on a date.'

'You don't understand how that sort of thing works in our community, do you?' Mr Eskowitz looked to his wife for corrob-oration.

There was a heated exchange between the bereaved parents in what Shazia guessed was the Germanic-sounding Yiddish.

The old man slammed his hand down on the desk, making his wife jump. He turned to Shazia and Jackie. 'I can't believe you think my respectable, highly observant daughter would be tied up in a serial-killer case involving common prostitutes and single mothers. It's an insult. And you're absolutely not rummaging through her personal affairs, like she's a suspect. My daughter was the victim. Now do your jobs.'

He got up from his seat and stormed out of the office. They heard the front door slam.

Jackie turned to Mrs Eskowitz. 'I'm so sorry. This must be heartbreaking to find out your daughter has been murdered and then to hear she's somehow been involved in something that doesn't sit right with your community's expectations of women.'

The old woman nodded, wiping her eyes. 'Do you have children?'

'Three,' Jackie said. 'Two boys and a baby girl.'

'Lovely. Lovely. Children are our diamonds and rubies. My Esther was a good girl.' Mrs Eskowitz screwed the fabric of her long skirt in her fist. 'She was my third eldest. Third out of seven. Three girls, four boys. But being a child from a large family doesn't make you any less precious to your parents. May you never know such pain,' she said.

She got to her feet and walked around to the side of the desk where her husband had been sitting. She opened a slim drawer beneath the desktop – a concealed drawer. Took out a key and walked over to a filing cabinet. She unlocked it and opened the bottom drawer. From the back, she took out a MacBook Air and a mobile phone. Wordlessly, she handed them to Shazia.

'I don't understand,' Shazia said. 'Whose are these?'

'Esther's,' Mrs Eskowitz said. 'My husband took them from Esther's house after the paramedics and your lot had gone. He said he wanted to keep her reputation safe, and didn't want anyone noseying into her financial affairs or the circumstances surrounding her divorce. Just in case it came to it.'

Shazia looked at Jackie, bemused. If only Jackie could hear her thoughts. *How did he know to hide the devices? Could he and the ex-husband be involved? Or are we just lucky the old lady is helping us out?*

Jackie took the MacBook and phone from Mrs Eskowitz. 'I'm sure your daughter was an innocent in all of this. We're not trying to make assumptions or doubt her good character, I promise.'

Mrs Eskowitz wiped away a tear and patted Jackie's forearm. 'My daughter was human. Fallible. Gullible. Lonely. And whatever she got herself into... she's left a young family behind. And the only way you're going to find out what happened and bring her killer to justice is to seek the unvarnished truth. Now take these with my blessing and go. Before my husband gets back.'

TWENTY-FOUR

'Want a slice?' Dave asked, pushing the box towards Jackie. His eyes were smiling. His facial features had relaxed, taking away those deep furrows in his brow. Even his body language, as he leaned back in his chair, talking with his mouth open as he chewed his own slice of pizza, said here was a man who was at one with the world.

Jackie took a deep breath and threw her bag onto her desk. She sat down heavily, feeling the disappointment weighing her down. Wishing Shazia could unsay her revelation about Esther Glickman. 'No. I won't. Pepperoni gets into my breast milk and plays havoc with Alice's guts.'

Dave curled his lip. 'Thank you, Jackson. Thanks a bundle for that. Are you trying to sabotage my dinner? Because everyone knows pepperoni pizza is the dinner of heroes.' The smile on his lips slid suddenly. 'Hang on.' He sat up straight. Swallowed noisily. The tautness in his face returned, along with the furrows. 'Why have you got a face like a smacked—?'

'You're not going to like this.' Despite her best intentions, the smell of savoury grease and oregano was too tempting; her appetite too ferocious; her need to comfort-eat too strong.

Losing her baby weight could wait. She grabbed a slice of pizza. 'I don't think Fleming's our man.'

Like a crab, Shazia wheeled her computer chair around to their side of the partition. 'It's true. We've just got back from the home of this ultra-Orthodox Jewish woman's parents – Esther Glickman. I've been looking into her death, and it turns out she had a roll of ten-pound notes in her throat, same as your victims. Rohypnol in her bloodstream and evidence of a jab to the thigh.'

'Exactly the same MO,' Jackie said. She growled with frustration. 'Can you believe it? We're right back to square one.'

Dave looked at them both blankly. Blinked repeatedly. 'How does this rule out Fleming? I don't understand.'

'Think about it,' Jackie said. 'Tyler Fleming has been kerb-crawling. We're pretty certain he's the Col that Shereen and Daisy were talking about. They ID'd him, right? And he'd definitely been hassling Faye Southgate on social media as Cool_col88.'

'Yeah, and I bet we find out he's our Nice Guy too, seeing as he was sacked for sexually harassing your pal at the biscuit factory.' Dave picked at his teeth. 'We've got his motive for catfishing them on Facebook and online dating sites. He's an incel! Occam's razor, isn't it?'

'What?' Shazia asked.

'The truth is usually the most likely, logical hypothesis... or something like that.' Dave waved his hand dismissively. 'Hannah uses that phrase all the time.'

'Hannah's a philosophy graduate from Oxford, isn't she?' Jackie asked. 'I'm not sure long words and difficult concepts are safe in your hands though, David.' She turned to Shazia. 'He's just trying to sound impressive, love. Take no notice.'

Shazia hid a smile beneath her slender hand.

'Point is though,' Jackie said, 'Fleming might be Col, the weirdo punter, and he might have had a connection to Claire and the biscuit factory, but surely Claire wouldn't have willingly let a known sex-pest into her house, and it certainly doesn't mean he's Nice Guy. Col the kerb-crawler having a similar MO to our murderer could just be coincidence.'

Dave shook his head. 'I don't believe in coincidences, and neither do you.'

Clearing her throat, Shazia spoke. 'Not being funny, but we've seen the family this Esther Glickman comes from. There's no way she's been on Tinder and Connection. No way.'

'Well, Fleming met her online some other way then.' Dave pointed at Shazia with a fresh piece of pizza. 'A Jewish dating site maybe.'

'If she'd been a regular Jew, I'd agree,' Shazia said. 'I had a look on the way back from her parents' house, and there is a Jewish dating service called JDate. But the ultra-Orthodox don't meet partners that way. I googled it. They have matchmakers. Old-fashioned ones, where everything's fully vetted in advance, with the involvement of parents, and it's all in person.'

'Well, don't rule it out,' Dave said. 'And don't let Venables hear this theory until you're absolutely sure Fleming *isn't* the murderer. She'll fry you both alive.'

'Well, let's divide up the work.' Jackie turned to Dave. 'How about you keep going, checking in with the victims' friends and neighbours and colleagues? Try to establish the relationship – if there is one – between the Steve James avatar, Nice Guy and Tyler Fleming. Meanwhile, me and Shazia, here' – she turned to the junior detective, who was eyeing the pizza box with curiosity – 'start looking at other possible connections between the victims. Women are getting killed. We've got four and counting. What we can't afford to do is stick with one line of enquiry doggedly and then find out – months and several more bodies down the line – that we were wrong. Right?'

She slapped Dave's hand as he picked up yet another slice of the giant eighteen-inch pizza. 'And how can someone your size eat all that junk and never put any weight on?'

Dave chuckled and started to roll the slice up. 'I'm a Chinese man. My brains and good looks demand massive fuel consumption. Calorie black holes, see? That's philosophy for you.'

Jackie took up the takeout menu and started to dial the number. 'No. You're just a greedy sod with a fast metabolism. Occam's razor.' She winked and ordered a vegetarian pizza for her and Shazia. It was going to be a long night.

Unlocking Esther Glickman's laptop had been surprisingly easy for Clever Bob, whom they'd caught just before he was leaving for home. Now Jackie, Shazia and Bob were sitting in a spare meeting room with the MacBook Air open in front of them and Esther's phone placed next to it, free of its screen lock.

'So what are we looking for?' Shazia asked, taking a bite from the last remaining slice of their pizza.

Jackie massaged her temples, trying not to think of the children she was failing to kiss goodnight yet again. Still, tonight was Gus's night. The boys would be tucked up in their bunk beds in Catherine Harris's guest room. Jackie silently prayed that Gus had had a word about Taylor taunting Percy.

'We'll examine Ether's finances in the morning. If there *is* a link to the world of online dating, her direct debits will tell us straight away. For now, let's step away from the dating angle completely and look at the thing that unites them. All four women were divorced. Right? Even if Esther's divorce was one of those religious ones that the rabbis sanction...'

'It's called a "get" apparently. Mrs Eskowitz told me.'

'Okay, a get then. But I'm assuming that in this country, Orthodox Jewish divorcées have to get the religious divorce and then a civil one too, for the thing to be legally binding.'

At her side, Shazia was googling it. Jackie could see her eyes move from right to left as she scanned the information on the web. 'Yep. Unless one half of the couple is living in Israel at the time of the split, there has to be a civil divorce too. Shimon Glickman only moved to Israel *after* the divorce. Wow. The religious side of it all sounds really...' Her eyes widened.

Jackie could see a Venn diagram developing in her mind's eye; the lives of the four very different women intersecting where the legal process of spouses parting company took place. 'We're looking for letters from solicitors, mediators, children's services maybe. Even estate agents and removal men. Check for invoices. Any correspondence from the courts – perhaps there's a common contact who wrote to all of them. You just never know.' She nodded to Bob.

Bob saluted and opened the MacBook's files. 'Oh,' he said, his eyebrows shooting up. He smiled. 'You're in luck. There's a folder called "divorce" right here.' He clicked the folder open but it was empty. 'Weird.'

'Could it have been wiped?' Jackie thought about Mr Eskowitz seizing the computer equipment before a suspicious death had even been determined.

'Maybe she was just terrible at admin,' Shazia said. 'My dad runs his own electricals business, but he keeps his receipts in a flower vase. My brother's an accountant. He's always going mad at Dad for being disorganised.'

'It's okay,' Bob said. 'I can search the whole hard drive. Look at her internet history too. Nothing gets past Clever Bob.' He tapped his forehead and winked, the sarcastic intent of the nickname still lost on him.

Before long, Bob had a selection of documents and websites open. They started to go through them, one by one, and Jackie noted down the names of anyone who had had correspondence with Esther Glickman.

'Right. We've got the rabbi and his clerical people. That's Eli Neiman, Dovid Levy, Avraham Knopf...' She wrote down the names, deciding that it was deeply unlikely that any of the other victims had ever had any contact with these insular, religious men. 'Now how about the court?'

With a click of the mouse, Bob moved to Esther's court documentation. 'Well, she lived in Broughton, so her divorce court was in Salford.' He accessed the public divorce records for each of the victims. 'Nope. They all lived in different boroughs, so you've got each of the four women attending different local courts in different years. Obviously, we haven't got any of the devices for Claire Watkins, Faye Southgate or Marie Grant, but from what I can tell, the correspondence sent out is all pretty routine and anonymous. When the courts are open tomorrow, I can get copies of anything they were sent.'

Jackie drained what was left of an acrid cup of instant coffee that had been on the go for two hours. 'Right. Let's try Esther's solicitor. That's got to be our most obvious port of call, right?'

Bob switched to a string of email correspondence, some two years old, between Esther Glickman and a woman called Avril Steadman at Black, Black and Fein solicitors.

Jackie looked at the e-signature at the bottom of the emails. 'Avril's the associate. She's a lackey. Who was Esther's lead lawyer?'

Bob put the law firm's email address – blackblackfein.co.uk – into the Hotmail search engine. Two screens' worth of emails popped up, going back two and a half years. He clicked through to the initial enquiries and found that Esther's first few emails had come from one of the partners – Samuel Black. 'Here you go. Sam, he signs off as. Sam Black.'

He clicked on an attachment to one of the early emails. It contained the firm's T&C and a lengthy contract, complete with a schedule of fees. 'Esther signed up to this guy, and then he's obviously passed the work onto his underling, because in later emails, Esther says she's stretched for cash, and this Sam Black says she can deal with Avril, because...' He squinted at the screen to read what had been written in the email in question. 'She's apparently good, and her fees are lower.'

Jackie nodded, writing *Sam Black* in her notebook. 'Right. Next is any mediation. Did Esther get a mediator involved?' She considered her own financial position and how she'd recently spoken to a mediator, who had promised she could get the cost of her and Gus's divorce right down to perhaps as little as £5,000, as opposed to £50,000–£70,000, simply by having them both get legal advice first, and then sit in a room to decide like civilised adults who should get what. She saw the mediator's face in her mind's eye, all flawless make-up yet approachable. Her voice had been more comforting than the solicitor's, but her words no less uncompromising. *Obviously, if he won't play ball, it's back to the drawing board, I'm afraid. Mediation is a collaborative process.*

Jackie swallowed hard. 'If she was hard-up, I'm guessing she wanted to avoid those £300-an-hour fees like the plague.'

Bob searched through the remaining tabs for correspondence. He clapped his hands. 'Bingo. You're right. She did have a third party involved. An Olivia Armstrong. Family Mediation.'

Shaking her head, Jackie thumped the table. 'Olivia's no good. Our killer's not a woman. I'd bet my pension on it.'

She pushed her chair back and looked at the clock. Appraised her colleagues. They looked grey-faced and dark underneath their eyes.

'Let's sleep on this and carry on tomorrow, when we can do more digging. We need more information on the other victims. One woman's hard drive does not a multiple murder case make. Get some sleep. I'll see you in the morning.'

TWENTY-FIVE

'I feel just as exhausted as ever,' Jackie said, yawning at her monitor. She glanced over at Dave. 'Would you believe it? No breakfast mayhem to deal with this morning. No getting up in the middle of the night with a baby who won't accept that she's old enough to sleep through the night. All that was Gus's responsibility last night. And yet, I'm whacked.'

There was no response from her partner, who was typing an email with two fingers, his tongue sticking out of the corner of his mouth.

'Are you listening to me, Tang?'

'Nope. But Venables was in early. She wants to see you.'

'And you're telling me this now?'

Dave shrugged and continued to jab at his keyboard. 'Don't worry. I didn't say anything about you and Shazia's side hustle. But you might wanna stay out of Venables' way this morning. She was being a bit... asking a lot of questions, you know?'

Jackie turned back to her screen, where she had displayed a PDF of Esther Glickman's latest bank statement. Her eyelids started to feel heavy as she tried to find anything that stood out in the woman's outgoings. 'This is no use,' she said.

She forced herself to her feet and peered over the partition. 'Get your coat,' she told Shazia. 'We're going on a world tour of dead women's filing cabinets. First stop, Claire Watkins' place.'

'But Venables wants me doing door-to-doors with Connor on some Cheetham Hill shooting.'

Jackie waved her hand dismissively. 'Don't worry about her. I'll deal with her.' She looked over at Connor's empty seat and glanced at the clock on the wall. 'Connor's not due off the toilet for at least another twenty minutes. It takes him that long to read the captions beneath the pictures in *The Sun*'s sports' section. Let's go now. Neither of them will even notice you're gone. I promise.'

When they arrived outside Claire Watkins's house, Jackie switched off the engine of the Ford and stared at the nonde-script front door of her old school friend's terraced house.

She frowned at the sight of blue-and-white tape fluttering loose in the breeze. 'Someone's cut through the police tape.' She gazed up at the bedroom window and was certain she'd caught sight of someone hastily backing further into the room. 'I think they're still in there. You go round the back. I'll go in the front.'

While Shazia jogged towards an arched cut-through between the house and its neighbour, Jackie got out of the car and walked up to the front door. She took out the key to Claire's place. No signs of a break-in, she noted, yet the door was standing slightly ajar and had been put on a latch. Pushing it open, Jackie kept her breathing shallow and her footsteps light, wondering who had seen fit to access a crime scene that had been sealed off. A squatter? Unlikely. Or somebody looking for something perhaps?

Inside the house, the air was warm and stale. The only sound came from the traffic of the nearby high street and the blood rushing in her ears.

Maybe I imagined the person at the window, she thought. *Yes, I'm just tired and overwrought.* But then, Jackie heard a floorboard creak above her. She considered her next move. Should she surprise the intruder or announce her presence?

Peering through to the kitchen, she saw Shazia, staring through the window set in the back door. Good. Two against one, though they'd lost the element of surprise if the person upstairs had seen them pull up.

With the lightness of a ballerina, Jackie crept quickly through to the kitchen and let Shazia in. She pressed her index finger to her lips and pointed to the bedrooms above. Put her hand on her baton. Shazia nodded.

Jackie climbed the stairs, careful to walk on the sturdy sides where the wood wouldn't creak. She imagined the scenarios she might happen upon. Someone with a key: a nosey neighbour; the ex-husband; the murderer.

As she got to the top of the stairs, a shadow flashed across a brightly lit doorway in her peripheral vision. She swung around to face the direction of the shadow, her heart thudding inside her like a bouncing ball. She felt a hand on her shoulder.

Jackie shrieked. She turned to see the intruder. A woman. The woman yelped too, seemingly just as surprised as Jackie.

'Police!' Jackie yelled. 'Hands in the air.'

The woman did as she was told. 'Sorry. Sorry. I'm not a burglar. It's okay.'

Shazia bounded up the stairs. 'Shall I call for backup?'

Jackie held her hand up, breathing raggedly. 'Who are you?' But she already knew. She'd spotted the likeness as soon as the woman had stopped yelling.

'Kylie. My name's Kylie Watkins. I'm Rachel Hardman's daughter.'

'Aha. Finally. I've been waiting to speak to you in person.' Jackie dropped the hem of her jacket back over her baton and cuffs. 'Shall we go and sit in the living room and have a chat?'

The living room looked much as it had done on the day that Claire Watkins had been found, except now, the architrave of the doorway and the surfaces were covered in grey, dusty marks, where the forensics team had searched in vain for a set of fingerprints that hadn't belonged to Claire or her neighbour.

Studying Kylie's face, Jackie realised that the woman was little more than a girl. Her eyes were bloodshot and her nose red. 'I'm really sorry for your loss. I knew your mother. We went to school together. She was lovely. Really lovely.'

'Thanks,' Kylie said in a small voice. 'I'm sorry I didn't call or FaceTime so we could have a proper chat. I work funny hours at a club, so... I booked the earliest flight I could and well, if I'm honest, I'm so carved up by the news, this is the first day I've been able to speak to anyone really. But you got my email, right?'

'I did. Thanks. And Luke's safe and sound with your grand-mother for now...'

'For now?' There was panic in her eyes. 'What do you mean "for now"?'

'Well, social services *have* been trying to get in touch with you about Luke.' She laced her hands together and pondered how she would react if Beryl disappeared. Then she thought of Lucian and pushed her heartbreak back into Pandora's box.

'Oh, they're not going to try to dump him on that piece of crap Greg, are they?' Kylie started to bite her fingernails, frown-ing. Even beneath the heavy foundation and contouring, a flush of consternation blossomed in her youthful cheeks. 'Because if they do, I can't stand for that. I'd – I'd sooner take him on myself.'

'You're barely out of your teens,' Shazia said, shuffling forwards in her seat.

Kylie's eyes wandered over the cluttered living room, seeming to rest on some framed family photos on the shelving of a corner unit, showing Kylie and her mother, with little Luke sandwiched between them. 'Plenty of young mothers do a good job of bringing their kids up. My own mum, for a start. So I wouldn't be the first, and certainly not the last.'

Jackie cleared her throat. 'I'll make sure social services deal with Luke's case sensitively. Now, what kind of a relationship did you have with your mother, Kylie?'

The girl shrugged. 'She was my mum. What can I say?'

'Well, you can say what kind of relationship you had, given it's taken you so long to come back to England?' The hard set of Shazia's face suggested judgement.

'Hey! I adored my mum.' Kylie's tone was one of outrage. 'I told you. The flights were rammed. Struggling to get on a flight back doesn't mean I didn't love the bones of her. When I was younger, it was me and her against the world. Then Greg came on the scene. Things started to turn sour, if I'm honest.'

She looked at Jackie. Her eyes suddenly narrowed to reveal undisguised venomous intent. 'I *hated* him. He's a pig. An absolute pig and a bully and couldn't keep his trousers zipped. But Mum was so desperate to find love, she chose him over me.' She looked down at her knees. 'I got out as soon as I could. Slept on mates' couches and floors, even though she begged me to come home.'

'You felt betrayed?' Jackie asked.

Kylie nodded. 'Yeah. But mostly, I was worried about Mum. Greg... I never trusted him, and I knew he'd break her heart. I told her, but she just wouldn't listen. Anyway, I couldn't stand there anymore, watching her ruin her own life. So when I got the chance to go to Spain, I jumped at it.'

Jackie appraised the girl's body language and facial expressions. If Shazia was wondering about murderous intent, where Kylie might have paid someone to kill her own mother, Jackie could see no signs of it in the girl.

Kylie started to sob. 'I should have stayed. I should have looked after her.'

When Shazia nodded in agreement, Jackie shot her

colleague an admonishing glance. 'Your mother was an adult, Kylie,' she said. 'I knew her when we were your age. Turns out, she was impressionable and made bad decisions – especially where men were concerned. I didn't see that side to her, back then. But it was there, even twenty years ago. She was bright enough to realise the choices she was making.'

Kylie slapped her hands to her tearful eyes. 'No! I'm the worst daughter in the world. My mum's gone, and I feel like I've lost everything.'

'So, what *were* you looking for upstairs?' Shazia asked, clearly deciding the girl's anguish was a case of crocodile tears.

Kylie wiped her eyes with the cuffs of her hoodie. 'Sorry for breaking down like this. I must look a right mess.'

Jackie noticed how the girl had sidestepped the question of what she'd been doing in the house. 'What were you looking for, Kylie? It would be really helpful if you can just tell us. We're trying to find your mother's murderer. Every piece of information you give us could be important.'

Kylie blushed. She cocked her head to the side and pursed her lips. 'If I'm honest, my first thought was to look for Mum's stash of cash and her will. I know how that sounds, but she saved and saved over the years, and she had this pot that she was gonna give to me to help me get my own place eventually. She kept it secret from Greg. She didn't want that useless lump coming after her hard-earned money. And I wanted to check it hadn't been taken by the cops, because I'm not stupid. I know stuff goes missing during searches.'

'Did you find it?' Jackie asked, imagining her old school friend squirreling money into some hiding place, for fear of Greg Hardman squandering it on drink and other women. Jackie wondered then if *she* might have been more sensible, had she creamed a just-in-case fund off the top of her salary every month, rather than allow Gus to ransack the family pot at will for his musical 'necessities'.

Kylie nodded. 'It's mine though.' She folded her arms tightly. Her chin jutted defiantly. 'Me and Luke's.' She looked back to the family photos. 'I'll keep his share for him for when he's older.'

'I'm afraid you'll have to declare the money, Kylie,' Jackie said. 'You'll need to speak to a solicitor. Find out your financial position in terms of inheritance tax—'

'Jesus. My mum wasn't a rich woman.'

'Well, make sure you do it right, Kylie. Get it safe in a bank, and get it in writing that you're leaving some cash to Luke. Keeping cash under the floorboards is a terrible idea. What if there'd been a fire? What if the murderer had taken it? All your mother's hard saving would have been for nothing.' Jackie thought then about Claire's divorce proceedings. 'Talking of solicitors, do you know the name of the firm your mother used for divorcing Greg?'

Kylie shook her head.

'Did she use a mediator?'

'What for? Poor people don't need mediators. They just need to split and go their separate ways.'

'Any idea where she kept her filing then?' Shazia asked.

The girl got to her feet and went upstairs. She came back down with a cardboard concertina file and handed it to Jackie. 'Here. I've got nothing to hide. I thought Mum had nothing to hide either. Shows how wrong you can be.'

Jackie leafed through the various tabs, easily finding divorce correspondence filed under D. She recognised the headed stationery immediately but took out the initial letter that accompanied the contract and showed it to Shazia. 'Look what we have here.'

Shazia leaned in and read the signature at the bottom of the letter. 'Samuel Black, Head of Practice, Family Law, of Black, Black and Fein.'

TWENTY-SIX

'What do you mean Sam Black's our man?' Dave asked. He started to count off his discoveries on his fingers. 'Tyler Fleming stalked Claire Watkins at work, he met Marie Grant through speed dating and he'd been blocked by Faye Southgate on Insta.'

Jackie looked at Shazia for support. 'But the solicitor, Sam Black... He acted for all four women. *All four!* We already knew he was the solicitor for Esther Glickman. So then we went to Claire Watkins' and saw the documentation for ourselves, and on the way back, we got in touch with Faye Southgate's and Marie Grant's ex-husbands, who rooted out their copies of correspondence. Sam Black is the common denominator.'

Dave frowned at her and scratched at his spiky hair. 'Well, Fleming's got the profile and the motive for a sexual killer. How does a lawyer compare to a publicly misogynist kerb-crawler that's on the sex offenders register?' He threw his hands in the air.

Shazia perched on the edge of Jackie's desk, cradling a takeout coffee. 'Could they be in cahoots?'

Jackie studied the girl's thoughtful brown eyes – they still sparkled with the professional curiosity of a recent recruit. 'It's possible. Good call. We need to look into Sam Black and see if that gives us any answers.'

Dave snapped his fingers. 'Oh, by the way. Venables wants you to swing by her office ASAP.' His right eyebrow arched.

Feeling the blood drain from her face, Jackie groaned.

'She's not going to be happy with your new line of investigation. She's *very* excited about Fleming. Think she's already seeing her photo on the front page of the *Manchester Evening News*. Just saying.'

Get it over with, imagined older Lucian told Jackie. *It's just like ripping a plaster off*. She could see her brother in her mind's eye, dispensing the wisdom and comfort she desperately needed. *It always hurts more if you prolong the agony*.

Shrugging her coat onto her chair, she marched across the floor and down the hallway to Venables' office – once her own office, filled with plants and photos of Gus and the kids. It felt like another life. She knocked only once and walked straight in.

Venables was on the phone, wearing a sycophantic grin. Maybe Dave had been right. Maybe Venables was already onto the editor of the local paper, boasting prematurely about her success in tracking down a serial killer before the month was out.

'Dave said you wanted me.'

'Danny, let me call you back.' Venables' smile soured though the sugar was still in her voice. She ended her call and turned to Jackie. 'What exactly are you up to? You and Tang are supposed to be putting together a court-worthy case for Tyler Fleming, and here you are galivanting with Malik on a totally different line of enquiry, when Malik is supposed to be partnering with Connor.'

Jackie shrugged. 'What can I say, Tina? The truth is not

always convenient. Shazia's Jewish lady turned out to be part of our case, and I can't connect Fleming to her. But I can connect the family lawyer, Samuel Black from Black, Black and Fein, to all four women.'

Venables blinked hard. 'I know Sam Black. I sat next to him at a Chambers of Commerce dinner. He's... there's absolutely *no way* he's a serial killer. I mean, that is just damned ridiculous, and I want you to get back onto Fleming now, and stop wasting everyone's time. Black, Black and Fein sponsored a charity football match between our lot and Manchester's leading law firms, for God's sake. It was in aid of the NSPCC or something. Maybe Barnardo's. Some kids' charity anyway.' She waved her hand as though the gesture would get rid of Jackie.

'I can't ignore a line of investigation just because it's bad politics, Tina. You know that. You have to pull on the threads and see where they lead.'

Tina pressed her fingertips to her temples. 'We're going to get sued.'

'We're not. I'll make subtle enquiries.'

Venables shot her with a disparaging look. 'You wouldn't know subtle if it came at you, wearing a placard round its neck saying "subtle" in capital letters.'

'I'm a detective sergeant, Tina. It's my job to solve cases. It's your job to balance the books and report to committees, remember? You opted for the management post that I deliberately gave up.' She tried and failed to keep the weariness out of her voice, biting back all the told-you-sos regarding the previous case that were on the tip of her tongue. 'Now just let me do my job.'

Over the years, Jackie had amassed quite a little black book full of useful contacts, including the details of the city's best and most disreputable solicitors. Now she handed a photocopied list of names, numbers and email addresses to Shazia.

She leaned over the partition, raising her voice to be heard over Connor, who was bellowing into his mobile phone at someone who he'd clearly decided didn't speak perfect English. 'Call first,' Jackie told Shazia. 'If they won't take your call, then email, asking them to call you back. But be discreet. Don't leave a message. Don't put any detail in the email. If you don't write it down, it can't be screenshotted and forwarded to Sam Black. If he turns out to be our man, we mustn't forewarn him.'

Shazia nodded. 'Shall I mention you?'

Jackie considered the suggestion. Would these people be willing to help Jackson Cooke – a dogged detective who had put some of their clients behind bars? Maybe honesty still stood for something in Manchester. 'Yes. You might as well. They won't divulge any sensitive information if they don't know who's asking. Just don't tell them why. We're getting a feel for the man. Not going on a witch hunt. Not yet anyway.'

Taking her own half of the list, Jackie started to dial numbers. She began with a criminal prosecutor called Neil Saffman, whose secretary reliably informed Jackie that he was at court. Jackie left a message.

The next call was to a criminal lawyer called Karen White. She managed to get put through almost immediately.

'Jackson! Long time, no see. Congrats on your recent triumph. That was quite a case.'

Jackie chuckled and was glad the solicitor couldn't see her blush down the phone. 'Oh, well... you know. All in the line of duty, blah blah blah. But listen. I need to get your take on another lawyer for this case I'm on.'

'Hit me.'

Wondering how to play it, Jackie realised she could just be direct yet economical with the truth. 'Samuel Black. Black, Black and Fein. He's the family solicitor who acted in a divorce for a victim. I just need to get the lowdown on him.'

'Are you investigating *the* Sam Black?' The surprise in Karen's voice was evident.

'Just gathering information. It's a fact-finding mission. Trying to get all the pieces on the board. You know? Divorce is maybe at the heart of the case.' She gritted her teeth and winced.

'Well, you know Sam Black's one of the most respected CEOs of one of the best law firms in Manchester, don't you?'

'Okay.' Jackie was sure she wasn't going to get anything bordering on gossip out of Karen White. 'What kind of a man is he? Family guy? Single? Easy to deal with or one of those old-fashioned types who act like they live on Mount Olympus with the other gods?'

'Really nice guy. He's got a beautiful wife, if memory serves. Three kids. Pillar-of-the-community types. Honestly, I doubt you'll get anything but glowing reports on Sam Black. If he was creepy or unpleasant, I'd tell you.'

Hanging up, Jackie felt a little crestfallen. But she had to keep going. She dialled a further fifteen solicitors, who covered legal disciplines ranging from criminal law to probate. They all said the same thing.

'Sam Black's lovely. Oh, he's such a kind man. He gave my son work experience over last summer so he could put it on his university application for law.'

'Sam Black? Oh yes. He's a good golfer. I played a charity tournament with him. His handicap puts me to shame. Brilliant legal mind. Any divorce he presides over... well, he's worth every penny, and he does lots of reduced rate work too, for poorer clients.'

The recommendations went on and on. It seemed Sam Black was beyond reproach.

As the weak autumn sun started to sink towards the city's industrial skyline, Jackie hung up the phone and turned away from her computer monitor, feeling not crestfallen but downright low. Missing her children. Shuddering at the thought of Gus's solicitor, who was gunning to set Gus up for life financially, funded by her modest detective's salary.

Feeling that everything below the waist had gone numb, she stood up and stretched. Then she leaned over the partition, to find Shazia crossing out the last name on her list. 'Well?'

Shazia looked up at her. The shine had gone from her eyes now, and she sat in her chair with slouched shoulders. 'Nothing. Sam Black is squeaky clean. Either that or Manchester's legal eagles are closing ranks.'

She smoothed her hijab over her forehead and frowned. 'Who's Black, Black and Fein's rival firm? Because maybe we should be calling them. My brother's an accountant, right? And honestly, you should hear him slagging off his rivals. He's got this opposite number in some big accountancy firm in Spinningfields, and he's constantly out to dig dirt on this guy, so he can drip poison in potential clients' ears. Mum and Dad tell him he's being unprofessional, but will he listen? Will he heck!'

Jackie clasped her hand to her mouth and nodded. 'You're right. I can't believe I didn't think to do that straight away. Question is, who's the biggest competitor of Black, Black and Fein? Who would give me that sort of information?'

She looked again at her list and realised there was one person whom she hadn't yet crossed off. Neil Saffman, the public prosecutor. Yes, it was perfect. He would hopefully be impartial but would know everything going on in the circuit. Jackie dialled his direct line for the second time.

This time, she got put through after several minutes of being on hold.

'To what do I owe this pleasure, Jackson?' Saffman was ever the charmer, but an end-of-the-day yawn seemed to be bubbling just beneath his effervescence.

'Sam Black. Family solicitor. CEO of Black, Black and Fein.

Who would be his arch-nemesis, who might give me an honest appraisal of the guy?'

A few moments of silence ticked by. Then Neil Saffman spoke. 'Er, why?'

'I just need to speak to someone who isn't going to tell me he sits at God's right hand and doles out gold stars to all the angels.'

Neil sighed heavily. 'Okay, but this is strictly between me and you, right? If you tell anyone I said this, I'll deny it. And I'm only telling you because it's you.'

'Go on.'

'Black is a total philanderer. He literally can't keep it in his pants.'

Jackie barely stifled her stunned laughter. 'What? I thought he was a happily married man. Everyone's been telling me how his wife's "gorgeous" and an ex-model who now does charity, and his kids are delightful and don't even smell of farts like my two – I mean, three.'

'They don't call him Snakey for nothing.'

'Snakey?'

'Like a boa constrictor, I've heard.'

By now, Jackie was laughing so hard that Shazia's head popped above the partition, looking down at her with a confused expression. Dave turned away from his screen to face her, blinking hard.

'So his fragrant, perfect wife puts up with *that* for... what? Appearances' sake?'

'Oh, they're not together anymore. They split years ago. Acrimonious too.'

'But everyone says they're together.'

'They attend functions together to keep "brand Black" going, and because she's got a *massive* interest in his entrepreneurial side projects. Property development mainly. A fashion business too. His brother's listed at Companies House as the owner, but everyone knows it's Sam Black behind the façade. You want my opinion? I think he's money laundering because he represents a lot of gangland types.'

The fatigue had gone from Neil Saffman's voice now. On the other end of the phone, Jackie imagined him leaning back in his chair, grinning like the proverbial Cheshire Cat as he dished the dirt on one of Cheshire's fattest cats.

Right now, she could see that loose thread dangling in front of her yet again. She mentally reached out to pull on it. 'Was their split really that nasty, if they're still playing at happy families? I mean everyone – apart from you – thought they were still together. Everyone. So I can't see them sparring in public.'

'Like I say, Black's always had an eye for the ladies. Snakey likes the new recruits, fresh out of college. It's a #MeToo situation. But the wife – Linda – got full custody of the kids. He never gets to see them alone; unchaperoned.'

'I was told his kids were delightful, so he clearly rolls them out at professional functions. I can't believe the Cheshire set would sit on gossip like this.'

'But you're not talking Cheshire set, are you? You're talking about top-dollar solicitors. They don't gossip about their own to gen-pop, and especially not to cops. Me, on the other hand...'

Jackie smiled. She caught Shazia's eye and gave her the thumbs up. 'How come you can't stand him?'

'I've seen him represent too many wife-beaters and abusers, who have gone back and ruined their wives' and kids' lives. It doesn't sit well with me. I'm a public prosecutor. I earn a fraction of what Sam Black and his ilk earn. I'm not swayed by fat fees. I'm on the side of the victim, me.'

'So Black's wife wouldn't give him unsupervised access to the kids?'

'Nope. Linda Black was *livid* when she discovered the extent of his infidelity, I heard. That's why she bent him over and showed him who was really boss in their divorce proceedings. The kids – that hit him where it really hurt. She knew his weak spot, and she went for it.'

'So he's a sex pest with an axe to grind against divorcées?'

'Oh yes. Yes, siree. You bet your bottom dollar. And you know me, Jackie. My word is my bond.'

TWENTY-SEVEN

'Venables went *ballistic*,' Shazia said as they drove into Manchester city centre. 'I couldn't believe it. It's like she doesn't want you to solve the case.'

Jackie nodded, staring out at the autumn rain, praying that they would find a parking space close enough to the restaurant where Black was having pre-dinner drinks with a client, if his secretary was to be believed. 'Venables likes to think she mixes in rarefied circles. She's forked over huge amounts of cash to go to a couple of charity dinners with Black, so she's scared that if I go wading in with questions and a warrant to examine his devices that she'll be blackballed by Manchester's elite.'

At her side, Shazia snorted with derision. 'She's shameless. Her first priority should be to take the bad guys off the streets. I mean, we're looking at Sam Black potentially for murder.'

'Well, she did at least sanction us questioning him. It's better than nothing, even if she said yes through gritted teeth.'

'It shouldn't have to be through gritted teeth though. Whose side is she on?'

Jackie cocked her head to the side. What more was there to say? Shazia Malik, the fresh-faced recruit on a graduate fast

track had an infinitely better developed moral compass than
Tina Venables, who had trained with Jackie, almost two decades
ago. 'You hang on to your principles, Shazia. This job can suck
the good out of you.'

They parked in a backstreet in the triangle between
Piccadilly, Market Street and China Town and walked down to
the King Street eatery that boasted a Michelin *bib gourmand*.
How Manchester had changed, Jackie thought. For all its
poverty and crime and rain, there were restaurants that now
charged more for dinner for two with a bottle of wine than she
paid for her entire weekly family shop.

Catching her reflection in the gleaming plate-glass window
of the restaurant, she felt suddenly shabby and ashamed of her
dog-eared anorak that had seen too many winters; her suit
trousers hanging beneath it, turning slightly shiny at the knee.

'You okay?' Shazia asked, holding the door open for her.

'Fine.' Jackie patted her on the shoulder. 'Now remember,
we want to corner Black at his table so he doesn't have chance to
delete any phone or chat records before we arrest him. But let's
keep this as low-key as possible.'

The stylish young man who greeted them looked them up
and down. A glimmer of disdain shone through the professional
smile. 'Can I help you, ladies? I'm afraid we're fully booked.'

Jackie flashed her ID. 'We're not on a social visit. I need to
speak to one of your diners.'

The smile fell from his face. 'Of course. Can I ask who?
Perhaps I can get them to come and speak to you outside.'

'Samuel Black. And we'd prefer to surprise him at his table.
Don't worry. We're not intending to curdle your custard.'

Jackie could sense confusion in the lad as he led them
upstairs to the dining area. There, he whispered discreetly in
the maître d's ear.

If it was confusion she'd smelled on the front-of-house
greeter, she could see fear in the maître d's affected smile.

The maître d' approached her and Shazia with hands held together in supplication. 'I'm really sorry, Detectives...'

'Detective Sergeant Jackson Cooke and Detective Shazia Malik.'

'Yeah, well, I'd be really grateful if you could—'

Jackie locked eyes with the maître d. 'Please don't obstruct justice at 5 p.m. on a weekday night, love. You'll put me off *my* dinner, and I don't even get to eat 'til about 9 p.m. Later than that, if I have to make and arrest and process *you* down the station.' She winked.

They were shown to a table where six sharp-suited men were all studying menus half-heartedly while laughing at an older man's joke. The table was already full of drinks – several wine buckets at the side with bottles on the go. Jackie immediately recognised Sam Black among them. He was facing her, looking just as he had done in his corporate profile picture on the law firm's website. Short dark hair, starting to recede in earnest and with grey flecks at the sides. Neither handsome nor ugly, but with the heavy features of a stolid-looking middle-aged man that had been made the best of with a gym-trim physique, expensive glasses and bespoke-tailored clothes. Was this her murderer?

Jackie introduced them both. 'Can we have a word please?'

Black looked up at her, clearly irritated. 'Sorry, Detective. Can this wait? You could call my secretary and make—'

Jackie inclined her head to a couple of empty seats at the bar. 'It won't take long.'

As Black got up from the table full of Manchester's movers and shakers, she could feel the other men's eyes boring into her back. She could almost hear them wondering why she could possibly want the great Samuel Black in the middle of a corporate love-in with the boys. It wasn't unusual for the police to speak to solicitors, but it was unusual for them to accost family law solicitors – CEOs at that – in the middle of a fancy restaurant.

'Look, what's all this about? You're embarrassing me.'

Jackie waited until he met her gaze and then, as she spoke, she watched his reaction. 'Claire Watkins – or should I say Rachel Hardman, as she was known, Marie Grant, Faye Southgate and Esther Glickman. What do these women mean to you?'

Black looked at her blankly, the furrows in his brow deepening. He shook his head. 'You've lost me.'

'All women you represented in divorce proceedings.'

He smiled then. 'Yes. Yes, I remember. Well, nothing unusual there. You had me worried for a minute.'

'These women have all been murdered. We think they were targeted because they were single mothers.'

Now Black's face looked a picture of concern. 'I'm so sorry to hear it.'

'I'm afraid you are the common denominator in all four cases, Mr Black. Can you tell me where you were and what you were doing on the following four dates?' She took out her notepad with some ceremony, flicked to the right page and read out the approximate times and dates of each of the women's deaths.

The concern was all gone, replaced by an ashen mask of dead-eyed fear. Sam Black's Adam's apple peeped up above his shirt collar as he swallowed. 'This is nonsense. Have you ever been sued for defamation of character, Detective?'

At Jackie's side, Shazia stood tall. 'Just because you're a solicitor doesn't make you above the law, Mr Black.' There was a slight waver to her voice. She cleared her throat and the wobble was gone. 'You're a suspect in a murder investigation.'

Black gripped the bar top. The sinews in his hand looked like iron rods beneath his tanned skin. 'Keep your voice down, for God's sake! Look, I had nothing to do with any of those women beyond the strictly professional.' He looked at his own reflection in one of the gleaming surfaces behind the bar. 'In fact...' He turned back to Jackie. 'I think I passed all of them on to a junior associate to save them legal fees. Having them sign a contract was the extent of my dealings with them, and you can ask my secretary, Barbara, what I was doing on the dates you gave. She'll show you the paper trail too for these women's divorce proceedings.' He straightened his tie and leaned forwards in his seat, looking poised to stand.

'Well, that's good to know,' Jackie said. 'But there's the small matter of me having a warrant to examine your phones and your computers.'

Like the lights going on at the end of a cinema viewing, revealing the truth of the litter on the floor and the stains on the upholstery, the curtain dropped on Black's friendly, professional exterior. Only a grimace on his lips and fury behind his eyes remained. 'You *what*? Are you bloody kidding me, you cheeky cow?' His voice was a deadly whisper.

'My name is Detective Sergeant Jackson Cooke. Not cheeky. Not cow.'

Realisation seemed to dawn then as Black blanched. 'Wait. You're the crazy bitch who took on the Necromancer when you were practically giving birth. I saw you on the cover of *The Times*.'

Jackie bowed slightly and smiled. 'Lucky the photographer caught my good side. I'm not normally photogenic.'

She withdrew from her pocket the legal documentation that she'd fought to get at short notice. She held it out for him to see. 'But like I say, I've got a warrant for your devices, including any phones. Oh, and you're under arrest too.'

She cautioned Black, whose mouth hung slack, presumably in disbelief or perhaps in shock.

Shazia held up an evidence bag. 'Just drop the phones in here please. We've already sent uniforms to pick up your PC, laptops, any tablets. Your secretary told us your housekeeper would be in, so at least our lads won't need to trash your front door. Don't think your secretary likes you much.' She tutted and raised her eyebrows. 'Did you forget her birthday?'

'This is harassment,' Black said. He glanced over at his friends, who were busy ordering food. 'You don't know who you're dealing with. I'm a respected legal professional and a family man. And anyway, my electronic devices all contain documents subject to legal privilege.'

'You're being arrested on suspicion of having murdered four women, Mr Black. I don't think you should be looking for legal loopholes right now. I think *if* you're innocent, you should be bending over backwards to help us and clear your good name.' Jackie tried to ensure her tone was recognisably tart. Payback for the crazy bitch comment. She *wanted* him to feel angry and frustrated.

'Now hand over your phones – work phone and any personal device you've got too – because I sincerely doubt you keep your client's legal documents on there, and I need immediate access because I reckon your reluctance to hand them over could seriously prejudice my murder investigation.'

Jackie wrote in her notebook, ensuring Black could see she'd put *On the defensive and threatening*. 'How about we have a little trip down to the station now?'

'No way.' He looked over to his friends, perhaps trying to decide whether or not to ask for their help. 'You are *not* frog-marching me out of here wearing cuffs like a common criminal. This murder charge is a flight of fancy – the ramblings of a madwoman.'

Jackie leaned in until their faces were almost intimately close. She spoke quietly but clearly. 'I think you're failing to comply, Mr Black.' She backed away abruptly and turned to Shazia. 'Do you think he's resisting arrest, Detective Malik?' She took out her cuffs.

'Don't put those on, for God's sake.' Black's face was shiny with sweat now. His previously composed demeanour was jerky like a junkie's. 'Please. It doesn't have to be this way. Cuff me outside when they're not watching.'

'Put the phones in Detective Malik's bag.'

Black finally acquiesced. They had their man. She was certain of it.

TWENTY-EIGHT

'Do you think we'll find incriminating evidence on this one?' Shazia asked, staring at the unlocked personal phone.

Jackie looked at the wallpaper of a photo of Sam Black's children. She looked at the various app icons on Black's phone, trying to decide where to start. 'No idea. I didn't expect the work phone to reveal any dirty secrets, and it hasn't. But this personal one... I guess there's only one way to find out.'

First, she opened Gmail. 'Let's search for any correspondence with the four women. We may not have three of the women's phones, but if he's been stupid, maybe, just maybe, we can find his end of any conversation.'

She typed Claire Watkins into the search facility. Nothing. She tried Rachel Hardman. Nothing. Faye Southgate yielded only two emails to a man called Jim Southgate, who had apparently fixed a sticky electronic gate on Black's driveway for the sum of £250 + VAT. Marie Grant solely brought up an email Sam had forwarded to his wife – subject: grant stuff – regarding applications to the student finance people for his eldest's university fees. Esther Glickman yielded nothing at all.

'No emails then,' Shazia said. 'But hardly anyone communicates through email anymore, unless it's work related.'

Jackie resented the sinking feeling that had started to squeeze tightly around her heart, tugging down, down, down. 'What's next?'

'Text?'

Opening the texting facility, Jackie felt suddenly like she'd missed a step. 'Hang on. Let's see if the women were contacts on his phone first.'

Scrolling through the long list of contacts, Jackie smiled when she came across the mobile numbers of all four women. 'They're here. But did Black talk to them outside of a work context, and did he leave evidence behind?'

She reopened the texting app and didn't even need to scroll. Black kept his inbox incredibly tidy. 'Dentist, his mother, United Utilities, HSBC Bank, the plumber, by the looks, and the electronic-gate repairman. That's it.'

'WhatsApp,' Shazia said. 'Everyone uses that the most.'

Nodding, Jackie opened that app. In here, it was far less spartan and ordered. There was thread after thread, going back years. She sighed. 'Okay, what have we got? His wife, sending brusque notes about the kids and some charity function. The kids, mainly asking him for money and demanding to know why he couldn't make it to some concert at school.' She skimmed through each thread. 'Neighbourhood watch group; his brothers; football over-40s; lads' cycling on Sunday; some sort of legal professionals' dining club. It goes on and on.'

'A man like Black... all that charity work he does and then he's got his business interests on the side. Lawyers do golf and that too, don't they?' The enthusiasm in Shazia's voice was audible. Clearly she wasn't yet in the grip of the dreaded sinking feeling. 'It's bound to take a while, but our evidence might be in there, so... if you want, I can read through.'

Jackie shook her head. 'I'm fine. It's just... even when you've got a good solve rate, you still worry that you're heading down an investigative dead end. I don't want to let my school friend down. Or those other women. I don't like being wrong.'

For another twenty or so minutes, Jackie and Shazia pored over the messages. Then...

'Bingo! Faye Southgate.' With soaring optimism that pulled her heart free of the leaden feeling, Jackie read out the correspondence from the beginning of the thread, some months before Faye Southgate had engaged the legal services of Black, Black and Fein.

Sam: Hey Faye, hope you don't mind me getting in touch. It was great to meet you last night.

Faye: Hey yourself. I really enjoyed it. It's such a lovely venue

Sam: Do you mind that I got your number off Kim? I just felt we had a connection.

Faye: Why would I mind chatting to a nice guy like you? I'm flattered you should get in touch with a lonely housewife like me.

Sam: A beautiful woman like you shouldn't feel lonely. Maybe Mr Southgate doesn't realise how lucky he is.

Jackie turned to Shazia. 'He's flirting with her.'

'She's flirting back.' Shazia was twisting the fringes on her hijab. She turned away from the screen to Jackie and grinned.

They continued reading. Over the course of several days, the conversation between Faye Southgate turned from the suggestive into the overtly sexual. There began an exchange of erotic selfies that made Shazia blush and Jackie think ruefully of Gus and Catherine Harris.

'I can't believe he never had the sense to wipe these,' Shazia said.

'It's as we thought. Too stupid or too arrogant.' Jackie turned back to the thread.

As the weeks progressed, the nightly sexting thinned, and it was replaced by regular arrangements to meet in Manchester's better-quality hotels.

'They were having a full-blown affair,' Jackie said, wondering if Gus's affair had unfolded the same way – starting with a few gateway flirtatious messages and leading to adulterous trysts, whenever the opportunity arose. 'Maybe this is how Faye Southgate consoled herself when her ex came out as gay. Or maybe it was before Miles came out, and he found out about Faye's affair and thought, "What the hell? Why should I pretend when she's sleeping around too?" Maybe Faye thought it was the start of something more with Black.'

'Well, if Black's our murderer, how did they go from signing off...' Shazia read from the phone screen. '"Faye, baby, I can't get you out of my mind. Every minute I'm not with you is a minute wasted..."'

'To Faye Southgate's accidental auto-erotic death being faked in her own home?' Jackie finished.

The messages continued after Faye had signed the contract for Sam Black to act as her solicitor in her divorce proceedings.

'I can't believe he didn't declare a conflict of interest,' Jackie said.

'He quickly passed her on to the associate though, didn't he?'

Scrolling further, Jackie noticed how the messages started to spread out in frequency and become more perfunctory on Faye's part. Black was still gushing and suggestive in everything he wrote and every photo he sent.

'Faye had stopped reciprocating,' Jackie said. 'In fact, the messages from her stop about a month before her death.'

'She ghosted him,' Shazia said. 'The affair must have ended because look – she's left him hanging twice.'

Sam: Why aren't you answering me back, darling? I came to your house and I know you were there. Why didn't you answer the door? I drove all the way to see you because I love you. Is everything all right?

Sam: You're being cold, Faye. I don't like being treated like this. I thought I gave you what Miles couldn't.

Sam: Stop being a bitch. Stop avoiding my calls. What the hell have I done wrong?

There was only one message back from Faye before the thread ended.

Faye: Leave me alone. We're just not a good fit. Don't contact me again.

'Faye was dead a fortnight later,' Jackie said, setting the phone down. 'Wow.' She frowned and chewed the inside of her cheek, wondering what, if anything, the thread revealed about Faye's fate.

'It's got to be him,' Shazia said. 'They were having an affair and she ended it. He felt humiliated and rejected. There's your motive.'

Jackie studied the blemish-free features of her colleague's youthful face. 'But there's nothing on the others. We've just not got enough here. We need to find out more about Black's relationships with the other women.'

'Time to interview him?' Shazia glanced at the clock that was slowly ticking its way to 9 p.m.

Shaking her head, Jackie stifled a yawn. 'No way. Not at

this hour. Not without his lawyer present. He can sit and stew in his cell overnight and get a feel for how the other half lives. I think we should sleep on this and then go into the firm first thing. Speak to any colleagues who also had contact with the women and quiz them about Black's behaviour. Once we've got our facts straight, *then* we interview him.'

Later that evening, when the children were asleep and the only sounds in the house were the cracking and creaking of the floor-boards as they cooled and contracted overnight, Jackie lay in bed. Her eyelids felt heavy as she reread the sequestered divorce files of all four victims.

Her focus started to drift. She thought about the letter that had awaited her on her return from work – a demand from Gus's solicitor for a monthly maintenance payment that she couldn't possibly afford. It was official. He was gunning for full custody of the children, and Jackie was expected to accept this and simply hand over the kids that she'd given birth to, the family home she'd bought and a generous stipend, taken from the lacklustre salary she earned.

There was that sinking feeling, weighing down Jackie's heart yet again.

'Kiss my arse, Augustus Rutter,' Jackie whispered beneath her breath.

She wiped a tear away defiantly, shifted the paperwork to the foot of the bed, threw off the duvet and padded through to the baby's room. Standing by the cot, she peered down and could make out Alice's tiny form: head to the side and little fists balled and held high. She was out of the swaddling and into a sleeping bag now. Jackie leaned in and kissed her baby daughter's peach-like cheek. The little girl made a snuffling noise and then fell silent again.

Jackie backed away and paced to her sons' room. The air

smelled of freshly washed pyjamas with a note of boyish testosterone. Percy was snoring gently, limbs splayed as if he'd fought sleep, before sleep had won. Lewis was curled up in a foetal position, breathing softly. Jackie crept forwards and kissed them both.

Over my dead body Gus takes these kids off me, she vowed to imaginary older Lucian. *I'll fight to the death for them. Gus just can't love them the way I love them. I'm their mother.*

In her mind's eye, her brother put his hand on her shoulder and squeezed supportively. *Damn straight. These are Cookes,* he said. *Not Rutters. Cookes. Look at them. These amazing babies are yours, Jackson. Gus is weak. He'll back down. You have to be strong. Can you be strong, Jack?*

Jackie nodded and closed the boys' door, full of resolve. A light bulb went on inside her head as she thought about the women whose murders she was investigating: they too had had to protect their children against neglectful or abusive or merely disinterested fathers. Had the court employed the services of a social worker to assess the situation? Might someone going into the women's homes to speak to their children, as well as interviewing the divorcing parents separately, have a better insight into any additional drama or intrigue that might have been unfolding behind closed doors? Maybe someone like Andy Dewhurst at the Children and Family Court Advisory and Support Service.

Clambering back into bed, she checked through the files and saw that in the cases of Esther Glickman and Marie Grant, Andy Dewhurst *had* been employed by the Children and Family Court Advisory and Support Service to determine the circumstances of the children and their relationships with both parents. Had he had involvement with Claire Watkins' divorce? No. Faye Southgate's? Dewhurst had told her during their first exchange at Black, Black and Fein that he hadn't needed to be involved in that case either, and there was no evidence of it in the paperwork. But Jackie reasoned that speaking to Dewhurst again would be worth ten minutes of her time.

She opened her notebook and scribbled a reminder for the morning, set aside the paperwork and finally fell into a fitful sleep, where the rug was not only being pulled from under her, but it was also rolled up and carried off by Gus and Catherine Harris.

TWENTY-NINE

Jackie stifled a yawn, feeling her tired, stinging eyes threaten to water. 'So, Andy, thanks for speaking to me again – especially coming all the way down here.' She drank some of the espresso she'd ordered from the almost empty Spinningfields coffee bar, feeling certain that the terrible night's sleep was showing through her friendly, encouraging smile.

'Not a problem,' Dewhurst said. He sipped his steaming tea and set his cup back down with precise movements. Raised an eyebrow. 'I was *very* sorry to hear about Esther Glickman and Marie Grant.'

'Both clients of Samuel Black at Black, Black and Fein. Both women you investigated for the family court.'

He nodded, wearing a serious expression. 'I put together section 7 reports. Yes.'

'And now they're dead.' Jackie was interested to see Dewhurst's reaction.

'Poor, poor women. Like I told you last time, I deal with a lot of vulnerable people as a CAFCASS social worker. I'm no stranger to tales of domestic and child abuse, believe me. I wish I was.' He smiled sadly. 'But *murder*? It happens. We know it happens – rarely, thankfully. But it doesn't make it any easier to hear.' He laced his fingers together, twiddled his thumbs and then slid both hands beneath the table.

Jackie eyed her interviewee. With his blue shirt – open at the neck and with a slightly frayed collar – and his battered old leather satchel, he was reminiscent of every social worker she'd ever met. Could it be that this unpretentious, slightly awkward man might offer her useful insight into a slick operator like Sam Black?

'Tell me the nature of your involvement with Esther Glickman and Marie Grant,' she said.

'Okay. So, I looked over their case notes before I came to meet you.' Dewhurst unzipped and removed his windcheater, folding it neatly and setting it down beside him on his bench. 'Never saw it coming, if I'm honest.' He blushed. 'Both women had problematic husbands: abusive men. Gaslighting and controlling, you know? They were both fighting any kind of amicable child arrangement order just to be difficult as hell. Esther Glickman's husband... we know there are problems in the ultra-Orthodox Jewish community, but it's very rare that they get brought to our attention. It's a closed world.'

'How come Esther was different? How come she spoke out?' Jackie had started to scribble notes in her notepad.

Dewhurst frowned. 'She has... *had* spirit. She'd taken years of flack from a bombastic, unfaithful man, and I guess she decided enough was enough.' He shrugged. 'Esther dared to step outside the boundaries her parents and husband had set for her, you know?' He squeezed his eyes shut momentarily. 'Shame her heroism put her in a body bag.' Shook his head.

'And Marie Grant?'

'Similar story. Married to a real bruiser. I'm pretty sure he was sexually abusing the oldest daughter, Lisa, but the family closed ranks about that. One day though, Marie just reached the limits of her patience and apparently threw all of the husband's stuff into the front yard; had all the locks changed. He fought and fought for custody, even though he'd broken the youngest daughter's arm. That much we did know about.'

Jackie remembered that Lisa Grant had mentioned nothing about Sacha being physically abused by their father. The Grant family story was an onion with many layers.

'Grant was just utterly bloody-minded. So was Shimon Glickman. Obviously, the judge had no compunction about ruling in favour of both women. Supervised access was requested in the case of Grant. I understand Glickman gave up the ghost and went to live in Israel.'

'Yes. He was thousands of miles away at the time of his ex-wife's death, and her parents insist he completely severed contact with Esther after the divorce. His alibi is cast iron.

'Were you aware of any other men in the lives of Marie or Esther at the time you were reporting on their circumstances?'

Dewhurst shook his head. 'None.' He chuckled. 'They both seemed to have had enough of men for several lifetimes.'

'And Samuel Black. Tell me about him.'

The social worker shrugged. 'What's there to say? I don't know him, except in the context of: he's a family lawyer and the senior partner of Black, Black and Fein. He's got a formidable reputation and he's meant to advise his clients well.' He looked down at bitten but clean fingernails. 'If I'm honest, I'm surprised he was representing such... well... women of modest means. Lawyers like Black don't charge bargain-basement fees. Know what I mean?'

He locked eyes with Jackie and leaned towards her unexpectedly, his voice loaded with intrigue. 'Wait. Sam Black's not suspected in the murders, is he?'

Jackie leaned away from him. 'I can't discuss the details of the case, I'm afraid. But it would be helpful if you could tell me anything you know about Black's dealings with both women. In fact, any female clients.'

The conspiratorial air dissipated. Andy Dewhurst sat back; merely shrugged again and shook his head in answer. 'Sorry, I can't help you. Sam Black and the likes of me don't run in the same circles. Occasionally, his secretary will reach out on his behalf to try to ferret out of me what I'm going to put in my report, but that's about the extent of any contact I have with him.'

'Faye Southgate,' Jackie said, feeling herself deflate like a sagging party balloon as Dewhurst's insights dwindled to nothing. 'You said you didn't work on her case.'

'No. Afraid not.'

'And Claire Watkins? Also went by the name Rachel Hardman. That didn't ring a bell either, when we last spoke.'

'Sorry. I only ever get to speak to mothers where there's a possibility that a child needs to go into care, or else in a sticky divorce like Esther Glickman's and Marie Grant's, where the parents are fighting like cat and dog, using the children as bargaining chips. If these other two women were able to come to an amicable agreement with their exes over who got the kids and when, I wouldn't ever get involved.'

She only had one more question left to ask. 'Did either of the women ever mention a Tyler Colin Fleming?'

The social worker peered wistfully through the window. Finally, he turned back to Jackie and shook his head. 'No. Sorry. Never heard that name in my life.'

Disappointed with the meagre fruits of her interview, Jackie left the coffee shop and crossed Deansgate, heading deeper into Spinningfields. The tall, gleaming buildings on either side acted as a wind tunnel, and now the bitingly cold gusts barrelled into her, making her already sensitive eyes stream in earnest.

As she pulled on her hood and zipped her anorak to her chin, she wondered if she and Gus would end up being investigated and reported upon by a social worker like Andy Dewhurst; their lives dissected and their children interrogated, all because neither of them would concede any ground in the fight over custody of their children. Jackie sighed heavily, realising that her obstinacy would ultimately hurt the people she loved the most. She made a mental note to sit down with Gus and try to reason with him. Wasn't Percy already putting out distress signals with his disruptive behaviour in school?

You're a terrible mother, Jackson Cooke, her alter ego said.

But imaginary Lucian put his hand on her shoulder. *Stop being so hard on yourself, sis. You're a great mother, trying to do her best under impossible circumstances. Let Gus be a good father, but don't let him use his own children to write himself a blank cheque at your expense. Fight, Jackie! Fight for your babies, and fight for justice for these women.*

She knew he was right.

Inside the offices of Black, Black and Fein, Jackie showed her ID to the receptionist.

'My colleagues, Detective Sergeant Dave Tang and Detective Constable Shazia Malik are already here.'

'I'll take you through.'

The receptionist smiled at her, but there was something else behind her heavily made-up eyes. Was it fear? Loathing? Clearly news had travelled. Jackie felt sure she wouldn't have had an icier reception had she been an auditor.

Jackie could see Shazia in a small room on the far side of the admin pool, interviewing a woman who looked to be in her early thirties. She guessed it was the associate who had ended up handling all four divorce cases at a lower hourly rate.

'Can you take me to my colleague DS Tang please?'

'No problem.'

The receptionist led Jackie to a large office where Venetian blinds had been dropped but twisted horizontally, so that the people inside could see out. Jackie was sure she'd caught sight of an older man staring out at her, but at a second glance, he was gone.

The receptionist knocked on the door. 'The DS lady's here.'

Jackie was ushered inside, relieved to see Dave, seated in a visitor's chair scribbling in his notebook. In another visitor's chair was a red-faced woman who looked thoroughly flustered. She was leafing through a large desk diary. Behind the desk sat the older man Jackie had seen staring out at her.

The older man stood up. 'You must be the famous Detective Jackson Cooke,' he said. He held an outstretched hand. 'I'm Gerald Fein. Senior partner.'

Jackie shook his hand. She looked questioningly down at Dave and then turned her attention to the woman.

'Sorry,' the woman said, standing abruptly so that the diary fell from her lap. 'I'm Samuel Black's secretary, Barbara. I'm helping your colleague, Detective Chang, here—'

'Tang,' Dave said. 'Detective Sergeant Tang. Chang is a brand of Thai beer. Tang is tasty and Chinese. Easy to remember.' Dave turned to Jackie. 'We're checking Mr Black's whereabouts on the dates when our victims died.'

Gerald Fein sat stiffly down. 'Is this really necessary? I'd testify to Sam Black's good character under oath. What you're doing here... it's defamatory.'

'We're just following our lines of enquiry, Mr Fein. We have rock-solid evidence that shows Mr Black had been having an affair with one of the murdered women. When it fizzled, he turned nasty.'

Fein waved his hand dismissively. 'Consenting adults. Sam is divorced, as were all of your murder victims. I don't know which woman you're referring to, but last time I checked the law, there's nothing says a red-blooded man can't sleep with a consenting adult woman.'

'Do me a favour. Sam Black is no angel,' Jackie said. 'There was a clear professional conflict of interest. He signed up to be the acting solicitor for Faye Southgate in her divorce, *after* he'd started sleeping with her.'

'That doesn't make him a murderer,' Fein said. 'This whole nasty business is pure conjecture and fantasy.'

Dave held his hand up and Fein fell silent. He picked up the diary and handed it to Black's secretary. 'So you're saying that Black was in court at the time of Claire Watkins' aka Rachel Hardman's death, but you can't account for his whereabouts on the evening that Faye Southgate died, and you can't find the diary going back to Marie Grant's death.'

'That's right.' The secretary's hands shook as she leafed through the pages of the desk diary. 'I don't keep tabs on Mr Black in the evening of course. He has a lot of charity functions to go to. I don't manage his diary for the things he does outside of the practice. He always tells me his ex-wife takes care of that.'

Dave crossed his right leg over his left knee, licked his index finger and started to rub at a scuff mark on the sole of his otherwise immaculate shoe. 'What about Esther Glickman, then? Around lunchtime on September twelfth? It was a Sunday. Her younger kids were all out at the park with the older kids. But her murderer was in the house with her, because they drugged her, and she either fell down the stairs or they pushed her.'

Jackie noticed that he kept back the detail of the roll of money down her throat. She watched Fein and the secretary to see if there was any sign that they were privy to some terrible secret.

The secretary shook her head. 'There's nothing in the diary for that day.' She looked at Fein and bit her lip. 'I'm sorry. I can only confirm Mr Black's whereabouts on one occasion.'

'And the other three?' Jackie asked.

'I just can't give him an alibi.'

THIRTY

'I'll ask again,' Dave said, locking eyes with Sam Black across the interview table. 'Where were you on those dates?'

For many long and fruitless hours, Black had sat impassively in the hot seat, arms folded and mouth steadfastly shut, with his astronomically priced legal representation – Diane Haslam – butting in at every possible juncture, decrying the interrogation as harassment. Now Jackie could tell by the ragged edge to Dave's voice that the deliberate attempt to block their line of enquiry had truly got to him.

'It will be a lot easier if you just answer the question, Mr Black,' Jackie said. 'We know you were having an affair with Faye Southgate, and we have evidence that you turned nasty on her.'

'I resent the use of the word "nasty",' Diane Haslam said. She toyed with the large diamond stud in her ear. 'Try using that in court, Detective. You'll soon lose that professional good reputation you value so much.'

Jackie turned to Dave. 'Let's take a breather.'

They left Black and his lawyer sitting with arms folded,

both wearing wry smiles that said they knew who was in control of the questioning process.

In the corridor, Dave looked at his watch and growled with frustration. 'We're getting nowhere. It won't be long before we have to cut Sam Black loose.'

Jackie leaned against the opposite wall and squeezed her eyes shut. She clasped her fists to her temples. '*No comment, no comment, no comment.* I mean, I know he's a lawyer, but... You'd think he'd answer some of our questions, if only to appear innocent and helpful.' She opened her eyes and appraised the telltale dark rings beneath Dave's eyes that said he was stressed to breaking point.

He shook his head ruefully. 'Black knows exactly what he's doing. No alibi for three out of the four murders, but he doesn't need to worry, because he's got the best criminal lawyer in the city repping him. They know we haven't got a shred of evidence good enough to convict him.'

Jackie was just about to suggest they grab a cup of coffee, giving them both time to talk through how they might go at their last round of interrogation, when Venables stalked down the corridor towards them.

'Cooke. Tang. A word.' She glowered at them – a dangerous glint in her eye said trouble lay ahead. She opened the door to an adjacent empty interview room and marched inside. 'In here. Now.'

Following in the wake of Venables' strong perfume and flowing knitwear, Jackie felt certain they were about to be given another dressing-down for having pulled in one of Manchester's most respected legal minds, when they had already had a perfectly good case against Tyler Fleming. But then Jackie noticed Venables had blanched. Something else was afoot.

'Drop the charges against Black and apologise like your life depended on it,' Venables said. 'Right now.'

'Ah, here it is.' Jackie perched on the edge of the table that was bolted to the floor. She undid her ponytail and retied it. 'And there was me thinking there was something about the look on your face that spelled—'

'There's another body. A fresh one.' Venables' lips trembled as she spoke.

'Same MO?' Dave asked.

'Where is the victim?' Jackie asked.

Venables held her manicured hands up. 'Chorlton. Another divorcée and she's called Emma Thomas. I've left the address with Malik. Just get yourselves down there. Swinton and his crew's already on the scene. I suggest you ask him about the finer details of the MO, but I do know it's another roll-of-cash-down-the-throat affair, dressed up as suicide. And I also know the body's not been there long enough for it to be Fleming *or* Black.' She pointed at both of them as though she were aiming a loaded gun at their hearts. 'So you two had better pray for a breakthrough, because you're back to square one, and now you can bet your bottom dollar you're going to be slapped with a harassment suit from Sam Black. I did warn you. I'll make damn sure Diane Haslam and the commissioner both know you arrested him against my wishes.'

'But you gave us the green light!'

'It's my word against yours, Cooke.'

Jackie could feel cumulative frustration and fatigue chipping away at her professional boundaries until her true feelings spilled out like toxic waste. 'Jesus, Tina. Would it kill you to support the people who work for you every once in a while? Honestly. You know we're underfunded and understaffed. Me and Tang sacrifice a normal family life to do the right thing for victims – long into the night, and often seven days a week. We miss our kids growing up, okay? But all you're ever bothered about is how things reflect on *you*.' She was dimly aware of Dave grabbing her forearm, but she shook him off. 'Well, guess what – not everything's about you, okay? So take a damn day off with the finger-pointing and gloating and blaming. It's like we're back in junior school! Get a grip of yourself.'

Without waiting to see Venables' reaction, Jackie strode out of the interview room, grinding her teeth in frustration not just at her boss's attitude, but principally at the thought that the killer was still out there, clearly spiralling into a spree. She poked her head into the room where Black and Diane Haslam were ensconced.

'You can go now,' she told Black. 'My colleague, Shazia Malik, will process your release. But if we need to speak to you again, make sure you're available.'

'Well, about time,' Diane Haslam said. 'But don't think we won't be lodging a formal complaint.'

Jackie waved and started to close the door on them, but not before Black managed to bombard her with a threat that turned her blood to ice.

'I hear you're getting divorced, Detective Cooke,' he said. 'I'm feeling pretty charitable after this overnight stay with one-star hospitality. I think I might return the gesture by offering your husband some top-drawer representation in your proceedings. Diane tells me his name is Augustus Rutter. That's right, isn't it?'

Jackie froze and met Black's gaze. She could see from the set of his jaw and the ferocity behind his eyes that he'd meant what he'd said.

Slamming the door the rest of the way shut before she said something she'd regret, she hastened away from the interview rooms. As she contemplated Black's threat, she thought about all she *currently* stood to lose. If Black really did offer Gus pro bono representation just to spite her, she would be left with nothing. Everything that defined her life, apart from her job, would be taken away from her. And if Black did hit her with some embellished harassment nonsense, the job she cared so much about might go too.

Hastening back to her workstation, she spotted Shazia. The junior detective looked up and waved a piece of paper in the air. She was already pulling on her jacket and slinging her bag across her body.

'I've got the address,' Shazia said.

'What have we got?' Jackie asked, pushing Sam Black and Gus into an imaginary locker and pressing the door shut until their goading was silenced.

'A thirty-eight-year-old woman – single mother, with a boy of seven and a girl of four. Nick Swinton says we need to get down there pronto, because it's the same as the others but not quite.'

'Not quite in what way?'

'He says we've gotta see it for ourselves.'

Jackie looked over her shoulder and saw Dave was on the other side of the forest of desks, clearly still trying to talk Venables down. She beckoned him over and turned back to Shazia, whose face was flushed with eagerness. 'Look, I'm sorry to break this to you, but you're going to have to deal with Black. We're cutting him loose.'

Clearly crestfallen, Shazia opened her mouth to speak but seemed to think better of it. She placed a hand on Jackie's shoulder. 'Look after her,' she said.

Jackie patted her hand. 'Don't worry. I will.'

'Looks... ordinary,' Dave said, peering through the windscreen at the house. 'A bit like a student house with all those dream-catchers in the living-room window. Bet a big Victorian semi like that is worth about half a mil or more, round here.'

Outside, two forensics vans were parked – one on and one across the driveway. Beyond the one on the street was a squad car. Beyond that was the coroner's black van, ready to take the body to the mortuary.

Jackie tugged at the collar of her tight turtleneck, feeling suddenly claustrophobic. 'Looks like my house.' She shivered involuntarily. The memory of Sam Black threatening her with pure poison in his voice pushed its way out of the mental locker she'd secured it in. He seemed to sway and jeer at her like a malevolent Jack-in-the-box. She blinked him away. 'Looks like my life from where we're sitting.' She swallowed hard. 'Come on. Let's see if our killer's genuinely struck again.'

Inside, Nick Swinton's forensics team were systematically combing the place for stray hairs or other damning evidence. Two uniforms were in the living room, talking about Manchester United's latest efforts against Arsenal. Dave had been right. The place did have a hippy, studenty feel about it, Jackie noted. But the sight of kids' toys in the dining-room alcove made her stomach tighten. *Come on, Jackson Cooke. Stop this sentimental crap. You're a professional. Work the case. This isn't your house. This isn't your story.*

The dining room opened onto a galley kitchen that ran the length of the detached side of the house. The place was lit brightly with Nick Swinton's kit. And at the far end of the kitchen, there he crouched in his white protective suit, trying to manoeuvre his tall body correctly to photograph the corpse at his feet.

He turned to Jackie and smiled warmly. 'Cookie.'

'Don't call me that,' Jackie said. 'You know it drives me nuts.'

The forensic pathologist frowned momentarily. His eyes moved from side to side as though he was thinking hard. Finally, he smiled again and snapped his fingers. 'Ah, you *take the biscuit.*'

'Have you been at the formalin again, Swinton?' Dave asked. 'Your puns are worse than mine.'

Nick chuckled and set the camera on his knee so he could peer closer at the body. He beckoned them both over. 'This is

Emma Thomas. I've tried not to disturb her, but I did check her over for a needle mark, where she may have been jabbed, and I've looked down her throat of course.'

'Well?' Jackie craned her neck to get a proper look at the woman's body, but the space was incredibly tight and Nick was in the way. She moved closer.

Nick nodded and took an evidence bag out of his toolbox. 'It was the same as with the others. I looked down her throat and caught a glimpse of a foreign object, rammed quite far down. I got my tweezers on the job and...' He waved the baggie at them.

Through the transparent plastic, Jackie saw a tight roll of twenties, similar to what had been found in the gullets of three out of four of the existing victims. 'So what's new?'

Finally, Nick got to his feet and backed away from the body so that they could get a clear view of it.

Jackie looked down and gasped. Clasped tightly against the victim's heart was a child's baby doll – stripped of all clothing and staring blankly, ghoulishly up at her.

'Who found her?'

'The window cleaner spotted her. He put the call in to 999.'

'Kids?'

'At school, according to the next-door neighbour. That's what the first responders told me.'

'Same as Claire Watkins, aka Rachel Hardman.' Jackie thought about her old school friend, lying lifeless by her kitchen table; that startled look on her face.

'I heard you had a couple of guys in custody,' Nick said. 'But unless they're accomplices in some kind of incel murdering team, I'd say you've got the wrong ones. Our killer is still at large.' He pressed his lips together and his nostrils flared. He raised one of his bushy, dark eyebrows emphatically.

'Damn it. We're no further forward,' Jackie said, almost in a whisper. 'This piece of crap is running rings round us. I feel like he's taunting us that we've got the wrong men in custody. It's like he knows our every move. And the doll... His modus operandi is maturing, but what's the doll telling us? Is it about mothers? Children? Is the toy an actual metaphor for toying with everyone involved?'

She felt the ground undulate as stress threatened to pull the rug from under her.

'You okay?' Nick asked. 'You look pale.'

Jackie dragged her palm over her furrowed brow and pressed down over her right eye, behind which a headache was starting to throb in earnest. 'I need to take a step back from this. A night off, just to recharge my batteries and get some distance from the case. I feel like I'm going insane and no way am I letting this game-playing monster get the better of me. For the sake of these women, I need to take a breath and then come back fighting.'

THIRTY-ONE

'Come on, Jackie,' Hannah said. 'We're going to have a ball, I promise. A night out in female company will do you good.' She patted Jackie's hand, full of well meaning.

'I should be with my kids or working to solve a murder case, never mind sipping overpriced G&T in a wine bar in town.' Jackie looked down at the baggy jumper she'd hastily thrown over a pair of skinny jeans. The only nod to evening wear was the silver lamé thread woven into the black acrylic. At least it covered her new-mum body.

'Dave said you desperately need a break. Think of this as therapy.' Hannah paid the barman and carried their drinks to a table.

Jackie followed and took her seat opposite Dave's glamorous wife, feeling shabby in comparison. 'You look amazing. I wish I had the energy to make an effort.' She sipped her drink and realised when the alcohol hit her bloodstream that perhaps this *had* been a good idea. The image of Emma Thomas, clutching a baby doll, started to recede in her mind's eye.

Hannah raised her glass to Jackie and laughed. 'Most of the time, I look like I sleep rough. But that's having kids for you, and thankfully tonight, ours are tucked up with their dads.' She reached out and squeezed Jackie's hand. 'And don't be hard on yourself, Jackie. You're a cop after all. Dave's a cop. I don't think I've seen him look anything but exhausted since our honeymoon, and he certainly never has the energy to think about his appearance if we go anywhere nice. If he's clean, that's good enough. A Hawaiian shirt hides a multitude of sins.'

Jackie looked down at the baggy black jumper. 'Maybe that's where I'm going wrong. I need to get me an entire wardrobe of Dave shirts.'

'Good birth control, if nothing else,' Hannah said, winking.

For the first time in a long while, Jackie laughed. But no sooner had she suppressed the worry of the case and the possibility that Sam Black would exact the worst kind of revenge on her for having humiliated him so publicly than something caught her eye on the other side of the busy bar.

'Is that...?' Blinking hard, Jackie looked again, but the familiar face she'd spotted had gone.

'What?' Hannah asked, looking around to see what had transfixed Jackie.

Jackie shook her head. 'It's all right. I'm going mad. I thought I just spotted an old friend. I hadn't seen her in about twenty years, and suddenly, I see her twice in, like, a week. Maybe I'm wrong.'

She looked back at the booth where she'd seen the familiar face, and a man sitting with his back to her leaned to his left to pick something off the floor. With his head out of the way, she got a proper look at the woman he was sitting with.

'No. It *is* her.' She turned to Hannah. 'Just give me five seconds. I've got to go and say hello to this woman. Sorry. Five seconds, I promise.'

Shooed merrily away by Hannah, who had already taken out her phone and begun to scroll, Jackie made her way over to the booth. As she approached, she caught the eye of her old school friend, who looked nonplussed when they first locked eyes. She then grinned in recognition.

'Jackson Cooke!' the woman said. 'We meet again.'

'Katie Pritchard,' Jackie said. She was just about to lean in for an embrace when she caught sight of Katie's date. Jackie turned and looked properly at the man. 'Andy?'

Andy Dewhurst raised his glass to Jackie and chuckled. 'What are the odds, eh?'

Jackie looked back at Katie. 'Andy was assisting me with my enquiries yesterday. In a professional capacity of course.'

'What can I say?' Dewhurst said. 'It's a small world.'

'So, tell me, are you two married?' Jackie asked.

Katie blushed. 'Oh no. We're just on a date. Our third.'

Jackie clasped her hand to her mouth in horror. 'Oh, of course. I'm so sorry to intrude. I'll leave you guys to it.' She took hold of Katie's hand. 'Look, give me a shout before you leave. I'll give you my personal number. We can keep in touch if you like.'

'I'd love that.' Her friend nodded energetically.

Noting the delight in her shining eyes and the radiant smile on her lips, Jackie decided not to mention the case or Claire Watkins' death again. Katie and Andy Dewhurst were on a date after all.

She made her way back to the table to find Hannah had ordered them a second round of gins.

'Really?' Jackie asked.

'It's medicine,' Hannah said, popping an ice cube into her mouth and crunching away. 'Anyway, Dave said your ex was giving you a hard time, so maybe it's anaesthetic too, just for one night.'

'My milk's all but dried up anyway, with stress and long hours. Thank God for formula.'

As the gin gained a foothold in her bloodstream and the evening progressed, Jackie realised how much she'd missed the company of another adult woman who wasn't her mother. She joined in with mothering anecdotes and listened to Hannah's tales of being the wife of a cop. Two hours and two more gins ticked quickly by.

'What's really hard – even harder than having to do everything while Dave does overtime, when you guys work a murder – is the worry. The worry.' Hannah gazed ruefully at the slice of lemon at the bottom of her glass and sucked the liquid remnants up through her straw with something bordering on aggression. 'Many's the night I lie in bed, wondering if he's gonna come home at all. I mean, you two are out there 'til the early hours sometimes, staking out drug dens and brothels and... anywhere where there's a possible killer inside, you guys are there. Putting yourselves in harm's way for a crappy cop's salary and pension.'

Jackie stared into her glass and thought about Gus, running to his band rehearsals, being tempted by the pneumatic and uncomplicated Catherine Harris.

'You okay?' Hannah asked, jolting Jackie out of her reverie. 'Only you seem miles away.'

Smiling, Jackie nodded. 'Fine. Absolutely fine. Just thinking that people who are married to cops deserve a medal.'

'Or danger money,' Hannah said.

She checked her watch. 'Wow. Is that the time? Look, I've got to go or this Cinderella turns into a pumpkin.'

'Me too,' Jackie said, thumbing the screen of her phone into life to check that there were no tidings of sick or injured children.

There were none.

'Look, I really appreciate you doing this. I needed to get out of my own head for a couple of hours. This case... this divorce... it's all getting to me.'

'I know,' Hannah said. She leaned over and squeezed Jackie's hand. 'Just remember I'm only on the end of a phone. Don't bother talking to Dave though. He's your archetypal stoic man. Only opens his mouth to chew noisily or scream instructions at

Man City on the telly.' She laughed at her own observation. 'But you know where I am if you feel overwhelmed or just want to chat.'

Hannah gathered her belongings, kissed Jackie on the cheek and was gone in a flurry of long hair and full-length fun fur, leaving only a cloud of fading perfume behind.

As soon as Hannah had departed, Jackie slipped on her own coat. She was just about to head for the tram when Katie called her over.

'Jackie! Why don't you come and join us for a nightcap?'

Realising she had nobody to go home to, Jackie glanced at her watch and reasoned she had another hour or so until the last tram departed. 'Why not? It would be nice to have a proper catch-up – *not* with my notebook and pen in hand.'

Dewhurst went to the bar, leaving Jackie and Katie to talk.

'So, how's the last twenty years been treating you?' Jackie asked, setting both her work and her personal phones down on the table, in case an urgent message came through. 'You look amazing, by the way.'

Katie ran a manicured hand through her tonged hair. 'Divorce suits me.' She giggled. 'Me and my ex *consciously uncoupled* about eighteen months ago. I really enjoy being my own boss, to be honest. I go where I want, when I want, with whom I want. When I go on a date, I get wined and dined and treated like royalty, not like a cheap afterthought.'

Jackie looked down at her own unadorned hands. 'Oh, yeah? You got any kids? I've got three – twin boys of nine and a baby of four months.' She lifted her personal phone and showed her old pal the wallpaper photo of Lewis, Percy and Alice.

Katie cooed over the photo. 'A *baby*. I haven't looked after babies in years. Aw, your daughter's adorable, and your sons are so handsome.' She showed Jackie a photo of her own brood. 'Kieran's fifteen, Thomas is twelve, Sophie's nine and Rose is seven.'

'You've been busy.' Jackie studied the photo, nodding approvingly. 'Do you share custody with their dad? "Conscious uncoupling" sounds amicable. Very grown-up.'

'Oh, you're kidding, aren't you?' Katie asked. She glanced over at the bar, where Dewhurst was placing their drinks on a tray. Turned back to Jackie and shuffled forwards to close the gap between them. 'That lousy arsehole, my ex, was controlling. A narcissist. I kicked him out because I didn't want him ruining our kids. Kieran's in therapy.' She waved dismissively but there were tears in her eyes. 'It's a long story, but basically, I made damn sure my ex never got a sniff in, where custody was concerned. He doesn't even get to visit them. He's scum.' She almost spat the word and dabbed at her eyes. The sorrow seemed to lift. 'Anyway, once the judge told him to get back in his box, the kids haven't had so much as a phone call from him. Loser. They're at my folks' tonight. What about you?'

Jackie noticed Dewhurst turn away from the bar, poised to walk back to them. 'Oh, we're trying to keep it all friendly. Being a detective isn't a profession that's conducive to a stable marriage.'

The social worker began his journey across the busy bar. He stopped to talk to a man who clearly knew him. Jackie turned her attention back to Katie. 'Don't suppose you had any more thoughts about Claire?'

Katie's eyes dulled. She fell silent and frowned, as if wracking her brain. Then she looked up. 'Actually, I think she might have mentioned some guy she'd been talking to online.'

'Oh? What was his name? Guy? Steve? Col? Sam?'

Katie shook her head. 'Sorry. I honestly can't remember.'

'Can't remember what?' Dewhurst said, setting the drinks down carefully.

Jackie was just about to answer him when her work phone lit up with a text. It was Shazia. At a glance, she could see that it was about the latest victim.

Catching sight of Dewhurst reading the preview over her shoulder, she snatched up the phone. 'Oh, excuse me, guys. I'm just going to have to deal with this. It's work.'

In the relative privacy of the toilet, Jackie read the text.

Andy Dewhurst from CAFCASS involved in Emma Thomas's custody battle.

She sprinted back to where she'd been sitting with Katie and Dewhurst, but when she got to their booth, there was no sign of either of them.

THIRTY-TWO

Jackie ran out of the bar and onto the rainy street. It was deserted but for a speeding taxi, spattering water over the kerb, and one gaggle of girls, click-clacking along the pavement that was slick and wet, giggling and screeching excitedly with the collars of their coats held high over their heads.

'Damn it!' Jackie shouted, her breath steaming on the cold, damp air.

She dialled Katie's number first. 'Pick up! Pick up!' But the phone rang out. Either Katie had switched her phone off for the night or else... Jackie shook her head at the thought that the truth had dawned on her too late.

Next, she dialled Dave's number. It went straight to voicemail. 'Come on!' She dialled his landline. After a couple of rings, he picked up, sounding bleary, smacking his lips and coughing. 'Jackie? What the hell kind of social call is this? Did you and Hannah drink too much lady petrol? Wait, she's not home yet.'

'Don't worry. She left not long ago. She'll still be in a taxi. Listen. This case – it's all about the children,' Jackie said. 'These murders –

they're not sexually motivated. They're not about divorced women or single mothers – not *just* about that anyway. It's about fighting men for custody and getting their access rights taken away.'

There was the sound of something being knocked from a nightstand perhaps, and then a light being switched on. She could hear Dave rustling his covers. 'I don't get it. Isn't that exactly the same as the killer targeting women because they're single parents?'

'You're not listening!' Jackie raised her voice. 'This is only about women who have split acrimoniously and then tried to get the kids taken away from their fathers. Don't you see? These are revenge murders. And I've got a horrible suspicion that I know who our man is.'

'Who?'

'Andy Dewhurst, the social worker who reported on at least three of our victims' custody battles – Esther Glickman, Marie Grant and the latest dead woman, Emma Thomas. He works for the courts, so I'll bet even if he's not supposed to look into anything beyond his official caseload, he can get access to any divorce record he likes.'

'So, wait. You're saying Dewhurst is the killer?'

'It makes sense,' Jackie said. 'But we need to find him and bring him in. My friend's dating him, for God's sake. She's with him now. I was drinking with them both. Shazia sent me a text about his involvement. I'm sure he caught sight of the preview over my shoulder because when I came back from reading it in the toilet, they were both gone. My friend could be next. She fits the bill – nasty divorce and wrangling over the kids. But, Dave, we have to do our homework. Dewhurst knows the judicial system inside out. He's part of it. And he's been prewarned. I've interviewed the son of a bitch twice already, without realising.'

A few moments of silence on the line ensued. Then Dave

groaned and spoke again. 'Right. I'm getting dressed. Let's get an address for Dewhurst and pick him up.'

'Well, you'll have to collect me because I'm still in town.'

Within the half hour that it took Dave to get into Manchester city centre, Jackie had downed a cafetière of coffee, giving herself enough of a boost to temporarily drive away fatigue.

Dave pulled up outside the bar at just after 2 a.m. He lowered the driver's-side window. 'Ready?'

'You bet.' Jackie got into the car, her heart thumping with adrenalin and caffeine. 'Where are we going?'

Dave pulled away from the kerb. 'He lives in Salford Quays. You get hold of your friend?'

Jackie shook her head. 'Nope. I've asked the uniforms to go round to her house though. Did you manage to get hold of Bob? We need to find out everything we can about Dewhurst. I want to go back down that incel rabbit hole to see if we missed anything – especially now the killer's MO has changed to include dolls. I'm really worried about Katie. If I'm right, and Dewhurst is our man...'

Jackie allowed the possibility to take shape in her imagination and felt panicked tears stab at the backs of her eyes. She willed the image and the fear to subside. They were going to catch Dewhurst before it was too late. Katie would be fine. She and Dave would make it so.

As Dave thundered through Manchester's streets, crossing the postcode boundary into Salford, Jackie dialled the number of Bob's girlfriend, Zoe. She picked up just as Jackie had given up hope that she'd ever get through.

'Jackie?' Zoe's voice was bleary.

Grabbing hold of the handle above the passenger seat, Jackie leaned heavily against the door as Dave took a corner at speed. 'Zoe, I'm so sorry to wake you, but it's a matter of life and death. Is Bob there?'

'No. I never let him stay over. He snores.'

'Well, I need you to do me a favour, and I know Bob's not up to it. This started out as staged suicides, but our guy's now not even bothering to dress up his murders as something else. He's got a vendetta against mothers who fight for custody of their children in acrimonious splits. So I need you to go back onto those incel forums and look for a guy who talks about single mothers and child custody battles. I'm looking for a guy who fantasises about killing women and posing their bodies with their children's toys. Anything about ramming money down their throats is obviously something to watch out for too.'

Zoe yawned. 'But you caught your incel guy.'

'Wrong guy. I think he was just a copycat, targeting prostitutes. Now, can you do this for me, Zoe? Can you do it *now*? I'm counting on you.' Jackie could feel the pulse in her neck pounding. She encased her throat in her hand, imagining what it must be like to have money rammed down your throat; choking to death and unable to scream. 'Please.'

'Come on, Jackie. You know I want to help, but I'm not a charity case. I've got undergrads to teach in... seven hours. I've got bills.'

Feeling tension mounting inside her, Jackie balled her fist. Her fingertips were prickling. 'I'll make sure you get paid, even if me and Dave have to do it out of our own pockets. I swear.'

'Two hundred. In cash. But I want you to get me set up as an official computer consultant on the payroll after this. It might make me look like a fascist, but to hell with it. I can get more freelance work off the back of that on LinkedIn.'

Jackie swallowed hard. 'Done.'

Hanging up, Jackie looked out of the window to see Salford Quays glittering all around them in the glow of the moon that had just broken through the clouds. The rain had stopped. The water in the central bay and on the Manchester Ship Canal beyond it was almost dead calm, reflecting back at her the executive apartments that were studded with constellations of light where night-owl residents dwelled. Was Andy Dewhurst in one of those living rooms? Was he with Katie?

'We're here.' Dave drew up outside of a ten-storey block, not far from the twisted metallic mass of Lowry Theatre.

In the distance, sirens heralded the approach of the squad cars. With one last glance at her phone to see if Zoe had sent through a message, Jackie got out of the Ford. The cold night air whipped off the water and slapped her across the face. She had never felt more awake.

Dave pressed the buzzer for Dewhurst's apartment. No response.

'Try one of his neighbours,' Jackie said.

After several attempts, an older-sounding woman spoke on the intercom. 'Can I help you?' she asked.

Jackie laid her hand on Dave's arm before he could speak. 'Police,' she said. 'Are you the neighbour of Andy Dewhurst?'

'His next-door neighbour. Yes. It's very late, you know.'

'Can you let us in please? It's an emergency. I'm Detective Sergeant Jackie Cooke. I can show you my ID if you'll just let me in.'

Would the woman help them or leave them on the doorstep?

'Come up. Second floor, dear.'

The buzzer sounded, and Jackie and Dave sprinted up the stairs, rather than wait for the lift. With adrenalin coursing through her body, Jackie barely felt the limits of her new-mother's body.

On Dewhurst's landing, the woman was waiting for them, clad in an old-fashioned robe. 'I've just knocked, but there's no sign of life. I hope he's okay. He's a nice boy.' Her eyebrows shot up, as if something had occurred to her. 'Oh, actually, I've got a key for when I cat-sit for him. He's often away, you see.'

'That's great,' Jackie said. 'Can you let us in please?'

The neighbour eyed Dave with undisguised suspicion. 'ID first.'

Jackie and Dave submitted their credentials to her scrutiny and were then let in.

Holding her breath, Jackie pushed past the neighbour. 'Andy! Andy, it's the police. If you're hiding, give yourself up and come and talk to us.'

While she spoke, Dave crept through the flat, armed with his extended baton. Each time he emerged from a room, he shook his head. It was a tiny flat. If Dewhurst was there, Jackie was sure they'd find him, and judging by the sirens, the uniforms and the dog handlers were already outside.

'Oh! I just remembered,' the neighbour said. 'Andy's not here at all. He said he was staying at his girlfriend's.'

THIRTY-THREE

'What do you mean there's nobody there?' Jackie asked.

The uniform on the other end of the phone sounded like he was coming to the end of a long, long shift. 'I mean there's nobody at Katie Pritchard's address. The place is all locked up and in darkness. Nobody home. Nada.'

Jackie pressed her finger and thumb to her temples. 'Are you sure you got the right address?'

'That's the address we were given – 205 Fog Avenue. I've spoken to the neighbours. They've not seen her since yesterday.'

Jackie thanked the uniform and hung up. She turned to her partner. 'No sign of her.'

'What do we do now?' Dave asked. He slowly turned to take in Andy Dewhurst's minimalist living room, which looked like it had been furnished with charity-shop finds from the eighties.

The uniforms that had arrived on the scene looked expectantly at Jackie.

Feeling suddenly overwhelmed by the disappointment of not having found Dewhurst, the worry that Katie was missing, and the hiss and garbled chatter of the radios strapped to the uniforms' shoulders, Jackie merely shook her head. 'I don't know. I – I need to think.'

She pushed past three of the six uniforms who were milling around in the cramped hallway to the small but tidy bathroom. Locked herself in and sat on the toilet, feeling impotent. Her head had started to pound.

Jackie glanced over at the bathroom cabinet above the sink. She was just about to get up and see whether Dewhurst had any painkillers in there when her phone rang. It was Zoe.

'Zoe. Any news?'

On the other end, Zoe sounded wired, as though she'd downed a triple espresso. 'You bet. Listen to this. It was written a week ago on an incel forum. The guy's avatar is Beta_Warrior. He's a real charmer. It goes: *"What I've been thinking about is snuffing the life out of one of these bitches and leaving them clutching at their kids' toys. That would teach them a lesson. The last thought they'd ever have is regret that they tried to take away their children from their fathers. The fathers get the kids. The manipulative witches die alone, thinking about everything they lost because of their selfishness and arrogance."* What do you think of that?'

Looking blankly at her reflection in the bathroom cabinet mirror, Jackie felt the hairs on her forearms stand proud. 'Have you been able to identify who this Beta_Warrior account is registered to? Is it our guy?' She held her breath, praying that Zoe would be able to eradicate any doubt.

'Not yet. But I'm working on it,' she said.

The pain lanced through Jackie's head. She opened the cabinet door and scanned the contents, taking a latex glove out of her jacket pocket in the hope that there would be some ibuprofen among the razors, mouthwash and Tiger Balm. 'Okay. You're doing great. Keep at it. Let me know as soon as...'

Jackie's gaze had wandered to the door of the bathroom cabinet that held thin packets of tablets on a narrow shelf. It took her a moment to make sense of what she was looking at, but then she realised that behind the metal rail, behind the baggie of what looked remarkably like Rohypnol, were photos.

'Are you all right, Jackie?' Zoe asked.

'What?'

Jackie put her phone on the side of the sink, snapped on her latex gloves and pulled the photos out from behind the Rohypnol. 'Christ. You're not going to believe this,' she said.

'Jackie? Jackie? Have you fallen? You sound weird.' Zoe's voice was tinny and far away.

Studying the photos carefully, one by one, Jackie whistled softly. There, caught on camera, was Marie Grant, lying glassy-eyed on her kitchen floor; Faye Southgate, trussed up in the garb of auto-asphyxiation and wearing a dead-eyed look of horror on her face; her old school friend, Claire Watkins, staring at the future she'd never get to see, beneath the kitchen table; Esther Glickman, with her arms and legs at awkward angles at the bottom of her stairs, reaching out as if to claw her life back; and Emma Thomas, propped against her kitchen base cupboards, clutching a child's toy.

'We're hunting the right man, all right,' Jackie said.

'Dave! Dave!' She was shouting now, almost overcome with emotion as she thought about the grave danger that Katie Pritchard was in. 'David, get in here!'

Jackie unlocked the bathroom door and held up the photos for Dave to see. She was dimly aware of Zoe on the other end of the phone, still calling her name to check she hadn't passed out.

Dave snapped on some gloves and took the photos from her. 'Bingo.'

'Jackie! Jackie! Wake up!'

Jackie was dimly aware of Dave calling her name from the depths of her slumber. She started to surface towards wakefulness when she realised how stiff her neck was; how her head still throbbed; how the interior of the car smelled of fried food. She opened her eyes and looked up at the building where Andy Dewhurst worked. Turned to Dave. He was taking a large bite out of a sausage and bacon roll.

'Were you calling me?' she asked, straightening up in the passenger seat and rubbing her neck. She stretched and yawned.

'Yeah.' Dave wiped ketchup from the corner of his mouth. He took a parcel of greasy paper and handed it to her. 'Here. One of the uniforms picked us up some breakfast. Get something inside you. Got you a bottle of Coke too.'

Jackie's stomach growled as she unwrapped the package. A sausage bap was inside. 'Was that it? No sign of Dewhurst?'

'Not a thing.' Dave belched softly. 'We've got people watching his flat, Katie's place, and obviously, we're here. I just got off the phone from Bob's girl though.'

'And?'

'This Beta_Warrior *is* Dewhurst. There are messages from him on two different incel forums, listing all the ways he'd like to wipe out single mothers. Seems Tyler Fleming was a bit of a fanboy, trying to copycat him. But the link to Dewhurst's IP is indisputable. All registered to his home address in Salford Quays. Oh, and Bob's been in touch from HQ, while you were asleep. Apparently Dewhurst got divorced eight years ago. His wife fought him, tooth and nail. Said he was a gaslighter but couldn't prove him an unfit father. When she couldn't get the judge to rescind his parental access, the ex just upped sticks and moved to Southampton. Seems Dewhurst started to trawl incel forums and spread hate after that.'

'Less effort than driving down to Southampton,' Jackie said. 'But he clearly found enough energy to stalk and kill Marie Grant.'

'You got it,' Dave said. 'Marie Grant was found dead a couple of weeks after Dewhurst's ex-wife and kids left town.'

'He couldn't bring himself to murder his own ex-wife so he killed somebody else's.' Jackie tutted. 'He knew Marie Grant's circumstances because he'd investigated her years before. Maybe she stuck in his mind all that time. Or maybe he bumped into her and she just happened to be low-hanging fruit. And that's presumably where this case began, seven years ago.' Jackie sighed and checked her personal phone, refreshing WhatsApp to see if there'd been a problem with Lewis, Percy or Alice. It was only 6 a.m. though. Chances were, they were all still asleep. 'Do we have proof that Dewhurst's our Nice Guy from Facebook, Connection and Tinder?'

Dave started to pass on the update that Bob had relayed to him, but Jackie had stopped listening. She was looking at a message that had just landed in her WhatsApp inbox. It appeared to be from Katie, but the shiver that rippled across Jackie's skin told her this wasn't her school pal, apologising for having left the bar without saying goodbye.

Jackie held her left hand up and Dave fell silent. 'I've got a message. I think this is Dewhurst. He must have Katie's phone.' With a shaking finger, she opened the missive.

'What does it say?' Dave asked.

'Oh, Jesus. There's a video clip.' The film was prefaced by a still of Katie, head lolling on her shoulder, encased in what looked like a concrete storeroom. She was sitting on a chair.

Jackie pressed play and the image came to life. Katie was out cold, at first, but quickly came round. She looked around at the claustrophobic grey walls and started trying to scream; clawing at her mouth but only able to issue muffled cries through it. Had her lips been glued shut? Yes. It appeared so. One moment, she was looking straight into the camera – all flaring nostrils and pleading eyes. The next, she looked down and everything seemed to change. Her eyes widened; snapped tightly shut. Katie started to shriek, but the nasal shrieking didn't last for more than a few seconds. Whimpering after that. She became almost perfectly still – her body perfectly taut – occasionally glancing down and then squeezing her weeping eyes shut.

From behind the camera, Jackie and Dave heard Dewhurst speak.

'Jackson Cooke. Listen carefully. This is Andy Dewhurst speaking – the fabled Beta_Warrior. I'm prepared to avenge every wronged father out there. Every man who's had his God-given rights snatched away from him.' His voice sounded ragged with adrenalin. 'If my children aren't delivered to the safe location of my choosing within six hours, Katie's dead. She'll meet the same fate as my other victims, except this time, I'll teach her what real suffering feels like. I won't just choke the life out of her. You want to see how far the mighty fall? I'll show you.'

He brandished a zombie knife in front of the camera lens. From her vantage point inside the strange concrete space, Katie obviously caught sight of the grim blade and started to scream again behind her glued lips. But her body remained rigid, and Jackie could see the tendons in Katie's bare arms and legs, where she seemed to grip the chair with every ounce of strength she had.

'See this?' Dewhurst said. 'When I've finished with her, I'll slice her up and leave that pretty face so badly disfigured, even her own family won't want to say goodbye to her. But the world will see. Oh yes. I'll send the footage to every incel group in the world to show my brothers how mighty we are and how ugly a woman is, inside and out.'

Finally, Dewhurst was in full shot. He came closer and closer to the lens until Jackie felt like there was no space between them. She could see the hatred in his eyes, and the delight in causing Katie – in causing all women – pain. More than that, Jackie could see that he was crazy. There was an insanity to his stare that made her certain he would never be reasoned with. He was beyond that.

'My God,' Dave said. 'He's unhinged.'

Dewhurst spoke again. 'Six hours from now.' He held a digital clock up in front of the camera and started a countdown. In his left hand, he still held the zombie knife. He set the clock down onto a stool, positioned in the foreground, so that the countdown was visible as he crept towards Katie, reached into the space that held her and pressed the tip of the blade to her throat. A fat bead of blood tracked its way down her neck and onto her breast.

Her attempted screams were futile.

'Six hours, Cooke,' Dewhurst said, turning back to the camera. 'I'll be in touch on WhatsApp with a drop-off point – a safe place for you to take my children to. If you try to intervene or don't follow my instructions to the letter, I'm going to carve Katie up and then I'll hack her head off. And when I've finished with her, Detective, I'm coming for you and your children.'

He winked into the lens of the camera and then the footage went black.

THIRTY-FOUR

'He's gonna kill her,' Jackie said, barely able to catch her breath. There was that tingling feeling in her fingertips again. 'I know it. I mean, there's no way his ex is going to deliver her children into the care of a deranged killer. No way on God's earth. In fact, we shouldn't even let her know what's going on. But if he doesn't get what he wants... He's been so careful until now, but I can feel it in my bones, Dave – this bastard is gunning for some big public showdown. He's going to make an example of Katie for every grubby little incel idiot on the internet to see, and it's going to end very badly for her.'

'Breathe, Jackie. Wet your whistle and get some caffeine down you.' Dave offered her the bottle of Coke. 'I know Katie's your friend, but you've got to keep a cool head here. First thing's first. We need to tell Venables. Get all hands on deck.'

Jackie nodded. 'We've got to work out where the hell he's keeping her. Let's get out of town. We're wasting our time. There's no way he's holding her in the commercial centre, with all the shops and offices. There's too many potential witnesses.'

As Dave sped through the empty, early morning streets out of the Piccadilly area, Jackie made a call to her mother.

Beryl answered, agonisingly on the final ring before voice-mail kicked in. 'Jackson, do you know what time it is? What the hell are you doing, ringing—'

'Listen, Mum. Just shut up and listen. Me, you and the kids are all potentially in danger. I need you to pick them up from Gus's *now* – wake Gus up and don't take no for an answer. Get the kids and take them as far away as you can. Somewhere nobody will find you. Maybe...' She rifled through the flotsam and jetsam of accumulated facts and memories in her brain and found one crystal-clear thought. 'Dad's. Go to Dad's. He's totally off grid. Only me and you know his address. You'll be safe there, so get the kids, get in the car and get yourself to Ken's – *immediately*. Tell no one where you're taking them. And no fannying around to get your hair done or to pack like you're off to Thailand for a luxury fortnight. Get the kids in the car and drive. Okay?' She heard her mother draw breath. 'And there's no negotiating here, so don't try. Text me when you're on your way.'

She hung up before her mother could argue. It was a good plan, wasn't it? She turned to Dave. 'Wherever he's holding her – it's somewhere concrete and basement-like.'

'Or a lock-up type of place.' Dave brought the car to an abrupt stop that had a bus driver behind him honking with outrage. 'Listen, we're wasting time going back to HQ. Send the clip to Bob and let him try to triangulate Dewhurst's signal or whatever the hell it is a cyber-boffin like him does. In the mean-time, we're good old-fashioned detectives. Let's do detective work. There's a tonne of places on the edge of the city where your pal could be. How about we start with... the railway arches?'

Jackie nodded. 'Let's do it.'

As Dave drove, she put the call in to Venables. She knew that, even with a superior officer as obsessed by appearances as Venables, the footage would trigger a city-wide hunt. The complex web of alleyways and subterranean hidey-holes and still-derelict mills of Manchester demanded it.

'Does this look like the sort of place he's holding Katie?' Dave asked, slowing the car.

The railway arches at the back of Piccadilly Station were only a couple of hundred metres from where Dave had come to a halt. Yet, out of view of Manchester's tax-paying citizens, the arches afforded shelter to a good number of the city's homeless. With the sun only just coming up, most were asleep in their sleeping bags and cardboard boxes.

'Hey, mate,' Dave shouted to an old homeless guy who was already awake and pushing a supermarket trolley over the rough surface of those back roads. 'You seen a mousy-haired man and a dark-haired woman in her thirties round here? Not homeless though. He would have been dragging her against her will, or maybe even carrying her?'

The old man responded with a barrage of unintelligible salutation, grinning and waving.

'Forget it,' Jackie said.

Dave pulled up further down the street, and they started to explore on foot. Wherever the concrete and brick interior of a railway arch was accessible, they walked among the rats and the dispossessed, looking for some kind of enclosed space or store-room where Dewhurst might have taken Katie. An hour passed. By now, the police helicopter could be heard overhead, and still there was no sign of their quarry.

'We're wasting our time,' Jackie said. 'It looked like a basement to me.'

'Ancoats,' Dave said. 'There's a load of converted mills round there. A few are still derelict. He could have taken her there.'

'Worth a try.'

Hastening along the ring-road, they pulled up in front of an old mill that was earmarked for renovation but which was still surrounded by the developer's hoardings, with no construction work afoot.

'Maybe here?' Dave asked.

'Worth a try. It's like finding a needle in a haystack, but if we don't look, she'll definitely die.'

As they clambered over fallen brickwork and picked their way carefully down some stairs to a basement that dripped with foreboding, Jackie said a silent prayer for Katie. Shining a torch light into the murk, she whispered a promise to Claire Watkins that her killer would be caught. But with the damp sting of mildew in her nostrils and the almost impenetrable black yielding nothing but discarded syringes from the city's junkies and spray-painted graffiti from rebellious teens, Jackie's precarious optimism started to disintegrate.

'It's no good,' she said, feeling like there wasn't enough air in that godforsaken space. 'We're going about this the wrong way. We're missing a trick. Let's get back to the car and look at that footage again.'

Holed up in the Ford with a fresh takeout coffee, Jackie checked her watch.

'We've got three and a half hours,' she said. 'Bob's come up with nothing useful whatsoever. Dewhurst clearly knows how to cover his digital tracks. We've got people turning the city upside down, and me and you have combed through every archway and derelict basement we can think of.'

Dave's eyes narrowed and then he smiled. 'I've just thought of an old boxing gym that might fit the bill. It's in Moss Side.'

Jackie was just about to shake her head and tell him they were grasping at straws when her phone rang. It was Zoe.

'Zoe. What have you got?'

Zoe's normally strong voice sounded shaky. 'He's broadcast a clip of the woman he's abducted on the incel forum, and he's boasting that he's going to kill her and stream it for all those creeps to see.'

Jackie inhaled sharply. 'This is not good. Damn it. He's gone from being secretive and careful to sheer exhibitionism.'

At her side, Dave was listening in to the call. 'He's escalating. He knows he's not going to get his kids and he feels backed against a wall. There's no happy ending to this.'

'Keep an eye on his livestream, Zoe,' Jackie said. 'Let me know if he lets slip where he's keeping her.'

She hung up, feeling like her heart was being torn in two. 'Let's take a breath and watch that footage again,' she told Dave. 'Because there's something about Katie's body language that bothers me. We're just not looking... in the right way.'

Sipping her scalding coffee, Jackie thumbed her phone to life yet again and played the footage – this time at half speed.

'I don't see anything different,' Dave said. 'She's in a store cupboard or something. It's concrete. Maybe a bunker. I dunno, but the woman's tied to a chair and there's concrete walls and that's that. Honestly, we've viewed this about ten times. I don't think we're going to find anything different by watching it again.'

'The sands of time are bloody running out, David,' Jackie said. 'I could have warned Katie, if I hadn't been so goddamn intent on enjoying my night out with Hannah. I had Dewhurst within my grasp and I let him go. This is on me.'

'It isn't. It's not always about you, Jack.' Dave spoke quietly, carefully.

Feeling the weight of guilt press her into the passenger seat of the car, Jackie ignored him. She froze the footage.

Focus, Jackie, imaginary Lucian said to her. He laid his hand on her shoulder. *Don't let your fear get in the way of the truth. Trust your instincts.*

'Okay, so Katie's in the chair, but she's not tied up, which is weird. Just the glue on her mouth. Why can't she escape?'

'Paralysed by fear?' Dave suggested. 'Maybe he's threatened to kill her kids if she makes a break for it.'

'Well, no. I don't think that's it, because look – she glances down and balks. Right? What is freaking her out so much? Is she above a pool of acid or something? And see the space she's in? It's concrete, but it's smooth concrete. New. Not crumbly or covered in mossy residue or some other crap. It's brand, brand new.'

'Where would you get a square space that's about six by six feet and that's new?' Dave asked, his brow furrowed deeply.

Jackie considered the options. 'A new wine bar maybe? A walk-in shower on a building site?' She felt her consciousness snag on something vital. 'A building site... a building site. Manchester's full of them, but where might you be if you look down and what you see puts the fear of God into you?'

In unison, they answered. 'A lift shaft.'

'I don't believe it,' Jackie said. 'He's rigged up that chair so she's suspended over a lift shaft, with an almighty drop beneath her. That *has* to be it.' She could almost feel Lucian patting her on the back.

'Question is,' Dave said, eyebrows raised over fearful eyes, 'in a city full of high-rise building sites, where is she, and do we have a cat in hell's chance of finding her before time's up?'

THIRTY-FIVE

'Bob, you've got to get in touch with the planning people, or the council or whoever the hell it is that knows what's being built in the city,' Jackie said, peering at a skyline that was punctuated by towering cranes in every direction she turned. 'We've got too little time and too much at stake.'

She glanced at Dave, who was sitting on the bonnet of the car. Thanks to Shazia emailing through a list of every major construction company that was working on a new build in the city, Dave had just started to make calls to ascertain if any builders had arrived on site that morning only to happen upon a serial killer, holding a woman hostage, suspended above a lift shaft. In an ever-expanding city being rebuilt upwards, it seemed as smart a move as anything.

On the other end, over speakerphone, Bob's voice wavered. 'How long we got?'

Jackie looked at her watch. 'Couple of hours. Not enough. Even if every available uniform was out there, checking every building site, there's no guarantee we'll find where Dewhurst is keeping Katie before it's too late.'

'No joy so far with this,' Dave said, putting his reading

glasses on his head. 'It's ten in the morning. Builders start at about eight. If she's in one of these half-built office or apartment blocks...' He described a slice of the high-rise horizon with the arm of his glasses – 'they'll find her before we do.'

Jackie nodded and turned her attention back to Bob. 'Did you hear all that? We need you to speak to planning. Right? Find out which building sites have ground to a halt because of planning issues or maybe the developer has run out of cash.'

'Planning officers are up in everybody's business,' Dave said. 'Believe me. I found that out the hard way when we extended the—'

'Are you listening, Bob?' Jackie could feel impatience taking bites out of her professional composure.

'Yes. Building sites that have ground to a halt.'

'And they'll have architect's blueprints to hand. So we want a building with a lift shaft that's about six or seven feet wide, judging by this footage. No idea on how many storeys, but it's definitely not low-rise.'

She hung up, feeling impotent. 'All we can do is wait.'

But Dave wasn't listening, he was talking to some site foreman, by the sounds. 'All right, mate. Cheers. So where would you be looking if you wanted a lift shaft where a member of the public could gain access?' Dave grimaced as the person on the other end spoke. Nodding.

He ended the call and turned to Jackie. 'Guy I just spoke to said there's a tonne of development going down between the Ordsall Lane end of the Irwell and Bridgewater Canal, near Deansgate. He heard one of the blocks has stalled because of Covid supply issues. No materials coming through from China. Different trades have been coming to him, grumbling and asking if he wants subcontractors for extra hours, because they can't get onto their own site to work. Maybe that's our place.'

'Worth a try, while we're waiting on Bob,' Jackie said. 'Got an address?'

Dave nodded, brandishing his notebook.

'Damn this traffic,' Jackie said, wishing she'd stayed in the passenger's seat. Her skin itched with frustration at the sight of the roadworks that stretched all the way along the ring road. Even with their siren on, there was no way for the queue of traffic to go.

At her side, Dave continued to quiz every building site foreman he could get through to. There had been nothing untoward reported to 999. The city was keeping Dewhurst's secret.

Jackie thumped the steering wheel and then pressed hard on the horn. She leaned out of the window and screamed at the driver of a long-wheel-based van that was stubbornly blocking her path. 'Can't you see the flashing lights, you tit? Get out of the bloody way.'

But the driver merely treated her to a rude hand gesture, which she could see reflected in his side mirror. She glanced at the clock. Under two hours now.

Unable to bear the lack of control, Jackie let the engine idle, put on the handbrake and got out of the car. She could feel Dave watching her, but she didn't care. All she could see through the red mist was Katie's terrified, pleading eyes.

The driver of the van rolled up his window fast.

Jackie knocked on it and shoved her ID up to the glass. She held her cuffs out for the man to see. 'Police. Move the goddamn van before I arrest you.'

The man nodded, his florid colour draining fast. He mouthed, 'Sorry, love,' and finally inched forwards so that the Ford could pass.

Half an hour had passed before Jackie pulled up in front of the building site that Dave's contact had suggested. She looked up at the carcass of an apartment block that must have been twenty storeys high at least.

'Okay. Here's the plan,' Dave said. 'I've spoken to Venables. Uniforms are scouring Salford Quays, where there's quite a few new blocks going up, but we're too thin on the ground to cover all the developing areas of the city centre. Not in the time we got.' He looked up at the police helicopter, slowly circling. 'So if this looks like it's our man, we call and wait for backup. Nobody's far away. We've been told not to try anything stupid.'

Jackie nodded. 'Venables. Venables expects us to sit on our hands if we find Katie suspended above a lift shaft?'

'Orders are orders. And she's got a point. We'll potentially need the fire brigade to get her out in one piece. And Dewhurst's tooled up. You saw that zombie knife. We haven't got a taser between us. It could take an armed unit to tackle him.'

'Why are you telling me all this, Dave?' Jackie said, slinging her bag across her body. She had already started to walk towards the hoarding that surrounded the site. Knocked on the makeshift door.

Dave jogged behind her to catch up. 'Because you've got that glint in your eye, Jackie. The Lone Ranger look. And I don't like it, because whenever you get that, I'm left to pick up the pieces. I'm not your Tonto.'

Jackie wasn't listening.

A security guard opened the door to her. 'Can I help you?'

She showed her ID. 'I understand the contractors from this site have been sent home temporarily. Is that correct?'

'Yes, love. Why?' The guard was looking her up and down, half grinning, as though he'd never seen a female detective before. His eyes came to rest on Jackie's chest.

She snapped her fingers in his face and pointed to her eyes. 'Hey. Come on. Pay attention. Eyes up here. We're looking for a dangerous individual who may be with a woman he's abducted. We have reason to believe the woman's being held on a building site just like this. Maybe this one. Can we take a look at the lift shaft please?' Jackie's gut felt like it had been tied in a knot; her heart was pounding hard enough to make her breathless.

'I think you need a warrant, don't you? I should call the boss.'

Dave gently manoeuvred Jackie aside. 'This is an urgent police matter, mate. See that chopper circling above us? That's there because we asked it to be.'

The guard scratched his head. 'But you're meant to wear a hard hat.'

'Don't worry about health and safety. Lives are at stake. All right? A criminal's potentially on this property, and you're the security guard. So how about you just help us, pal?' Dave asked. 'We're all on the same side here. Show us where the lift shaft is.'

Finally, seemingly puffed up with manly pride, the security guard let them in and led them to the shaft.

He looked upwards. 'There you go. Twenty floors. Don't know what you're expecting to see, but there's nothing there.'

Jackie peered up into the dizzyingly tall, narrow space. There was nothing to see but the dark grey, rolling Mancunian clouds, where the shaft was open to the elements. 'This isn't it.'

Back in the car, the rain started to fall in fat spots.

Jackie thumped the dash. 'We're going to lose her. Katie's going to die and it will be my fault.'

Dave shook his head. 'You're not the one with a zombie knife to her throat. Look, there's still time. We can find her.' He picked up her phone. 'Has Dewhurst been in touch with the drop-off location for his kids? Maybe that will give us a clue.'

Taking the phone from him, Jackie refreshed her texts and her emails. As she did so, a WhatsApp message appeared in her inbox. She felt the blood slow and cool in her veins as fear took hold.

'It's him.' She opened the message. Read the words. 'He wants them to be left in the middle of the main concourse at Piccadilly Station.'

There was an accompanying sound recording. When she played it, she gasped. It was fifteen dreadful seconds long: the sound of Katie's muffled screams.

'She's still alive at least,' she said. 'We've got to hurry. Think. Where could she be?'

'Could he have Katie near Piccadilly after all?' Dave asked. 'Surely he's got eyes on the station, if he wants his children to be dropped there.'

Jackie nodded. 'It's worth a try.'

They drove in silence back across town. Every minute or so, Jackie glanced at the clock on the dash. Time seemed to spool forwards faster than she could bear.

'Come on, come on, come on,' she said as they got stuck behind a queue of traffic on Aytoun Street, skirting past the crown court to her left.

Finally, the lights changed and Jackie was able to gun the Ford up the concourse that led to Piccadilly Station. They were just about to get out of the car when her phone rang. It was Bob.

'Jackie. I finally got through to the right person in planning. There's three building sites with lift shafts that have recently had to down tools. One's near South Tower at the end of Deansgate.'

'How many storeys?' she asked.

'Ten. It's not huge.'

She gnawed at the inside of her cheek. 'Go on. What else?'

'One's near Ordsall Lane. In fact, we had a complaint come through that a couple of cops matching you and Tang's description already barged your way in.'

'Yep. Done it. Nothing there. What's the third?'

'Big apartment block in New Islington. The developer's built it two storeys higher than it should be. Planning has shut the build down while the developer applies for retrospective permission. The dimensions of the lift shaft fit the bill.'

'That it?'

'That's it. Everywhere else is crawling with tradesmen. If your killer was on a live building site, we would have heard by now.'

Jackie made a note of the address and ended the call.

Dave looked hopeful. 'New Islington's not far, but I doubt you can see Piccadilly from there.'

'Don't kid yourself,' Jackie said. 'There's only a ten-minute brisk walk between them. If Dewhurst's as high up as we think, he might be able to monitor the station concourse through binoculars. I've got a feeling this is our place, Dave.' She looked at the clock yet again. 'We've got half an hour before he kills Katie, and there's roadworks on every damned street. We'd better pray we're not too late.'

Speeding back down the concourse and hanging a right, they headed for the ring road and found themselves almost immediately in New Islington, behind the old Express building. The building site they sought loomed above them – a Jenga-like towering concrete carcass, open to the elements on all sides.

'Call for backup,' Jackie said.

'What if we're wrong?' Dave asked.

'What if we're right?'

When they found the door to the site in the otherwise impenetrable wooden hoarding that surrounded it, Jackie noticed the bust padlock. Wordlessly, she pointed to it and nodded at Dave. Watched as he thumbed a text straight to Venables, Shazia and his contact in the armed response unit.

They both looked up at the helicopter, which was still circling, but in the wrong place.

'Let's go?' she asked.

'What choice do we have?'

Creeping inside, Jackie pushed all thoughts of her children and the limitations of being a breastfeeding new mother aside. Now she needed to be Detective Sergeant Jackson Cooke: principled and fearless, though the weight of the many floors of concrete above her seemed to make her legs sluggish and her thoughts slow.

They found the lift shaft among the shadows on the ground floor of the dripping concrete shell. Dave peered up into the tall, tall aperture. In silence, he gestured that Jackie take a look.

Steeling herself to look up, Jackie could see that right near the very top, a chair had somehow been suspended on scaffold planks, precariously laid across the fatal drop. It was clear that Katie was seated on the chair. Jackie closed her eyes and said a silent prayer for her old school pal.

Dave grabbed Jackie and pulled her back into the shadows. 'We need to find a temporary lift or something,' he whispered. 'There must be one, like a window cleaner's basket maybe, else how do they get materials all the way up there?'

Jackie nodded. 'It'll be on the outside.'

Together, they walked around the sizeable footprint of the block, glancing up regularly to check they weren't being watched. No security guard or guard dog here. The developer had clearly cut corners.

Finally, they found a builder's lift on the far side of the site. The basket was at ground level. Dave tried to open the barrier, but it was locked. There seemed to be no power in the building either.

'There's no way we're getting up that way,' he said. 'We're gonna have to walk it.'

'How many floors is this?' Jackie asked, looking up.

'Thirty,' Dave said. 'Actually, thirty-two.' He crossed himself.

Adrenalin powered Jackie up the first three flights. By the time she got to the fifth, she was flagging. By the time they made it to the tenth, she was barely able to breathe, and vertigo had started to kick in as her brain realised that, with no banister yet in place, there was nothing between her and certain death, should she stumble too far to her right. Jackie clung to the wall then, edging up reluctantly, step by step.

By the penultimate floor, they could hear Dewhurst talking. The searing pain of the lactic acid in Jackie's legs was trumped by a new wave of adrenalin, and finally, she dared to let go of the wall.

'Not long now,' she could hear Dewhurst saying. 'Another ten minutes and either my children will be delivered to me, or you'll be a slick of red at the bottom of this lift shaft. All my incel boys are watching us. You're famous. How do you like that, bitch?'

Katie shouted an angry response that was obscured by the glue. Her voice ricocheted off the concrete structure that held her.

Dave opened his mouth to speak, but Jackie held her hand up, signalling they should listen.

'Your head's going to explode like an overripe melon,' Dewhurst said. His voice was whipped by the wind. 'I won't even need to cut you up. The impact will do it for me.'

Jackie pulled Dave close and whispered in his ear. 'He's not standing by the lift shaft. Sounds like he's on the edge. Facing Piccadilly?'

Dave nodded, grabbed Jackie to him and whispered his response. 'You get to her. I'll take him on.'

Glancing down to the ground floor, all those storeys below, Jackie willed herself to leave all her fears in the stairwell. *Come on, Jackie. Katie needs you to be strong. What kind of a world will Alice inherit if men like Dewhurst get to go free?*

On the count of three, Jackie and Dave bounded up the last few stairs, batons drawn. They found themselves on an apparently empty penthouse floor: the city laid out before them in 180-degree splendour, punctuated only by the monolithic bulk of the lift shaft.

Katie saw them and started screaming.

Jackie started to turn her head to check behind them when she heard the whistle. By the time she realised a scaffold pole was whizzing through the air towards them, it was too late.

THIRTY-SIX

'Where are my kids?' Dewhurst screamed. 'I told you if you didn't bring them to Piccadilly when time's up, I'd kill her. I told you to await instructions, and you didn't. You're trying to ambush me. So now that bitch's blood is on your hands.'

Jackie looked up. The scaffold pole had taken her legs out from under her and she'd fallen hard, hitting her head on the unforgiving ground. She felt dizzy. The wind was gusting through the open concrete structure, but she could hear Katie weeping, off to her left. Where was Dave?

Jackie followed Dewhurst's incensed stare and the line of the scaffold pole, which he was brandishing like a spear. Caught sight of Dave standing behind a supportive column. She could see he was scanning his surroundings for a weapon that would match up to the pole.

'Come out from there, you little jerk, and fight me like a man,' Dewhurst yelled.

'Give it up, Andy,' Dave said, taking several quick steps backwards. He ducked behind a tall stack of breeze blocks and was momentarily out of sight. 'This place is going to be crawling with my colleagues in a few minutes. The whole of Greater

Manchester Police knows we're here. If you were looking for a reaction, you've got it. Okay? Now drop the pole and put your hands in the air.'

Dewhurst ran towards Dave's hiding place, holding the scaffold pole as though he was a decathlete, about to vault into the air.

Now was Jackie's chance. Getting to her feet, she tried to blink away the woozy sensation and weaved her way over to Katie. Finally, she appreciated how insanely dangerous Dewhurst's rig-up was. Katie was seated on an old wooden chair, balanced on scaffold planks that had been slung across the aperture where the lift doors would eventually go. They had been wedged into the meagre crack where the top section of the lift shaft's pre-cast structure had been craned on top of the section beneath. But Jackie could see that the rickety chair wasn't fastened down in any way, and Katie had clearly been wriggling about. One of the chair's legs had shunted right to the edge of the plank. Another inch, and Katie would topple and plunge to her death.

'Katie, listen to me,' Jackie whispered. 'Shush, shush, shush now.'

Her old friend stretched out her arms towards Jackie. The movement made the chair leg shunt away from the edge of the plank and then edge back again. Now the margin between life and death was even tighter.

Jackie pressed her index finger to her lips. 'I need you to keep quiet and keep absolutely still, because that chair's right on the edge. Okay? If you move, you'll fall.'

Katie looked down and started to whimper. She shut her eyes tightly, and fresh tears leaked onto her already tear-streaked cheeks.

'Keep still and follow my instructions,' Jackie said.

What exactly were her instructions though? She looked at the impossible situation and realised that she didn't have a clue how to rescue Katie. Dave had been right. It was surely a job for the fire brigade.

She dared to peer over the edge of the floor into the abyss below. Saw the ground, thirty-two storeys down, and bit her lip. It was no good waiting. Though she could hear sirens in the distance, the fire brigade would take too long to climb up to this windy death trap of a penthouse shell. With Dewhurst and Dave fighting precariously near the edge of the building, Jackie knew anything could happen. The key was to keep Katie absolutely calm and somehow stop her from falling. *Don't show any fear. Make her think you've got everything in hand.*

Peering over her shoulder, she could see Dave uselessly heave a breeze block at Dewhurst, who was still waving the heavy pole around – dangerously out of control. Jackie scanned the floor and came to rest on a pile of electrician's cabling. A plan began to form. It was her only hope.

She turned back to Katie. 'I need you to sit tight. Whatever you do, do *not* move 'til I say so.'

From behind her glued lips, Katie screamed her protests.

Jackie kept low as she scrambled over to the cable. She reached into her handbag and pulled out the Swiss Army knife that doubled as her key ring. Cutting a long length of cabling, she coiled it up quickly.

There was a loud clang.

Looking round to see what had befallen Dave, Jackie realised Dewhurst's arms had finally tired, and he'd dropped the pole. Only now, he'd snatched up a hammer drill that still had juice in its battery back. He came at Dave, squeezing the drill's trigger.

She saw Dave dash to the scant cover provided by a pile of timber, destined for stud walling. Dave snatched up a length of wood and sprinted towards Dewhurst, knocking the drill from his grasp. Now the men were wrestling one another, scrabbling back and forth but inching towards the edge, some four or five metres behind them. Jackie stifled the urge to call out to Dave. She'd seen him take down men far larger than Dewhurst before. Her task right now was to secure Katie.

Returning to the lift shaft, she unravelled the long piece of cable. 'Now listen, Katie. We need to get you safe, so I'll throw you this cable, and I want you to grab it and carefully triple knot it around your waist. Okay?

Katie nodded.

'Don't look down and *don't* move your body. Okay, I'm throwing it now.' Jackie hurled the coil of cable to her friend, but it fell uselessly to the side and swung down into the lift shaft. 'We'll try that again.'

Jackie turned momentarily to see Dave drop-kicking Dewhurst. But Dewhurst sprang to his feet, powered by the determination of a deranged killer. He lunged at Dave, and again, the two men shunted a few feet closer to the edge.

Turning back to Katie, Jackie gathered the cable up. 'Ready? Again.'

With all the precision she could muster, she threw the coil of cable to Katie. This time, it hit her in the face. Katie grunted and tried to catch it, but the cable seemed to slide from her clumsy fingers and tumbled into the abyss.

'Sorry.' Jackie pulled the cable back up from the shaft. 'One more try.'

Glancing back, she was horrified to see that Dewhurst had gained the upper hand and was on top of Dave now, squeezing his neck.

Jackie had to be fast. She turned back to Katie and slowed her breathing; steadied her hand; focussed on the trajectory the cable would have to follow to land in the right place. She threw the coil in a fluid movement, and this time, it landed in Katie's lap. 'Now tie it around you – quickly.'

Katie nodded, whimpering as the chair shunted closer to the edge of the planks with every slight movement.

'You won't fall, if you stay calm and follow my instructions,' Jackie said.

While Katie fumbled with the cable, Jackie turned to see Dave, prone on the ground. She gasped. Dewhurst was getting up off her partner's motionless body. He looked around and locked eyes with her.

Feeling the blood drain from her extremities, Jackie knew the killer was coming for her. She prayed Dave wasn't dead. Where the hell was the armed response unit?

Quickly, she tied her end of the cable around her own middle and anchored herself on the ground. Turned to Katie. 'Get up out of the chair and walk along the planks to me. Slowly.'

Turning slightly, in her peripheral vision, she could see Dewhurst pick up a discarded wood saw. She had seconds. Turning back to Katie, she saw the woman had stalled.

'Keep walking. Don't look at him and don't look down. A couple of feet and you're home and dry. Then I want you to run for the stairs and keep going.'

Dewhurst's footsteps scuffed across the concrete floor. He was stalking slowly towards them. As Katie stumbled to safety and Jackie undid the cable around her own waist with fumbling fingers, he spoke.

'You should have left her in the chair and saved your own skin, Cooke.'

Jackie rose up and shouted to Katie. 'Run! Run and don't come back for me.'

Katie fled.

Now Jackie was alone with Dewhurst. 'You killed my partner!'

'Don't worry about him. I don't kill men. He's just sleeping. When he comes round, this will all be just... not a bad dream. More a waking nightmare.' He laughed.

Jackie glanced over at Dave. 'You jabbed him with

Rohypnol?'

Dewhurst ignored her. 'This works out well for me actually,' he said. 'You're a thieving witch, like the one I just let go.'

Think, Jackie! Improvise! Jackie heard the voice of imaginary Lucian resound all around that windswept, half-built penthouse. *You're smart enough to get out of this. You can't leave Beryl and Gus to bring up the kids.*

The comfort she might have gleaned from her long-lost brother's imagined words of encouragement were consumed by her red-hot anger. 'You didn't let Katie go. I freed her.'

'Thieving witch! Burn the witch! That makes me a modern-day Witchfinder General. *I* know you're in the process of getting a divorce, and *I* know you're trying to swindle your ex out of access to little baby Alice and the twins, Lewis and Percy.' He said the children's names in a mocking, babyish tone.

'You know nothing about me,' Jackie said. 'And don't talk about my kids as if you know them, you murdering piece of crap. Don't you even say their names.'

There was suddenly a break in the thick clouds, and a shaft of sunlight plunged through the top of the lift shaft, still open to the elements. An object on the floor just beyond Jackie's reach caught the light and glinted.

'I'll say what I like,' Dewhurst said. He flexed the blade of the saw. 'I have the power of life and death over you. You don't get to tell me what I can and cannot say. That's how good men have ended up living on their knees, while women turn the world on its head.' He grinned nastily. 'Speaking of which, you should know I'm going to hack your head off like the Medusa you are.'

He was almost upon her now. With a thirty-two-storey drop behind her and Dewhurst blocking her escape to the stairs, Jackie had no option but to lunge left for the thing on the floor that glinted in the sun. Mere feet away. She realised what it was now.

Dewhurst switched the saw to his left hand, and with his right pulled the zombie knife from a sheath, attached to his belt. As he leaped forwards, Jackie threw herself onto the shining thing – a circular blade from an angle-grinder. Though it sliced into the soft pads of her fingertips, she darted swiftly towards Dewhurst, sinking the blades deeply into the flesh of his upper arm.

Dewhurst's eyes widened momentarily; then his mouth opened in a silent scream. With a clatter, he dropped both weapons, clutching his left hand to his injured right arm. The blood gushed deep red through his fingers. 'What have you done?'

His features collapsed into an ominous glare. Letting go of the wound, he tried to grab Jackie with blood-slick hands.

Yet, despite Dewhurst's malevolent intent, Jackie saw he'd paled immediately. Had she hit an artery with the circular saw blade?

As she side-stepped his reach, she caught sight of Dave getting to his feet and staggering drunkenly towards the edge of the building.

'No!' she yelled. 'Dave, watch out!'

Again, Dewhurst reached out to grab her, encircling her middle with a still-strong left arm. The pair tangoed into one of the concrete walls by the lift shaft, where exposed electrical cabling hung down from the ceiling. Dewhurst wrapped a length of it around Jackie's neck. She started to choke; felt her eyes bulging, though she never took them off Dave, who was tottering too close to the edge, clutching his head.

Determined to get to her partner, Jackie bit Dewhurst's shoulder. Perhaps he was weakened by blood loss and surprise. Jackie wasn't sure, but momentarily, mercifully, he loosened his grip on her – long enough for Jackie to wriggle free.

The sound of sirens was just below them now, echoing up the lift shaft and stairwell. They were accompanied by the voices of men and barking police dogs. There was a deep *thunk* from somewhere below, and the building started to thrum with electricity. Fluorescent building-site lights dazzled suddenly – strings of what looked like industrial fairy lights overhead and floor-standing floodlights on the concrete floor. There was the clunk-clunking sound of the temporary lift ascending on the outside of the building.

Jackie squinted in the bright light. Her eyes adapted to the glare just in time to see Dewhurst twitching as if caught in the grip of a fit, with the frayed copper wire at the end of the cable he'd tried to strangle her with still clutched in his wet, bloody hand. He collapsed to the ground and was still.

Jackie sprinted over to Dave and wrestled him away from the edge of the building.

'It's over, Dave. It's over.'

THIRTY-SEVEN

'Comfortable?' Jackie asked as the hospital tannoy binged and bonged in the corridor, just beyond the door to the private room that had been allocated to Andy Dewhurst.

Dewhurst tugged at the handcuffs that secured him to the metal frame of the bed. The chain clanked. 'Go to hell.' He tried to spit at her but missed.

Jackie leaned back in the vinyl visitor's chair. 'Why, Andy? That's what I want to know? Why did a staid, dependable social worker turn into a murderer? An *incel*, for heaven's sake?' She leaned forwards and anchored her elbows on her knees. Clasped her hands together, as if praying for enlightenment in a case that had confounded her and her colleagues.

Looking wistfully out of the window to the reddening autumn foliage on the trees beyond, Dewhurst sighed. 'Why do you think? After my divorce, my wife took my world away. I was impotent. She left me with nothing.' He looked back at her. There was loathing etched into his cruel features. 'Do you know what it's like to have your babies stolen from you? My goddamn kids. Mine! And I worked in this perverted, leech-like industry that's grown up around failed relationships, deciding which parent gets to keep their precious progeny. I was part of the problem, but the mothers – they're always the ones really to blame.'

'Oh, and all those abusive men are clear of conscience?' Jackie sat up straight, not trying to disguise the sarcasm in her voice. 'The beatings and the infidelity and the gaslighting – that counts for nothing, does it?'

'Women are nothing. They deserve *nothing*.' He was shouting now. 'Women like Marie Grant and all those others deserved a terrifying and painful end for what they did to their menfolk.'

'Why did you leave all those years between Marie Grant and Rachel Hardman? Were there others we haven't found yet?'

Dewhurst looked at her. There was some mischief behind his dangerous, glittering eyes. 'Maybe there are. Or maybe I regretted Marie and swore I'd never do it again, until Rachel came along. Maybe I'd killed before all this. You'll never know, because you're too stupid. Or *maybe* Marie was the first, and for seven years, I was just waiting; planning a showdown. You'll never know, will you?' He started to laugh heartily.

'You were Guy Schön and Guy Sympa and Steve James, weren't you? An identity thief.'

'I'm a master of disguise, you idiot.'

Jackie ignored the niggling frustration that made her skin itch. 'You're the idiot actually, Andy. Because you're going to spend the rest of your life eating slop on a high-security wing of a category A prison. You'll die in there, and you won't be an incel hero. You're a middle-class almost-pretty boy. All you'll be is a punchbag for every angry lout inside. And prison's full to the rafters with those. What fun! Well, you made your bed, Andy. Enjoy lying in it.'

She got to her feet and walked from the ward back down to A&E, happy, at least, that she'd gain justice for five women who had had their futures stolen by a weak and hate-filled excuse for a man.

'David Tang?' The nurse checked her paperwork and looked out among the sea of faces in A&E.

Jackie nudged Dave. 'Here we go. You're up.' She patted him on the back.

As he got to his feet, he looked down at her with a vacant smile. 'Are you getting déjà vu? Because I sure as hell am.'

'Go.' Jackie waved him away. 'Call when you're done. I'll pick you up out front. You've got at least a couple of hours in there, and I've got some loose ends to tie up in the meantime.'

Satisfied that Dave was in good hands, Jackie made her way out of the emergency waiting room and breathed in the damp Mancunian air. She walked past the smokers, huddled together with their plastered arms and bandaged heads, and returned to the Ford. Got in and dialled Venables.

'Ah, Cooke. Just the person I wanted to speak to,' Venables said.

'Dave's just been called to get checked over.' Jackie rubbed at her head, still sore where she'd fallen and bumped it the concrete floor. 'I've been up to the ward to visit Dewhurst too. He's awake, cuffed to the bed, and sadly no more palatable as a human being for a little light electrocution.'

Uncharacteristically, Venables chuckled. 'Ha. Very good. It makes for much better headlines when we catch these morons and put them behind bars instead of in the ground.'

Jackie was prepared to let the 'we' go. Right now, she didn't have the energy to fight with her superior. 'He's confessed anyway. Decided he wants to be some kind of infamous, international poster boy for the maritally hard done by, the lunatic. And I caught up with Katie Pritchard. They've managed to dissolve the superglue he used to stick her lips together. She's being kept in hospital overnight for shock and dehydration, but she's going to testify in court. Coming in later this week to make her statement. We've got everything we need.'

'And are *you* all right?' Venables asked. 'I heard you took a beating.'

Running her stinging fingertips, covered in sticking plasters, gently over the raw skin on her neck, Jackie allowed herself to entertain the memory of Dewhurst strangling her with the electrical cable. Then she let go of the horror, because she knew he would end his days in prison, and, more importantly, she knew she would get justice for Claire Watkins and the other women whose lives Andy Dewhurst – the self-proclaimed Witchfinder – had snuffed out. 'I'm fine.' She smiled. 'Look, I'll see you after Dave's finished and I've dropped him home. Oh, and, Tina... thanks for asking.'

'Don't think a bump to the head will get you out of any kind of disciplinary action for not following protocol in a hostage situation, Jackson Cooke,' Venables said. 'You and Tang played fast and loose with the rules. You're a law unto yourselves, you two. There will be consequences.'

Jackie chuckled, almost comforted by Venables reverting to type. 'We'll live with those, I guess.'

She hung up and checked her watch. Dialled her mother, who picked up almost instantly.

'Jackson! Are you all right?' There was a manic quality to Beryl's voice. 'Are we in danger?'

'No, no. You're safe. And I'm A-okay. More to the point, are the kids all right?'

'Depends what you call "all right". Lewis and Percy are plastered in crap. Your father, the old reprobate, had them digging up onions the minute we got out of the car. He's showing them how to milk a goat right now. A *goat*. Alice is good as gold of course.'

Jackie exhaled heavily, feeling her shoulders drop as the tension leached from her body. 'Good. Brilliant. Thanks for looking after them. Kiss them for me, will you?' She said a silent prayer of thanks to a god she wasn't sure was listening. 'Anyway, I'm pleased to say it's over, Mum. We got our guy, and you can bring the kids home.'

'About time. You know, there's no hot running water in this shambles of a hippy commune, and they won't let you flush the toilet after a wee? Your father lives like a farmyard animal. *And* I left my thyroxine tablets and hair straighteners at home.'

'I'll see you later, Mum. Dinner's on me. Drive safe.' Jackie blew a kiss to Beryl and hung up, grateful for her family; happy to be alive.

Checking her watch, she saw that she had time to tie off a final couple of loose threads.

Gus was sitting in the living room of Catherine Harris's house, strumming his acoustic guitar. Jackie knocked on the window and noted the brightness of his smile when he saw her. By the time he came to the door though, the smile was gone.

'Oh, it's you,' he said, leaning against the architrave of the front door. 'You're alive then?'

'Seems so.' Jackie looked down at his hairy toes in those yellow flip-flops he always wore indoors. Same old Gus. 'Beryl's bringing the kids home tonight.'

Gus folded his arms. 'I should hope so. It's not right that you keep putting the family in danger. I had a call from a solicitor called Sam Black, you know. I wanted to let you know—'

Jackie held her hand up. 'Just stop for a minute, will you? This isn't war games, Augustus – this is our family. Look, if this case has taught me anything, it's taught me that we should come to an amicable arrangement for the good of the kids. I won't let you trample all over my parental rights, and you *can't* have the house, so just drop it. I bought it by working my fingers to the bone. The kids live in it. I'm still breastfeeding our daughter in it, and my mother lives in the basement. You *always* refused to get even a part-time day job. We could never afford for one parent to be a 24/7 stay-at-home mum or dad. You knew it, but you wouldn't look for work.'

'You're—'

'Gus, we need to be realistic. I acknowledge that you're their father, and they love you and need you in their lives. We need to share the parenting like responsible adults. We need to stop arguing over money and power. The fighting's killing the boys. Is that what you want?'

Gus pressed his lips together and stared at her until his hard eyes seemed to soften. 'Have you finished? Because I was going to say that I told Black to go to hell. We loved each other once, Jackie. I still do...' His cheeks coloured up. He looked down at his toes. 'I realise Percy's acting up is down to me. I don't want us to be like this.'

'Well, you chose another woman.'

He locked eyes with her then. 'You chose your career over me, Jackie. But none of that is the point. We are where we are, and this is about doing what's right for the kids. You just said so yourself. So I've decided: I'm going to get a part-time job. We'll go through a mediator. I'll need *some* money – only what's fair and practicable after years of marriage where you were the main—the *only* breadwinner. But you can keep the house.' He waved dismissively. 'I just want to be part of our family's life. I want my kids. I want... I don't want to lose you entirely.' He blinked hard. His features softened.

Nodding, Jackie looked at his yellow flip-flops and smiled. 'Good. Okay. Well, that's start. Let's take it a day at a time.'

. . .

She drove over to Agecroft Cemetery, hoping to catch Claire Watkins' funeral, only to find she'd missed it by twenty minutes. Jackie navigated her way through a maze of graves to find the freshly dug mound of earth beneath which her old school friend had been laid to rest. The grave was festooned with glorious white and lilac floral tributes. Roses, lilies, chrysanthemums, whose heady scent and pure beauty seemed wasted on the dead.

'Oh, Claire. I wish they'd all cared as much when you were alive, love. I wish you'd let me be there for you too. In fact, no. It's on me. I should have tried harder to reach out. Forgive me.' Jackie wiped the tears from her eyes.

Crouching down, she read the accompanying cards:

You'll always be the best mum in the world. Love forever, Kylie and Luke xxx

Our daughter lives on in our hearts forever. Sleep well, beautiful girl. Mum and Dad xxx

To our much-loved colleague, RIP, from the biscuit gang.

'So much talk of forever, but there's no such thing, is there?' Jackie spoke to the mound of earth, imagining her friend below it, encased in an expensive casket, cocooned in crushed velvet and dressed in her Sunday best, as though the murder had been just an inconvenient footnote in an otherwise wonderful life.

Jackie thought about the lies the living told themselves to cope with loss. *They'll live on forever. They never really leave you. They're with God now. We were great parents. We all loved each other so much. They had such a happy life. She never wanted for anything.* The dead were rendered mute, as if their truth no longer counted, while those that were left behind rewrote the narrative to suit themselves.

'You deserved so much better. You and Faye, Marie, Esther and Emma.' Jackie looked up to the bruising rainclouds. 'I'm sorry we live in a world where this was allowed to happen to you. Goodbye, sweetheart. See you on the other side.'

Jackie took one last look at her friend's final resting place and turned to face the grey Mancunian day, satisfied, at least, that her job allowed her to give a voice to the city's silent dead.

A LETTER FROM MARNIE

Dear reader,

I want to say a huge thank you for choosing to read *The Silent Dead*. If you did enjoy it, and want to keep up to date with all my latest releases, just sign up at the following link. Your email address will never be shared and you can unsubscribe at any time.

www.bookouture.com/marnie-riches

If you've already read the first book in this series – *All the Pretty Ones* (formerly called *The Lost Ones*) – you'll know that my new detective Jackson Cooke is a plucky woman who loves her children deeply and who struggles to juggle her somewhat dysfunctional family life with a very demanding job. I hope you can relate to Jackie, because her plight as a working mother is not dissimilar to that of so many women across the globe. In any case, I hope you loved reading *The Silent Dead* as much as I loved writing it. If you did, I would be very grateful if you could write a review. I'd love to hear what you think, and it makes such a difference helping new readers to discover one of my books for the first time.

I love hearing from my readers – you can get in touch on my Facebook page, and through Twitter or Instagram.

Thanks,

Marnie Riches

www.marnieriches.com

 facebook.com/MarnieRichesAuthor

twitter.com/Marnie_Riches

instagram.com/marnie_riches

ACKNOWLEDGEMENTS

The Silent Dead was written at the start of another busy year for my family – a year full of exams and university applications and the various mini-dramas that are recognisable features of house-holds where middle-aged parents and older teenagers are all trying to juggle too many responsibilities in a post-Covid world. Yet, it is my rich family life that partly inspired this story. So I'll say a huge thank you, as ever, to Christian, Natalie and Adam: for all of the love and proud moments and sleepless nights and worry and inspiration they give me.

An author's most important ally is always their agent, and mine is one of the finest people I know. So thanks, as ever, to my splendid partner in crime[1], Caspian Dennis, for his ongoing support, encouragement, sage advice and hilarious anecdotes. Thanks too to his colleagues at the brilliant Abner Stein literary agency – especially Sandy, Felicity and Ray.

I owe a huge debt of gratitude to my editor, Ruth Tross at Bookouture, for her savvy editorial input into this series and her unflagging professionalism and attention to detail in getting the covers, title, blurb and all other marketing matters just right. The Bookouture team is an incredibly dynamic bunch, so thanks are also due to Sarah, Kim, Alba, Mandy and those others behind the scenes, who make publication run so smoothly and who whip readers up into a frenzy about every new release!

Thanks must go to Linda Price for her extensive knowledge regarding Jewish burial and the procedures that are put in place when a death is suspicious. Any errors in the book are my own and for dramatic reasons. The same applies to any legal or police procedure in the story. I do carry out extensive research before and during the writing process and I often consult experts when I can't find answers for myself, but these folk don't always wish to be named in the acknowledgements section. Sometimes, for the sake of a good yarn, I just ignore what they say! But thanks anyway to those anonymous types who let me pick their brains from time to time. You know who you are.

I'd like to thank the inimitable Anne Cater, Ayo Onatade and Gordon Mcghie for their continued support of my writing. Thanks are also due to the book bloggers who participated in the blog tour of *The Lost Ones* – or *All the Pretty Ones*, as it's now called. Thanks too to online book clubs THE Book Club, UK Crime Book Club (especially David Gilchrist) and Crime Book Club (especially Lainy Swaanson). Without these crime-fiction enthusiasts, readers wouldn't get to hear about half of the incredible books that get published in the course of the year.

Finally, thanks to my readers. Without their ongoing enthusiasm for my stories, I wouldn't have a career as a published author – a career that I worked extremely hard to get off the ground and which I now wouldn't change for the world. Every time someone buys, reads and favourably reviews one of my books, I feel like I have done my job well in bringing a little thought-provoking joy to someone's life. Readers and authors have a symbiotic relationship, and my readers are definitely the best! So thanks, guys! I hope you've enjoyed *The Silent Dead*.

* * *

1. That's to say, partner in crime fiction – not actual fencing stolen goods, stealing cars or dealing drugs, in the Mancunian sense of the word.

Made in United States
Orlando, FL
04 November 2022

24189898R00183